WITHDRAWN

EMERALD ENCHANTMENT

YOLO COUNTY LIBRARY
226 BUCKEYE STREET
WOODLAND, CA 95695-2600

EMERALD ENCHANTMENT

S S
EMERALD

Raine Cantrell

Emma Merritt

Bonnie Pega

Marylyle Rogers

SMP

ST. MARTIN'S

EMERALD ENCHANTMENT

"The Fairy's Tale" copyright © 1995 by Marylyle Rogers.
"Green Willow" copyright © 1995 by Emma Merritt.
"The Bride's Gift" copyright © 1995 by Theresa DiBenedetto.
"The Lady in Green" copyright © 1995 by Bonnie Pega.

Photograph of Emma Merritt on inside back cover by F. E. Alexander.

All rights reserved. No part of this book may be used or reproduced in any manner whatsoever without written permission except in the case of brief quotations embodied in critical articles or reviews. For information address St. Martin's Press, 175 Fifth Avenue, New York, N.Y. 10010.

ISBN: 0-312-95448-4

Printed in the United States of America

Contents

EMERALD
ENCHANTMENT

THE FAIRY'S TALE

Marylyle Rogers

Chapter One

Through the drifting mists of a distant time danced a sylphlike figure. Garbed in a gossamer gown seemingly spun of moonbeams and rose petals, Lissan whirled and dipped in time to the melody flowing from her wooden pipes. Tiny feet hardly touched the small woodland meadow's green carpet while the light of a new-risen sun accented the red sheen in golden curls swirling around her dainty figure.

Lissan halted abruptly. Her silver-green eyes narrowed to peer through the lingering lavender haze of dawn at the unexpected discovery of a dark object laying where bright glade met mysterious forest's deep shadows.

This glade and the tor behind were her home. She knew every pebble, every blade, and every bright flower intimately, but this intrusive shape was foreign to her. Hesitant, yet drawn by the unknown, Lissan's curious nature urged her forward. Still, mindful of possible peril, Lissan paused far enough away that she might disappear at the first hint of a threat.

It was a man—a *human*. Rarely had Lissan seen one of their number and never at this close a proximity. Wary but wanting to know more, she edged nearer and then nearer until by the dappled light falling through

Prologue

Ireland, early spring, 450 A.D.

Pained by his wounds, dizzy with loss of lifeblood, Killian stumbled over a half-buried root. Where forest opened to meadow he fell. His strong body, gone limp, made an ominous thud as it landed hard atop a thick mat of tangled spring grasses.

Though enveloped by the darkness of night, Killian fought to stave off the threat of Death's infinitely more ominous gloom while wondering, *Why?* Why had he alone among the Knights of the Red Branch survived Queen Maeve's treacherous assault upon warriors diverted by a hunt for deer in the forest beyond Emain Macha, their king's fortress? *Why?* Killian wondered again. Why had he lived when even their leader, Cuchulain, had fallen prey to her vicious band?

Thick black lashes closed tightly over Killian's turquoise eyes. Why had he been spared when Ulster's legendary golden warrior had fallen? Better that he had not lived to see the destruction of the Red Branch and with it a perilous weakening of King Conchobar's realm. Killian let his dark head fall back into a patch of lush clover and glared up at the star-speckled sky.

There must be a reason for his survival. But what? What use a lone knight?

overhanging branches she clearly saw the lines of a powerful form topped by a strong, handsome face.

Handsome? Aye, handsome. And, curiously unlike the golden members of her own race or any figure from humankind she had ever glimpsed. Hmmm . . . Lissan's thoughts whirled. In the first instance, she'd been led to believe the physical appearance of a human could never meet—even less over-match—the high standards set by inhabitants of her world. In the second, a person with a mane so dark was a thing she'd never dreamed existed.

Tsk, tsk. Lissan could almost hear Gran Aine's voice clicking with disapproval. Yet, despite refreshed memories of her grandmother's oft-repeated warning that unfettered curiosity beckoned danger, Lissan stepped closer still to her exciting discovery. Once standing above the unmoving mortal, she not merely saw the red-brown streak running across his temple and cheek but realized it was dried blood.

Without a moment's further hesitation, Lissan sank down to kneel amidst dense grass at the wounded man's side. She reached out and pressed her fingertips against a sun-bronzed throat. The faint throb thus detected proved him alive—although only just.

After quickly unfastening the red-enameled brooch holding his black cloak closed, Lissan laid back its edges and loosened the laces of the tunic beneath. These actions enabled her to judge the depth of a shoulder wound plainly the result of the same blow which had bloodied his temple and cheek.

"Compared to our kind, humans are quite primitive. They lack the power either to fly or to become invisible."

While Gran Aine spoke, Lissan was helpless to prevent her gaze from shifting to the fascinating, wounded stranger who at her first glimpse of his face had fostered within her a peculiar awareness. After seeing the dark man safely ensconced inside her cozy hill-home, she'd discovered the blow to his head and shoulder was but one of several injuries. Thus, she had beseeched this powerful woman's aid in tending him and already the wounds first uncovered had been treated—but only those.

"Worse," Aine added, anxious to rid her plainly intrigued granddaughter of a dangerous interest in this mortal. "They are easily maimed, even killed during their endless petty wars."

Lissan recognized the words for the intended warning they were. Pale green eyes lowered although not before glimpsing her companion's dismissive wave toward the unconscious man laying atop a large downfilled mattress covered in the sheerest of linen.

"And so vulnerable are humans to almost any ailment that even under the best of circumstances their frail forms can sustain life for only short spans of time."

"Yes, Gran Aine." Lissan knew her position in the order of their world and respectfully agreed with her grandmother, the queen. However, even due deference could not stifle her desire to seek more by winning the answer most fervently besought.

"But can you heal him?" This human was Lissan's discovery and from the moment she'd noted his wounds, a protective instinct had sprung to life. In the brief time between that moment and this she'd grown determined to ensure his survival.

"Aye." Penetrating blue eyes leveled on the younger

female. "Humans *are* fragile but their battle-torn flesh is easily mended—so long as the spark of life remains."

"Tell me what I can do to help fan his faint spark back to roaring flame." Lissan's eyes darkened with the earnestness of her plea.

"Tsk, tsk . . ." Aine shook her head in faint despair. Her descendants included a small multitude of grandchildren but Lissan was a favorite amongst them. This fact left Aine both more likely to indulge the girl and to fret over the pitfalls of any path she chose.

"You can help me rid him of his tunic." With a deep sigh of reluctant tolerance Aine answered Lissan's question. "Then while you wash away the blood, I'll blend the healing potion." Aine's eyes narrowed meaningfully. "But you must understand that, restricted by the limitations of human flesh, my salve will require more time to work the deed on him than when applied to one of our own."

Lissan realized the latter statement had been added for the sake of further emphasizing the vast differences between herself and the patient. Instantly obeying with a sweet smile of dubious consolation to her grandmother, Lissan pulled wider the laces untied in the glade.

This action eased the way for Aine to tug the wounded man's dark tunic from his inert form. While the older woman performed that task, the younger prepared to do as commanded by quickly mixing an astringent herbal solution into a basin of fresh water.

Lissan began carefully bathing dried blood from wounds which thankfully proved to be more superficial than feared. Freed from that immediate concern, her attention was claimed by another matter—an unquestioned belief disproved. Long taught that no human male could be as handsome as one from her own world, Lissan studied the figure beneath her touch and acknowledged that claim as clearly an untruth. Unable to resist the compulsion, her gaze moved down from a stunningly handsome face to trace the magnificent planes and ridges of a powerful chest half-hidden by a wedge of dark curls. Captivated by both sight and touch, an unfamiliar tension made her heart pound harder and breathing erratic.

By virtue of both age and position Aine had learned to be uncommonly perceptive and had no difficulty in recognizing the reason for Lissan's rapt expression. Thus, once blood had been soaked away by the drenched cloth wielded all too attentively, Aine's more experienced hands took over.

Lissan was uncomfortably aware of her grandmother's disapproval. Still she felt safe in watching as the other deftly applied a creamy, soothing salve to livid gashes marring a bared expanse of bronzed skin before covering each with a clean pad of folded linen.

"Come away and leave your patient in peace while I explain what must be done in continuing the treatment of torn flesh in need of mending." Aine motioned Lissan to follow as she stepped to the far side of a hearth containing an unusual fire that burned without smoke.

Despite a viciously pounding head, Killian fought through a disorienting fog of pain to surreptitiously peer between thick lashes at two unknown women. A warrior well-trained, he knew better than to betray his wakeful state. Moreover, because they were strangers to him he deemed it wiser to first seek answers to several troubling questions: Who were they? And how had he come to be under their control? Of more import, what had happened to bring him here? Indeed, where was here?

While unfamiliar feminine voices spoke in tones so quiet Killian was unable to make out their words, he attempted to win answers by giving full attention to examining these sources of sweet sounds. Each female was daintily formed, with delicate features and unusual grace of movement. Both possessed a pair of thick braids, one woman's of a gleaming hue to match the golden torque fastened about the base of an elegant throat and the other's of purest silver. 'Struth, uncommonly lovely they were although one must be considerably older than the other. But in the end their appearances provided no clues able to reveal their identities.

Hoping for better fortune with a study of his surroundings, Killian slowly glanced about, turquoise eyes widening in awe. This chamber, neither small nor large, was filled with items of rare beauty and of a making such as he'd never seen before. There were vivid wall-hangings in undreamt-of shades echoed in the hues of softly padded seats, and an iridescent pitcher with goblets that seemed formed of pearl. Stranger still, light seemed to come not from the fire alone nor any other identifiable source. Rather it seemed as if beams of sunlight had been captured by the very air within.

Nonsense! Utter nonsense. Killian clenched his eyes shut. The bash on his head must have completely knocked right senses from him. That thought brought a glimmer of relief. Leastwise now he remembered the battle and the fight which had ended with that blow . . . but it did nothing to explain how he'd come to be here.

After a few calming moments, Killian again peeked

warily at his surroundings. Only a single female remained in the chamber. Despite a throbbing head he
immediately began looking about for the door. He
found none. Impossible. With eyes narrowed to penetrating slits he renewed the search.

Lissan heard bedclothes rustle and turned to approach her guest with a winsome half-smile and con-
cern-darkened green eyes.

"Now you are awake, how fare you?"

A melodious voice, clearly-heard for the first time,
instantly won Killian's attention although an emotionless mask guarded his expression. He gazed directly
into magical silver-green eyes heavily fringed with
lashes of deep auburn and found himself unable to
look away from the loveliest sight he had ever beheld.

As no response was forthcoming, Lissan dipped the
cloth dislodged by his actions into a bucket of icy
spring water. Nervous as she could never recall having
been, Lissan wrung out the excess and neatly refolded
soft linen before brushing black hair aside to place the
pad's reviving chill across his forehead.

"Would that I knew what laid you low at the opening
of my glade." When there was still no response, a flus-
tered Lissan continued, "Whatever the cause, I will see
you restored before you leave my care."

"Who are you?" Killian's eyes narrowed. Clearly he
owed this amazing creature his gratitude for rescuing
him and treating his wounds. And yet nowise could he
ignore the ingrained distrust which had helped him survive many a hazardous challenge.

"Lissan." The answer was given without an instant's
hesitation.

"But of what family?" Killian quietly persisted.
"What kingdom?"

This time before responding Lissan took a moment to consider possible repercussions. But what choice was there? She had never willingly lied and suspected that this man would not allow silence to be her refuge.

"I am a member of the Tuatha de Danann."

Killian frowned. Did this woman mean to mock him? Or did she truly think he might believe she was a part of the Celts' mythical other world? He was not native to Erin and in the land of his birth these superstitions were unknown. He'd never heard of such beings until after he'd been taken captive by a Celtic slaver decades past.

"But from whence came you?" Lissan promptly decided the best defense against uncomfortable questions would be to ask her own. "You look not to be a part of any race who has crossed this way."

"I'm from Gaul." The growing look of confusion on a face of such perfection that he could near believe her born of an otherworldly fairy breed left Killian feeling compelled to explain. " 'Tis a land beyond the sea and on a far, far distant shore."

Sensing an interesting tale behind these words, the curiosity her grandmother had warned against urged Lissan to learn more. "How came you to the Isle of Erin?"

Killian took a slow, deep breath. "A slaver, King Niall of Tara, took me from my home while I was but a child."

"Truly?" How could a slave be so incredibly handsome? Lissan's first misdoubts were quashed by the fact that she'd thought the same impossible for *any* human. And how could she know what was possible when she'd never before met a slave, even less conversed with one. In the next instant the memory of one certain fact lent strength to her suspicions.

"If you are a slave, then how is it that I found you wearing the garments of a warrior?"

"Many years gone by I was given to King Conchobar of Ulster as part of a tribute owed." Killian was more amused than offended by the beauty's skepticism. Many members of Conchobar's court still found his position of respect difficult to accept. "My new lord had me trained to arms and added to his army. In time—by my feats of strength and proven valor—I earned a place in his elite guard of champions, the Red Branch."

A solemn Lissan recognized the depth of pride in his voice and accepted his flat claim for truth. "But if you were wounded in battle, then surely your companions-in-arms must be searching for you."

As if a cloud had passed over the sun, Killian's brilliant blue eyes darkened while his face went as still and cold as granite. "They are all dead." Only his hands moved, curling into tightly clenched fists. "I alone survived Queen Maeve's assault."

"Queen Maeve?" A third voice intruded.

Killian's attention shifted to find the same silver-haired woman seen earlier in conversation with Lissan. A tight frown emphasized the core of strength in her unique, ageless beauty.

"Are you certain it was an assault made at Maeve's behest?" Aine demanded.

Killian's lips firmed into a tight line against this implication that he might either have misidentified the singular Maeve or have knowingly made a false claim.

Annoyed, Aine shook her head and absently waved aside the human's profitless affront while relentlessly seeking information she deemed imperative. "Does Maeve know *your* history?"

The wry humor which had seen Killian through any number of difficult confrontations came to his aid. With a half-smile of great charm he obliquely stated, "I expect Maeve knows all that can be known of any foe's strengths and weaknesses."

Aine's expression was grim, and she abruptly cut off the conversation with Killian by pointedly turning toward the younger woman.

"Don't you see, Lissan? Before you lays the fulfillment to the prophecy of our doom?"

Lissan glanced sharply from grandmother to Killian, green eyes widening while a stricken look tinted her delicate face with soft color.

"But there are many, many slaves abroad in Erin," Lissan argued, desperately wanting to believe her grandmother's suggestion unfounded. "How can you say that *he* is the one?"

Aine immediately countered, "How many of those slaves are warriors, champions for a king?"

"The prophecy says nothing of either warrior or champion." Lissan was quick to point out this favorable fact. For, in truth, the seer had stated only that a slave would bring an end to the Tuatha de Danann in the world of mankind.

Killian's brilliant gaze met his sweet, unexpected defender's sea-green eyes. In their stormy depths he saw the waging of a powerful battle between hope and fear.

"Does it not?" Aine quietly asked the plainly distracted girl, forcing calm over a growing irritation aggravated by concern. "Best you further ponder the meaning of 'clad in unexpected human garb' more closely."

Killian glanced toward the older woman only to discover she wasn't there. Startled, he ignored the contin-
uous painful thumping in his head and twisted about
looking for her. She was gone . . . completely gone.

Chapter Two

Harp strings issued a shimmer of notes and through their glittering strands wooden pipes wove a wild melody. The gentle music, which had filled the fairy queen's court while a rich feast was consumed, changed into this sprightly tune as a summons for the bright company to merge in joyful dance. Yet before the first steps could be taken, the merriment was interrupted by a deep voice.

"Queen Aine, I beg your ear."

Perched atop a chair lushly padded with silk cushions, Aine shifted her attention toward an unexpected arrival. It was her much-beloved grandson, a golden-haired, powerful figure with potent smile and charm of manner that enabled her to proudly claim him one of the most attractive examples of all the best in their race.

"Comlan, what odd imp lends so stiff a tone to your words?" Rarely in all the years since the days of his childhood had the pleasant-natured prince adopted such an air of solemn ceremony.

Bronze brows arched in question while a mocking sparkle danced in emerald eyes. "I bring Maeve's formal 'request' for an audience with you."

Aine restrained the hiss of disgust inspired by that

name but few others amongst the many present in her
court wasted the effort. By blood half of fairy-folk and
half of humankind, the despicable Maeve was truly
welcome in neither world.

"Request? Hah!" A smile not of pleasure but rather
of cynicism curled Aine's lips. Oh, how it must gall that
imperious woman to be forced into such a deed. Not
for the first time, Aine thought how fortuitous it was
that although Maeve could sense where the Tuatha de
Danann abided she lacked the ability to enter the
Realm of Faerie without the aid of its inhabitants.

"How did she inveigle you into importuning me on
her behalf?" Aine knew very well that Comlan would
never have willingly agreed to do the deed.

"Maeve lay in wait for me and my companions on
our favorite riding path. She blocked my cavalcade by
placing a hazelwood fence across our path and refused
to command her minions to see it removed until after I
brought her request for an audience to you."

Aine was not surprised by Maeve's trickery. The
woman could work little magic of her own but knew
enough of fairy ways to make a nuisance of herself.
Wands of hazelwood could aid a fairy in wielding
power to cast spells but that same power could be
worked against them when employed as nearly the only
barrier impassable to one of their kind. There were few
who knew the secret of that fairy bane and fewer still
those who would dare to wield it against them.

Aine's eyes snapped with irritated displeasure. Yet
she had not reached her advanced age and supreme
position without first mastering the subtle mysteries of
judicious timing for all actions taken.

"Comlan, wrap your cloak about Maeve, from head
to toe. Bring her to me now."

In the instant following Comlan's disappearance, Aine turned toward her watching subjects. "Once I've had done with the annoyance Maeve embodies, we'll return to the joys of our gathering."

Mere moments after these words left Aine's mouth Comlan reappeared with a cloak-bundled figure at his side. Even as Maeve fought free of rich velvet, she spouted a foolishly bold ultimatum for one standing alone in the midst of another's court.

"I have come to demand that you surrender to me the wounded warrior wrongfully given safe harbor."

The words won more soft laughter from onlookers than gasps of shock, but Aine's expression remained unchanged. "Demand?"

"Aye," Maeve instantly responded. "To do else than I have asked will be the worse for you and yours."

"This warrior . . . whose warrior?" Aine moved a short step nearer to her uninvited guest. "Surely you'd not be so foolish as to ask that I surrender one of my own?"

Maeve grimaced and shook her head, impatient with the obvious attempt at diversion. "Nay, a human warrior. As well you know."

"Human?" Aine's brows rose in exaggerated surprise. "And by what witless reasoning would you dream I might have an interest in protecting any such lesser being?" Her contempt for humankind was well known, and she now donned the image of that emotion as a most believable mask.

"My army followed the wounded warrior's trail to the area where your granddaughter lives. There they found a great puddle of lost blood . . . but no body." Maeve willingly spoke of this proof of a wounded warrior but chose not to reveal the discovery of the brooch which might yet prove a useful tool in her scheme.

"And because you've lost a body—a *human* body— you leap to the conclusion that I might have rescued him?" Aine slowly shook her head in feigned amazement over Maeve's reasoning. In reality her surprise came from the fact that this woman hadn't intruded earlier when by the reckoning of mankind more than a sennight had passed since that warrior's wounds were treated.

"I am not one to be so easily mislead, Aine." Maeve steadily glared into the fairy queen's eyes, hating her the more for a beauty so little marred by passing time. "After a thorough search 'tis clear that the only remaining place where a gravely injured human could be is inside the very hill at whose base he fell . . . and it a part of your realm. Yield him to me now and avoid the grim consequences in which doing else will surely result."

Adopting a fine expression of pity, Aine responded, "Do you expect me to tremble at the prospect of a battle between my powerful fairy legion and your puny mortal army?"

Maeve sneered her disdain and shrugged. "The consequences my warning speaks of may well be war— abetted by my knowledge of fairy vulnerabilities—or may be so simple a penalty for denying me what I seek as the seizing of something . . ." A brief pause echoed with dire portent. ". . . Or some*one* you treasure."

Watching the confrontation unfold, Comlan had initially been amused by Maeve's unfounded arrogance in making threats she could nowise fulfill but he took her last menacing words a great deal more seriously. Comlan recognized, as surely his Gran Aine must, that this was a thinly veiled threat against his only sister, Lissan.

Killian struggled to rise, alone in a dwelling of uncanny beauty that was a perfect background for its owner's beguiling allure. Because this chamber lacked windows he'd no way to determine whether 'twas hours or days which had passed since he'd first awakened atop Lissan's down-filled mattress. Though it seemed the former, if judged by the healing state of his wounds, it must be the latter.

However, the headaches which returned whenever the normally fit Killian attempted too strenuous a physical activity lingered to remind him of new and deplorable limitations. He'd begun to worry that without consistent exercise his strength could but dwindle.

With that concern in mind, Killian moved carefully from his comfortable bed across a floor that was softened by a scattering of thick carpets. In an arm's span of the wall, he paused and reached out to peek behind the large, iridescent tapestry hanging there. Beneath was strangely smooth and unbroken stone. He moved further along to look under the next tapestry and then the next and the next until he again stood facing the first, perplexed.

In a single instant Lissan silently appeared in the chamber's midst, unobserved by Killian. She waited, motionless and watching, curious about the purpose for her patient's actions while at the same time falling prey to the irresistible lure of admiring him.

During the length of his convalescence Lissan had found it difficult to prevent her eyes from straying to this devastating human although she'd valiantly fought to keep her fascination unseen. Only while Killian slept under the influence of Gran Aine's healing potions had she felt free to study his superb masculinity. And only while applying unguents to rapidly mending flesh dared she touch him.

By those treatments she knew how soon he'd be restored—a fact which first had inspired melancholy but then had deepened to dread. She fought to block that gloomy thought. Nowise could she confess that from the physical nearness and quiet conversations of recent time together had come a closeness of more than mere proximity and assuredly wrongful longings. This admission of forbidden feelings tinted smooth, creamy cheeks with a wild rose hue and hastened her into unwary speech.

"You should be resting," Lissan softly chided.

Killian whirled about and, almost losing his footing when his head began to swim, stumbled awkwardly back against the wall. "Nay, I should be out in the fresh air, striving to recover my good health and rebuild my stamina." The irritation in his frown was more a response to his faltering action's shaming betrayal of weakness than to her gentle suggestion.

Lissan nibbled her lips, uncertain how best to counter Killian's claim. Gran Aine was rarely truly annoyed with her yet Lissan had sensed it was that emotion which laid at the base of a warning given. Her grandmother had cautioned Lissan against the further transgression of sharing with this human more fairy rites or abilities than already she had.

Before the maid could marshal an acceptable response to her guest's words, Killian made a sweeping motion. "I searched for the door but found none. Are you holding me prisoner?" He pushed himself away from the wall he'd fallen against. "Mayhap all your actions have been plotted in league with Queen Maeve?"

"Maeve?" The shocked horror in this single word made it clear the suggestion was unthinkable to Lissan. "You are not a prisoner but rather a guest, a wounded man to whom much needed aid was freely rendered."

Guilt for his completely unjustified assault upon a plainly innocent damsel brought a rare heat to Killian's cheeks. "I pray pardon. Seldom have I been plagued with any ailment and never do I accept physical limitations easily, hence my hasty, ill-conceived words."

Lissan promptly glided toward the rueful man while extending her hands palm up. "Lay your fingers in mine and close your eyes."

Bemused by the odd request, Killian's dark brows furrowed. But contrary to recent words that implied elsewise, he'd come to trust this maid for the sweet-natured yet sharp-witted being their quiet, pleasant conversations had proven her to be. Without hesitation Killian did as Lissan asked.

In the next instant Killian felt a cool breeze lift the weight of black hair from his neck. His eyes opened to discover that the two of them were standing in the midst of a meadow lent a silvery sheen by the glowing sickle of a quarter moon.

"You *are* a fairy." Killian said it with a charming grin and mock astonishment. Whenever he had awakened from a sleep no doubt induced by the potions Lissan provided, he'd found her hovering near. It was during such moments that they'd settled into the habit of discussing many subjects. But, despite her frank answer to his initial questions on first waking, she'd gently avoided any further revelations concerning her heritage.

Lissan smiled in response to Killian's statement yet remained mute as she backed several paces away from the too-intriguing human. Already she'd confessed her nature once. Since then, in deference to her grandmother's fervent words of caution, Lissan had accepted that admission as an error which daren't be repeated.

"I shouldn't be surprised." Killian's rueful grimace gave way to a potent smile. "You are the loveliest creature I have ever seen . . . far too beautiful to be a mere human." When Lissan still failed to respond—beyond an unpreventable blush of pleasure—he inwardly acknowledged her long-suspected quandary. To ease her way, Killian posed another question, one Lissan would likely find easier to answer.

"Where did you find me wounded and when?"

"One morn I discovered you laying on the meadow's edge just this side of that great oak." A slender arm gracefully motioned toward the imposing silhouette of a massive tree towering on the glade's far side. "I was frightened but my curiosity prodded me to investigate." An impish grin turned into a less-than-repentant pout. "Grandmother swears curiosity threatens to be the end of me."

"Frightened?" Killian was startled. Considering his injured state when she'd come upon him, how could that be true? "You were frightened of me?"

"Not frightened of *you.*" Lissan gave her dainty head a slight shake. "Simply frightened by the nearness of any member of your race."

"Why?" Killian found the concept of fairies fearing humans inconceivable. Surely in the tales he'd been told it had always been the reverse with humans apprehensive of the Tuatha de Danann's otherworldly powers.

Lissan saw Killian's incredulity and immediately sought to explain her reaction. "Humans seem a violent folk, prone to taking more pleasure in a battle than in merry festivities."

Killian did not immediately respond. A slight scowl knit dark brows while for the first time he saw himself and his manner of living through the eyes of another who existed outside his sphere. As this was the first opening to a topic of serious substance since their initial exchange of words, he treated it with the solemn thought it deserved.

"I fear you mistake pride in a duty well done for pleasure in the fight in and of itself. As one of King Conchobar's champions 'tis my duty to defend him and his realm. I worked hard to win that honor and have continued to work as hard to justify the gift."

Knowing it was as mere slave that Killian had begun his struggle for acceptance, Lissan had no doubt he spoke true of the toil required. The night's faint light seemed to collect and burn brighter on a thick braid falling forward as Lissan inclined her head, accepting her companion's comments in the same spirit with which they were offered.

"Now it is my turn to beg your forgiveness for an unintentional slight. Even in my land we've heard praises sung about the Knights of the Red Branch. Never did I mean to denigrate your honorable feats of valor." While lifting small cupped hands daintily joined together in tender supplication toward the dark man, Lissan made a quiet plea. "Pray forgive me?"

"Done," Killian responded with a devastating smile that robbed Lissan of steady breath. And yet it was the man who learned anew the folly of ignoring his unaccustomed weakness in an unwise attempt to move toward her too quickly. Dizziness accompanied a renewed thumping in his head, and he slowly sank to his knees atop the glade's grassy carpet.

Nibbling a full lower lip, a concerned Lissan wondered what she ought do to best aid him. But then, on seeing self-disgust curl his lips, potential words were stalled by the opening of her soft heart. She recognized how difficult it must be for a man whose form demonstrated formidable strength to find his natural abilities even temporarily limited.

"You were right in saying I needed time to heal." Though embarrassed by his sudden weakness, Killian chose to use it to good advantage as explanation of his search for her home's outgoing portal and desire for exercise. "But I also was right in claiming the importance of rebuilding my strength."

Despite the lingering, limiting effects of Killian's injuries, Lissan saw by his unaltered aura of physical power that such energies could be no more than temporarily thwarted. While his talk of regained strength was a goal she shared, at the same time his determined words lent vivid details to Lissan's vision of the moment he'd wish to leave her company. That thought reinforced the dread she'd already recognized as a confession of wrongful emotions.

Killian was *human*. She was not. It was a bald fact which made any consideration of a bond between them the dream of a fool. And though Lissan knew that Gran Aine might be justified in naming her both too curious and too daring, she was no witless simpleton.

"Are you going to stand there frowning down at me until the dawning?" Killian recognized his previous, defensive words as a likely cause of the sudden, unaccountable gloom darkening Lissan's normally bright eyes and tried to revive her blithe spirit with gentle cheer. "Sit down, leastways for a while, and join me in a silly childhood game."

As Killian had hoped, the maid's curiosity overcame bleak thoughts. Lissan settled beside him before turning a questioning gaze his way.

"Before the slavers took me from my home in Gaul I lived on a small farm with my parents and two sisters." Killian hadn't allowed these desolate memories to surface for many a long year. But now with this exceptional companion it seemed a natural deed both comfortable and comforting.

Lissan heard the note of melancholy in his deep voice. She ached for Killian's past anguish although his usual tone of wry amusement soon obscured that revealing chink in his armor.

"During the shorter days of early spring and late autumn, when it soon grew too dark for chores yet remained too early for easy sleep, we'd gather in a small meadow much like this. With closed eyes and in sequence from youngest to oldest, we'd take turns identifying some living thing by its scent alone. Around and around the circle we'd go until one participant after another withdrew for lack of a suggestion. The sole person remaining at the end was the champion . . . leastwise until the next competition."

Lissan laughed with delight over this new amusement. However, she did wonder if perhaps her companion might either be unaware of how acute were a fairy's senses or simply thought her unacquainted with the lay of her own grounds.

"It sounds a jolly game, but I would win, you know." Lissan deemed it only fair to warn him. "It couldn't be elsewise."

"We shall see." Killian's slow, potent smile returned. "But first you must learn the rules. Either of us may challenge the other on any single item. Then, to verify their claim, the namer of the plant's presence must lead the way to where it grows."

"Plants?" Delicate brows rose in exaggerated surprise as Lissan leaned away from the man all too disturbingly near. "Do you not include animals amongst your *living things?*"

"In family contests of old the possibilities were restricted to plants. But since this challenge involves only we two, I'm willing to expand the choices and include animals."

Acknowledging his concession with a faint smile, Lissan began to suspect that the stunning man's disorienting nearness might prove her initial confidence folly. Eyes demurely lowered and attempting to tamp down a dangerous response to Killian's likely unintentional wiles, Lissan's heart skipped a beat when his strong hands swallowed her much smaller ones inside their gentle grasp. "Now close your eyes."

The game began in simple stages during which she listed a briar rose and day lily against his honeysuckle and daisy. But eventually the contest progressed to more difficult challenges—everything from holly to the reticent night blooming aster and from field mouse to ferret.

At length and after a long pause for careful consideration, Lissan came up with a single additional entry. "Wolves."

"Wolves?" Killian's surprise was apparent. Surely even the daring Lissan would be unwilling to calmly sit here if dangerous, unpredictable wolves lurked in the area.

"Aye," Lissan promptly confirmed. "There's a den full of nearly weaned cubs on the far side of my tor. Come, I'll show them to you." She made to rise but as Killian still held one of her hands he gently restrained her at his side.

"Nay, I concede you were right in predicting you would win." Killian's feigned chagrin immediately warmed into an appealing smile. "In truth, I knew it would be so at the outset but hoped you'd find this a sufficiently enjoyable activity to see us remain occupied out here in Nature's restoring embrace." He gazed into the beauty's delicate face and asked, "Do you resent giving me the boon of your company amidst such pleasant surroundings?"

Although a fairy's home could be deemed nature's equal, Lissan, too, valued her glade's sweet, reviving tranquillity. Thus she understood Killian's meaning and instinctively responded with a beguilingly gentle smile. But soon she glanced away from his intense scrutiny.

During time whiled away in a cheery game, the moon had slipped from the sky. Only starshine remained to provide the faint light against which Killian studied the perfect symmetry of his companion's profile. Hours spent together had not blunted his awed admiration of Lissan's incredible beauty. And why not? She was the embodiment of that illusive, magical creature: fairy.

Killian knew he must soon return to his own world, to his own duties. Indeed he'd warned Lissan that goal must be won. And yet it was uncommonly difficult to contemplate never again seeing this enchanting damsel whose loveliness extended beyond beauty of face and form to the fiery sweetness of spirit within. Born in separate if parallel worlds, there could be no future for them. Even as Killian stoically acknowledged this fact, it thrust an invisible dagger into his soul and delivered a pain sharper than could be produced by any well-honed blade.

All too sensitive to the potent lure in unwavering turquoise eyes, Lissan lost a prudent but doomed battle to prevent her attention from responding to his wordless summons. Helplessly turning toward the darkly handsome man, she found his heavy-lidded gaze so intent on her lips that it felt like a kiss and inspired strange, thrilling sensations to tremble through her body.

Driven by the prospect of shared time grown short and despite certainty in the wrong of this action, Killian slowly drew the yielding beauty's delicious curves into his strong arms. All rational thought of why this should never happen between two so different sank into oblivion beneath the searing river of passion in his blood.

As Killian's mouth began moving gently, enticingly across her cheeks, Lissan shuddered. And when he nibbled at the corners of petal-soft lips, she sighed. To tempt her into seeking the ever-deepening kiss he craved, Killian brushed his mouth lightly across her lips again and again until they fell open on an anguished gasp.

Lissan buried her fingers into strands as black as the night all around, urging Killian to give the liquid fire of his kiss to her yearning lips. At last he melded their mouths into a devastating kiss which both satisfied and increased a wild new hunger. She crushed herself against his powerful form, reveling in the pleasure of iron thews intimately near even while whimpering with untutored need for something more.

Met by this innocent's unexpectedly wanton passion, Killian felt as if he'd been swept into a swirling vortex of fire. Though to him these moments were worth any price, perversely it was Lissan's stunningly passionate response which doused him with the icy water of sanity. He would not see her pay the price for his wrongly taken pleasure.

Killian abruptly broke the seal of their mouths and lifted his head while cradling the gilded fire of Lissan's hair beneath his chin. The maid's lips parted but her protest went unspoken.

"Lissan!"

Had Killian not earlier seen stars scattered across a cloudless night sky, he might've suspected this ominous accusation to have been eerily delivered on a deep roll of thunder.

"Comlan—" Lissan struggled free of Killian's arms and guiltily straightened to sit bravely facing her brother.

"To my own disgust I see that Maeve was correct . . . likely for the first time. You *have* fallen prey to a mere human's wiles."

Lissan's cheeks flushed with uncomfortable heat. She didn't think Killian a *mere* anything. However, she could hardly deny an action so obvious as her willing participation in a shared embrace—nor could she truthfully claim any wish to do so.

Before the maid could speak, with more grace than he'd feared recent debilities would permit, Killian succeeded in gaining his feet. He immediately moved to place his body as a shield between the still-seated maid and this looming stranger.

"I stand as champion to Lissan," Killian boldly announced.

" 'Struth?" A harsh smile accompanied Comlan's response. "And I stand as her brother and closest blood kin. I'd ask you your purpose here but I've already heard that sorry tale tonight in the court of our grandmother, the queen."

"Sorry tale?" Finding her tongue, Lissan jumped up and stormed toward her brother. "No sorry tale was it but rather the rescue of a brave warrior sorely deceived and ambushed by the treacherous Maeve."

At this heated defense, Comlan's eyes narrowed in a less jaundiced scrutiny of the proud warrior who returned his gaze without flinching. Despite his grandmother's attempts to imbue him with her disdain for humankind, he chose to consider each specimen for their own individual traits.

Lissan was pleased by this signal of a willingness to hear what yet needed to be said. "Killian alone from among the Knights of the Red Branch survived Maeve's treacherous scheme to obliterate them all."

"You alone?" Comlan directed his question toward the other male and after winning the immediate, brief nod of a raven-dark head, softly mused, "This then is why Maeve demanded that Gran Aine surrender you into her control."

"She can't give Killian to Maeve!" Lissan's eyes narrowed into green slits of horrified disgust.

"Fortunately for the pair of you, grandmother agrees." Comlan's attention rested with heavy portent upon his sister. "Of course that response infuriated Maeve the more. And in reprisal she made a threat which she claims will either end in all-out war against our Faerie Realm . . . or the seizing of something precious to Gran Aine."

"Maeve's army could never stand against the force

of Faerie." Lissan promptly refuted the first danger but added a denial of the second with less confidence. "And what is the likelihood of a split-blood launching a successful raid against one of our kind?"

While brother wordlessly sent sister a look full of meaning, Killian clearly recognized the hazardous position into which his mere presence had placed his benefactors. As a warrior trained to stand strong and dare any personal danger in defense of others, this situation was untenable.

"I'm certain you know the folly you speak," Comlan quietly refuted his sister's claim. "And there's little point in debating the matter. Not when I've simply come to warn you that the only place either of you can be assured of safekeeping is within an abode impenetrable to either Maeve or those in her service—your hill-home."

Killian, appalled by the mere suggestion of cowering from a foe, startled siblings who seemed to have forgot his presence by flatly stating, "I will not hide from the fight."

"Humans are such fools." Disdain curled Comlan's lips as he slowly shook his golden-hair which, like Lissan's, glowed even in the moonless hours of night. "They permit pride to push them unprepared into dangers better defeated after calm advance planning."

Thick black lashes clenched tightly together while the truth in this sound observation swept over Killian.

"You are right." Killian's brilliant blue eyes opened to directly meet the other male's gaze as without hesitation he admitted his error and thus won a surprised Comlan's reluctant approval. "By harsh experience I've learned well enough the importance of never going forth ill-prepared for the challenge to be met." Killian

shifted his attention to the plainly concerned fairy
damsel. "I'll return to Lissan's home . . . for a time."

Lissan was pleased with Killian's immediate admission of initial poor reasoning followed by his wise
choice to seek the shelter of her hill-home. But beneath that warm response, she was discomfited by in-
tentions left unspoken yet as certain as if issued in a
royal edict—he meant soon to leave and valiantly face
Maeve's threat.

Chapter Three

"Where's my brooch?" a darkly frowning Killian absently muttered to himself while holding the right hem of a black cloak over his left shoulder. He studied both the intricate pattern of various carpets on the floor below and the smooth top of the trunk on one side where he'd found his neatly folded cape.

During the brief time since their return to her hillhome Lissan had watched with growing despair while her guest took stock of his belongings. His actions were clearly preparation for a final leave-taking. That certainty deepened her distress but even it couldn't block her guilty admission of a forgotten deed. And it was guilt Lissan felt for the fact that between the morn she'd discovered the injured warrior and this moment she hadn't once remembered the red enameled clasp removed from his cloak.

"Was it of great value?"

"To me." Startled from preoccupation with his search, Killian instantly glanced up into repentant green eyes.

"Its loss is my fault."

By Lissan's immediate acceptance of blame Killian realized his words had contained an unintentional re-proach. And the rueful explanation she next gave increased his regret.

"After finding you I pulled it loose, permitting me to move obstructing cloth aside and better judge the extent of your wounds."

Anxious to prevent Lissan from suffering guilt over a deed whose purpose had been a generous act of kindness, Killian sought to mitigate the damage of his previous words. "It was an item of little worth to anyone save me and certainly not treasure of such price as to justify distressing you."

Although the handsome man negligently shrugged, Lissan was nowise convinced and probed for the truth. "But it *was* valuable to you . . . yes?"

Realizing this damsel was too perceptive to be easily misdirected, Killian made a calm admission. "It was a token presented by King Conchobar as he welcomed me into the elite ranks of the Red Branch."

Though these words were flatly stated, the acute senses of her kind enabled Lissan to detect a regret tinged with dismay. She murmured aloud what surely those emotions further revealed. "As symbol of that bond it has become your personal talisman."

" 'Struth." Black hair brushed across broad shoulders as with a wry smile Killian deeply bowed his head in concession. "My personal talisman, and never since the giving have I gone into battle without it."

Lissan felt wretched about causing the loss of an item so important to this exceptional human who had captured her interest at first sight. And then with the potent charm of a valiant spirit had conquered her fairy's heart.

"I went back for your cloak but didn't think to look for its clasp."

Renewing his attempts to lighten her gloom, Killian's smile warmed while he gently proposed a solution. "The clasp may still lay where it fell." His smile brightened into a roguish grin. "Let's go see if we can find the missing treasure."

In that first moment, the daring nature of Killian's bold challenge sorely tempted Lissan to join her companion in the quest but . . .

Lissan gave a gentle shake to a cloud of hair freed from restraining braids, and light from the central hearth's flame emphasized its fiery glow. " 'Tis best we both take seriously Comlan's warning to remain safely here."

These words startled their speaker. Yet the next instant Lissan was pleased. Surely her brother, even her grandmother would be proud, although surprised, by this exercise of good sense and wise restraint from a maiden too oft lacking in those attributes.

Killian was mesmerized by the myriad emotions quickly flashing across a beautiful face—surprise, dimple-peeking merriment, pride, and then—before he could assimilate and form a response—wistful regret.

Lissan was still troubled by Killian's loss and her rueful but prudent rejection of his suggested remedy. In a hopeful effort at restitution she made a gracious offer —one more generous than he was likely to understand.

"I'll give you my brooch to use in your clasp's stead." Lissan promptly hastened to where her velvet cloak hung. She pulled free the sharp, emerald-topped pin fastening together two of its layers through an intricately wrought circle of gold.

Killian gazed into Lissan's solemn face as she turned to approach with the prize cradled in her hand. Lingering regret darkened green eyes like a smoky haze drift-

ing across the woodland. Recognizing her anxiety to
ease his feeling of loss, he knew that to refuse would be
an insult to her generous intent. Without further words
he allowed small fingers to place the rich ornament
into his much larger palm.

"I thank you for entrusting me with so precious an
ornament." Killian immediately attached the priceless
piece to his cloak. "I will take great care to see it re-
turns to you unharmed."

Lissan wished she dare explain that it was the brooch
which would see him unharmed rather than the other
way about. Unfortunately, Gran Aine had forbidden
her to speak with Killian of such mystical matters as
that the brooch's worth went far beyond mere beauty
to the protective powers vested in amulets wrought
amidst her world.

Her brooch could be of more literal use to Killian in
any battle, but Lissan realized his inability to understand its purpose meant the absence of his own might
limit the good effects of hers. The mere presence of his
own talisman doubtless imbued him with an intangible
power: a confidence of equal value. That lack was her
fault and guilt added to the anguish in a vision of him
departing into danger. As Gran Aine had said, humans
were easily maimed. So, by the lack she'd caused he
might never return at all.

"I can't bear for you to leave me." Lissan hadn't
meant to speak her thoughts aloud and immediately bit
her lip to prevent further useless admissions.

"I would gladly stay here and count the world well
lost for the pleasure of your company were it not for
duties owed, oaths made that must be kept."

"But surely your people already believe you are lost
to them and thus your oaths are negated." It was a

desperate argument and one Lissan didn't truly expect a man of honor to accept. Nor, she'd later admit, would he have kept her admiration by committing such an act.

"Queen Maeve clearly knows I survived . . ." Killian grimaced. "But even if she did not . . ."

Lissan's cause was lost and she knew it. Though she said nothing more, a single tear welled from brimming eyes to lay its silver track down one softly rosed cheek. She recognized this rarity as shame to a fairy whose breed seldom cried. Joy. Love. Anger. Passion. Even hate. These were all emotions valued by the Tuatha de Danann, but to them sorrow was anathema.

"The challenge goes beyond even the importance of preserving my honor," Killian quietly reasoned while gently brushing loose golden tendrils back from the wistful damsel's damp face. "For the sake of both my king and the peace of your Faerie Realm I *must* thwart Maeve's schemes."

Fearing to further shame herself by attempting to speak around tears forming an uncomfortable block in her throat, Lissan firmly bit at her lower lip.

Against her silence, Killian made a final resolute statement. "I refuse to be the freed slave your grandmother's seer has predicted will see an end to you all." A muscle jerked in his clenched jaw and he instinctively gripped the hilt of his sword. "Nor will I let the foul Maeve, Queen of Connaught, claim victory over King Conchobar of Ulster by virtue of having utterly destroyed the whole of his Red Branch."

"But you can't go tonight." Alarmed that he meant to insist on pursuing perilous goals immediately, Lissan unthinkingly pressed small hands against a broad chest while in desperation offering the only argument which came quickly to mind. "You'd forfeit the weapon of surprise."

"Nay." Although Killian deemed this a most woefully inadequate reason for remaining, the mere fact that the beauty temptingly near cared so greatly for his safety deepened his useless wish to stay forever at her side.

"I'll not leave this night." Killian gave Lissan a wry smile full of self-mockery. "Nor likely until the morrow is far advanced."

Even a reprieve severely limited ignited in Lissan's green eyes so many sparkles of relief that they seemed to turn all of shining silver.

Killian found Lissan's further demonstration of emotion for him incredible and it proved too potent a lure. Wrapping the precious creature fully within his embrace, he cradled her close against his chest while burying his face into fragrant masses of coppery hair.

Once inside the circle of Killian's arms, the feel of his muscular body overwhelmed Lissan with burning sensations. Too aware of how likely these were to be their last moments of complete privacy, Lissan refused to heed the inner warning bells of unwelcome sanity. Rather, she rose on tiptoes to align herself more closely with him while wrapping her arms about his neck and tangling fingers into cool strands of black.

Reacting to Lissan's honey-sweet temptations, Killian twined his fingers into silky curls and gently pulled her head back until he could gaze down into eyes darkened to the hue of a stormy sea. Voice dropping into deep velvet tones, he made one final, half-hearted attempt at calm reasoning.

"Will our actions be judged defilement by your kindred?" Killian gently growled the words into an ear he

sted urgently across the breadth of his
n welcomed her onslaught of wild, untu-
on and responded with a deep, devastating
maginable pleasure. And when his mouth
id flame down her throat to the laces there,
k deeper into his thrall while tingles of ever-
light rippled over her.

gh shudder ran through Killian, a just reflec-
Lissan's trembling hunger. Having passed be-
ol reason, beyond sensible restraints and into a
hunger become almost a tangible thing, he
neither of them were capable of remaining up-
much longer.

ile reclaiming her mouth in a kiss of passionate
sity, Killian first swept her up into gentle arms and
slowly laid her atop the down-filled mattress. As
ame down at her side, he again let his lips savor
addictive delicacy of her long, elegant throat.

Lissan's world spun with wickedly sweet sensations
the trail of consuming flames climbed back up to
ke possession of her sigh-parted lips. Masculine lips
emanded and received even as caressing fingers alternately stroked and loosened the front laces of her gown
until its top half lay an unwanted barrier about her
waist.

With this first goal achieved, Killian rose above to
permit a burning gaze to drink in the full measure of
her truly remarkable loveliness. From slumberous eyes
to half-parted lips to the ripe curves and gentle valleys
of her body. It left him further convinced of the imperative need to ensure their single experience of mutual
love must be as incredibly memorable for them both.

Under the gleaming blue admiration revealed from
beneath desire-heavy eyelids, Lissan felt only pride in

couldn't help but
lieve the fairy-folk
matters than human
he knew it unlikely t

"If you'll be deemed
release you." Even whil
slid down the curve of l
nearer still.

Having already refused
welcomed the smoky haze
intimate touch. Under a deli
ever stronger, her eyes drifted
terly pliant in his arms. Nuzzlin
her tongue taste the expanse of

A harsh groan rose up from K
blood in his veins caught fire fr
touch. Despite a lack of verbal answ
he chose to accept the beguiling b
wanton actions as a far more effective

Killian pulled back but only far en
him to rain short, teasing kisses on cheel
the corners of her mouth. She gasped her
his lips lifted before fully claiming hers and
stead to press whisper-light caresses into th
hollows beneath her ears. All were a temptin
but achingly unsatisfying.

With fingers that had never loosed their hold
midnight mane, Lissan tugged her tormentor's r
back to hers. Yet still his mouth merely bit soft.
hers, tongue entering and withdrawing in teas
strokes.

After repeated tastes of the honeyed nectar inside—
brief and unsatisfying—Killian's breath came as fast
and ragged as hers. Driven by anguished need, Lissan

suddenly tw
chest. Killia
tored passi
kiss of un
trailed liq
Lissan sa
hotter de
A rou
tion of
yond cc
greedy
feared
right
Wh
inter
ther
he
the

as
ta
c

couldn't help but caress. He desperately wanted to believe the fairy-folk might feel differently about such matters than humankind but in the depths of his soul he knew it unlikely to be so.

"If you'll be deemed tainted, though it kill me, I will release you." Even while Killian spoke his errant hands slid down the curve of Lissan's back to clasp her hips nearer still.

Having already refused to count future cost, Lissan welcomed the smoky haze of pleasure roused by his intimate touch. Under a delicious new hunger growing ever stronger, her eyes drifted shut, and she went utterly pliant in his arms. Nuzzling his throat, Lissan let her tongue taste the expanse of skin beneath her lips.

A harsh groan rose up from Killian's depths as the blood in his veins caught fire from the tantalizing touch. Despite a lack of verbal answer to his question, he chose to accept the beguiling beauty's recklessly wanton actions as a far more effective response.

Killian pulled back but only far enough to permit him to rain short, teasing kisses on cheeks, eyelids and the corners of her mouth. She gasped her dismay when his lips lifted before fully claiming hers and moved instead to press whisper-light caresses into the sensitive hollows beneath her ears. All were a tempting delight but achingly unsatisfying.

With fingers that had never loosed their hold in his midnight mane, Lissan tugged her tormentor's mouth back to hers. Yet still his mouth merely bit softly at hers, tongue entering and withdrawing in teasing strokes.

After repeated tastes of the honeyed nectar inside— brief and unsatisfying—Killian's breath came as fast and ragged as hers. Driven by anguished need, Lissan suddenly twisted urgently across the breadth of his chest. Killian welcomed her onslaught of wild, untutored passion and responded with a deep, devastating kiss of unimaginable pleasure. And when his mouth trailed liquid flame down her throat to the laces there, Lissan sank deeper into his thrall while tingles of everhotter delight rippled over her.

A rough shudder ran through Killian, a just reflection of Lissan's trembling hunger. Having passed beyond cool reason, beyond sensible restraints and into a greedy hunger become almost a tangible thing, he feared neither of them were capable of remaining upright much longer.

While reclaiming her mouth in a kiss of passionate intensity, Killian first swept her up into gentle arms and then slowly laid her atop the down-filled mattress. As he came down at her side, he again let his lips savor the addictive delicacy of her long, elegant throat.

Lissan's world spun with wickedly sweet sensations as the trail of consuming flames climbed back up to take possession of her sigh-parted lips. Masculine lips demanded and received even as caressing fingers alternately stroked and loosened the front laces of her gown until its top half lay an unwanted barrier about her waist.

With this first goal achieved, Killian rose above to permit a burning gaze to drink in the full measure of her truly remarkable loveliness. From slumberous eyes to half-parted lips to the ripe curves and gentle valleys of her body. It left him further convinced of the imperative need to ensure their single experience of mutual love must be as incredibly memorable for them both.

Under the gleaming blue admiration revealed from beneath desire-heavy eyelids, Lissan felt only pride in

Killian's approval. She wanted nothing more than to please him and lifted her arms in a wordless enticement and welcome.

Smiling through his own intense excitement, Killian needed no more specific invitation and a deep groan came from his throat as he swept her gown completely away before bending to savor her delicious offering. With lips and hands he brushed slow, searing paths and trailed fires of tender torment until she melted against him like wax turned pliant by the sun. Breath caught in her throat to sigh out in little gasps as he purposefully stoked the fires of pleasure all around, teasing her senses unmercifully until, overwhelmed by blazing sensations, she instinctively clung to him and arched into the center of his need.

The searing heat of their embrace forced a harsh groan from Killian's throat and his hands pulled her even tighter while her enticing, exciting motions pushed him perilously near an inevitable culmination. Pulling from her arms, he fought desperately to rip open the laces of his tunic and in great haste rid himself of it, along with his cross-garters and chausses. All this giving no thought to recent efforts to bring order to his belongings.

As oft in recent days, Lissan's starving gaze feasted on the magnificence of his bare chest—a powerful expanse of bronze muscles partially covered by an arrow of dark curls spreading across its width and down to a flat, firm belly. From there the territory was new and her eyes shyly skittered away.

Amused by her shyness even amidst this shared fiery need, Killian stretched out at her side and for long moments again stroked hot pleasures over her willing body with both hands and lips. Not until she was burning with unimaginable heat, wordlessly begging for an unknown surcease, and smoothing her hands over him in helpless fascination did he rise above before coming down, crushing her beneath his full weight.

Lissan welcomed the power of his form, reveled in their closeness and in the torment hotter than wildfire . . . but not enough . . . not nearly enough. Yearning to be yet nearer, she urgently ran her palms over the hard contours of his back and up to dig nails into the smooth flesh of his shoulders as she writhed against him.

Battling against his own unmanageable hunger with determination to see her initiation into this magical rite as wonderful as she was, Killian gazed down into her eyes. Losing the battle to devastating desire, his hands swept down skin like hot satin to tilt her hips into his and ease the joining feverish need demanded.

Immediately lost in a vortex of stinging pleasures, Lissan moaned with erotic delight, aware only of the gentle abrasion of skin against skin, surging wildly against him until he took command and began rocking them ever deeper into the firestorm's fury, driving them beyond sanity and into an abandon that tumbled over the precipice to shatter into a thousand shards of unfathomable ecstasy.

"I wondered why I alone was spared but now I think I see the purpose. By defeating Maeve's schemes I have the chance to protect both my king and your Faerie Realm."

Lissan pulled a small distance away to gaze up into Killian's remarkable eyes.

Fearing she meant to argue the point, Killian restated his meaning from the opposite angle. "You must see that by failing to accept Maeve's challenge myself, I might in truth be the catalyst of a conflict deadly to your world. And I cannot bear to be the source of such danger to my beloved's very existence."

Lissan went motionless beneath the joy of hearing Killian proclaim the love which in so short a time she'd come to crave. She welcomed this admission even while a tiny corner of her mind hosted amazement that he'd understood and remembered a conversation overheard between herself and Gran Aine.

"I dare not allow myself to be waylaid from going out to face my destiny on the morrow." He held Lissan a brief distance above while his penetrating gaze melded with hers. "But you've my oath that if I survive, no force on earth will bar me from returning for you."

Lissan buried her forehead into Killian's powerful chest, nestling closer to prevent him from seeing either her fear for his survival or concern for his ignorance of forces beyond human comprehension. Perversely it was the horrible possibility that he might not return which kept her from warning him of the block to any future between them. With her grandmother's disdain for all humans it seemed an unalterable barrier despite the certain fact that no matter how long her fairy life might last, she could never love another.

But then of what value that life?

Chapter Four

Lissan awoke smiling under the lingering pleasure in visions half dream and half precious memory. Thick lashes lifted a fraction allowing her to confirm that she was truly in her own hill-home and laying atop her own soft bed . . . but for the first time she was wrapped in the comforting warmth of her lover's arms. Her contented smile deepened until a glimpse of other items not commonly a part of her surroundings intruded upon her happiness with reminders of looming peril. These were the weapons of strife gathered hours earlier by a warrior intent on resuming the fight.

Anxious to avoid disturbing the sleeping Killian, Lissan eased carefully from his arms. She was determined to see one task done before he awoke. But, uncomfortably aware of possible dangers in her intended action, she cast a fleeting glance toward Killian's cloak and the golden brooch fastened amidst its dark folds.

No matter. Lissan attempted a less than convincing shrug of unconcern while telling herself that its protection was surely not necessary so early in the morn or on so simple an errand. Nay, she'd have done with the deed and be safely returned in a trice.

One instant later Lissan hastened across dew-damp grass to where the undergrowth at forest edge trapped dawn mists around an aged oak's base. An inexplicable sparkle amidst a shadowy cluster of ferns caught her attention and won the sweetness of a dimpled smile. Her quest was blessed with this almost immediate giving of its prize.

Lissan leaned forward, stretching out a dainty hand to retrieve Killian's red-enameled, bronze brooch.

Whoosh! Thump!

Startled, Lissan straightened. Tightly clutching the recovered item, she blinked rapidly against the unexpected sight of a loose-woven cage abruptly dropping over her. It had fallen from the same thick-leafed branches spreading above as those from which a band of human warriors were lowering themselves while others stepped free from the forest's dark green veil.

"What nonsense is this?" Lissan demanded the explanation with anger deepened by an alarm shameful to one of her kind.

" 'Tis a hazelwood fairy trap," a stocky, red bearded man sneered, planting meaty, scarred hands firmly on hips while turning to face the penned fairy.

"Fairies can't be trapped," Lissan announced an instant before making herself invisible to human eyes.

"We've been forewarned to expect your tricks." The response was immediate. Putting confidence in his queen's account of the power-hindering effects in the fairy bane she'd suggested, the speaker was smugly pleased even though the cage he slowly circled seemed empty. Motioning his companions to stand in a ring about the crate formed of flexible green limbs, he announced, "Aye, forewarned is thus forearmed. And by this knowledge, we can defeat your attempts to escape our snare."

Although Lissan's heart thumped with an agitation

that roused self-disgust, she stood perfectly still in order to prevent either sound or motion from betraying her unseen presence.

"Quickly, lads. Lash plank flooring to the frame." Feeling certain of success in this assigned feat and the good favor it would surely bring, the red-bearded man issued both orders and obvious explanations with glee. "By its weight when the whole is lifted you'll have proof that our prisoner remains in our hold long before we deliver her as trophy to Queen Maeve."

"Our queen would rather have had Conchobar's last remaining champion." The cynical warning came from a small, wizened man amazingly spry for his apparent age.

What fear Lissan had felt for herself instantly fled beneath the much heavier weight of terror inspired by this unveiled threat against Killian.

"Nay." The first speaker snorted his scorn for the second's statement. "You underestimate the pleasure Maeve will take in proving an ability to thwart fairy powers to her old foe, Aine, queen of the Tuatha de Danann."

As rough human hands hastily brushed aside leaves shed the previous autumn and lifted away clumps of sod, Lissan comforted herself that Killian was safe—leastways for a time. The next instant she nibbled her lower lip in remorse, knowing he would not likely thank her for protection provided by truly making him a prisoner as once he'd accused her of doing. She helplessly watched her captors work strong twine in attaching her cage's frame to newly revealed planks and regretted her wrong in leaving Killian inside her hill-home alone and unable to win free.

Aye. You acted the impetuous fool that Comlan ac-

cused all humans of being. She further acknowledged the error in not lending greater credence to her brother's warning. That and even more. She certainly shouldn't have departed so blithely from home without even the simplest device for safekeeping.

The crate tilted wildly as Lissan's captors awkwardly hoisted their burden. To hold her balance, she tightly grasped the cage's hazelwood bars. Reminded by their nature, Lissan took what limited consolation might be found in the fact that not even her magical brooch could have saved her from this humiliation.

Killian stalked from one side of the chamber to the other. Where was Lissan?

After waking he'd initially overcome the disappointment of her absence with the certainty that she'd surely be gone for only a brief time. She'd left him alone several times since his arrival but never for extended periods of time. While he dressed and checked over his weapons one more time, he reasoned that by her brother's warning and by the fears expressed for him Lissan knew better than to be gone long.

But hours had passed . . . at least it seemed so to Killian. He'd never felt more helpless in his life, not even during his days as a slave. Though his surroundings made for an incredibly beautiful prison, a prison it was and one with no door at all!

In the next moment disgust swept over Killian for this selfish preoccupation with his own difficulties. Here he stood amidst luxurious comfort while Lissan's absence raised the bleak likelihood that she had fallen prey to Maeve's dangerous snare. Killian knew too much of the Queen of Connaught's greedy, calculating and vicious habits to feel else than horrified by any thought of Lissan within her reach.

Frustrated by an inability to take action, Killian's hands curled into fists even as the thunderous voice which had startled him in the past night's glade reverberated through the room.

"Where is my sister?"

"Would that I knew," Killian answered, whirling toward Comlan. "She was gone when I awoke."

Emerald eyes narrowed in judgment of the truth in this dark warrior's claim. The next moment broad shoulders shrugged, disturbing the flow of a thick, golden mane.

"Lissan too oft acts without prudent forethought." Even the smooth veneer of annoyance covering Comlan's words failed to conceal the anxiety beneath.

Killian instantly defended Lissan despite his own recent anxiety over her foolish deed. "Pray forgive me, but when last we spoke wasn't it you who stated that going unprepared into danger was purely a human folly?"

This human's prompt response won a wry smile of approval from Comlan. He'd earlier recognized Killian as an exceptional example of his kind. And yet Comlan immediately questioned the depth of this man's awareness concerning a menacing probability.

"Do you have any idea where Lissan has gone?"

"No matter Lissan's intent," Killian answered with deceptive calm considering the animosity roused by the prospect of his beloved made captive, "I doubt she'd any part in choosing where she is now."

"But where do you think she is?" Unasked by the human, Comlan was not able to freely share his species' mystical practices. However, by insisting on such definite answers as this, he could point the way toward a promising path.

"If not already," Killian promptly answered, "then she'll soon be an unwilling guest in Queen Maeve's Connaught fortress."

"I agree." Comlan's smile was bright.

"Then free me from this place." Killian deemed the other's pleased expression an utterly inappropriate response to such a wretched probability for his own sister. "And I'll lose no moment in hastening into Connaught to see Lissan liberated."

"You . . . alone?" Golden brows arched over dancing green eyes.

Although not spoken aloud, Killian was certain the plainly incredulous Comlan was inwardly repeating his mocking assessment of human fools who act impetuously. Moreover, Killian was sharp-witted enough to see that a particular motive rested behind both these words and the other's previous questions. He was unsure only whether their intent was to raise suspicion on the strength of his honor or to lend aid by nudging him toward some mysterious goal.

"We both know Lissan was taken as a bargaining tool to force the Queen of the Tuatha de Danann into surrendering me." Killian gave his response with the forthright manner of an honorable Knight of the Red Branch—in truth, the last of his kind. "My going is likely the single action lending any hope of seeing Lissan returned to your realm."

"You intend to surrender yourself without a fight?" A peculiar mixture of expressions flickered in the green depths of Comlan's eyes, ranging from approval to disappointment.

"Nay!" Killian directly rebutted the other's miscon-

ceptions, wondering what strange manner of creature
might imagine such a thing possible. "Not merely will I
fight but I'll claim a goodly number of lives in retribution for this wrong done Lissan. Then only by falling in
honorable battle will I forfeit my own life."

Comlan was pleased to learn his admiration for Killian justified, a fact which increased his wish to aid this
human's quest to rescue Lissan. However, despite the
Tuatha de Danann's deep distaste for conventional
rules, there were limitations and principles that had to
be respected. The words must be chosen carefully, but
a warning he could give and did.

"Gran Aine and Maeve have been poised at daggers'
points for a very long time. Because of their enmity I
fear your sacrifice will go for naught. Maeve is certain
to enjoy exhibiting her captive fairy princess far too
thoroughly to cede her so easily."

"Have you an alternate plan to propose?" As Killian
asked it, he sensed that here by this question he'd
turned the key to open a door on the very goal Comlan
wanted him to find.

"Aye," Comlan quickly answered, relieved to have
the human ask for this aid he couldn't give without it
being requested. "By joining our singular gifts there
may be a better and—for both of us—an ultimately
more satisfying method to win Lissan's release."

Anxious to clear away nebulous mists and learn the
details of so welcome a possibility, Killian returned
Comlan's grin with a quizzical smile.

In the next instant Comlan disappeared.

An impatient Killian felt as if an eternity had limped
past on hobbled feet before Comlan again returned to
Lissan's hill-home. The tension of that experience was

in no way lessened during moments when, following the return of the Tuatha de Danann's prince, the man initially refused to fully explain the reason for his absence. Yet that prickling annoyance swiftly sank into nothing beneath the weighty importance of information at last given.

" 'Tis as we feared. Maeve has Lissan"—Comlan no longer smiled—"in a trap."

"Trap?" Killian was baffled. Could their kind be trapped? For a man who had rarely been confused by any of life's myriad complexities, this was a new and unpleasant sensation. "How can you know?"

"I saw it myself." Green eyes met blue unblinking.

Dubious, Killian's chin lifted. "You've been to Connaught?"

"Aye." The mocking smile returned. "And as soon as my warriors respond to my call, we'll take you there as well."

"But Maeve's fortress is a two-day ride from here."

"For you." Comlan's mocking smile deepened.

Killian's own lips clamped together. Whatever must be done and no matter the unnatural methods required, he would rescue Lissan. A more suspicious question abruptly popped to his mind and tongue: "If you can come and go in Maeve's fortress with such ease, why didn't you simply free your sister?"

"Hazelwood," Comlan succinctly answered.

"Hazelwood?" This strange response more thoroughly convinced Killian of just how incomprehensible was the logic of the Tuatha de Danann.

For the sake of achieving their goal Comlan took pity on his ally and provided a more detailed explanation of one of the Faerie Realm's limits than Gran Aine would ever have permitted a human to know.

"Hazelwood is a barrier to our kind. We can neither pass through it nor break it. Nor will it take fire from our hands."

Killian nodded while his faint smile appeared. He now saw how the "diverse gifts" of the human warrior he was and those of this magical prince might be joined to each balance the other and secure their goal.

"Then take me to Connaught and I'll break this hazelwood cage and set Lissan free."

"Nay." A golden head shook sadly. "Bars formed from green branches would take far too long for the strength of any human to sunder."

"Then how?" Killian asked, wasting no useless thought on the likely unintentional slur. He felt certain his new cohort knew of some method to overcome this challenge.

"Fire."

Turquoise eyes darkened against the unpleasant vision of his beloved threatened by flame.

"Calm yourself." Despite the return of a wry smile, Comlan immediately sought to placate the plainly worried human. "I forgot to first tell you that we of the Faerie Realm are able to walk through fire unscathed."

Killian sent Comlan a speaking glare that won a short bark of laughter.

"And while you work on turning Lissan's cage to useless ashes, I and my legion will keep Maeve's warriors too busy to interfere."

After nodding acceptance of tactics surely capable of confounding the Queen of Connaught, Killian motioned Comlan to join him in settling upon nicely padded chairs on either side of a hearth whose unnecessary fire had been allowed to go cold. They had as well wait for the coming of others important to their plan's next step in as much comfort as possible under the tension of their soon-to-be-faced challenge.

Silence stretched while sober thoughts of the task ahead occupied each. It was Killian who made the first effort to stem that dark flow. He asked about the prediction in whose execution he'd sworn to Lissan he would never willingly be a part.

"Do you agree with your grandmother's belief that I am the fulfillment of a seer's prophecy that a former slave will bring an end to the Tuatha de Danann?"

Comlan frowned slightly while sending a considering glance over his companion. But although this human was more likable and even trustworthy than he'd ever thought one could be, neither of those traits were factors in the answering opinion he gave.

"Nay. You are a warrior, doubtless fierce and greatly skilled, but none of your weapons could present a serious danger to one of our number."

"Do you mean to say you are all immortal?"

Comlan grinned. "Not quite but in human terms we do live very, very long lives."

"Then if you are not vulnerable to human ailments and injuries, the seer must have been mistaken."

" 'Tis an enigmatic puzzle to which even the seer swears there will be no answer until it begins to unfold."

Killian was reluctant to accept this explanation as an end to the subject it was plainly meant to be. In truth, it seemed to him the seer's oblique statement was simply an admission that here was a riddle which even he couldn't solve. Intrigued, Killian sought one further clue.

"Is there no way in which a human represents danger to you?"

Comlan was surprised by the other's persistence but willingly answered. "As you say, we are not vulnerable to the hazards of humanity." He shrugged and absently continued with an unimportant addition. " 'Tis only a human's disbelief that renders us permanently invisible to that being. And even then our world abides unchanged."

Choosing not to further pursue the matter in which Comlan seemed to have nothing further to reveal, Killian turned his attention to one thing the golden prince had said which raised a new question.

"You say you live great lengths of time?"

Comlan nodded, suspecting the direction of his companion's thoughts and mentally forming a response that while true still kept secret such matters as were not to be shared with humans.

"How old is Lissan?" Killian asked the expected question, earning the other's flashing grin.

"Truly—" Comlan forced a solemn expression over his face while teasing the dark man with an evasive answer. "Our time is not human time nor is it ruled by sun and moon."

Killian steadily watched the other, willing him to answer.

At last Comlan gave in, sharing more than he ought. "By human reckoning Lissan is in the spring of life's cycle."

Killian nodded, aware that this much was a concession and that he'd win no answer more definitive. It was just as well as a golden warrior abruptly appeared at Comlan's elbow.

Chapter Five

A banquet celebrating the capture of a fairy progressed with roisterous laughter and bawdy jests rolling from the warriors and slaves crowding Queen Maeve's great hall. The feasters consumed barrels of liquor and platters of hearty food, gleefully tossing bones stripped of meat into the seemingly empty hazelwood crate atop a table in the chamber's center.

It was not in Lissan's nature to patiently wait for others to act. However, now caught in bonds she could neither break nor transport herself free from, Lissan was forced to accept the frustrating fact that the very essence of this cage made doing else impossible.

Lissan found a crumb of consolation in the simple pleasure of frustrating her captors by remaining invisible. But this action required no thought, leaving Lissan little to occupy her attention. It was thus that she fell to studying Maeve's sour expression. Plainly the red-bearded man overheard during her capture had been wrong to claim the taking of a fairy sufficient for pleasing this split-blood woman. That harsh truth was proven by the lingering dissatisfaction marring coldly beautiful features more than a decade past their prime.

While ever wilder festivities continued Lissan's attempt to bar negative thoughts was forestalled by the increasing strain of worry for a man likely as thoroughly confined as she. Lissan feared Killian might be blamed for her disappearance. Or, worse, if somehow freed (no matter how remote the prospect), that Killian would valiantly offer himself in exchange for her safe return. He surely knew she would deem this a very poor bargain, just as she knew this fact would make no difference to his actions.

Lissan purposefully shifted her thoughts from current bleak realities toward the challenge of finding some means of escape. Green eyes narrowed on leaping flames. It would be impossible for her hand to set hazelwood afire but . . . To be better seen by all, her cage had been placed very near the hall's central hearth. If she rocked the crate from side to side, it might tip—

Suddenly the rafters shook under the roar of an eerie battle cry. And simultaneously two towering, iron-bound doors burst open.

Pandemonium erupted as the Tuatha de Danann's golden host fell upon the unprepared warriors of Connaught. Sotted defenders lurched to their feet. In awkward haste they overturned benches and knocked against tables still bearing the remnants of a celebration feast. Hunks of roasted meat spilled from greasy platters sliding across hazardously tilting surfaces. They thudded down, joining shards of shattered earthen pitchers to litter the floor.

Fallen food mixed with the spilled honey-mead and bitter ale splashed in wide arcs to make the planks beneath Killian's feet a slippery mess. Yet, despite either the treacheries of this path or the lethal peril of weapons slicing the air all around, he dashed through the dangerous fray.

Lissan watched as with amazing masculine grace Killian ducked beneath slashing swords, evading both poorly aimed blows and randomly thrust blades. Heart pounding loudly and breath caught painfully in her throat, Lissan fervently hoped that the gold-and-emerald brooch she'd given him would prove a shield as valuable for human as for fairy.

No weapon made contact with Killian's flesh until he leaned forward to snatch a flaming branch from the fire. In that instant a long dagger thrown with deadly accuracy stabbed to the hilt in his back. For a moment Killian arched against the piercing pain. Yet he maintained a tight grip on the burning limb while turning to stagger toward an apparently empty cage.

Killian thrust his firebrand into the crate, and as it skidded across a crudely hewn floor Lissan materialized. He froze, seemingly suspended between the stinging agony of his fresh wound and awe for the ethereal vision of this dainty beauty. Lissan's distress for his peril was unmistakable even though it was she who stood amidst flames which soon took hold. Jagged tongues of blue-tipped yellow and orange leaped upward to sear the green hazelwood branches loosely woven around an unfazed Lissan.

That Lissan's cage had yet to disintegrate into ashes prohibited her from offering her beloved the physical comfort she longed to share. Her heart ached for Killian, injured anew and this time on her behalf. His pain brought to Lissan's eyes a shimmer of crystal tears which lent them the same glow as a rain-blessed forest.

The noise of a fierce battle being waged faded beneath the voiceless yet insistent warnings clamoring for acknowledgment in Lissan's mind. An action must be taken before her magical brooch could achieve its purpose.

"Killian," Lissan softly called to the warrior still upright though his brilliant eyes had begun to glaze. "Reach behind and pull the dagger from your flesh. Try," she implored with a gently pleading smile on rose-petal lips. "Please try."

Despite limbs going numb while he rapidly slipped beyond either sane thought or rational endeavor, Killian sought to perform the feat she asked. It was difficult to force arms losing their coordination into the unnatural position required, but after repeated attempts, he gripped the dagger's handle with the straining fingers of one hand, only to discover their strength ebbing.

"Please, Killian," Lissan cajoled, knowing his only hope lay in succeeding with this necessary deed. "See?" She lifted his red-enameled clasp as added inducement. "I recovered your brooch. Maeve used it to lay this trap. And if you fail in what I've asked, her wicked schemes will surely triumph."

Between Lissan's sweet entreaty and the goad delivered by the unpleasant prospect of a foe seizing and wielding his talisman to claim victory over him, Killian forced a renewed effort.

Lissan bit hard on her lip, watching the powerful man tense every muscle to arch an injured back while reaching behind with both hands. Despite unsteady stance and gritted teeth, Killian gave the exposed handle a mighty tug.

The dagger flew free. It plowed a furrow across the hall's rush-bestrewn floor before coming to a halt at the feet of an enraged queen.

"Maeve," Killian called out, choosing not to honor

her with the title *Queen*. He straightened without thought given the wound which moments past had nearly dropped him to the ground in ignominious defeat. "You have lost both this battle and your ill-conceived war of greed."

"By what right do you dare to tell *me* when my war is lost?" Maeve's nostrils flared with fury.

"He has eyes." An unexpected voice gave this response. "As do we all." Aine calmly stood just behind Lissan. "Your army was no match for my host nor your tactics a challenge for either my granddaughter or the human who rescued her."

"My army will recover and regroup for another assault," Maeve instantly responded, going rigidly straight to harness an anger so fierce she shook under its power and tilting a pointed chin upward into an imperious angle.

"Whatever you like." The confidence in Aine's smile increased Maeve's ire fourfold. "But as you see, your cohorts and minions suffer where mine do not and never will."

Remembering Comlan's talk of the Tuatha de Danann's ability to stand impervious to human weapons, Killian knew this was true. However, he was startled to realize that the piercing pain caused by a dagger no longer in his back was gone. He looked down to meet the gentle green eyes of the woman he'd rescued. Lissan's small finger brushed over the brooch she'd lent and by that action Killian recognized this golden piece as source of the mystical power responsible for his miraculous recovery. He gave her a smile almost as potent as the borrowed amulet.

While this exchange passed between two she'd thought to control, Maeve's piercing gaze moved from

one among the fairy host to another. She had watched
the struggle and gleefully observed many of Aine's sup-
porters struck down or maimed. Yet now here they
stood unharmed while the vast majority of her support-
ers lay either dead or badly wounded.

Maeve's attention immediately returned to the last
Knight of the Red Branch, the *human* she'd seen griev-
ously injured. His death, at least, would provide her
with the right to proudly boast of possessing the might
to destroy all of King Conchobar's champions.

But Killian, the dark Gaul, also stood at his ease and
unscathed. Maeve's brimming frustration turned to apprehension when the strikingly attractive man strode
purposefully toward her, turquoise eyes glowing omi-
nously.

"You stole my talisman," Killian accused, pausing a
handsbreadth away and towering above his foe. "But
with the aid of my allies I have recovered this symbol
of the Red Branch undefeated."

As Killian waved his red-enameled brooch perilously
near, Maeve's eyes widened. She took a step back but
not fast enough to prevent Killian from ripping her
own brooch from where it fastened together the neckline of a gown.

"Now I claim yours—and with it proof of how thoroughly you have been quelled by King Conchobar's
champion."

As if on cue, although unplanned, Maeve's hall went
abruptly empty of all save those defeated, wounded or
dead.

Euphoria filled the fair host savoring victory over the
vainglorious Maeve. Their merry laughter and proud
toasts reverberated through Queen Aine's luxurious

hall, fading into silence only after its mistress motioned for compliance. She rose from a throne on the dais at one end of her chamber to address the remarkable human in their midst.

"In honor of the aid you rendered to we of the fairy folk while the feat of securing Lissan's freedom was won"— Though relishing the joy of triumph and diverted by that pleasure, still Aine acknowledged her duty as monarch of the Tuatha de Danann. Anxious to prove that her kind left no debts unpaid, she made to the last Knight of the Red Branch an offer almost immediately rued. " 'Tis only just that I grant you the fulfillment of a single wish."

"I have but one wish." Killian wasted no moment in hesitation. Rather, inspired by a dream that had hourly grown stronger, he moved to stand directly below Aine while firmly stating his desire. "I would that this night Lissan be given to me as wife . . . if she can bear a human mate."

With his final words Killian turned toward Lissan and the bright happiness glowing in green eyes gave him the fairy damsel's wordless yet unmistakable acceptance. He opened his arms and she dashed into their welcoming embrace.

For long moments Lissan buried a bright face against the soft texture of the tunic covering his broad shoulder. She'd recognized in her grandmother's words the unintentional bestowal of a wondrous gift since, save for circumstances like this, never would the older woman have countenanced even the suggestion of such an alliance.

Aine grimaced but permitted the briefest of forced nods to the steadily watching Killian. The error had come in not placing limits upon the boon to be granted a human warrior. She should've expected his request for her beloved granddaughter. Now trapped by her own lack of prudent foresight, the best Aine could do was pursue her sole, improbable hope for nullifying this wrong by convincing Lissan not to accept the man as spouse.

"Think on the matter carefully, Lissan," Aine urged. "Remember that agreement will see you bound with this being likely destined to be our destroyer."

"But, Gran Aine . . ." Lissan turned to earnestly argue, affection strengthening her wish for the older woman to leastwise recognize that her choice represented no threat to the Faerie Realm. "That surely cannot be true. Only consider how Killian came to us in a season of regeneration, of beginnings not endings. Thus, how can he be the former slave predicted to bring an end to our kind on this earth?"

Although plainly reluctant, Aine's disapproval was warmed by a brief flash of indulgent pride in her favorite granddaughter's quick wits and sound fairy logic. And yet she struggled to sway Lissan's intent.

"It matters little whether or not Killian is the one foretold now that Maeve's challenge has been soundly defeated. But he is still *human.*"

" 'Struth, but neither the prophecy nor Killian's humanity matters in the least." Lissan's response was prompt. "All means naught save the wish you've granted which will see the two of us wed this very night."

Again Aine curtly nodded, hating to be forced into admitting the inevitability of her error. And it was with ill grace that the Queen of the Tuatha de Dannan motioned her subjects into the proper double ring formation necessary to see the binding rites of their kind performed. Joining the couple, to her mind unequally matched, in the circle's center, she took battle-callused fingers and tied them to Lissan's far daintier ones with silken ribbons pulled from her own crown of fragrant blooms.

Killian had no way to comprehend the purpose behind each meaning-laden action from the fastening of hands to the sharing of a single delicate goblet filled with a most flavorsome ambrosia. But nearly as quickly as the ceremony had begun, it appeared the deed was done. He was startled when onlookers abruptly returned their attention to eating and drinking.

" 'Tis our way." Lissan rose on tiptoes to whisper into Killian's ear. "So, please do not think it an insult issued against the nature of being that you are."

Killian cradled his new wife in a gentle embrace while lifting his chin to gaze across the top of bright curls to where Aine stood with Comlan at her side. "From the depths of my heart I thank you for the precious boon you've granted, although before I can claim Lissan in human terms, I must hasten to warn my king of all that has passed since last he and I spoke."

"I will see you delivered to King Conchobar in the blink of an eye." Comlan made the offer with the same wry smile that was habitually his. "And as quickly returned to Lissan once your duty is done."

A raven-dark head nodded and the two men were instantly gone.

Seeing this departure as an unexpected but longed for opportunity, Lissan immediately approached her grandmother with a wistful smile.

"Considering the many warnings you've given that unions between fairy and human are never happy, how is it that my union with one of their number has been permitted?"

This question Aine refused to answer. As the eldest and most powerful individual among the Faerie Realm, she was rarely confounded and in this moment was deeply uncomfortable to discover that she even could be. Irritated, Aine silently gazed at Lissan through narrowed eyes.

"Was it not you who taught me that split-blood turns sour like wine gone to vinegar?" Lissan had often inwardly questioned the truth of this claim, but was merely repeating what the older woman had many times stated with unwavering certainty. "And will not my children be among the split-bloods you despise?"

Aine remained mute though she fervently believed her oft given warning was true. Indeed, had they not just fought a battle against a frightful example of that very woe? In the next instant her self-righteous defense wavered under the weight of flatly stated facts. By a promise injudiciously made, she'd been forced to see her granddaughter become part of just such an alliance. She wished it were possible to do more than desperately hope that the doom predicted for their offspring need not always come true.

"You can prevent such an ill-fate from befalling my children," Lissan solemnly claimed after rightly reading the source of Gran Aine's faintly regretful frown.

Aine was again startled. She hadn't expected the bride to change her mind so rapidly as to renounce her new mate so soon.

"You cannot make Killian one of us," Lissan quietly stated, losing no moment to specifically outline her carefully conceived plan. A pause ensued during which Lissan's heart broke from wise constraints. It thumped

wildly as she squeaked out a single all-important fact.
"But you can make me one of his kind."

Aine went white while a soft gale of gasps came from
the throats of many others supposedly involved in their
own interests rather than hers.

"Consider all that you would forfeit—" Aine began,
only to be interrupted by Lissan's immediate response.

" 'Tis what I desire more than any treasure in either
our realm or his world." Lissan's soft lips were curved
with a sweetly confident smile.

"Nay." Aine lifted her hands palm-out as if to hold
back Lissan's words. "I insist that you pause to seriously consider the depth of your commitment again.
Remember, once this rite has been performed, even I
can never see its effects undone." Strain left her melodious voice abnormally flat while she gracefully waved
toward the incredible beauty of their surroundings.
"All this will be beyond your reach. You will be a fairy
no more, unable to fly or disappear at will. And worse,
once subject to the roughness of human possessions, to
their habits and weaknesses your life will be much
harder and *much* shorter."

"I have thought of little else but my goal and its cost
since near the moment I first set eyes upon Killian."
Lissan's smile drooped forlornly. "And I'm certain that
I had rather *be* dead than exist without him in my life."
That she would miss the Faerie Realm was true, yet not
with the same depth of anguish as she would find in
missing her beloved were he no longer near.

Two absent men silently reappeared just in time to
hear Lissan's last quiet but fervent assertion. Though
Killian had no idea what had precipitated her avowal,
he quickly strode to Lissan's side and wrapped a powerful arm about her slender shoulders.

Wise enough to recognize defeat when meeting it face to face, Aine yielded with a slight shrug. "As 'tis nearly dawn, let us hie away to the brow of your hill so that as sunlight breaks across the horizon I may see this terrifyingly final deed complete."

Of a sudden Aine swept the hem of her cloak upward. With that motion the whole of her company were transported to the summit of Lissan's tor.

Wondering if he'd ever become accustomed to this mode of unexpected coming and going, Killian gazed down at the precious creature still in the circle of his arms. He'd thought their marriage rite complete but apparently that assumption was false. No matter, he was willing to do whatever was required to claim Lissan as his own.

"Come, Lissan," Aine imperiously demanded.

Lissan instantly pulled free of Killian's hold. And when he made to follow she glanced back over her shoulder to startle him with a purposeful command.

"Wait for me there."

Thick black lashes blinked and Killian's jaw dropped but he froze in place while onlookers made a wide ring about the hill's top and Lissan moved to stand at its apex. They sang a mournful tune as Aine began an eerie, awkward dance. She dipped and twirled, tracing a slowly widening circle all around the younger woman's dainty figure. Voices dropped deeper and ever deeper until all the notes seemed to crash together in a strange cacophony of harsh sounds.

Lissan went limp but only slowly sank to the ground. And as she did, Killian was awed by the amazing sight of a ring of buds bursting through the lush grass carpet. They almost instantly blossomed into lovely, fragrant flowers which perfectly encircled his fallen wife.

Killian rushed to kneel at Lissan's side, unconsciously aware that they were suddenly alone. And when she drew his mouth to hers, he welcomed their soul-binding kiss as magic far more powerful than any mere fairy spell.

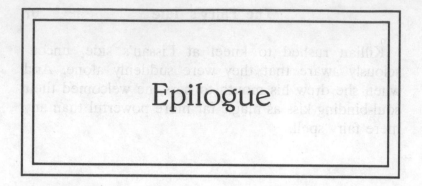

Epilogue

Spring, 453 A.D.

The first gentle shades of a fresh dawn lay across the horizon while from her hilltop home's open door, Lissan gazed contentedly out over a onetime meadow now become tilled field.

"Do you regret your choice?" Killian asked, coming to stand behind and wrap strong arms about his wife.

The bright grin Lissan cast over her shoulder was a blatant denial although delicate brows teasingly arched. This question had become a game with them since the moment he'd been thunderstruck by her sharing of a final fairy secret. That revelation had been given on their wedding night—after the Tuatha de Danann's bright host disappeared, leaving the pair of them alone in the ring of flowers which had magically appeared and ever bloomed to one side of their house. Lissan had spoken of an incredible gift already given for love of him; she'd told of how the ring of blossoms had sprung up as her fairy powers drained into the earth, leaving her as human as he.

Killian was still overwhelmed by Lissan's willing surrender of so much in order to fully share his mortal life. And he'd sworn to see that she need never regret the loss—hence, the repeated question.

His acceptance of her precious gift had been eased when in the following days and weeks it became clear that Aine had exaggerated the price Lissan would pay for her choice. That Aine had exaggerated was proven by their many visitors from the Faerie Realm and rich presents left behind in sufficient numbers to furnish a human home with indescribable luxury. Then after the birth of their small daughter, Tansy, even Aine had come calling.

That they would share both the good and bad of a human life while growing old together was a burden greatly lightened by deep and abiding love.

But this needless query was not the reason Killian had joined Lissan in the open doorway. It was late the previous night when he'd returned from a journey to Emain Macha, the King of Ulster's court. He had heard there the latest news and freshest gossip—one nearly indistinguishable from the other.

It seemed that since their confrontation, Maeve had retreated and stayed close to her own in Connaught. However, Killian did not fool himself that this tranquil condition would long last. And it wasn't this talk of lingering peace between the two kingdoms which most roused Killian's interest. Nay, his attention was claimed by another morsel of idle information, an insignificant shred of talk which had shifted the oblique pieces of an old riddle into a new and logical pattern.

Bending a dark head, Killian whispered into Lissan's ear. "I have the answer to a seer's prophecy."

There was no need to ask which seer or what prophecy. Trying not to look dubious, Lissan twisted in her husband's hold while green eyes studied the warrior she still thought the most stunning man alive. "Have you?"

"Aye." Killian gently stroked the thick copper silk flowing loose down her back. "Remember, Gran Aine said that the former slave would appear in unexpected garb."

Lissan nodded while turning in Killian's arms to face him as he continued.

"And Comlan told me that no human weapon can harm your kindred, so how could a warrior be the answer?"

A mock frown accompanied Lissan's response. "I thought you claimed to have *the answer* when all you've done is tell me who it is not."

" 'Struth." Turquoise eyes gleamed with amusement.

After a long, wordless pause, in frustration Lissan demanded, "Then tell me!"

Killian grinned and spoke again although with a further clue rather than the immediate giving of what she sought. "Comlan also explained that only when a human stops believing does the world of fairy permanently vanish from his sight."

Lissan's eyes narrowed. And though she refused to beg once more, Killian yielded.

"There is a former slave who has returned to Erin as the priest of a new religion. This Patrick teaches the people to believe *only* in his God and *never* in the Tuatha de Danann."

Lissan laughed, throwing her arms around Killian's neck to give him a tight hug before leaning back to say, "Even Gran Aine will be relieved by your discovery. It means her *Faerie Realm* won't be destroyed but merely fade from contact with the humankind she'd rather were unable to intrude."

Killian cradled her closer, pleased to think his decoding of the prophecy was some small reparation for the treasure he'd won from the Tuatha de Danann.

Yielding against her warrior's strength, Lissan buried a warm smile into his broad shoulder. There was joy in knowing that it was a human who'd first deciphered the seer's meaning . . . *her* human, *her* exceptional mate . . . and a fairy's dream tale come true.

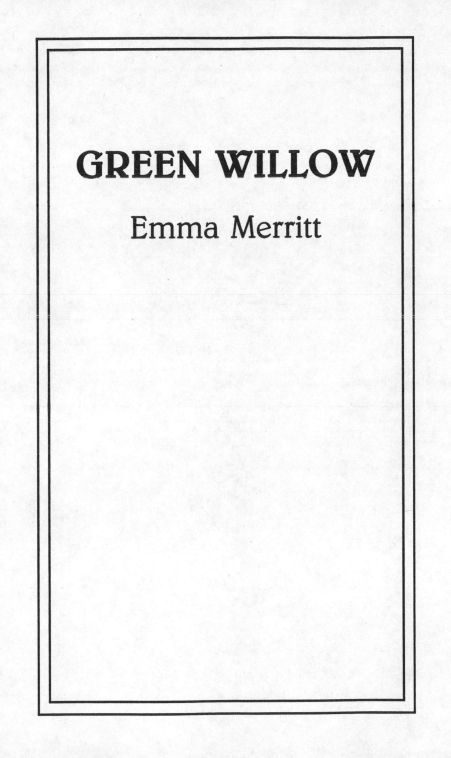

GREEN WILLOW

Emma Merritt

Chapter One

June, A.D. 864
Village of Forestgreen, Ireland

An ominous silence, heavier and darker than the night shadows, hung over the village of Forestgreen. Light from scattered torches and fires flickered. Women, children, the elderly and infirm, all who had remained behind when the warriors had ridden out to battle six days earlier, went through the motions of working. But their hearts were not in what they were doing.

Feeling the heat from the overhead torch, Willow stepped back into the shadows of the porch of Forestgreen Hall, the royal residence. Like her subjects, she too worried and wondered how the battle was going. Two days ago a messenger had arrived with news that the Irish of Forestgreen were losing. Since then the villagers had heard nothing.

A murmur caused Willow to look at the assemblymen who were bunched together to the right of the porch and who were also watching and waiting. One of them, an older, white-haired man, the tribal *brethim* or law-expounder, separated from the other council members and walked over to stand beside her on the porch.

Quietly he said, "Do not fret, my lady. We have the greatest of all champions fighting for us."

"Champions!" Willow scoffed. "We have mercenaries fighting for us, my lord Shamus. Mercenaries that you and the other councilmen demanded that I hire."

Willow would never forget that last meeting of the *óenach,* the tribal council. Because Forestgreen had no warriors or a king to champion their cause, the council members had demanded that she hire mercenaries, their recommendation being Hugh MacDougald and his warriors. Even in Ireland, they told her, the Scottish warlord's name was spoken in awe and he and his men were hailed as heroes by all who knew—who had ever heard of—them. She didn't doubt the man's prowess as a warrior, but she had deplored the idea of hiring a mercenary to fight for Forestgreen.

"The king's death made our demand necessary, my lady queen," Shamus reminded her. "His dishonor could not go unavenged."

By habit, Willow reached up and clasped the amulet she wore around her neck. A small locket, given to her by her mother before she had died, it contained a magical four-leafed shamrock and was Willow's talisman.

"Garret—the treacherous murderer!—allowed you two seasons in which to mourn your loss," Shamus continued, "but he would have been back demanding more tribute . . . and you."

Remembering the bloody massacre, Willow squeezed the amulet so tightly the edges bit into the softness of her palm. Her husband, King Angus, and his warriors had fought valiantly, but they had been no match against Garret's far superior forces. Garret had not only killed Angus, but he had shamed the king and Willow by parading the king's mutilated body up and down the main street before he dumped it on the village dung heap.

Tears warmly coursed down Willow's cheeks. Even now she could not bear the thought that her honorable husband had died such an inglorious death.

With all that Garret had not been satisfied. He had stolen all of Forestgreen's cattle and foodstuff and had taken captive many of the women and children.

During the autumn and winter Willow's tribe, the *Tuatha* de Forestgreen, had mourned the loss of their king. Willow had mourned the loss of her husband. Deep down she regretted for both her and Angus' sake that she could not mourn the loss of her lover. But she did not delude herself. Hers and Angus's marriage had been one of necessity, not of love. Now he was dead, and during their year of marriage she had not conceived a child—the blessed child who would deliver the *tuatha* from their curse. Now she would not. Angus was dead.

"Had there been another way, my lady queen," Shamus gently said, "the *óenach* would have taken it. Always your well-being is our major concern."

"Aye, Shamus," Willow admitted grudgingly, wiping the tears from her cheeks, " 'twas necessary. But to think that we had to go abroad to hire a Scotsman to help us Irish fight our own battles."

"Garret de Ywnson may have been born an Irishman, my lady," Shamus said, "but he is not one of us. He is a greedy and power-hungry overlord who preys on smaller and weaker *tuathas,* like ours. With the passing of the seasons, he demands more and more tribute and always becomes the liege for our most valiant warriors. Nay, my lady queen, I do not reckon Garret de Ywnson to be one of us."

"Neither is the Scotsman even though he fights under the colors of Forestgreen," Willow said. "Hugh MacDougald is in our service at the moment, my lord Shamus, but he is not much different from Garret. Both are motivated by greed and power. Both are for hire, one collects tribute, the other bounty. I fear we shall live to regret our having given hire to the Scotsman."

Willow and Shamus lapsed into silence, both of them gazing at the frightened villagers. The tension was palpable. At each little noise everyone jumped. Not knowing how much longer she could endure the suspense of wondering what was happening on the battlefield, Willow leaned against the porch pillar and closed her eyes. Breathing slowly and deeply, she relaxed and silently begged God for a miracle.

After a while, she thought she heard a distant noise. She moved her head and listened more closely. "My lord Shamus," she said, "I hear something. Perhaps the returning warriors?"

"I have heard them so many times in my mind during the past few days, my lady queen, that I no longer listen." He laid a hand on Willow's upper arm and squeezed reassuringly. "Our warriors will return when they return."

"They must come back in victory, Shamus," she whispered. "They *must.*"

"Aye, lass." Shamus, like a father, draped an arm around Willow's shoulder and comforted her. "They will. Have no fear. The warlord will rid us of Garret. Then he, too, will be gone from our shores."

"You have more confidence in the Highlander than I do, my lord jurist." Willow gently moved away from Shamus. "I hope you are right and I am wrong."

"Aye, lady," Shamus said, "I do, too. I like the man.
For a verity, he is a mercenary, but he is honest about
it. In all his dealings with us, I have found him to be
forthright."

"And conceited and arrogant," Willow added. "Unwilling to invite or to listen to the opinions of others."

Shamus chuckled softly. "You really do dislike the
Scotsman, don't you?"

"Aye."

From the time the Highlander had walked into
Forestgreen Hall and had been introduced to Willow,
he had upset her by not showing her the proper respect
due the queen of a *tuatha*. There had been no negotia-
tion. He had stated his terms, had assumed command
of what few warriors remained in the village, and had
kept his own counsel about his battle plans.

Willow also didn't like the Highlander because he
evoked all kinds of sensations in her, sensations she did
not wish to experience because they took precedence
over reason. Tall and rugged, with a darkly chiseled
handsomeness, he was an extension of the sword and
dirk strapped at his side, that he wielded with ease and
expertise. Like his weapons, Hugh MacDougald was
hard and lean and deadly.

Even now Willow could see him as plainly as if he
were standing before her. His thick black hair and
steely gray eyes. She would never forget the way he had
stared at her the first time he had seen her. His gaze
was filled with pure, undefiled lust. For her. His leering
made her feel as if she had been standing naked in
front of him. More, his gaze seemed to pierce through
to her very soul and to ignite a flame of desire deeply
within her . . . a fire she could not allow to burn.

Breaking into her thoughts, the jurist said in a low,

pensive voice, "The Highlander will make some woman a good husband, my lady."

Willow looked directly through the glimmering torchlight at her chief advisor. "Not for me, my lord. True, I was born under the curse, and I shall do my duty by remarrying and by bearing a child. Hopefully it will be the chosen one. But I shall not marry the Highlander."

"As you say." Shamus smiled kindly at her. "The choice is yours to make."

"I won't let you or the *óenach* forget that," she muttered.

Everyone was falling under the Highlander's spell. Willow could only imagine what would happen when . . . if . . . he returned victoriously to the village. How easily he could persuade the assemblymen that he —the man who had defeated the powerful overlord Garret de Ywnson—should receive the queen's hand in marriage. Aye, she was prepared for this. He was a crafty man, Willow had no doubt, and would not be gone soon enough for her. He was also one of the most handsome men she had ever seen.

Time passed slowly. Then from afar a lur sounded, the deep and raspy bellow of the horn slicing through the night shadows.

Shamus snapped to attention. So did the villagers. Tension reverberated through Forestgreen.

"The horn, my lady," Shamus said, his voice shaking. "Did you hear it?"

"Aye," she murmured and prayed they would hear two more blasts to announce the victory.

Shamus stepped closer to her, and both gazed beyond the gate into the darkness.

"The battle is over," Willow heard someone mumble.

"Why only one signal?" another cried.

"Why doesn't the horn blow a second and a third time?" still another wondered aloud.

"We have lost," came the dismal answer.

Paralyzed by silence, all anxiously waited. Then the lur's gusty voice was raised a second . . . a third time. For the blink of an eye silence cloaked the village to be shattered by the wail of the bagpipes as it heralded the song of the *Tuatha* de Forestgreen.

They had won! Garret de Ywnson had been defeated!

Shamus turned to Willow, clasping both her hands in his. "I told you so, my lady. I told you so."

"Aye, my lord jurist, you did." Weak with relief, Willow slumped against the wall of the house.

The villagers, jarred out of their paralysis, shouted and leaped to their feet. Hugging each other, they cried and danced in the street. Soon all had lit their torches and gathered the willow branches they had cut in preparation for victory. Rejoicing and anticipating the triumphant return of the mercenaries and the Irish who had been taken captive by Garret, the villagers strewed the branches up and down the main street.

From her vantage point Willow kept her eyes pinned to the black horizon. Her first glimmering of the warriors was a tiny dot of light that bobbed through the thick darkness: the torch carried by the standard bearer. As the warriors drew nearer, the light grew larger, the creak of leather and rumble of horses louder.

Soon the conquering heroes rode through the gate, the Highlander in the lead. Willow could not recognize his features because the torch bearer rode so far ahead of them. But she knew by the way the rider held himself that it was the Highlander. No man rode a horse like him. His back was erect, his shoulders straight, his head forward. Then the full glow of the village torchlights captured him. His helmet, cast in silver and decorated in gold, and his chain mail glistened and gave him an otherworld appearance.

Riding double with many of his warriors were the freed captives. Villagers swarmed around them, the rescued slipping to the ground, racing to their families, hugging and kissing.

"Hugh MacDougald! Hail, Hugh MacDougald! Our hero! Our champion!" The deafening chant rang throughout the village.

All but one joined in the adulation, not that Willow was not elated over the victory. She was. The Scotsman had rescued the hostages. No longer were she and her people the subjects of Garret de Ywnson. And the honor of the royal house had been avenged. For that she was grateful. But the victory was hollow. Would they now become subjects of Hugh MacDougald?

The Irish had won only because they had enlisted the help of Hugh MacDougald and his kinsmen, and it was his name the people were shouting in adulation—not that of their deceased king. Willow could not bring herself to hail the Highlander as a returning hero.

As the warriors neared Forestgreen Hall, she pushed further back into the shadows to watch. Hugh MacDougald would be making and receiving the hero's demands . . . and the demands that he might make frightened her. Heat rushed through her body as she recalled his blatant stares.

The Scottish warlord and his warriors dismounted

from their magnificent steeds and released them to the care of their own stable lads. The MacDougald refused to let any but his men handle the Scottish horses.

"Give the horses special attention, lads," the Highlander commanded, his deep voice carrying above the crowd. "They have done well by us these past days and are battle-weary."

Gilded by the flickering light of the torches, he removed his helmet with gloved hands and tucked it beneath his left arm. The evening breeze gained momentum, and he stood for a moment, his face uplifted and his eyes closed.

His cloak billowed away from his body, revealing the silver glint of chain mail that he wore over his long-sleeved white tunic. From either side of his waist hung a sword and a dirk—a favorite of the Scots. His thick black hair, cut short and usually brushed back in loose waves, blew about his face.

"He is indeed a handsome warrior," a young woman said to another as they walked by the porch of the Great House.

"Aye, a fit husband for some woman."

"Would that I was the woman."

It seemed the Highlander was winning some of her people over, Willow thought. While she agreed that he was a handsome warrior, she was also distrustful of the man. He was an outsider, a mercenary, and she wanted him out of Forestgreen, out of Ireland.

Yet she did not take her eyes off him.

One of the Scottish warriors called James, standing next to the MacDougald, spoke and the warlord lowered his head and opened his eyes. As he listened to his comrade-in-arms, he nodded from time to time, but his gaze was fastened to the porch of the royal hall.

"Now, men, let us collect our bounty," the MacDougald barked and rested his hand on the hilt of his sword, drawing Willow's attention from his broad shoulders and chest to the muscular sleekness of his lower physique. Tight brown trousers encased long, lean legs that slid seductively into calf-high boots.

He began marching toward Forestgreen Hall. His warriors, as huge and fearsome as their chieftain, fell into step behind him. The thud of his footfalls were firm and determined, those of the conquering warlord. The MacDougald wore his battle-soiled clothing with pride and a leisurely grace that belonged to a king, not a barbaric Scottish warrior. Oddly, Willow could easily imagine him wearing the rich, royal robes of a king.

The man who occupied her thoughts stopped in front of the porch. Even though Willow was cloaked in the shadows and was hidden behind her assemblymen who were now bunched together in front of the royal residence, she felt as if the Highlander was looking directly at her. A tremor ran through her body. No matter how much she disliked him, or how barbaric she thought him to be, his gaze made her aware of herself as a woman . . . as a desirable woman. And his look proclaimed to her in no uncertain terms that he desired her. Irritated with herself for thinking so much about him, irritated because her thoughts of him excited her, Willow stepped forward.

In the glimmering light of the torches attached to both sides of the building, she could see him even better. Up close he was bigger and more fearsome. His visage was hard and indomitable, a small scar running across his right temple. Again the summer wind blew strands of black hair across his face and brought Willow's attention to his silver-gray eyes that were framed with long dark lashes. His lips were tipped at the corners as if he were smiling, but his steely eyes were serious.

"Welcome home, my lord Hugh MacDougald." Shamus moved to stand beside Willow. "God has given you the victory."

Cold gray eyes pierced the *brethim*. "No one gave us the victory, jurist. We fought for it, leaving many good men dead on the battlefield."

Shamus seemed unperturbed by the warrior's sarcasm. "I have been told, my lord, that the warrior lives to die. That is the glory of battle."

"Aye, my lord jurist, if a man dies bravely that is the glory of battle, so the philosophers say." The MacDougald's gaze raked over all the assemblymen who now seemed to be huddling together. "As you can see, my lord, your captives were returned."

"What of Garret de Ywnson?" Shamus demanded.

"He and the majority of his warriors are dead," Hugh reported, "and his village razed. His power is broken."

"The cattle?"

"We found no cattle. Evidently they had hidden them elsewhere before we engaged in battle."

Shaking his head, Shamus sighed his regret.

"I delivered what I promised," Hugh said. "You and your people are safe once more, and you owe Garret no tribute."

"You have our gratitude, my lord."

"Gratitude is for crusaders. I am a warrior who fights for hire."

"Aye, my lord, so you are." Shamus nudged one of the assemblymen who stood close by. "Get the bounty."

The man nodded and waved. Two of the men brought a huge chest and set it before the Scottish warlord. Shamus lifted the lid while someone else held down a torch so that Hugh could see the gleam of riches—gold and silver studded with precious gems. The villagers, pressing closer, caught their breath at the splendor of such wealth. With renewed fervor, they began to shout and to stamp their feet. Those who were not holding torches or willow branches clapped their hands. The MacDougald gave the trunk a cursory glance, then returned his gaze to the *brethim*.

"When you invited me to come fight your battle for you, you neglected to inform me of an important custom, my lord Shamus." Hugh spoke quietly but his voice resounded with such authority that the crowd quietened and moved back. "I have learned that since you have no living king and I am your champion, I am entitled to the king's portion, as well as his title and all his possessions." The MacDougald pinned Willow with a steely gaze. "Including his wife."

Chapter Two

Willow stiffened. The villagers gasped, their gaze shifting in puzzlement from the queen to the Scotsman then back to the queen. Shamus looked at Willow.

The silence overpowered her. More frightened than she had ever been in her life, she wanted to run, to run as far away from this man as possible, but she could not. One, she had never run from unpleasant situations in her life. Second, whatever she may want for herself, she must first think of her people. She was the queen of the *Tuatha* de Forestgreen. She was the Lady of the Willow, the protector of Bishop Patrick's sacred grove of willows.

Rubbing her amulet for luck, she stepped between Hugh and the assemblymen. "In so far as you know the law, my lord Hugh, you have interpreted it correctly. But in the case of our tribe, the *Tuatha* de Forestgreen, our leadership is determined through the queen, not a king. My husband, who died two seasons ago, was king by virtue of my having selected and having married him. I do not choose to be married to you." Willow cast Hugh MacDougald a disdainful glance. "We are quite willing to give you the honor of being a hero and to award you the hero's portion, even the king's portion, but I am not part of the bargain, my lord. I am not for the taking." *Especially to a man like you.*

The warrior laughed softly. "Ah, my lady, I feel as if you have issued a challenge."

Apprehension, like an arrow nocked in a bow and drawn back for the shot, stretched tightly among the villagers.

"Nay, lord." Willow kept her voice steady, but inside she was trembling. "I have spoken the truth."

" 'Tis also a truth, madam, that as queen it is your duty to marry and to provide your people with a king."

Irritated with the man, Willow said, "I shall remarry when I have finished my period of mourning. Until such time, my lord Hugh, I shall dedicate myself to God and to the keeping of the grove that once belonged to our beloved Bishop Patrick." She smiled, hoping the gesture was condescending. "As queen of the *Tuatha* de Forestgreen, I give you permission, my lord, to select a wife from among our maidens."

"Thank you, for your generosity, my lady."

The people relaxed.

"I choose you."

They tensed again.

"I have explained—" she began.

"Brethim," Hugh bellowed, "stand forward."

The villagers stepped back from the bellowing man.

"Our law-expounder?" Willow demanded. "Why do you want him?"

Hugh took a step so that he stood immediately beneath the burning torch. His gray eyes locked with hers. He was so close, she felt the warmth of his breath on her face. She saw the texture of his skin, the beard-stubble that darkened his jaws and chin. Her heartbeat and her breathing quickened. She wanted to touch him, wanted to feel him.

"My mother's mother came from the land of the Irish, my lady," Hugh said, "and she told me the willow's tale."

The willow's tale! The words echoed through the village.

Shamus and the members of the *óenach* shuffled nervously about, murmuring among themselves.

Willow felt a chill of fear run down her spine. She had been right not to trust the Highlander. Why in the name of the blessed mother was she so attracted to him?

"Close to your village, madam, is a beautiful pond and circling it are lush willow trees."

He paused.

The people, seeming to be entranced with the seductive timbre of his voice and the sorrowful beauty of their legend, relaxed and closed in a semicircle around the porch of Forestgreen Hall.

"Bishop Patrick's grove," Willow said.

"Also, for the past six generations, the Lady of the Willow has not given birth to a male child. But this was not always so, my lady queen."

"No," Willow murmured.

"You and your ancestors are shamed and bear an ancient curse. You shall give birth to one child only and that is a woman child—the Lady of the Willow. Soon after this child is born, the mother dies. Until this curse is lifted, you and your ancestresses shall never have a direct male descendant."

Willow fought back the tears.

"Speak, my lady queen," Hugh ordered. "Is this not so?"

"Aye, 'tis the truth. Six generations ago, my ancestress, a devoted follower of Bishop Patrick, was forced to marry rather than allowed to enter into a convent. She—she—" Willow swallowed her tears as she recalled the incident. Time had not softened its atrociousness at all.

"She hated her husband," Hugh continued, "and when she had given birth to her twin children, she tried to kill them along with her husband. The husband and the girl died, but the boy lived—crippled and maimed, unable to be king because of his deformity."

Willow squeezed her eyelids tightly together, but a tear forced its way between the barriers and down her cheek.

"Through marriage she felt as if she had broken her vow of chastity to God," Willow explained. "Because she considered herself married to the church, she also felt as if she were an adulteress. Guilt caused her to go insane. She didn't know what she was doing."

"The day she killed her husband and daughter and herself, Bishop Patrick's willows changed their color, my lady. They turned from emerald green to blue."

"After my ancestress inflicted herself with the fatal wound, she lived long enough to place a curse on all her descendants. Never would the *tuatha* have a king from us. What her family and people had demanded from her, she determined they would not be able to demand from any of her descendants. We would never give birth to a child again."

Willow rubbed her amulet between her fingers.

"My grandmother told me, my lady," Hugh said, "that when the bards sing the willow's tale, they say the trees mourned the loss of the king and the princess, the injury done to the prince, and the curse. They cried so much a lake was formed."

Willow added softly, "The young child, our last direct male descendant, grew to manhood and met a wonderful woman who loved him despite his deformity. He stood beneath the Green Willow and begged Bishop Patrick to intercede and to give them a child. Seven months later, beneath the Green Willow she gave birth to her child, but she herself died a few hours later, leaving her daughter to be Lady of the Willows. From that time forward, shamrocks have grown in that very spot."

"There has not been a Lord of the Willows since that time?" Hugh asked.

"Nay," Willow said. "But all of us who are Ladies of the Willow have prayed to Bishop Patrick that our shame might be lifted. He appeared to my mother in a vision prior to her death and told her that the chosen one was coming and he would deliver our *ruatha* from its curse. Until then, we are destined—or cursed—to give birth only to girls." A strand of hair escaped Willow's wimple and fell across her forehead. She lifted her hand, her shawl draping loosely about her shoulders, and brushed the tendril from her temple.

"Even knowing this, my lady, I still claim you for my wife."

"That is a decision that only I make." What she said was partly true. She hoped that Hugh MacDougald was not familiar with their tribal customs.

"Are you afraid of marriage, my lady queen?" Hugh paused, then added, "Because you know that once you have delivered a child, you will surely die?"

Willow breathed deeply. "I have no fear of marriage itself, of bearing a child, or of dying, my lord. I know

and accept my duty to my people. I am frightened of
marrying the wrong man." She returned his steely gaze.
"I shall have only one child and possibly may not live
to see her a grown woman. I want her to have a father
of whom she can be proud, one who will guide her
through life with love and wisdom as my father did me.
I am afraid, Hugh MacDougald, that an unscrupulous
man would—"

"Would kill his daughter so that he might usurp her
kingdom," Hugh finished.

"Aye," the villagers murmured in unison.

"That is my greatest fear," Willow admitted, "and it
is not an unfounded one. Many leaders have done it."

"Madam, I give you my word before God that I am
not that kind of man. I would cherish any child that I
should father."

"Be that as it may," Willow said, "you are an admitted mercenary, a man who has sworn his allegiance to
money. I will not entrust my only child to a man who
sells his service to the highest bidder."

Assent lowly rumbled through the onlookers.

Hugh's jaws clinched. His lids lowered until his eyes
were mere slits. For the first time since she had met
him, Willow felt as if she had scored a winning point.

"As I said before, my lord, the decision of husband is
mine to make, and I do not choose you."

He smiled wickedly at her. "The decision is not altogether yours, my lady."

Once more palpable silence cloaked the village. Willow's heart skipped a beat.

The MacDougald taunted with the truth. "*Tuatha*
law must also be considered."

At the moment Willow despised Hugh MacDougald.

The man was ensnaring her in a trap from which there
was no escape.

When he spoke, his voice reeked with the insolence
of one who knew for certain that he held the upper
hand. "According to the laws of your land, madam, if a
man can perform three feats of virtue, he can win the
hand of any maiden of his choosing."

The people crowding around the porch looked to
their queen in question. The men of the *óenach* again
whispered among themselves.

Hugh looked at the *brethim*. "Is this not so, jurist?"

The old man looked from Hugh to Willow.

"Speak out," Hugh commanded.

Willow nodded to her advisor.

"Yes, my lord," the jurist replied. " 'Tis a custom and
law of the *tuatha*."

"Then, my lord Shamus, I lay my case before you
and the assembly. According to the laws of the *Tuatha
de Forestgreen*, I want Lady Willow to be my wife.
Stipulate the feats and the rules governing them."

A clamor of protest arose from the people, but Willow lifted her hands to quieten them. She understood
their outrage. She was consumed with it, too. But it
would do them no good to lose their composure, nor
she hers. Everyone needed to stay calm so she could
think, so she could outwit Hugh MacDougald.

"As you have said, there are three," the *brethim* replied. "The successful completion of each is to be
sealed by a kiss between the victor and chosen
maiden."

"What is the first feat?" Hugh asked.

"Before I answer that question, my lord," Shamus
replied, "I must warn you of the seriousness of this
challenge." He paused. "If you should fail to accom-

plish any of your feats to the *óenach's* satisfaction, you
will be killed."

"A serious judgment for a minor offense, my lord
jurist," Hugh said. "Especially when the one suffering
the humiliation and harm is the one to be executed."

"We take marriage seriously," the old man said.
"Consider this carefully, my lord MacDougald. Once
you have heard the first task, you cannot change your
mind."

The warrior called James moved closer to his chief.
"Hugh, you can't—"

"I accept," the MacDougald declared.

"By all that is holy!" his young comrade-in-arms
swore.

"My lord," the jurist said, "I beg you to reconsider."

"I have spoken!" The warlord's tone brooked no further argument.

"Hugh MacDougald," James said softly, "you are a
fool."

"I don't dispute that, Jamie lad." Hugh's voice was
as soft as that of his companion. Louder he added,
"Now, jurist, what is my first feat?"

"You will entertain us with the harp, Ireland's oldest
musical instrument, and with a dance."

"The harp!" Hugh exploded.

The villagers laughed at his expression of outrage.

"You say you take marriage seriously, and I am to be
killed should I fail to successfully perform one of these
tasks, yet you ask me, a warrior, to cavort about with a
harp? That, my lord Shamus, sounds like a ridiculous
request, one designed to humiliate."

Willow laughed softly. She could imagine this huge
warrior strutting about Forestgreen Hall, singing and
playing the harp. Yet she hoped to use his indignation

to her advantage. She laid her hand on the law-expounder's lower arm. "My lord Shamus, since Hugh MacDougald is a stranger to our shores, could I persuade you and the *óenach* to let him change his mind?"

Immediately the assemblymen began to nod their heads.

"Aye," Shamus answered.

"Nay, madam." The MacDougald's voice held a quiet, ominous ring to it. "I have spoken and so be it."

Shamus sighed. "Not only must you entertain us with the harp and dance, my lord, but like the gods of old you must play a wail strain to make the people weep, a smile strain to make them joyful, and then a sleep strain so that all who hear will fall into a blissful sleep."

Shouting their agreement, the people stamped their feet and clapped.

Hugh frowned. "What are the other two feats?"

The old man shook his head. "Each successive feat is revealed only when the one prior to it has been successfully accomplished and the kiss of confirmation has been exchanged between you and Lady Willow. This first one is stipulated by *tuatha* law."

"Are the last two as ridiculous as this one?"

"I don't know," the jurist replied. "The other two will be issued by the lady herself."

"So be it," Hugh muttered.

"You will have three days in which to prepare for your first challenge. And I would encourage you to practice, my lord. This is no simple feat."

Willow said, "There have been many who have challenged for me, or should I say my kingdom, and as many are dead, my lord. I advise you to change your mind while the assembly and I have compassion for you."

"Save your compassion for another," Hugh replied. "I don't want it. I want only your passion."

Anger roiled through Willow. "You have as much of my passion as you are going to get, Scotsman. I despise you and everything you stand for."

The villagers, as if not sure what the mercenary's response would be, sidled away from him.

He grinned. "Aye, madam, I knew that a woman with fiery brown hair like yours had to have a spark of fire within her. And you do. I like it when you are impassioned. Your green eyes flash with the heat and fire of summertime. Your . . . er—" His gaze fastened to her breasts. "Your *chest* rises and falls with your quickened breathing."

Glad that she was fully hidden by her loose shawl, Willow felt her breasts swell at the man's tormenting. Trembling uncontrollably, hiding it by slipping her hands into the long, bell-shaped sleeves of her tunic, she drew in a badly needed breath of air. The man was unnerving her. She couldn't allow him to do this to her.

When she felt that she had composed herself enough to speak calmly, she said, "Don't attempt to turn this into a jest."

"Never have I been more serious, my lady."

The deep timbre of his voice ensnared Willow, and she felt herself swaying toward him. Bemused, she stared into his eyes. The color had deepened until it was a hot, smoldering gray. Consumed by the passion, by the promise she saw in his eyes, Willow forgot who and where she was. Easily she could have lost herself in the heated depths.

"The challenge stands, lady. I won't be persuaded otherwise."

"Many have won the first kiss."

"I would think so. Entertaining with a harp cannot be too difficult."

"Not if you're a harper," Jamie muttered.

"A few have won the second kiss," Willow admitted.

"I shall be among the few."

"None has won the third."

"Be assured, madam," the rusty tones washed over her, "I shall be the first man to win all three kisses. You *shall* be my bride." The gray eyes pierced hers.

"I see that you lack not for arrogance and conceit, my lord."

"Nay, lady, my only lack at the moment is a beautiful woman in my bed."

Heat infused Willow as the Highlander blatantly gazed at her body, slowly moving from her head to her feet and up again. Shamus snorted his indignation at the insult and moved forward as if to challenge him. Knowing the old man was no match for the warlord, Willow laid her hand on her advisor's arm and stopped him.

"In due time, my lady," Hugh promised, "I shall have that."

"That remains to be seen." Again taking refuge in her defiance, Willow summarily dismissed him with a disdainful look. Then she smiled at her subjects. "My people, the night soon comes to a close. On the morrow we shall celebrate our victory over Garret de Ywnson. We shall begin with a mass of thanksgiving and end with a feast at Forestgreen Hall."

Hurrahs swelled into the air.

"Now, let us retire for the night."

"Get the treasure chest and carry it to our quarters," Hugh ordered two of his warriors.

Willow turned, her long forest-green tunic rustling

about her ankles. Although she was covered from head to foot in tunic, shawl and veils, she was one of the most beautiful women Hugh had ever seen. He had been besotted with her from the moment he had first looked into her green eyes and had seen her long, auburn hair cascading down her back. He had wanted her and wanted her even more now that he had seen the spark of fire in her. He would have demanded her as part of his bounty if she had not been the queen of the *tuatha*. As it was, he had found a legitimate way by which he could have her.

Willow swept regally into the great house. The two Scottish warriors closed the chest, hefted it between them, and started toward the conical-shaped building where Hugh and his men were lodging while they were in Forestgreen.

"I have never seen you so taken with a woman before," Jamie said.

"I had never met Willow of Forestgreen before," Hugh admitted. "For a verity, James MacDougald, my blood races hot for her, but it races even hotter for her kingdom. In Scotland I am a hero and a chieftain of a sept, a small branch of the MacDougalds, but I am not a chieftain of a clan. Here in Forestgreen, I shall be king and you and my other warriors shall be noblemen." Hugh paused, then added, "Jamie lad, I want Willow of Forestgreen for my wife, and I shall do whatever it takes to win her."

"Aye," Jamie muttered, "even to the death."

"To the death."

Chapter Three

"You are daft, Hugh MacDougald!" Jamie exclaimed. "No woman is worth this."

Hugh shifted his helmet from one arm to the other. "I'll not comment on that, Jamie lad, until I have tasted of her beauty."

Jamie snorted. "By that time, my friend, it will be too late. You will be stuck with her as your wife."

"In order to get me a kingdom, I'll take the wife," Hugh said.

"One who disdains you. A mercenary who fights for money not for loyalty, land or kinspeople."

"At least she has sentiment for me. I would be worried otherwise." Grinning at his young cousin, Hugh started walking toward their quarters. "I've discovered that one woman is much like another, and all come with the same equipage. If I find the Willow enjoyable in bed that's an added pleasure. If she's not, then I shall find me a mistress."

"All of that will happen if you successfully complete the tasks," James grimly reminded Hugh. "Otherwise, you'll be dead."

"Death shall not have me so easily, my friend," Hugh promised.

"But it will come to her once she has born her

daughter," James said. Then he peered intently at Hugh. "Is that what you're counting on?"

" 'Tis nothing more than a tale, lad."

James cut his eyes over at Hugh. "You sound as if you don't believe the curse."

"I don't, but for those who do believe in curses, they are real, laddie. I shall have to prove to my lady Willow that she is not cursed."

"Pray tell, how are you going to do that?"

"Impregnate her with a male child."

"A chieftain you are, but not god."

"Mayhap not a god, lad. But I am the chosen one. Lady Willow shall conceive our son."

"You are a fool, Hugh!" James made a face and shook his head. "The queen said many have accomplished the first feat, but you shall not be among them."

Hugh laughed.

"There's no way you can learn to play the harp in three days."

Hugh playfully clapped his young cousin on the shoulder. "Three days, lad? For a verity, you know me better than that. I shall dispense with these silly tasks as quickly as I can. I am a man sorely in need of a woman."

"They have whores for that."

"Nay, Jamie, none but the Lady Willow shall do for me. Tomorrow night at the feast I shall entertain with harp and dance as the jurist has stipulated. The first kiss between the Willow and me shall be witnessed by all who celebrate in Forestgreen Hall."

James stopped walking and turned to face Hugh. "Don't let your whimsical jesting get the best of you,

Hugh. Remember, you're a chieftain, the leader of our sept, and a hero. You can't humiliate yourself."

"Are you worried about me humiliating myself or you?" Hugh asked.

James thrust his hand through his brown hair. "Hugh MacDougald, I know you and that jesting streak in you. You love to cut the fool, but you can't do it in front of these people."

"Have you been with me so long, Jamie, and do not yet know that Hugh MacDougald does what he damn well pleases, when he damn well pleases?"

"Damn the man!" Willow muttered.

Wearing a yellow long tunic, she tossed her gauzy veils back on the bed where they joined her wimple and rose-gold diadem. She strode through the generous spill of morning sunlight, past Shamus who sat at the small table drinking a cup of mead, to the opened window. Playing with her talisman, she gazed at the frenzied activity of the mercenaries.

Some of the Scottish warriors were rolling casks of mead into the small house where they were quartering during their sojourn in Forestgreen. Others were bringing in sacks of vegetables and grains. The MacDougald and Jamie walked onto the porch when a large, empty cart rumbled up.

Willow said, "They stole anything that was worth stealing from Garret's village."

"Aye, 'tis the victor's right," Shamus reminded her.

"And they have not offered to share one whit of it with us."

"Also—"

"—the victor's right," Willow finished.

Across the street, the MacDougald opened one of

the food sacks, pulled out a handful of scallions and laughed. Then he tossed them back in and handed the pouch to Jamie. Speaking quietly, his voice not carrying across the street, he waved his hands toward the barrels. Then turning, the Scottish warlord reentered the building. Jamie, smiling grimly and shaking his head, followed.

"Whatever can he be doing?" Willow murmured.

Shamus laughed. "Certainly not practicing the harp, my dear, which is what he should be doing."

"They've been moving those casks of ale all night, Shamus. And laughing." Willow pushed a tendril of hair from her face. "Damn him! I wish we had never hired him. That he had never set foot in Forestgreen. I knew our hiring Hugh MacDougald was a mistake."

"It will be all right, my dear." Shamus soothed her. "You and I know that no man has lived to collect the third kiss. Mayhap, the MacDougald might perform the first feat successfully, but surely not the second, considering what you have planned for him."

Shamus chuckled softly. "I have heard the many tales about the sacred circle of lights, lass, and during my lifetime, I have seen many a saintly man try to conjure it up so that his people could be healed. I've yet to see someone do it."

During the night Willow had carefully planned her feats, making them as difficult—well, making them *impossible*—to complete. Still she worried. Hugh Mac-Dougald was different from any other man she had ever met. He unnerved her to such an extent that she did not want him to claim even the first kiss.

Putting her thoughts into words, she said, "My lord jurist, Hugh MacDougald is most unlike any man who has challenged for me before."

The most frightening and the most determined.

"From the way he assumes command of a situation," she continued, "I would say he is a man who always gets what he wants. And he wants my kingdom, my daughter, and me." *And he wants us in that order.*

Shamus finished off his glass of mead, then rose and laid a comforting hand on Willow's shoulder. "Don't be worried."

" 'Tis not your hand in marriage that he has demanded, jurist, or you would be worried."

Shamus grinned and winked at her. "Aye, Willow, that I would." He walked to the door, and said over his shoulder, "I shall await you in the great room. Hasten your dressing, my lady, and we shall lead the procession to the church for Mass."

When the door closed after her chief advisor, Willow continued to gaze at the activity in front of the small house. Scottish warriors loaded the barrels of mead—enough to fill the bellies of several armies—onto the cart.

"Good morning, my lady!"

Willow jumped. The MacDougald's voice startled her. Blinking, she lifted her gaze from the cart and saw him standing to one side of it on the porch.

"Good morning," Willow muttered as she visually devoured the Scottish warlord.

Although he still wore his mail and weapons and had been up a major portion of the night, he looked refreshed. His face was shaven. His hair, brushed back from his face, was burnished to shining jet by the sunlight.

He stepped off the porch and moved toward her window. "Your hair is beautiful, madam. It gleams more richly than all the precious metals or gems in the world."

Willow reflexively touched her hair and wished she had thought to put on her veils and wimple.

"Truly, my lady, you have no need of headdresses or headbands. The golden-red gleam of your hair is crown enough for any queen."

"Does poetry always flow so glibly from your tongue, my lord MacDougald?" Willow hid behind sarcasm.

"Nay, lady, only when I find inspiration."

As he moved closer to Forestgreen Hall, Willow stepped further back into the chamber. Reaching up, she caught the thong that held the window covering in place.

"Pray excuse me, lord. I need to complete my dressing so that I may attend Mass. I presume you will honor us with your presence." She jerked the cord, and the shade fell into place.

His soft laughter mocked her.

"Aye, my lady."

With shaking hands, Willow quickly adjusted her veils around her head and neck. She donned her wimple, making sure that it hung low over her forehead, and settled the rose-gold diadem over it. She glanced a last time at her image reflected on the oval piece of polished copper that hung on the wall. Satisfied that she was as covered as she could be, as hidden from the MacDougald's sight as she could be, she walked out of her sleeping chamber into the corridor that led to the great room.

"My lord Shamus," she called, "let's be on our way. The sooner we get started, the sooner we can get rid of this loathsome mercenary."

"Madam," the MacDougald's voice dripped with

feigned injury as he stepped out of the shadows to stand before her, "is that any way to talk about the man who liberated your village from bondage to a tyrant?" His cloak swayed from his broad shoulders and brushed against his muscular legs.

Her face burning with embarrassment, Willow asked, "What are you doing here?"

Hugh grinned. "Escorting you to the church, my lady."

"I shall walk with my advisor."

The grin faded. "Nay, lady."

"Shamus," Willow called.

"I have sent him away." Hugh caught her hand. She tugged, but he clasped it firmly. "I am a mercenary, madam, and that you knew from the beginning. As to my being loathsome, I don't think so. But I do know—as do you and all your villagers—that I am the returning hero and your champion. It is I who will escort you to church." His gray eyes glittered. "And who shall sit beside you and will take communion after you."

"You are most presumptuous," Willow grated between clenched teeth.

"Aye," he agreed as he placed the palm of her hand over the top of his. "I've had to be, madam, else I would not be a warrior of repute."

"I would say a warrior of ill-repute, my lord."

"Sometimes, my lady, it doesn't matter whether the reputation is good or bad, so long as one has it."

She frowned in disgust, and he laughed.

"Now, shall we proceed? Your villagers are waiting with eagerness to begin their day of festivities. And so am I. The day shall go all too quickly for me."

"Not for me," Willow muttered.

"Would it make you feel any better, my lady," Hugh

said, "to know that I shall perform the first feat tonight at the feast?"

Willow stopped in her tracks. "Tonight?"

"Aye, lady, tonight. I shall collect my first kiss."

Unable to comprehend this man standing beside her, Willow stared at him.

"You're beautiful when you look at me with those challenging eyes, madam." The MacDougald's voice was thick as he leaned so close to her that their faces nearly touched. She could feel the warmth of his breath on her skin. "I'm tempted to take my first kiss now."

He touched his finger to her bottom lip, breaking the spell, and Willow jumped back.

He smiled. "But I shall wait. I don't want to do anything that would nullify the challenge."

Chapter Four

Willow had been in a daze ever since the Highlander had announced his intention of performing the first feat of the challenge at the victory banquet. Even now that night had fallen and the banquet about to begin, Willow could hardly believe that he meant to follow through with his announcement. Sitting at the head of the High Table in Forestgreen Hall, she gazed through the opened entrance doors, impatiently awaiting his arrival. Both the challenge and the man hung like a storm cloud over her.

As if he were a god, the Highlander stepped out of the silver-hued twilight into the doorway and paused, his powerful physique dwarfing all who stood around him. Although he wore his weapons, he had taken off his mail and had flung his tartan over one shoulder. The gold cloak brooch glittered in the firelight. A white tunic and midnight-blue trousers accentuated his broad shoulders and muscular hips and legs. Cinched about his waist was a black leathern girdle with three gold latchets.

After a moment's pause, he strode arrogantly through the crowded room to the High Table where he bowed to Willow. Then he straightened, his gaze fastening to her face. Slowly his eyes moved, and she felt his visual examination as he looked first at her crown and wimple . . . the veils she had wrapped around her head, neck and shoulders . . . the long-sleeved tunic . . . the fur-trimmed long cloak.

"The evening is mild, my lady queen," he said. "You're bundled up as if it were winter. Aren't you rather warm?"

"I'm quite comfortable," she answered, even as perspiration beaded her upper lip.

"Aye, lady, I can tell," he said dryly. "Still you look beautiful. That is, what little I can see—your face and your hands—peeking out from among your clothing."

The MacDougald's voice flowed seductively over Willow.

"You're seeing all that is necessary for you to see, my lord. After all, I am not a heifer who is being sold and is in need of an inspection."

The Highlander laughed softly, the sound pleasing to Willow.

"I thank God that you are not, madam, but I believe the cost of winning your hand is high enough that I might be permitted to see a little more."

"We shall save the *little more,* my lord, for after the completion of the feats. Perhaps it will give you added incentive."

The color of his eyes deepened, and Willow caught her breath at the unspoken promise she saw in them. "Aye, my lady, it does indeed." He walked around the table, stepped onto the dais, and pulled out the King's High Seat.

Shocked, Willow stared at him. The hall grew quiet.

"That's the—king's—"

"Aye, madam, I know, and he was a brave man. He

would be honored to have another warrior of such repute to claim his chair."

In one moment the warrior could seduce her with his smiles and caresses and winsome ways. In the next he infuriated her with his arrogance. She rose. "I don't think, my lord, that there is any comparison between you and my husband."

"My lord Hugh," Shamus called out from the entrance doors, "do I understand that you are going to attempt your first feat tonight?"

Frenzied murmuring buzzed through the hall as the villagers turned to look at the law-expounder who walked toward the High Table and his chair to the left of the queen. Willow glared at Hugh. He gave her a condescending grin.

Easing into the King's High Seat, Hugh said, "Aye, jurist, that I am."

Humiliated that the MacDougald was already acting as if he were the king and angry that her chief advisor had interrupted, Willow slid back into her chair.

The Highlander waved a hand, and several of his warriors rolled mead barrels into the hall and set them upright in front of the kitchen door. Jamie, a large harp in his arms, followed. Only the thud of the lad's boots on the planked floor resounded through the room. When he reached the High Table, he handed the instrument to his liege.

Hugh accepted the harp as if he were as familiar with it as he was with his weapons. While his men rolled in more barrels of mead, he stood and walked to the center of the hall.

"Pull the plugs, laddies and lasses," Hugh shouted. "Serve the ale."

As servants hastened to obey, Hugh strolled leisurely

among the tables of villagers. When all glasses and tankards were filled, he raised his. "To the joyful note which I shall play."

The people shouted and raised their ale in reply.

When he had drained his glass, Hugh motioned for a refill. "Drink heartily, my friends."

Willow leaned over to Shamus and said none too quietly, "They're going to need to drink heartily in order to endure this night."

"I heard that, my lady queen." Hugh turned to her, his eyes twinkling. "I promise this will be a night to remember rather than one to endure."

Several toasts later, tankards and glasses had been refilled and everyone was ready for the next salutation. Hugh set down his tankard and situated the harp on the edge of the High Table in front of Willow.

"Now, lads and lasses, I shall play you a joyful note from Ireland's oldest musical instrument, the harp." Hugh lightly ran his fingers across the strings, a whine reverberating through the hall. The villagers grinned. So did Hugh.

Willow did not.

"And the sound is going to be more joyous, people of Forestgreen, when you realize that you are drinking the best ale in all of Ireland." He plucked the harp.

The discordant tones caused Willow to wince.

"Provided to you by Garret de Ywnson," Hugh announced with a pinging flourish on the strings. More disharmonious notes swelled through Forestgreen Hall.

The people laughed. Some of them leaped to their feet and danced a jig; others waved their tankards for yet another refill.

"Are you happy, people of Forestgreen?" Hugh shouted.

Ayes resounded all over the room.

Hugh turned to the jurist. "My lord Shamus, I believe I have successfully performed the first part of the feat."

Furious, Willow glared at him. "You didn't play, my lord. You plucked the strings, filling the hall with a horrid sound."

Hugh's expression was serious, but his eyes glittered with devilment. "Madam, I was not instructed to play tunes, and I believe that all harping is a matter of plucking the strings."

"You did this through trickery and deceit, my lord."

"A little," he admitted, "but the Forestgreen jurist did not exclude such tactics, madam."

Shamus rose. The people slapped their palms against the table, stamped their feet and yelled, "Hail, Hugh MacDougald!"

Willow grew even grimmer.

"My lord Hugh, you have made us laugh," the *brethim* announced, "but can you make us cry?"

"Cry, my lord?" Hugh exclaimed. "A few strains of music from this harp shall have tears running down everyone's cheeks." He looked over at Willow and winked. "To show how much I dislike turning your laughter into tears, I shall give you drink from Garret's best."

Hurrahs swelled through the building.

"No more ale," Willow declared.

The people quietened and looked curiously back and forth between Willow and Hugh.

"Madam, is it right to add to the rules once the challenge has begun?"

"Nay," the crowd roared.

Willow breathed deeply.

"But, my lady queen, I shall defer to your wish. I will serve no more ale."

A groan of protest rose from the villagers.

Hugh laughed aloud and announced, "We shall drink Garret's best imported wine."

The cries of the people were deafening.

"One condition," Hugh shouted as servants moved through the hall refilling glasses. "Once you have put the glass to your lips, you shall not set it down until it is empty."

To show their agreement, the villagers slapped their hands against the table.

"Are you sure you want to do this, Hugh MacDougald?" Jamie asked, his face grim, his tankard brimming with the deep amber liquid.

"Are you not man enough for the challenge?" Hugh countered.

" 'Tis not a question of manhood but one of stupidity," Jamie muttered, his eyes fixed on his glass.

" 'Tis time for the *wail strain.*" Hugh lifted his glass to his lips and drained it in several deep swallows. As the villagers followed his example, he began to pluck the strings of the harp.

When Willow set her glass down, her mouth and throat were on fire. Tears streamed down her cheeks. She looked around. Everyone was gasping, coughing and holding their throats . . . and crying.

"Scallions!" she croaked. "You mashed scallions and put them in the wine!"

Grinning, although tears tracked his cheeks, Hugh continued to strum the harp.

Willow pushed to her feet and balanced her weight on palms flattened against the High Table. "Don't deny it," she said. "I saw you bringing the vegetable bags into the small house last night."

"I'll not be denying it, lady. 'Tis true." He set the harp down. "But all are weeping."

"But they are not sad," Willow pointed out.

Hugh pursed his lips as if in thought and rubbed his chin. "In all due respect, my lady queen, I think wailing, not sadness, was demanded. Your jurist said that I must play a wail strain to make people weep, and I have done that." Hugh turned first to the villagers, then to his own warriors. "All are teary-eyed, my lady."

"Nay!" Willow exclaimed, trying to blink back her own tears.

"Aye," the people clamored.

Hugh leaned across the High Table and gently ran his thumb beneath her eyes. Softly he said, "Aye, madam. Even you."

Willow trembled but didn't move from the touch of his hand.

Shamus rose. "The Highlander has successfully completed the second part of the feat. He has succeeded in making us weep. What do you propose to do now, my lord?"

" 'Tis far too early in the night to put the villagers to sleep, lord *brethim*," he said without taking his gaze from Willow's, "so I shall dance."

More hurrahs sounded.

"Musicians play," Hugh called out. He straightened and walked to stand beside Willow's chair. "My lady queen, I should like for you to dance with me."

Lost in the fathomless beauty of his eyes, Willow said, "Aren't you supposed to be playing the harp at the same time that you dance, my lord?"

"Nay, lady." He caught both her hands in his and

gently tugged her from the chair. When she was standing close to him, he lowered his head and said, "What man would agree to hold a harp while he dances when he can be holding a desirable woman?"

Lost in the sultry beauty of his words and the sensuality of the man himself, Willow followed him to the middle of the hall. She was vaguely aware of scraping sounds as the villagers moved tables and benches out of the way. Music filled the room, and the mighty Highlander and the Queen of Forestgreen began to dance.

Willow was aware only of the man. Downy-gray eyes. Beard-stubbled jaws. His smile. His hand touching hers. The illusive promise of his body brushing past hers as he guided her up and down the room.

"Yesterday, my lord, you said you would look ridiculous *cavorting* about with a harp."

"Aye," he returned, "and I did." A mischievous smile glistened in his eyes. "As you can see, my lady, I risk much in order to have you for my wife."

"Me or my kingdom?"

"Both."

"But if you could only have one, which would you prefer?"

"Since that is not a question I must ponder, my lady, let us not trouble ourselves with it."

" 'Tis one that I always ponder," Willow returned.

"I shall be a good husband to you," Hugh promised.

"You're certain that you shall win?"

"Aye, lady, that's how much I want you."

Unable to look into the Highlander's eyes any longer, Willow lowered her own. He did things to her emotions that she didn't understand. He had confessed that he wanted both her and her kingdom, had refused to tell her which was the most important to him. Yet she trembled in his arms.

"You dance well," she said, trying to regain her aplomb. Her gaze went to the weapons strapped around his waist. As well as he wielded the sword and dirk. Oddly, he seemed to be as much at ease dancing as he did fighting.

"Aye, we Scots love our music and dancing."

The tempo of the music increased, and Hugh swirled Willow around the room. Only their hands touched, yet Willow felt as if she were bonded body and soul to the man. When the music stopped, Hugh caught her in his arms and twirled her around, the hem of her tunic swishing about her ankles.

Laughing and dragging in deep breaths of air, Willow threw her arms around his neck and laid her cheek against his chest. She heard the wild thudding of his heart and felt his chest rise and fall with his breathing. She lifted her head. Again their gazes caught and held.

"My lady Willow," he murmured, "I must have a taste of you now. If I tarry until I put this entire assembly to sleep, I shall have to wait for the morrow."

Willow had never really desired a man's kisses . . . until now. She wanted to know what the Highlander's lips felt like pressed to hers, but she could not. As he lowered his head, she lifted her hand, catching his chin and holding it still.

"Nay, my lord—"

"Nay," he muttered, his expression hardening.

"You wouldn't want to do anything that would nullify the challenge."

He stared at her for endless seconds before he laughed, deeply and richly. "Nay, madam, for verity, I would not."

He carried her back to the dais and settled her on the Queen's High Seat.

"Now, people of Forestgreen," he shouted as if he were the king, and Willow did not object, "let us dine."

Although Willow had celebrated many feasts before, this one was different. She ate her dinner with relish, accepting a bite from the Highlander every now and again, drank more wine than she customarily did, and listened spellbound as the Scottish bard sang of the great deeds of the MacDougald.

Every once in a while, she would look at Hugh at the same time that he gazed at her, and she lost herself in the depth of his eyes. Once he had brushed a droplet of wine from her lips, his fingers sending shivers of pleasure through her body. Again she had leaned over to brush a bread crumb from his chin, her fingers tarrying much longer than necessary against the abrasive caress of his beard-shadowed flesh.

Later she laid bets and shouted encouragement as the warriors competed among themselves in arm wrestling, darts, and board games. She even joined in the amusement, laughing and joshing the Highlander when she defeated him at darts. Deep down she knew that he had allowed her the victory. Hugh was escorting her back to the High Seats when Shamus rose.

"The evening soon comes to a close, my lord Hugh," he said, "and all shall naturally fall asleep. It is time for you to complete your first feat."

"Aye, my lord Shamus, 'tis time," Hugh said.

This was one of the most wonderful feasts Willow had ever attended, and she was saddened that it must end so quickly.

The Highlander waved to the servants. "Let us have

one more glass of wine to say good-night. Then I shall play the sleep strain."

Feeling quite mellow and magnanimous, Willow laughed. "My lord Highlander, I am getting altogether too familiar with you. I suspect that you have drugged our wine so that we shall go to sleep."

"You have reason to suspect, my lady Willow," he replied, "but I guarantee you have not grown familiar enough with me."

Willow felt her cheeks flush.

"I promise to remedy that, my lady. And very soon." He smiled at her, then turned to the jurist. "My lord Shamus, with the assembly's permission, I shall not cast a sleeping spell over you or myself, so that we shall know that all truly did go to sleep while I played the sleep strain."

Shamus nodded his head. "Agreed, my lord."

Hugh rose and moved to the center of the building. Picking up the harp in one hand, he held aloft a glass of wine in the other. "People of Forestgreen, tonight we end our revelry with gentle sleep and sweet dreams. On the morrow at the noon, I shall claim my victor's kiss from Lady Willow. All who wish to witness it may join us at the willow grove."

"Also, my people," Willow called out, "I shall issue the second challenge."

"Drain your glasses," Hugh shouted, "and listen to my song."

Their glasses emptied, the people settled back. Hugh plucked a string, the delicate sound winging through the room. He began to talk, his deep voice lulling Willow with its cadence and its sorrowful tale of a warrior who had gone to a far country to seek his fame and fortune. He said something about having found true love, but she was too sleepy to hear more.

"My lord," Shamus said, "everyone appears to be asleep."

Hugh laid down his harp. "Shall we put them to the test, jurist?"

"Nay, I am too tired to do it myself. I am sleepy."

Walking around the High Table, Hugh pulled out the queen's chair and scooped Willow into his arms. She roused, slowly lifting her lids.

"You did put us to sleep, my lord," she mumbled.

"Aye," Hugh grumbled, "all but me."

Willow burrowed into his arms, her diadem slipping to one side, veils falling away from her face to reveal a long slender neck with creamy smooth skin and a wealth of thick, auburn curls. Desire burned through Hugh, making him acutely aware of how long he had been without a woman.

But then . . . he had never wanted a woman as much as he wanted Willow of Forestgreen.

Long strides carried him across the great room into the corridor, then into Willow's bed chamber. Light from torches attached to the wall on either side of the door and the central fire illuminated a commodious room that was elegantly furnished.

A huge bed with ornately carved head- and footboards reposed against the far wall. Hanging behind it was a wall tapestry. A table and chairs were grouped together across the room. A large clothing trunk, as richly carved and decorated as the head- and footboards, sat to one side of the bed, another at the foot. Still a third one, a low one that doubled as a bench, had been placed beneath the window. Plump cushions and furniture covers decorated the trunks and chairs.

Hugh laid Willow on the bed and began to undress her. First, her shoes and her calf-high leggings, his eyes lingering on her lower legs. Wanting her with a hunger he had never experienced before, Hugh fought his desires. He lowered her skirt to cover her ankles.

Piece by piece he removed her clothing. Her diadem. The cloak. The numerous veils.

When they were removed, her hair spilled about her face. Unable to help himself, he ran his hand through the silken strands. With his finger, he gently outlined her face and brushed the fullness of her lips.

He picked up one of the folded covers on the trunk at the end of the bed and covered Willow. Then he bent and lightly kissed her forehead.

"Good night, my lady," he murmured.

Putting out the torches but leaving the fire to burn low, Hugh exited from Willow's bed chamber.

Her question came back to haunt him. Which did he want more, her or the kingdom? Warrior he was, he wanted the kingdom. Man that he was, he wanted Willow of Forestgreen.

Chapter Five

At noon the willow grove was a beautiful sight. The sweeping branches, in full leaf and bloom, danced gracefully in the early summer breeze. The Green Willow, the largest tree in the grove and the one from which all others were said to have sprung, grew close to the lake, its branches sweeping low, the tips of them dipping into the water. Ripples spiraled out from them as the sicklebacks and minnows played. All of the branches reminded Willow of delicate and magical silver-blue wands.

She stood beneath the Green Willow in a luxuriant bed of shamrocks, dotted with its tiny white blooms. Bees darted here and there as they gathered their pollen. Standing here, feeling the breeze on her face and inhaling the wonderful summer fragrances, Willow felt as if she were part of the mysticism of the grove.

Wearing white, she was once more clothed from head to toe in veils, tunic and cloak. But today her diadem was a wreath of tender willow branches, interspersed with shamrocks and blossoms. As usual when braiding it, Willow had searched for the sacred four-leaf shamrock but had not found it. She had her mother's, she thought, as she reached up and clasped the amulet between her fingers, but it was not the same as her finding her own.

Time and again she had prayed to God that she would be the one to lift the curse from the *tuatha* even if it meant her death. That would be a small sacrifice if she could deliver the first male child. She never ceased praying or looking for her confirmation—a four-leafed shamrock. If she found one herself, she would know without a doubt that the curse was truly broken.

Like those who gathered around her, Willow awaited the Highlander. But she was not sure that she was ready to see him, and she might not ever be. She was deeply unsettled and had been since Shamus had reported to her that the Highlander had put her to bed the evening before. She had thought of little else since.

Of the Highlander's touching her most intimately on the ankles as he had removed her shoes . . . on her face, neck and shoulders as he had taken off her cloak and veils. Of his having taken advantage of her drunken and drugged state. But a part of her would not allow her to think this of the Scottish warlord. For a verity, he was a mercenary, he was shrewd and crafty, but as Lord Shamus had said, he was honorable.

"He is late, my lord," Willow murmured to her advisor who stood to her left.

"Never fear, my lady queen," Shamus replied in a low voice. "He shall come. No man would go to such lengths to win a woman's hand—"

"—her kingdom!"

As if she had not spoken, the jurist continued, "—outwit us all to win the first feat, then forfeit the challenge. Nay, an honorable man would not intentionally heap shame upon himself in such a manner."

Willow looked around. The *óenach* clustered behind

her and Shamus, and the villagers fanned around them. At the thought of the Highlander making no appearance, Willow grew more nervous. With clammy hands, she lifted her kerchief and dabbed the sheen of perspiration above her upper lip.

How could she be so torn? She did not wish to marry the Highlander, did not wish for him to win the challenges, but she wanted him to claim his kiss. Deep down she desired Hugh MacDougald.

The wail of the Scottish bagpipes came from the village proper.

"The MacDougald is coming!" someone shouted.

All fixed their attention on the pathway, each wanting to be the first to spot him. Then they saw the piper as he topped the hill, his plaid tartan swinging about his legs. Behind him marched the MacDougald's best man, Jamie. The other Scottish warriors followed. The Highlander was not with them!

Willow's heart skipped a beat. What if after having won the first feat, he had decided that she was not worth the challenge? What if he had decided to forfeit? She did not know how she would bear such dishonor, heaped on top of what Forestgreen had already suffered.

The musicians and the Highlander's warriors grew closer. A murmur rippled through the crowd. They looked in question to their queen and her advisor; they looked at the approaching mercenaries. The music stopped at the same time that Jamie MacDougald did.

He bowed low. "My lady queen, I apologize for my lord's delay. A matter arose which needed his urgent attention."

Willow heard a soft rustle to her right. She turned and through the lacy curtain of willow branches saw the

Highlander. When she drew in her breath, her chest hurt and her heart lurched into erratic cadence.

A blur of darkness against the golden backdrop of noonday sun, he walked toward them. For a moment Willow wondered if he was one of the ancient gods. As usual he wore his weapons strapped about his waist, but wore no cloak. His form-fitting black tunic and trousers accentuated his powerful physique. The gentle breeze ruffled his hair. The sun gleamed off the gold shoulder brooches and the latchets of his black girdle. With one hand he brushed aside willow branches and entered the arbor.

"There he is," a woman whispered.

All turned.

The Highlander continued his steady march to the clearing where Willow stood. The people swung to either side, forming an aisle through which he walked. Hugh never took his eyes off Willow. She never took hers off him.

Excitement accelerated her heartbeat and shortened her breath.

Last night, he had put her to bed. Today he would claim the first kiss. Would the reality of his touch be as wondrous as the fantasies?

"My lady queen," Hugh said, "I apologize for my late arrival. My—"

Willow smiled. "Were you late, my lord?"

Hugh's eyes narrowed.

Shamus stepped forward. "My lord MacDougald, our queen, the Lady of the Willow, welcomes you to the sacred grove of Bishop Patrick. In acknowledgment that you have successfully completed the first feat of the challenge, she is prepared to bestow the victor's kiss on you."

Hugh's eyes were hot with desire, and Willow felt herself burning with the heated promise she saw in their depths.

"I am ready to claim my first kiss from the Lady of the Willow, my lord jurist," Hugh returned. He stepped closer to Willow and said in a low voice for her ears only, "My lady queen, as always you are beautiful . . . crowned with sunlight and embraced by the branches of the willows."

Not wanting her people to overhear Hugh's intimate comments, Willow stepped away from the crowd. Hugh followed.

"My lord warrior—" she couldn't help the huskiness that crept into her voice "—as usual you are most glib."

"But honest, madam." He kept his voice low. "Honest enough to admit that you are affecting me as much as I seem to be affecting you."

"I don't know how I affect you, my lord, so I cannot answer."

"When I am near you, my blood burns through my body like fire."

Willow's entire body flushed. "I'm sure I don't know what you're talking about," she said, flinching from the partial lie she told, but she was determined to protect herself. No man was going to sashay into her kingdom and demand her as if she were part of the hero's portion.

"Aye, lady, you do, else you would not be bundled so heavily in the summer season." He paused, his gaze searching hers. "The only thing about you that looks light and airy is your head garland."

" 'Tis made of willow branches and shamrock leaves, plants that are sacred to Bishop Patrick and sacred to

Ireland, sire, because they are emerald green as is our isle."

Hugh cocked a brow, and Willow grinned.

"As you well know, my lord, the willows were emerald at one time."

"The willow's tale, I have heard," Hugh said, "but not the shamrock's."

Willow bent and plucked a trefoil leaf. "Bishop Patrick is the one who converted the Irish to Christianity. 'Tis said when he explained the godhead, he used the Irish shamrock." Holding out the tiny leaf, she moved closer to Hugh. "Our mild, misty climate keeps the shamrock fresh and green, winter and summer. Its seed is everywhere."

Both of them gazed at the plant. "As you can see, my lord, 'tis one leaf, yet it is threefold. Like God, who is one but has three manifestations."

Hugh took the tiny leaf from her. "Does none ever have more than three segments?"

"Aye," Willow replied. "There are a few that are four-leafed. We always look for them because they are a blessed sign directly from Bishop Patrick himself." She raised her head and again looked directly into Hugh's beautiful gray eyes. "When we need or want something desperately, we of Forestgreen stand in this bed of shamrocks beneath the Green Willow and say our request aloud."

Silently she rehearsed hers once more.

"Then we search through the shamrocks."

Even as she spoke, her eyes skimmed through the thick pallet beneath her feet.

"If we find a four-leafed one, we know our prayer has been answered."

"Have you ever found a four-leafed trefoil?" Hugh asked.

"Nay, lord, we have had no recorded findings of the four-leafed shamrock from this patch, and we have been keeping written records for many generations. Since Bishop Patrick."

Hugh bent and picked a handful of shamrocks. With a grace that belied his huge, callused hand, he laced them together. He caught Willow's hand and slipped the bracelet of clover onto her wrist. He continued to clasp her hand in his.

"Note the ease with which I slipped this magical talisman onto your wrist," he said.

Willow's heart skipped a beat. How ironic that the Highlander would braid her a shamrock garland and call it her magical talisman.

"With that same ease, madam," he said, his voice low and seductive, "I shall soon remove your garments. One by one to slowly reveal the mysterious secrets of your body."

Anticipation raced through Willow's body. Keeping her attention focused on the wrist garland, she said, "From what my lord Shamus told me, sire, you did that last night."

"Whatever your perceptions of the events were, madam, let me clarify them." Hugh caught her chin and raised her face to his. "I removed your shoes, your diadem, your cloak, and your veils. I saw your ankles, but they were covered with your leggings. I saw your face and neck and a tiny bit of your shoulders that were revealed in the scooped neck of your tunic."

Willow stared at him.

"For a verity, I wanted to see more, was tempted to

see more, but I did not. I assure you I did not take advantage of you, my lady queen."

No physical caress could have touched Willow as much as the Highlander's confession. His words filled her with a warmth that burned deeper and truer than the flash fires of passion.

"Thank you, sire." She lifted her chin from his touch. "My lord Shamus told me that you were an honorable man."

"Don't thank me," Hugh replied. "While my actions seem to have been honorable, they were not. They were the selfish demands of a man who yearns for a woman. I want you to be fully cognizant when I next undress you, Lady of the Willows. My greatest desire is to have you want and invite my touch."

Willow burned with excitement.

He caught her hands in his and held them. "Until then, madam, I shall have to build a fire of longing in you that is so hot you will willingly dispense with all the coverings."

He leaned closer and touched her lips with his. The feel of his flesh against hers was more glorious than she had thought it would be. His lips were firm and warm and soft. Closing her eyes, she swayed toward him and moved her lips against his. She welcomed his touch, invited his possession. But he did not deepen the kiss. He lifted his mouth from hers. Surprised, Willow opened her eyes and stumbled when he stepped back.

Hugh smiled knowingly.

Desire slowly ebbed away to be replaced by frustration . . . and humiliation . . . and anger. If only she had a club she would have cudgeled him. How dare he treat her like this! To him this was only a game, she the prize.

"Until the next time, my lady."

Breathing raggedly, her emotions frayed, Willow stepped away from him and back toward the villagers. When she felt that she had her voice under control, she said, "There shall not be a next time, my lord mercenary."

Hugh cocked a brow in question.

"Your second challenge shall not be so easy as the first one, and trickery will not be the answer."

"The harder the battle, my lady," Hugh said, "the sweeter the victory. Now state the second feat."

"According to ancient legend," Willow said, "the Blessed Mother has been known to appear on special occasions when a circle of sacred light rises from the depths of Willow Lake. At this time she grants to those who see the lights a rebirth of spirit. Three days hence, my lord, you are to bring us the sacred circle of light so that the Blessed Mother will come and heal my people's spirits."

Hugh gazed at her for a long while before he said, "You ask the impossible, my lady."

"Aye, my lord Highlander, I do."

Several hours later dusk fell over Forestgreen. Lights glowed through opened windows as the people prepared their evening meal. Hugh paced back and forth in the bed chamber of the Small House. Jamie sat on the bed, leaning back against the fluffed pillows. His legs were stretched out and crossed at the ankles. Intermittently scraping and hammering sounds could be heard in the adjacent room.

"Scallions won't be the answer this time, Hugh," Jamie said.

"Nay, lad, they won't." Hugh stopped in front of the

trestle-table and poured himself a tankard of ale. "But there is a solution. I must find it."

Hearing a ruckus from outside, Hugh moved to the opened window.

"What's happening?" Jamie asked.

"Children," Hugh answered. "They're chasing fireflies."

Jamie joined his cousin at the window, both of them looking out. "Like we used to do."

"Aye, Jamie." Hugh sighed and wished that life could be so simple once again.

When the children's chase led them away from the small house, Jamie moved to the trestle-table. Picking up a piece of dried fruit, he said, "According to the legend, the candles come up from the depth of the lake and are burning as they break water."

"Aye, that's the tricky part." Hugh turned, leaning back against the wall. " 'Twould be simple if we could light the candles after the circle broke water."

"Hugh," one of the Scottish warriors called out, "we've finished. What now?"

"I don't know," he muttered and quaffed down his ale. "But God help me, I'll win this bloody challenge!"

"Aye," Jamie said dryly, "if it kills you."

Chapter Six

"Whatever can he be doing?" Willow murmured to Shamus. "He has been locked up in the small house for the past two days. When his men do come out, they run around like chickens with their heads wrung off."

"I would that I could answer you, my lady," Shamus said, "but I cannot. I trust he is ready to perform the second feat tonight."

"I trust so, my lord," Willow answered.

Knocking sounded on the entrance door. Then a young servant girl appeared at the bed chamber.

"Lord Hugh MacDougald wishes to see you, my lady queen."

Willow acknowledged with a nod. She quickly wrapped her veils around her head and neck, tossing the sashes over her shoulders. Without putting on her wimple, diadem or cloak, she walked into the great room.

"My lady queen." Hugh bowed low. "Did you order the harper and the piper?"

"Aye, and instructed the people that we are to form three large dance circles, and no one is to do anything until you give the command."

He nodded. "May I escort you to Willow Lake?"

"Before we go, my lord MacDougald," Willow said, "I must talk with you about a grave matter."

"Any more grave than that which we are already discussing, madam?"

"My chief advisor, Lord Shamus, and I met with the *óenach* earlier in the day. In an uncustomary vote, we have agreed that if you renounce your claim to my hand, we will release you from your vow and let you leave our shores with your life intact."

"Thank you and your council for your generosity, my lady queen," Hugh said, "but I would rather die than live without you."

Willow did not credit herself with hearing him correctly. "My lord, I am giving you an honorable way out of this challenge."

"I have given you my answer, madam." His face was grave, his expression filled with disappointment. "Surely by now you should know that I am not a man to make a commitment only to back out when the situation seems overpowering."

"Do you honestly believe that you are going to call forth the sacred lights?"

"Aye, I shall." The gray eyes gazed directly into hers. "Shall we go, madam?"

Leading the procession to Willow Lake, Willow and Hugh walked together. On either side of them were the torch bearers and behind was Shamus. Although no one was talking, anticipation ran high as the villagers followed. All had heard about the sacred circle of lights but none had ever seen it. Oddly none had any doubts that the Highlander would perform the feat successfully. They only wondered how.

When they stood beside the lake, Hugh turned to face the villagers. Pointing to a circular raft, large

enough for two people, Hugh said, "People of Forestgreen, your lady queen and I shall float to the center of
the lake on this raft that my men and I built. Your
queen shall instruct me where to stop. Then I shall
summon the sacred lights to appear from beneath the
water."

"You're not going to get out into the lake and light
those torches that circle the raft, are you?" one of the
women asked.

Hugh laughed. "I shall light them, good woman, but
not until after you have seen the sacred lights."

Shamus and the members of the *óenach* inspected
the raft, kicking at it, counting the torches, jerking on
the ropes. When they were satisfied, they stepped back
and nodded.

Picking up a long, slender piece of kindling, Hugh lit
it from one of the nearby torches and handed it to Willow. "Please hold this, my lady, so that the people will
be able to see us when we're on the lake."

Again he addressed the people, "When I call out,
you will douse your torches. Musicians, you will play
and dancing will commence."

Wondering how the Highlander was going to accomplish this feat, Willow let him help her aboard the raft.
She sat down but he stood, using a long pole to propel
them to the center of the pond. When she gave the
order, Hugh withdrew the pole and laid it across the
raft.

"People of Forestgreen," he called out, "douse your
torches and candles."

When all was dark, only the moonlight lacing the
people who stood beneath the willows and the blaze
from the kindling dimly glowing on the raft, Hugh sat

down. He yanked on one of the ropes that hung over the side of the raft. Then he and Willow waited.

She heard a soft noise in the water and leaned over the edge of the raft. Beneath the surface she saw a glow . . . a light? Shocked, she dropped the fire-starter. Hugh caught it. She scooted all around the raft and saw more globes of light. She turned back to Hugh. In the fragile glow of kindling light, they gazed at each other.

"You have done it!" Awe softened her voice.

A shiny object broke the surface.

"I don't know how you did it, but you did!"

All around the barge more of the objects began to appear. Willow couldn't make out what they were, but they rose higher and higher, lights—hundreds of lights glittering inside each one of them.

"The sacred circle," a villager shouted. "I see the sacred circle."

Deafening cries resounded from the shore. Then all was silent. With the kindling, Hugh lit the torches he had positioned around the outer edge of the raft.

"And our lady of the willow," another voice called out. "She looks like the Blessed Mother."

" 'Tis a sign!" many shouted in unison.

Reality setting in, her excitement and awe dying, Willow gazed through the blaze of torchlight but could not make out the kind of lights she had seen rising out of the lake.

"Musicians, play," Hugh shouted.

Slowly the mystical lights receded.

Willow returned her attention to Hugh. "I don't know how you did it," she said, "but I fear you have deceived my people, that these are not sacred lights."

"Villagers dance," Hugh called out. "You have cause

to rejoice this night. Let this be a sign to you from this day forward. No tyrant shall ever harm you as long as you have the will to fight for your freedom."

Music blared out, and the villagers began their dance of thanksgiving. Willow rose to stand beside Hugh.

"How did you do it?"

"Does it matter?"

"The circle of lights is sacred. How could you have reduced it to sacrilege?"

"You did that yourself when you made it a feat," he answered quietly. "You already knew that I would go to any lengths to perform the feats successfully and you also knew that it was virtually impossible for me to perform a miracle."

"Yet you seemed to have done so."

Willow glanced over at the shore, now ablaze with a huge bonfire and torches sitting upright in the ground.

"Nay, lady, the people created their own miracle. I only used what God has given us. My men filled clear water beakers with fireflies. Breathing through hollow reeds, they swam beneath the surface of the lake where they awaited a tug on the rope as a signal for them to rise."

Ashamed that she had used a sacred event as one of the feats, Willow said, "But we shall not receive a blessing from the heavenly mother."

"You already have, my lady. Your people have had a rebirth of their spirits. The scars will remain in Forestgreen forever, but the wounds are healed." Hugh dug the pole into the lake and started the raft back toward the shore.

"They didn't see the Blessed Mother."

"I believe they did."

Willow scoffed bitterly. "How so?"

"Mayhap I am wrong, madam, but is not any mother blessed? A woman who gives birth is in essence prepared to give up her own life to create a new one. According to the holy word no one is more blessed than the one who lays down his or her life for another. For the people of Forestgreen you are the Blessed Mother."

"You are twisting the word of God," Willow said.

"Nay, lady, I am interpreting it. Even when I explain to the villagers how I accomplished the feat, no one shall be able to take the glory out of the moment that they saw the circle of light, the hope they felt for a bright future, the renewed desire to fight for what they want out of life."

Willow said nothing.

"I don't believe in God as you do, my lady Willow, but I believe. Always we have miracles with us. It's just that many times we don't avail ourselves of them. Other times we cause them to appear but are too busy dissecting them to believe."

Still Willow could not speak.

"We are the human expression of God, madam, and he relies on us to bring about the miracle."

"Aye," Willow murmured.

The raft bumped into the bank, and Hugh leaped off and tied it to a tree stump.

Shamus rushed to greet them. "You have done it, my lord. You have created a circle of lights. 'Twas beautiful."

Hugh reached for Willow, assisting her to land.

"How did you do it?" the law-expounder asked.

The happy villagers crowded about as Hugh explained. His men rose out of the lake, holding their jars in one hand, their reeds in the other. The people clapped and shouted. The Scottish warriors unplugged their beakers, releasing the nocturnal beetles into the sky. As they flew out, they hovered over Willow and the darkened sky was filled with a brilliant explosion of light.

"Look!" a villager cried. "The queen. The fireflies are circling above her head."

"A halo!" Shamus whispered. "They've formed a halo around her head."

The people gasped and stood for a silent moment taking in the wondrous sight.

"My lady," Shamus said reverently, "this night we have seen the miracle of lights."

"Aye," Willow said softly, "we have."

"Aye," the people of Forestgreen murmured.

Willow looked at Shamus. "My lord *brethim,* do we concede that the Highlander has successfully performed the second feat?"

Shamus glanced at the members of the *óenach* who clustered together. All nodded their heads.

"We do, madam," the jurist replied.

"Then, my lady queen," Hugh said, "I claim the victor's kiss here and now."

Hugh stepped closer and for a moment gazed down at her. Light from the torches and the bonfire flickered around them, casting his face in ominous golden-brown shadows.

Slowly he raised his hands, his fingers deftly unhooking the brooch that fastened her cloak around her neck. With tantalizing slowness he pulled the material aside.

"I have never seen you without your cloak," he said.

His gaze swept down her figure . . . her breasts, her waist and her hips, clearly revealed in the form-fitting long tunic. So potent was his gaze that Willow would have sworn he had touched her.

He slid the cloak further aside. He touched the amulet, clasped it between two of his fingers and lifted it.

"It's beautiful, madam," he said.

"Thank you, my lord," she answered. " 'Twas a gift from my mother."

He turned it over, and she thought he was going to open it and see her four-leafed shamrock.

" 'Tis my sacred talisman," she whispered.

He gently replaced the amulet against her breasts. He once more began to brush the fabric of her cloak aside. Willow trembled as the fabric grazed her shoulder and arms. She trembled at the thought of the Highlander touching her.

He caught her hands, then pulled her into his arms. At last he held her closely and she felt the hard length of him against her body. Tilting back her head, she gazed up at him. His impassioned features filled her with awe. And his lips—she was fascinated with them. How could they be so firm, yet so soft? She burned with curiosity—nay, with desire—to feel them on hers, to taste their sweetness, to discover their mystery.

His hands tightened about her waist, his fingers splaying over her hips. Even through her clothing, Willow felt his strength and was reminded that he was a mercenary, a hard man who sold his services to the highest bidder. She was in no doubt as to his purpose. He wanted her because she was the *Tuatha* de Forestgreen. One part of her despised what he was doing to her. Another, the primitive part that she had not known she possessed until now, was excited and reveled in the challenge. It craved his touch, his possession.

"Willow." Her name was a ragged whisper on his tongue.

Her clothing could not shield her from the warmth of his hands. Nor could reason—that part of her that warned against her caring for the mercenary—shield her from the desire that raced hotly through her to take residence beneath his fingertips. She closed her eyes and gave herself to the pleasure of the moment, something Willow had never dreamed she would do. But which she now did with gleeful abandon. His lips captured hers in a kiss that began sweet and warm and tentative.

Without lifting his mouth from hers, he breathed, "Willow."

Then his lips closed over hers again, so that the kiss became hot, demanding and urgent.

His tongue touched her lips. She opened her mouth and welcomed him. As he filled her with the abrasive warmth of his tongue, Willow felt as if she had burst into flames. She answered his hunger with her own. He cupped her head with one hand, banded her waist with the other.

She clung to him and drank in the pleasure from his mouth and his strong, muscular body. She pushed her fingers through his hair, loving the feel of it against her flesh. She reveled in his arms about her. He was much stronger, more overpoweringly virile than she had dreamed possible. Willow wanted more than kisses. She wanted all of him.

He pulled her closer still, so that she felt his hardness against her pelvis. In the blink of an eye sanity returned. She pushed her arms between them to fight free of his embrace. She glanced around to see her people staring in dumbfounded silence at them.

Stepping back from him and speaking in what she hoped was a cool tone, Willow said, "You have overstepped your bounds, sire."

"I walked only where you guided me," Hugh answered quietly. "I took no more than was freely given."

Stung by the truth of his words, Willow said, "Then, my lord, let's see how well you take the last feat." She paused. "You will fight our village *shillelagh* champion."

A huge man, closely resembling an ox in size and shape, separated himself from the crowd. His hair was cut short, and he wore a leather sleeveless tunic and trousers. A large scar ran down the side of his face and across one eye. Hugh had met many enemies in his day, but this man was one of the biggest and most fierce-looking. The man held two short, stout clubs, one in each hand. With a casual grace that implied skill and ability, he tossed the clubs into the air. They twirled up and like spindles spun awhile, before they began their descent. With deceptive ease, the man held out his hands and caught both.

Willow waved to the man. "This is Eloign, our *shillelagh* master. You will meet with him in combat three days hence."

"*Shillelagh!*" Hugh muttered. "Whatever is a *shillelagh?*"

Eloign laughed, but his words sounded more like a snarl. "My lord doesn't know what a *shillelagh* is, lads."

" 'Tis time he found out," another returned.

Eloign held out his hands, once more swinging the clubs through the air and catching them as if they were juggling sticks. "These, Highlander, are *shillelaghs.*"

"Thank you, Eloign," Shamus said, moving to Hugh's side. Smoothly, he went on. "The word itself comes from an oak forest that stands in another part of Ireland, my lord. A club or cudgel cut from one of these oaks is called a *sprig of shillelagh.* Since the people of Forestgreen have the sacred forest of Bishop Patrick rather than oak, our cudgel is made of willow."

"Three days hence, my lord, at the nooning hour," Willow reminded Hugh.

"Where do I get my cudgel?" Hugh asked.

"Cudgels," Willow answered. "As you saw, there are two of them. You will cut them from one of the willow trees. Then you will whittle them to the proper shape. My lord Shamus shall instruct you in the making and the using of them."

Hugh raked his gaze over the old man, before he glared at Willow.

"Three days, my lady queen, is not long enough to make the clubs and learn how to use them."

"Three days," she repeated.

Chapter Seven

Hugh, clad only in his trousers and boots, stood in the center of the practice field on the outskirts of the village. The sun was high overhead, and he was hot, also weary. He lifted his arm and wiped perspiration from his forehead.

Yesterday under the guidance of Shamus he had cut two branches from the Green Willow, the largest tree in the grove. It was a magical tree blessed by Bishop Patrick himself, Shamus had told Hugh and would serve him well in the duel. Hugh himself didn't believe in the magical powers of the tree, but if the Irish did, that gave him a decided advantage. That was the tree from which his *shillelaghs* would come. He had cut off two branches and had carved his cudgels.

Remembering Willow's story about the shamrock, he had gone a step farther. He had searched for a four-leafed one. When he hadn't found it, he had carved one on each of his cudgels to bring him luck and magic. Since he had no skill in the handling of these weapons, he was going to need all the luck and magic he could get.

The better part of today had been spent in practice, but he could not get accustomed to the clubs. He had tried his skill at juggling them, but hadn't managed to catch them more than once, and only one club at a time. He glanced around to see two youngsters fighting with more skill and dexterity than he had been.

"You never swing a *shillelagh*, my lord," Shamus had instructed. "You grasp it in the middle. With one hand you deal a blow. With the other, you ward off the whack of your opponent. And your feet dance all about you."

Jamie sat on the grass, propped against the trunk of one of the trees. "On the morrow, Hugh MacDougald," he said, "you must fight the *shillelagh* master."

"Aye." Hugh looked at Forba, his young sparring mate who had succeeded in defeating him every time they fought.

"Well, sire," Forba said, "you're going to have to be getting a lot better before you can outdo Eloign."

Jamie grinned and said lightly, "Not to sound disloyal, cousin, but you look more ridiculous with these clubs than you did the harp."

"Jamie, lad," Hugh said, "sometimes it's a wiser man who keeps his mouth shut than one who tells the truth."

Jamie and the Irishman laughed.

Also laughing, Shamus pushed away from the tree where he had been standing. "You have a fair chance of winning, my lord, because you are a seasoned warrior."

"But not with these weapons," Hugh replied, "nor at fighting according to your rules."

"Rest for a while," the jurist advised. "Then we shall begin again."

"How about a glass of ale, Hugh," Jamie said, "to quench the thirst and to renew your spirits?"

"Nay, lad," Hugh replied, handing his *shillelaghs* to

his cousin. "I am going to refresh myself another way." He turned and walked toward the willow grove that was a distance away.

"Well, then, my friends," Hugh heard Jamie say to Shamus and Forba, "would the two of you share a glass of ale with me?"

"Aye," Shamus replied, their voices growing fainter as they moved in one direction and Hugh in the other. "We will, and I shall provide it. Let us walk to my house."

Glad to be alone, Hugh walked on farther, stopping when he reached the Green Willow. He plopped down in the bed of shamrocks and gazed at the clear cool water of the lake.

Unable to withstand its invitation, he stripped out of his boots, trousers, and leggings and slid into the water. He had swam several lengths when he became aware of a presence . . . of *her* presence. Even without seeing Willow, he knew she was here. As he had never been attuned to a woman before, he was attuned to Willow. He turned and slowly swam back toward her.

As usual she was garbed from head to foot with nothing showing but her face and hands, and today even her hands were hidden. She had them tucked into the sleeves of her tunic.

"My lord Hugh," she said. "I didn't know you were swimming."

"The water is cool and refreshing, my lady." Long, smooth strokes carried Hugh closer to her. "Why don't you join me?"

" 'Tis too public for me, lord."

"If you won't join me, lady," he said, "then I shall join you."

Before Willow could imagine what he was going to

do, he rose out of the water and began walking toward her. She couldn't . . . wouldn't . . . take her eyes off him. When he had walked through the willows two days ago she had thought he was one of the Ancient Ones; today she was sure of it.

Water dripped from his hair, little droplets glistening like jewels on his face and his chest. Rugged as if he had been chiseled from stone and bronzed by the sun, his body rippled with muscle from his shoulders to the bottom of his feet. Dark hair covered his chest and narrowed down his abdomen and waist to his groin.

He was magnificently endowed.

Willow's mouth was dry and she couldn't swallow . . . neither could she remove her gaze from him. Hugh bent and picked up his leggings. He stepped into them, drawing them up and tying the cord about his waist. As if she were not even there, he slid into his trousers and his girdle.

Embarrassed by her behavior, Willow turned. The man had succeeded in wearing her down, in making her want him. Not a minute went by that she didn't think of him, didn't yearn for him to make love to her . . . and didn't feel guilty because of her weakness where the Highlander was concerned.

"Where were you going when you saw me?" Hugh asked.

She heard him moving up behind her.

Softly she said, "I was coming to see you."

He caught her by the shoulders and turned her.

She gazed into his eyes. "I've been watching you practice all morning."

"You knew I was swimming?"

"Not at first." She pushed a strand of hair out of his

face, her fingers lingering on his cheeks. She gently outlined the tiny scar on his right temple.

"Does it offend you?"

"The scar?"

"Aye."

"It intrigues me." She thought it was a provocative diversion from an otherwise flawless face. "How did you get it?"

He smiled, and she noticed that it was lopsided and gave him a vulnerability she had not been aware of before.

"I wish I could say that it was a reminder of a wound received in a glorious battle, my lady, but I can't." He pressed his hand over hers. "Jamie and I were joshing one day, and I fell against the side of a house and severely cut my face."

Willow did not immediately remove her hand from his clasp. She liked the feel of his rough, callused flesh against hers. For a moment she imagined Hugh MacDougald shedding the vestiges of a warrior and being a man, laughing and having fun with his cousin. Mayhap making love to a woman. The thought saddened and sobered Willow. She withdrew her hand.

"The jurist has ordered me to practice all afternoon," Hugh said, "but even then, I shall not be able to defeat your champion. Fighting with your *shillelaghs* requires an art and dexterity that I do not possess."

"My lord, I could appeal to the assembly. They like you and would be willing—"

Hugh laid a finger across her mouth. "If the *óenach* were to release me from my vow, my lady, would you choose me to be your husband?"

"If I had the luxury of having a lover, my lord, I

should choose you, but I do not have that pleasure. I will not choose you to be my husband."

Disappointment shadowed his eyes. "Because I'm a mercenary?"

"At first, lord, that was my reason, but not any more."

As Willow gazed into Hugh's eyes, a deep gray now, she wondered why she had ever thought him to be hard and unfeeling.

"I am . . . learning to care for you," she said.

"You say that with the guilt of a person confessing her sins, my lady." He tugged her closer to him. Still their bodies did not touch. "Is it so wrong for you to care for me?"

"Aye."

"You cared for your husband?"

"Angus and I married, my lord, by decree of the *óenach,* and we mated. We treated each other kindly, but we did not love each other."

Willow lowered her head and gazed at Hugh's broad chest, covered in a thick pelt of black hair.

"He kept the woman whom he loved as his mistress." Willow breathed in deeply. "He knew that one day I would give birth to a child and would die soon afterwards, and he would be free to marry her."

As if he felt her pain, Hugh caught Willow in his arms and held her, tightly, protectively.

"My lady . . . Willow—" He caught her chin and tilted it up so that he could look into her face. "Willow, if you were to marry me, I would have no other woman."

"The *óenach* would not forbid it, sire, and while I would not like it, I wouldn't have the right to forbid it, either."

"Aye, if a man weds with you knowing all the conditions beforehand, my lady queen, you have a right to demand fidelity from him. I would pledge fidelity to you. That's how deeply my feelings for you are."

"My lord—"

"Hugh."

"Hugh. I cannot allow my own desires to interfere with my purpose. I am the Lady of the Willow, and it is my duty to bear a child . . . hopefully the chosen one so that the curse may be lifted from our *tuatha.*"

"Let us do that together, my lady."

"In caring for you," Willow confessed, "I would not want to conceive a child. Selfishly, I would want to spend as many years of my life with you as I could. That is not what Providence would have me do."

Hugh's arms banded so tightly around Willow that she wanted to cry out, but she didn't. She knew without his saying a word that he felt the same anguish of soul that she did.

"Please, Willow, let's dispense with this silly challenge. Tell the council that you want me for your husband."

"Nay, Hugh MacDougald, I cannot do that. I must think of my people and of the sacred grove more than of myself."

"Then, my lady, I will not . . . cannot . . . concede."

Chapter Eight

"Will not concede!" Hugh muttered. He thrust with such concentrated effort that the blow sent Forba stumbling backward. The startled look on his opponent's face was so comical that Hugh laughed.

Forba regained his balance immediately. "Laugh will you, my lord?" He lunged at Hugh, hitting him squarely on the right shoulder.

Pain shafted through Hugh's body in such proportion that he grimaced and almost lost his grip on the cudgel. He feinted the next blow and growled, "Cannot concede!" Then he rushed in for a quick, second thrust.

Forba danced aside. "Shall we rest a while, lord?" He sucked in deep breaths of air.

"Nay!" Hugh was as breathless. "I've a challenge to win, Forba, and I shall win it." *I shall!* He wielded the club again.

Tired and hot, perspiration moistened Hugh's hair and clothing and the band tied about his forehead. It ran down his face and neck in rivulets. Yet he would not stop. He dealt blow after blow, dodging those thrown at him. He pushed on.

"Dance, my lord," Forba shouted. "Dance about."

Laughing to himself, thinking he couldn't appear any

more the fool than he already had, Hugh lightened up, moving his feet to one of his favorite Scottish tunes.

"That's it, sire!" Forba shouted. "You're getting the rhythm of the *shillelaghs.*"

"By damnation, Hugh!" Jamie called out. "You're doing it. I believe you have a chance after all."

Villagers, hearing the commotion, raced out to see what was happening. Even Eloign gathered with them.

"Aye," Hugh muttered as he thrust with one club and feinted with the other, his legs and feet moving in time. Again he thrust, this time sending Forba sprawling on the ground. His *shillelagh* flew through the air to land with a thud at Hugh's feet.

"By all that's holy, Highlander, you did it!" Forba leaped up and clapped Hugh on the back. The blow jarred Hugh's bruised shoulder, and he grimaced from the pain.

"Aye," Eloign said with a grin. "You've done well for yourself, Scotsman, but the morrow shows us your mettle."

Hugh nodded his head. "Aye, *shillelagh*-master, it does indeed."

"Until then, my lord, I shall instruct you." Respect gleamed in the depth of Eloign's soulful eyes. "It won't be much of a challenge if I can easily outdo you."

Although he would have much preferred to halt practice and to put a soothing compress on his aching shoulder, Hugh nodded. "I accept your offer with gratitude."

The people cheered and enlarged their circle to give the men more room.

Assuming a fighting position, Eloign raised one cudgel in his right hand. The other he held close to his body. "This, sire—"

The lur sounded—one long blast, followed by two short ones. A warning signal! Fighting ceased. Chores and games were forgotten. The village became a flurry of new activity. Children hastened to gather and pen the domesticated animals; the elderly ran to the gates, ready to close them on order. Some of the women began to set huge cauldrons filled with water on the fire; others joined the men in hauling pails of rocks to the wall. Warriors raced to their armor and weapons.

An outrider galloped into the village, shouting over his shoulder, "Close the gates." He didn't stop until he reached the porch of Forestgreen Hall where he slid off the horse and curtsied before the queen. "My lady, warriors marching under the colors of Garret de Ywnson approach. I think he is in the lead himself."

"Garret de Ywnson?" Willow echoed.

Hugh, clad in mail and weapons, leaped onto the porch beside Willow. "Perhaps some warriors are championing his cause, my lady queen, but Garret is dead. I killed him with my own hand."

All around the village Hugh's warriors had moved into battle position, their horses also ready.

"Garret is dead," Shamus murmured, "but not vanquished. A man so evil is not easily vanquished."

"Then, my lord jurist," Hugh said, "I shall vanquish him."

Sounds of battle could be heard from outside the walled village. The heavy thud of horses' hooves, their snorting and whinnying. The creak and stretch of leather. The ting of the chain links in the mail.

"The warriors are stopping, my lady queen," shouted a man from atop the watch tower. "They send their standard-bearer forward."

Hugh to her right, Shamus to her left, Willow walked

to the wall. One by one, they climbed the ladder and moved to the watch tower. The standard-bearer rode forward, the other warriors halting not far behind him.

"My lord, Scannalan de Ywnson, cousin to Garret," the young messenger shouted, "demands retribution for the shame heaped on his family and liege. Death to all if you do not send us the head of Queen Willow of Forestgreen Hall."

As was customary, the *tuatha* champion—in this case, Hugh—showed his loyalty to the queen by stepping in front of her as a symbol to her and to all others of his promise to protect her with his life.

He felt Willow's hand resting lightly on his back, on his right shoulder—the one that was aching so badly that he could hardly stand it.

Softly she said, "Hugh, you don't have to do this for me."

"Nay, my lord," Shamus added. "We have no more bounty with which to hire your services."

Without turning Hugh said, "No bounty is necessary or demanded, jurist. I do this for myself and for the Lady of the Willow. My lady," he said quietly, still speaking over his shoulder, "I'll die before I let another person harm you."

Willow laid her cheek against his shoulder. "Thank you, Hugh MacDougald." As quickly she stepped back. She had to make way for the warrior.

To the messenger Hugh called out, "I, Hugh MacDougald, took your liege's life, and I alone. If Scannalan values his life and the lives of his warriors, he will return from whence he came. On my life, I promise him that we shall not send him the queen's head and he shall not harm this village."

Before the standard-bearer could turn his horse, his
liege galloped forward and joined him.

"You speak foolishly, Highlander." The warrior removed his helmet, a wealth of brown hair falling to his
shoulders. "My cousin was older than me. About your
age, I would say. You easily overpowered him. Had I
been in the battle, rather than moving the Forestgreen
cattle to safe pastures, the outcome would have been
different. You'll not get the best of me as you did Garret."

"You're a babe, my lord," Hugh taunted, knowing
full well that the warrior's youth was a definite advantage. "That's why your cousin had you tending cattle.
You'll be more easily vanquished than he was."

"Will I, my lord?" Scannalan grinned. "Let's see how
the babe handles the older warrior. I challenge you to a
duel, Highlander. If you win, you shall have my life. If I
win, I shall have both your and the queen's lives."

"Your stupidity is only outdone by your arrogance,
Scannalan," Hugh shouted. "You're not worth one life,
much less two, and especially not the life of the Lady
of Willow. I accept your challenge. When I win, and I
shall, all that is yours—people, foodstuff, cattle and
horses, and land—becomes mine, including the cattle
that your cousin stole from Forestgreen. Your family
must swear before me that no one will seek revenge
against the *Tuatha* de Forestgreen ever again."

Scannalan rode back to his warriors. Hugh watched
the heated and animated conversation ensuing among
them. Finally the young warrior returned to the gate,
four riders behind him.

"These are the heads of the houses of the *Tuatha* de
Ywnson," he said. "All are ready to swear."

As soon as the men had uttered aloud their oaths

and had sealed them with the brandishing of their swords, Scannalan shouted, "Choose your weapon, Highlander."

Disregarding the fiery pain that burned through his body, Hugh unsheathed his sword and held it aloft, the sun glinting on the long silver blade.

"So be it," the young warrior said. "At what time?"

"At mid-morning on the morrow."

Hours passed, and darkness gently descended over Forestgreen. The majority of the villagers were already in bed, but not Hugh. Restless after having treated his shoulder, wondering where his destiny truly lay, he had wandered down to the lake. Once more he sat in the bed of shamrocks beneath the Green Willow. His legs were stretched out, crossed at the ankles, and he leaned against the trunk of the tree.

He glanced at the shamrock that lay in his palm. Even in the moonlight it was easy to see that it had only three leaflets. He didn't believe in the magic of the Green Willow or the shamrocks, but he had plucked so many of the trefoils that it was a wonder any were left. And none had four leaflets!

"Day comes soon, my lord," Willow said softly.

Surprised, Hugh dropped the clover and looked up at Willow who stood in a bright spill of moonlight. She wore only a high-necked and long-sleeved long tunic, and her hair was hanging loosely down her back and over her shoulders.

"You moved so quietly, madam, I did not know you were near."

"I think perhaps you didn't hear me because you were in such deep thought."

"Perhaps."

"You should be getting your rest, my lord. You have a heavy day before you."

"Aye," he replied, "but sleep is far away tonight."

She sat down beside him.

"You couldn't sleep either?" he said more than asked.

"Nay. I, too, am thinking about the duel tomorrow."

"Are you worried that I shall be defeated?" Hugh asked, reaching up to gently massage his shoulder.

"It's not the defeat that worries me," she answered quietly.

"What's worrying you then?"

She hesitated so long he thought she wasn't going to answer him.

"The thought of you dying and my never seeing you again."

Unmindful of his shoulder, Hugh swiveled around and caught her in his arms. "My sweet Willow," he said tenderly, striving for a lightness that he didn't feel, "I have been walking in the shadow of death ever since I entered Forestgreen. How can I forget the ominous warning of Forestgreen's *brethim* when he told me the consequences should I lose the challenge? I had two choices, my lady. Succeed or die! Once I had heard the first task, I could back out only at risk of death and if I failed to accomplish a feat, I would surely die."

"That is to discourage men from taking it lightly," Willow said, snuggling closer to him, brushing her cheeks against his chest. "None has won my hand in marriage so far, and none has died."

"Then, my lady, I am left to assume that you and your council don't take your words seriously."

"Oh, but we do, lord." Willow laughed softly. "It has happened in the past that on hearing the second or third feat, the challenger has disappeared never to be heard from again."

Loving the feel of her in his arms, Hugh joined in her laughter. "The cowards."

"Nay, lord, reasonable." She ran her hand up the front of his shirt. "They figured no woman was worth death."

"They figured wrong."

She tilted back her head, and through faces christened by the pristine light of the moon, they gazed at each other.

"My father told me, lady, that love was not for the faint of heart."

"You learned your lesson well. You're certainly not faint of heart, lord."

Hugh's embrace tightened. The more he was around this woman, the more he loved her. The thought startled him. He had always lusted for her, had always wanted her kingdom, but what he felt for her now transcended all these sentiments. It went beyond loyalty and fealty. Both as man and warrior he loved her.

"I have never cared about another man as I care for you, Hugh MacDougald," Willow said.

He saw the sparkle of tears on her cheeks.

"And caring hurts. It has caused me to lose sight of what I must do. I want to put my personal feelings above what I must do."

"Aye," Hugh murmured.

"Before you came, I was resolved to my lot in life. My only thought was to be married and to conceive and to bear a child—hopefully the chosen one who would deliver my *tuatha* from its shame."

"And now?" He ran his hands through the silken strands of her hair, unable to get enough of her.

"And now all I think about is you, my lord, and how much I enjoy being with you." She smiled at him. "When I'm around you, I'm happy and alive."

"Then I shall have to make sure that I'm always around you," he said, trying to keep a smile in his voice when his heart was hurting from her confession. "Your mouth is made to smile, my lady, your eyes to sparkle."

He brought her into the full circle of his arms and laid his cheek against the crown of her head.

"Would you still like to marry me?" she asked.

Startled by the abruptness of her question, Hugh pulled back and stared at her.

"Would you?" she repeated.

"I thought you would never ask, lass," he whispered.

"I had hoped this would be your answer. I told Shamus and the *óenach* that I was releasing you from the challenge as I had chosen you to be my husband. Shamus has gone to get the priest to perform the ceremony."

"Why have you changed your mind about marrying me?" he asked. "Because you think I shall be dead on the morrow?"

"I have always lived for tomorrow," Willow confessed, "but this afternoon when Scannalan challenged you, I realized that I don't really have a tomorrow. Just the moment. And if only for the moment, Hugh MacDougald, I want to be married to someone who cares for me and someone for whom I care."

Thrusting his hands in the glorious red mane he lifted Willow's face and looked into her moon-kissed eyes. She had known great sorrow during her short life which pierced his heart. He kissed her, then rubbed a thumb across her cheek and felt her tears.

"I want to bear your child," she murmured. "But I

also don't want to bear your child, because I want to be with you . . . always."

"We shall find a way to have both," Hugh promised. He caught her hand, turned it over and kissed her palm. "When are we to be wed, my lady queen?"

"Now, if you're willing."

Facing each other, Hugh and Shamus stood in the middle of the great room of Forestgreen Hall in front of the dais. Clustered around the tables in front of the High Seat were the council members and Hugh's warriors. From the Queen's High Seat Willow observed what was going on. The village priest, having recently returned from a religious retreat, stood to her left.

His hands locked behind his back, Shamus said, "As the *tuatha* law-expounder it is my duty to specify the laws by which your marriage to the Lady of the Willow will take place and on which it will be predicated."

He paused; Hugh nodded.

"When you marry Willow, you will become our king, and it will be your foremost responsibility to protect Forestgreen and to impregnate our queen with a child, my lord, hopefully the chosen one."

As the jurist spoke, Hugh's gaze swept over the huge room, over the council members and his warriors who listened attentively to all that was happening. In particular he looked at his cousin, who leaned over the table, resting his upper weight on his folded arms.

All along Jamie had wanted only to return home, and he had advised Hugh of the folly of his actions. Yet Jamie would stay by his side and would always be his loyal advisor and warrior, always his honest cousin and friend.

Inadvertently Hugh moved his arm the wrong way,

and his body went weak with pain. He schooled his expression, not wanting anyone to know that he was hurt. Jamie looked up about that time. Hugh's heart went out to the younger man as he saw the shadow of concern on his face. The lad was the only one who knew about Hugh's bruised shoulder.

"Sometimes it is difficult to do one's duty, lord," Shamus said, "when that duty conflicts with what we personally want out of life."

Hugh returned his full attention to the jurist. He was clearly impatient with the proceedings and frustrated because there was nothing he could do to extricate Willow and himself from this situation that fate had thrust upon them. He was worried about his arm's being a disadvantage to him.

"My lord Shamus," he said, "you do not have to lecture me longer. I fully understand what my responsibility is. I swear before God that I have never forsaken my duty, and I shall not begin now."

Shamus nodded. "Then, my lord, we come to the most delicate part of this discussion, a part that I find most distasteful."

Hugh waited.

"Since the curse has come upon our village, not one of the Ladies of the Willow has lived many years after having given birth to her child. Clearly, lord, she has had to mate whether she loved a man or not or whether he loved her." Shamus paused and cleared his throat. "Quite naturally—"

Hugh glanced up at Willow to see her hands tightly gripping the hands of the armrests of the High Seat.

"My lord Shamus," Hugh interjected, determined that Willow would no longer be subjected to such humiliation, "I see no reason for you to discuss this matter further. The lady queen has already told me what the *tuatha* considers to be my rights."

Hugh lithely ran up the steps to stand beside Willow. He pried her fingers loose from the chair, caught them in his, and drew her to her feet.

"My lords of the assembly, lord jurist, holy father, and my fellow warriors, let me declare what I think my rights are. Before all of you, I pledge my undying love and fidelity to the Lady of the Willow. Before God and man—" he knelt before Willow "—and before you most of all, my lady-love, I troth my love and fidelity until death do us part."

Tears shimmered down Willow's cheeks as she knelt and captured Hugh's face in her hands.

"I love you, Willow."

She kissed him gently on the mouth.

"Hugh MacDougald, I love you."

" 'Tis easy for you to make such an oath," one of the council members railed. "You know that our lady shall not live long—"

"Don't say another word!" Hugh rose and slowly walked toward the accuser.

The man's eyes bulged, and his face turned white. He nervously backed up, wiping sweat from his face.

"I—I beg your pardon, my lord. I spoke too hastily."

"Aye, my lord, words are easily spoken," Hugh said, "but I am not a man who spouts words with the ease of an ever-flowing fountain. I would make the same oath if I knew Willow, Queen of Forestgreen, were going to live forever." Hugh turned and gazed up at her. "I would before God that she would live that long."

Willow held out her hands to him, and he returned to her. Standing beside her, holding one hand, his arm around her waist, he said, "My lord Shamus, I have a

question. In all of your legends has no one ever told
you how you'll know the husband who shall give the
Lady of Willow a man child?"

"Nay, my lord," Shamus answered sadly, "we know
of no sign."

"Then, jurist," Hugh said, "without more delay I
want to be wed to the Lady of the Willow."

"It shall be done," the old priest said. "If you and
the lady queen will follow me to the church—"

"Nay, Father," Hugh said. "My lady and I want to be
married beneath the Green Willow."

" 'Tis dark," the priest said. "Furthermore, weddings
are solemnized in a holy place, my son, in the church."

"Ours is not to be solemnized, Father," Hugh said,
"but rather celebrated. And it shall be done in a holy
place." Looking at Willow, he said, "My lady, direct
your servants to erect a pavilion beneath the Green
Willow and on the bed of shamrocks. We shall consummate our marriage there."

Willow's face glowed. Hugh didn't believe in the
magic of the Green Willow or the shamrocks, but his
lady-love did. He would make this concession for her.

"Aye, my lord."

Hugh turned to the priest. "Darkness is not an ob-
stacle, Father. We shall be wed in torchlight."

"As you say, my lord." The priest shook his head in
puzzlement.

"Awaken the villagers," Willow shouted. "Let them
celebrate their queen's wedding with her."

Chapter Nine

"Don't be so nervous," Jamie snapped, moving out of the way as Willow's servants hastily erected a pavilion. " 'Tis unlike you, Hugh."

"Aye, lad, it is," Hugh agreed. "But I've never been wed before."

He walked over to the lake's edge, his cousin walking beside him. The priest stood a good distance from them.

"Are you sure this is what you want?" Jamie asked.

"Aye," Hugh answered. "I've never wanted anything more in all of my life."

Pain shafted through his arm and side. Stopping, he caught his shoulder and grimaced.

"You are going to be at a definite disadvantage tomorrow," Jamie said kindly.

"Perhaps the shoulder shall be a slight disadvantage," Hugh said, "but I have one great advantage. I love Willow."

"Aye," Jamie murmured, "you are in love with a woman whom the villagers think is cursed. Mayhap she has brought a curse on you, my cousin."

Hugh didn't answer, because he couldn't. At one time he would have argued about the curse. But not any longer.

"When you first challenged for her hand, you told me you didn't believe in curses," Jamie said. "You claimed they were only tales."

"So I did," Hugh murmured, his heart heavy. "Now that I love Willow, it is easier for me to believe in magical things, lad, especially those that are harmful where she's concerned."

"If only you could find a sign."

"Aye."

"One that we're not responsible for creating," he added dryly.

"Where do you want the torches placed, my lord?" a servant asked.

Moving away from Jamie, Hugh showed the men where to set the torches; then he inspected the pavilion. When he had approved, he called out to the priest, "Father, are you ready?"

At the priest's nod, Hugh sent the servants to the hall to summon Willow. His warriors, their swords drawn, raised them in the air and crossed them at the tips to form an arch through which Willow would pass to join her husband-to-be. This was their sign that they swore their loyalty to Hugh's bride. Jamie, indeed Hugh's best man, stood beside his cousin to witness the marriage.

With an eagerness Hugh had never experienced before, he stood beneath the Green Willow waiting for Willow to join him. He waited in the same spot where she had stood only days earlier when she had been waiting for him to take his first kiss.

In the distance he saw the arc of light that announced the approach of the wedding procession. Then he saw the silhouettes of the people, of Willow and Shamus who were in the lead. Closer they moved, the torchlight growing brighter so that Hugh could distinguish their features. The jurist guided Willow to Hugh.

Truly Willow was the most beautiful woman Hugh had ever seen. Beneath her wimple and diadem, she wore a long diaphanous veil that flowed out behind her like a train. She wore no cloak, and the neck of her long tunic was scooped low so that her shoulders and the upper swell of her breasts were exposed. Long sleeves, parted at the shoulder seam, opened and flowed to the ground to reveal the length of her arms. A golden girdle hung loosely about her hips.

"My lady queen," Shamus said, "I give you to this man for marriage."

"Thank you, my lord Shamus."

"I accept the woman in marriage," Hugh said, holding out his left hand. When Willow laid hers on top of his, he whispered, "You told me that you would save *the more* for later, my lady, and that it would add to my incentive. Indeed it did, and it was worth waiting for. I have never seen so much of you."

"Nor have you seen as much as you shall see later this night, my lord."

Hugh grinned broadly. "You are most audacious, my lady, and I like it."

Willow laughed, her gaze running over the midnight blue shirt and trousers that he wore beneath his tartan. "You are the most handsome man I have ever seen, my lord, and the most glib. I like it. Your glibness brings me happiness."

They smiled at each other as they turned to face the priest.

* * *

Hugh stood outside the pavilion waiting for the ladies to complete Willow's toilet and to prepare her for bed. All the villagers were gone, and one torch burned low. Hugh moved closer to it and knelt down. He ran his hand through the shamrocks.

"My lord bishop," he muttered, "if these willows are your sacred grove, and the shamrock your sacred plant, then I beg you to give Willow a sign that I am the chosen husband."

Hugh kept running his hands through the clover, looking, searching for a four-leafed shamrock.

Only a sign for Willow? The thought shot through Hugh's mind with such intensity, he thought someone had spoken to him. Still unsure, he looked around but saw no one.

The ladies slipped out of the pavilion, nodding to Hugh that Willow was waiting for him. He stood, but didn't immediately walk into the shelter. He gazed upon the silver-blue lake.

He loved Willow, loved her more than he had thought it possible to love anyone, and he wanted to make love to her. But he could not bring himself to do it. He didn't want to impregnate her. He would go through life childless if it meant having Willow with him.

"My lord," she spoke from behind him, "I know what you are thinking, but we cannot give in to our personal wishes."

"Nor can I give in to my carnal desires, my lady love."

He turned to face her.

"But you must," she whispered.

"Not for all the assemblies in the world," he swore.

She caught his hands and tugged him closer to her.

"For me, Hugh. I have been mated, but have never been loved."

Her words pierced Hugh's heart and tore down his resolve.

"Aye, Willow, I shall make love to you."

He guided her toward the pavilion, but she shook her head.

"Nay, my love, let us consummate our marriage beneath the arbor of the Green Willow itself. Let Bishop Patrick's shamrocks be our marriage bed."

She knelt, drawing him down with her. When they were stretched out, he leaned over her, kissing her and running his hand over her back. She touched his chest, looked at his sun-bronzed chest covered with dark hair, at the strong column of his neck, his handsome face.

Still leaning over her, he began to unbutton her night tunic. "I promised that one day I would do this for you, my lady."

"I remember." Her voice was breathless. "You wanted me to be awake and aware of what you were doing. And I am, my husband. I have never wanted anything as much as I want your touch."

Hugh pulled her tunic aside and gazed down at her body. "You're more beautiful than I had dreamed," he murmured. "Your skin is creamy and smooth." He covered her breasts with his hands. She swelled to fill his palms, her nipples sensitive and eager for his touch.

As he kissed her, she ran her fingers through his hair. His hands began to touch her all over, in delightful but tormenting ways. The light touching, the teasing, became more than she could endure. She ached for more as he pulled the tunic from her body and kissed her thoroughly.

"I love you, Willow," he murmured, his voice thick and ragged.

"I love you," she whispered.

Cupping her buttocks, Hugh eased himself between her legs and pulled her against him. She wound her arms around him, her thighs trapping him in place. She returned his probing kiss, her tongue playing with his, answering his deep moan with soft cries of her own.

She had mated before, but never had she felt such wonderful sensations rushing through her body. She couldn't get enough of Hugh. She wanted to taste him, to touch him, to be part of him. She wanted him to be a part of her for as long as they could be together.

He broke the kiss, but only to trail his lips across her eyes, her cheeks, her throat. He bent to taste her breasts again. Such sweetness was almost unbearable.

"Your clothing," Willow said, and she began to fumble with them.

Hugh stopped her and rolled away. "I cannot," he whispered, plowing his hand through his hair. "Never have I wanted to love someone more than I do you, my lady, but I cannot. I cannot be the cause of your death."

Willow sat up beside him. "You will not cause my death, lord. That came with the curse. Mayhap, you are the one to release us from the curse."

"If only I could be sure." He lay down on his back and flung out his arm, his hand brushing through the shamrocks. He caught a fistful of them and pulled them loose. Holding them above their bodies and letting them drop a few at a time, he said, "I've made my request known, Willow. Then I searched through the shamrocks time and again, lady, hoping your blessed bishop would speak to us. But never do I find a four-leafed one."

"What is your request?" she asked.

"That I would be the chosen one to deliver you and your people from the curse."

"Would you believe if you found a four-leafed shamrock?" Willow asked.

"Only a few days ago," he confessed, "I would not have. But tonight I would."

"Then," Willow whispered, tears burning her eyes, "we shall have to find ourselves a four-leafed shamrock, won't we?"

Hugh laughed bitterly. "They are not that easy to find. Believe me, love, I have been searching."

"Perhaps, my love, you were searching amiss," she said.

Hugh lay back down and gazed at the ceiling of the shelter. Moving only her arm, Willow reached for her locket. Without Hugh's seeing what she was doing, she opened it and extricated the small shamrock—her talisman. Accustomed to the moonlight, she slowly picked up her shoulders and gazed at the dotting of tiny leaves on her stomach.

"Hugh," she whispered and reached down as if she were picking up one of them, "look!"

She held out her hand, and he gazed at the shamrock. "It has four segments," he murmured. Then he raised his head to hers. "Four leaflets, Willow."

"Our sign!" Willow whispered. "Our prayers have been answered."

"But it is dried," he said.

"What does that matter?" she whispered. She caught his face in her hands. "Always we have miracles with us, love. That's what you told me. It's just that sometimes we don't reach out for them. Other times we are too busy questioning them to believe."

He gazed at her.

"Let's reach for them. If only for a moment, let's just believe."

"Aye," he replied.

"I shall put it into my locket," she said, turning her head and hastily wiping away a tear, "and it shall always be my talisman."

Quickly Hugh undressed. Again she marveled at his beautiful body, at his taut muscles. When she opened her arms, they embraced and he eased her on her back, gently lowering himself over her. He kissed and caressed her until she was ready for him.

"Now," she said.

He moved inside her with great care, and she grasped his powerful shoulders as their hips rocked in unison. She lost all sense of time and place. Swept by the rushes of passion, she squeezed her eyes closed and hugged him tightly, letting his rapid thrusts carry her to a world where she had never been before and one to which only Hugh could carry her.

She reached a climax first, her world splintering into a million particles of pleasure. He exploded a moment later, his thrusts hard and fast, the completion all-consuming.

They held onto each other, neither willing to part from an embrace that had brought them such glorious satisfaction. It was a silently shared feeling, their only communication a gentle touch of his lips on her brow and a languorous stroke of her hand down his arm.

They made love again, then swam in the lake. Afterwards they moved into the pavilion and held each other the remainder of the night. Through the opening in the shelter, both watched dawn ribbon the sky.

"The sun is rising on a new day," Hugh told her. "The curse is broken, Willow. You shall give birth to a son, our son."

"Aye," she whispered, her heart heavy. In a way she had deceived Hugh, but she would not have changed what she did for anything. After all, it was he who had told her that miracles were all around and that humans had to make them happen. She simply made a miracle happen for him. She wanted Hugh to face his accuser with a light heart. If he died, she wanted him to die believing that he had lifted the curse from Forestgreen . . . and from her.

And deep within her heart of hearts, she knew that she had conceived her child and no matter whether it was a girl or boy, she welcomed it because it was Hugh's baby. It was a baby created in love, in her and Hugh's love, and it would be the baby that would break the curse, again no matter what its sex.

Chapter Ten

Morning sunlight glimmered golden on the clearing outside the village where Hugh and Scannalan were to duel. According to custom, a fighting arena had been designated, the boundaries clearly outlined by thongs stretched between metal stakes. Already the crowd had gathered. All quietly and fearfully awaited the outcome of the day's event. Willow, escorted by Shamus, walked to the opened pavilion that had been erected on a raised wooden platform especially for her.

Glad for the canopy of colored material, she sat down in her chair and gazed around her, at the anxious villagers, the Scottish warriors—worried frowns on their faces—and the Ywnson warriors. Anxious herself, she rubbed her amulet.

A murmur rippled through the crowd and they stepped aside. Hugh MacDougald, clad in his armor and weapons, marched proudly through to the fighting arena. Beside him walked Jamie, every bit as proud and courageous as his liege, Willow thought. Serving as Hugh's best man, Jamie remained in the fighting area; Hugh kept walking, not stopping until he stood before the royal arbor. He bowed low, then dipped on one knee.

"My lady wife, Queen of Forestgreen," he said, "today and for always I am your champion."

"My lord husband," Willow said, her voice strong despite her anxiety, "please rise. I am going to give you a talisman, a reminder of me, to wear in today's battle."

Hugh stood and walked closer to the dais. Slipping her sacred amulet over her head, Willow also rose, moved to the edge of the platform, and leaned down. She encircled Hugh's head with her necklace.

"Wear this, my love," she said, pressing the talisman against his chest, "and know that it will give you strength. It contains our four-leafed shamrock."

Hugh's hand caught and held hers. "I accept the talisman and wear it with gratitude," he said, "but 'tis your love, my lady, that will give me the strength to go through this ordeal. I have discovered, Willow, that there is only one miracle and that is love."

She felt the tears swimming in her eyes. "Then, my lord, you have a miracle, because I love you." She kissed him softly, then stepped back. "Go with God, my lord and champion, Hugh MacDougald."

The villagers clapped their hands and cheered.

The Ywnson champion strutted arrogantly into the fighting arena, stopping along the way to laugh and talk with his men, his loud boasts carrying to Hugh. Hugh observed Scannalan whip out his sword and brandish it. He was a brawny youth, Hugh thought, confident in his ability to win. And he was a braggart, ultimately a weakness. But he was also a skilled warrior. With expert proficiency Scannalan thrust with his sword.

The movement made Hugh's shoulder twinge. It was all he could do to keep from massaging it. Perhaps in his youth, Scannalan was overconfident. Hugh hoped so. That would be the younger's man's weakness, Hugh's strength.

Walking to the center of the circle, Shamus said, "My lords, it is mid-morning, time for the duel to begin."

"I'm ready," Scannalan bragged. " 'Tis the old man we have to worry about."

"Keep your concern for yourself," Hugh said with a smile. "You're going to need it before this day is over."

Hugh had been through enough battles in life to know that patience saw him through to the end and to victory more than might or strength or skill. Wearing down his enemy and outthinking them had always been his strongest points.

Knowing the rules of combat, Hugh listened halfheartedly as Shamus recited them. He used the time to study Scannalan. He watched his eye and body movements, the way he held his hands, the way he distributed his weight on his feet. He especially noticed the nervous way he twitched his lips.

"We're ready to begin," Shamus shouted, moving out of the fighting arena. "The challenged shall strike the first blow."

Hugh lifted his sword, his bruised body rebelling against such arduous movement. Down came his blade with a clash as Scannalan deftly feinted the blow. The clang signaled to the crowd that combat had truly begun.

Amidst the cheers and taunts, Hugh and Scannalan fought, blow for blow. Both were well matched. Although Hugh's experience far outweighed Scannalan's, Scannalan was the younger, the quicker and the lighter of the two. Landing several solid blows and laughing with each one, Scannalan danced out of the way of Hugh's sword.

The cooler of the two, Hugh quietly moved about, his eyes never leaving Scannalan. Always he measured his adversary's moves and calculated his accordingly. From the beginning he had known he could win this combat only if he outwitted, and thus outmaneuvered, the Ywnson champion.

The sound of steel against steel and the cries and grunts of battle-weary warriors filled the meadow. They exchanged blow for blow, wearing each other down. Then with a yell and a fierce lunge, Scannalan pierced Hugh's shoulder.

Willow leaped up and pressed her hand to her mouth to stifle her scream. She could not remember a time when she had been this anxious.

Blood gushed out of Hugh's wound to stain his tunic beneath his chain-mail. It trailed down his arm to drip off his wrist and fingers. It splattered to the ground.

Backing up from Scannalan, Hugh stumbled over an exposed root. As he fought to regain his balance, Scannalan came in for the kill. Hugh dove onto the ground, rolled away, but not before Scannalan had pierced his other arm.

Willow screamed.

Scannalan advanced, his sword swinging from left to right. The blows were coming so fast and furiously that all Hugh could do was hunker and ward them off. Scannalan's laughter rang louder than the clang of metal. He pressed forward. Hugh reeled from the fast and heavy assault. Then gathering all his strength he thrust. Again. And again. He startled Scannalan with his sudden offensive. The youth stumbled back, and Hugh stood.

Gulping needed air into his lungs, he glanced down to see the glimmer of gold on his chest. Willow's amulet—the four-leafed shamrock. Blinking his eyes, drawing new strength, he rushed toward the still shocked Scannalan and landed a blow that sent the youth reeling backwards.

He fell on his back, his legs swinging through the air. Before Hugh could strike him again, the youth rolled over and leaped to his feet. Once again he was in battle stance.

Willow watched Hugh's chest heave as he dragged air into his lungs. He wiped perspiration from his forehead with the back of his hand. Yet he never took his eyes off Scannalan.

"Dear Bishop Patrick," Willow prayed, "please help Hugh."

Shamus, standing beside her, laid a comforting hand on her shoulder. "Do not fret, my lady queen. Our Highlander is a wily man, the youth a fool. Hugh shall outwit him."

Willow looked at her old friend and advisor.

"Remember we have the greatest of all champions fighting for us."

Even in the heat of battle, Willow remembered the first time Shamus had uttered these words to her. She had scoffed them aside then, but not now.

"Aye, my lord," she said, "that we do."

An hour passed, and Hugh and Scannalan were slowing down. Their blows were not as heavy, as quick, or as clearly defined. Both had sustained numerous cuts and bruises, and the ground around them was stained with blood.

Scannalan moved forward, Hugh stepped backwards but not quickly or far enough. The Ywnson champion raised his sword and brought it down with all his strength. The blow, one too many to Hugh's previously bruised and now wounded arm, sent excruciating pain through his body.

That side of his body numb, barely able to grip his sword, Hugh fought to keep from losing consciousness. He drew in deep breaths and kept retreating, moving backwards, sideways, always away from the pounding blows of Scannalan's sword. In the fray of repeated impacts, the flat side of Scannalan's sword walloped Hugh again, hitting him fully on one of his open and bleeding wounds. Dizzy with exhaustion and pain, Hugh could no longer hang onto his sword. It spun through the air, landing close to the queen's open pavilion.

Willow gasped.

A cry of disappointment went up from the villagers.

Scannalan shouted his victory. His sword poised for the kill, purpose etched in the lines of his face and the gleam of his eye, he slowly advanced toward Hugh.

The initial fire of pain having subsided, Hugh closed his hand around one of the sharp, metal stakes that had been used to mark off the fighting arena. He tugged the stake. It wouldn't budge. He grunted and tugged again. He dislodged it from the ground.

Standing, Willow's heart pounded within her chest, and her breathing was shallow and painful. The stake looked so small and ineffective against Scannalan's sword.

Tottering to his feet, blinking perspiration from his eyes, Hugh gazed at his opponent. Scannalan slowly circled him, playing with him.

"The victory belongs to me, Highlander," he taunted.

Scannalan was only a huge blur to Hugh. He couldn't distinguish his features.

"Beg, and perhaps I shall be tempted to spare your life . . . or at least, the life of the Lady of Willow." Scannalan laughed, the mocking sound echoing through the clearing.

Several more deep breaths and Hugh's vision began to clear. His head spun less.

Scannalan stopped his circling and advanced. Again he laughed. He was getting cocky and overconfident, letting his guard down. What Hugh had been waiting for. His eyes pinned to Scannalan, Hugh drew back his arm and threw the stake.

"Damnation!" Scannalan cursed as the stake twinged through the air. It landed with a dull thud in Scannalan's shoulder. He screamed, and blood spewed out. His face white, Scannalan's sword slipped from his hand. He leaned over to pick it up, but Hugh stepped on the sword. Slowly Scannalan straightened.

"It's over," Hugh said.

"Kill me and be done with it."

"Nay," Hugh said, "you are no longer a threat to Forestgreen. I am going to let you live with your shame."

"Kill me!" Scannalan shouted. "Kill me."

Shamus shouted for all to hear, "Hugh MacDougald, king of *Tuatha* de Forestgreen, is the champion."

Willow raced from the pavilion and threw herself against Hugh, unmindful that he was soaked with blood and perspiration. He was alive, and he was her love. One arm circling his lady love, Hugh held his sword high in the air.

Those of the villagers who had weapons clanged

them together, those who didn't clapped their hands. All shouted their joy.

Although Hugh was engrossed with the victory celebration, he watched as three of the Ywnson chieftains walked over to Scannalan and carried him away from the fighting arena. The fourth one knelt before Hugh.

"I am Curadhan de Ywnson," he said, "now the chief of the *tuatha* since Scannalan has brought shame upon his name. You have defeated Scannalan in fair combat, and we shall honor the terms of the duel. From this day forward, you are our liege, Hugh MacDougald."

"Granted," Hugh said, growing weak from loss of blood. Light-headed, he thought he was going to pass out any moment. "My warriors, under the leadership of Jamie MacDougald, will ride with you so that we may reclaim all the goods you stole from Forestgreen, including our cattle."

"Aye, my lord king," Curadhan said.

Hugh lifted his head and smiled at the villagers. "We have won, Forestgreen. Our enemies have been vanquished, and we can turn our attention back to living."

Once again clapping, weapons clanging together, shouts, and whistling filled the air.

Willow held out her hand for silence. "People of Forestgreen, Hugh MacDougald came to us as a mercenary, his sole purpose to vanquish Garret de Ywnson. He did that, but in the process he and I fell in love. Last night we were wed beneath the Green Willow and our marriage bed was the patch of holy shamrocks."

Again she was so thankful, Willow couldn't keep the tears of joy from coursing down her cheeks. "My lord and I—we—"

"We found our miracle," Hugh said quietly. "Our request is that we bring an end to this curse that hangs over Forestgreen. We said it aloud beneath the Green Willow and we searched for a four-leafed shamrock as our sign that our prayer had been answered." He smiled down at Willow, love radiating from his eyes to her face. "And we found it!"

Aye, Willow thought with only a smattering of conscience, they had found it. As she had told him, one had to know where to look!

The previous victory celebration was nothing compared to the cries that went up with this announcement. The people thronged around them, laughing and crying and shouting.

"Tonight," Hugh cried above the noise, "we shall celebrate with a feast at Forestgreen Hall."

"Before then, my love," Willow said, guiding him toward the great hall, "we're going to take care of your wounds."

"Only my wounds, lady?" he teased.

"And whatever else might need tending to," she replied, her love shining in her eyes for him—for all—to see.

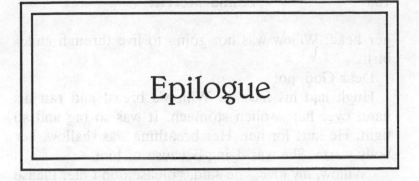

Epilogue

March 17, A.D. 865, Feast Day of Bishop Patrick
Village of Forestgreen, Ireland

"My lord," the midwife said, "it would be better if you waited outside."

Morning sun streamed in through the opened window to cast the royal bed chamber in a golden glow.

"Nay, good woman."

Hugh knelt at the head of the bed and wiped Willow's face with a damp cloth. Her long hair had been plaited, but it was soaking wet from her perspiration. Her clothing was also wet. Her eyes were sunken, and the skin around them was dark. Hugh's heart went out to her, and he wished he could endure this ordeal for her.

"How much longer?"

"I don't know, lord," the woman replied. "She has been travailing for two days now, and the babe seems no nearer to coming than it was when my lady suffered her first pains. Not many women pull through after this long."

Something in the woman's tone caused him to look up. She was wiping her hands on the huge apron she wore. Tears glistened in her eyes, and she was shaking.

her head. Willow was not going to live through childbirth.

Dear God, no!

Hugh laid his face on Willow's breast and ran his hand over her swollen stomach. It was so big and so tight. He hurt for her. Her breathing was shallow, her body warm. She was dying because of him.

"Willow, my love," he said, "please don't die. Please don't leave me."

Then he felt her hand on his head as she ran her fingers through his hair. "I'm so tired," she murmured. "So tired, Hugh. I don't think I can make it."

He lifted his face and gazed into her eyes, now dull with pain. "I wish I could undo this," he said, tears running down his cheeks. "I don't want to lose you. I can't lose you, Willow. You're my reason for living. I haven't had you long enough."

Even as he said the words, he knew that an eternity with her would not be long enough.

She brushed an errant strand of hair from his forehead. "Our—our child will be your reason for living from now on."

"Aye, I will live for him," he promised, "but it will not be the same without you, my love."

"If—if it's a girl," Willow said.

"I'll love and take care of her. I swear."

Willow dropped her hand and closed her eyes. He dipped the cloth into the bowl of water and wrung it out. As he washed her face and neck, he saw her amulet. He touched it.

"Willow," he whispered, "remember our four-leafed shamrock."

She spoke the word "aye" so faintly he could hardly hear it.

"Aye, our miracle."

Willow smiled, breathed deeply and went to sleep. Hugh leaned down and kissed her on the forehead. He rose and walked to the window, looking out in wonder and thinking about the four-leafed shamrock.

His gaze swept over the village to the grove of sacred trees. The Green Willow . . . that was really blue . . . He stopped. Something wasn't quite right! The trees—they weren't blue! They were green, emerald green. Unable to stop himself, Hugh raced to the bed.

"My darling wife, I know you're sore and tired, but you've got to see this."

"Later, Hugh," she protested.

"Now." Tenderly he scooped Willow into his arms, holding her protectively when she moaned softly, and carried her to the window.

"Look out, my lady. See the sacred willows."

Lying against Hugh, Willow wearily opened her lids and gazed at the trees. She tensed. "They are green," she whispered. "The willows are green. Truly the curse has been lifted."

She looped her arms around Hugh's chest and nestled close to him. "My lord husband, you were so right."

"Aye, my lady," he teased, "I always am. About what this time?"

"Love," she said. "That's the miracle."

"You and I," he said, "we've broken the curse, Willow. We have. Don't you remember our sign, our miracle."

She didn't answer this time.

"You've got to fight, my love. You have to."

As if the forces of nature obeyed his command, Willow's body contracted. As her body twisted in pain, she caught the travail-straps Hugh had tied to the bed, gripped them tightly, and summoned her last effort for the push. She grunted and shoved.

"The baby," the midwife cried. "It's coming, my lord."

"That's it, love." Hugh kissed her forehead. "You're doing wonderful."

"It's here." The midwife grunted. "It's here, my lord."

"You've given birth to our child."

"It's a—a beautiful—girl," the midwife announced.

Laughing for joy over the birth of his child, crying because he was afraid Willow would cease fighting, Hugh said, "Bring her to me, woman."

"My lord!" the woman shouted. "My lord, she's giving birth to a second child."

"Willow," Hugh exclaimed, "a second baby. We're going to have twins."

He heard the midwife moving behind him, but he concentrated on Willow. He dabbed her face with the wet cloth.

" 'Tis another girl, lord."

"Bring the babes to me," Hugh instructed. "I want my wife to see the blessings she has brought into the world."

The nurse placed two small bundles in Hugh's arms. "They look alike," she murmured.

Cradling them close to his body, swearing at that moment that no harm would ever come to his daughters if he could help it, Hugh held them down for Willow to see.

She opened her eyes. "Two girls, my lord."

"Not just two girls," he whispered. "Our daughters, the most beautiful girls in the whole world. They have their mother's auburn hair and green eyes."

One of the babies opened its mouth and gave a gusty cry. Then she flailed her fists in the air.

"And her father's conceit." Willow smiled and closed her eyes.

"Let my lady rest for a while, my lord," the midwife said. "And you need to rest yourself. You have hardly been out of this room since she began travailing."

"I don't want to leave," Hugh said.

"Go to the lake," the woman said, "and bring back some shamrocks and willow leaves to strew about the room. It will do my lady and the babies good."

With heavy heart, Hugh walked out of the great house to the willow grove. Kneeling beneath the Green Willow, he grabbed a handful of clover and threw them in the air.

"Bishop Patrick," he muttered. "Everything said about you must be stories and legends."

Then he glanced down to see one of the shamrocks flutter down to his leg. It was four-leafed. Time stood still as he stared at it. Gently, reverently he picked it up and held it on the palm of his hand.

Today was March 17th, the feast day of Bishop Patrick!

The four-leafed shamrock was the Bishop's holy sign!

Forgetting about the floor covering, Hugh leaped to

his feet and began to run toward the great hall. As he rushed into the building, the midwife ran out of the bed chamber. She held one of the babies in her arms. Tears streamed down her face.

"My lord king, you have a son!"

She shoved the baby into his arms, and Hugh looked at her—at it—at him in puzzlement. "How could you have made such a mistake, good woman?"

"I made no mistake, my lord. Our lady queen has given birth to twins and to a son, also."

"A son," he repeated.

Holding his son close to his chest, Hugh strode into the bed chamber. Gingerly he sat on the side of the bed.

"Willow," he said quietly, "do you know we're the parents of two girls and a boy?"

She opened her eyes and gave him a tired smile. "Aye, my love, all three came out of me."

Hugh laughed shakily. "Two daughters and a son, Willow. You and I have broken the curse. Have you seen him?"

She nodded. "He looks like you, my lord."

Smiling broadly, Hugh glanced down at his son. "Do you really think so, madam?"

"Let me wash and dress the babe, lord," the midwife said, "so that you can present them to the people."

Reluctantly, Hugh handed the baby over to her. Then he turned back to his wife. "Willow," he said softly, holding out his hand, "look what I found in the shamrock bed beneath the Green Willow."

She glanced over at him. "A four-leafed shamrock," she murmured.

"Aye, my love, and on Bishop Patrick's feast day, too. Our miracle."

THE BRIDE'S GIFT

Raine Cantrell

Chapter One

New Mexico Territory, 1878

Nicholas Dowling wished he had his cousin Patrick within arm's reach. He would throttle him. Cheerfully. A no-holds-barred whipping that would give County Donegal a new legend.

But Patrick was not there. No, a small voice reminded him, Patrick was in Ireland, and he was in New Mexico Territory.

Nick eyed the thickly woven blanket dividing his cabin in half. A scowl marred his strong features. His bride, his Irish mail-order bride, was on the other side making herself ready for their wedding night.

Somehow, someway, he'd get even with Patrick.

By the saints, how had he come to this?

He knew the answer, though it didn't please him to be reminded of it.

He'd foolishly trusted Patrick to follow his orders. If he continued to cast stones his own way, and if he was more the fool to believe in them, he'd swear Patrick was a changeling or the offspring of the *daoine sidhe*. But Nick did not believe in the fairy people of Irish legend and lore. He believed in none of the nonsense that people used to explain away bad luck, bad crops, or bad blood in the old country.

Hard work got a man what he wanted and needed. He'd come West to make his fortune, the only time he'd been lured by the promises of gold and silver to be found near Kingston, a mining camp on the Middle Percha. But there had been no big strike of gold, no silver. He had had nothing but hard, back-breaking digging and panning in ice-chilled mountain streams.

Nick thought himself smarter than most men who had come into the territory to find riches. He had used his small stash of gold dust to stake out land for a ranch in the vast thickets of walnut, cedar and pine trees east of the camp.

When he felt he had the good beginnings of his ranch started, he knew it was time for him to have a wife. He did not mind the loneliness, but a man had need of a woman and a family to carry on.

Respectable women were in scarce supply, and even if they were available, he didn't wish to spare the time necessary to court them. He thought it a grand idea, and a far easier one to write to his cousin Patrick and list his requirements for a wife.

He wanted a woman. A strong, sober-minded woman who would know her place. A plain woman unafraid of hard work who could come to love this new land as much as he did. He wanted a woman built for the bearing of sons. His large hands curled into fists. Damn Patrick!

He had none but himself to blame that he hadn't asked what his bride looked like. No, he'd agreed to the proxy marriage in Ireland to satisfy her family, and another in New York to still the tongues of his own relatives. It was his own fault he wouldn't take the time to travel East before he was doubly bound.

Never had he thought his wife would resemble

Brianna McPherson. She was young. Too damn young. If she had sixteen summers to her credit, he'd eat a bale of hay.

She was far more beautiful than Patrick led him to believe. *She's pleasing to the eye,* his cousin had written. Pleasing? Patrick must be going blind. But her beauty was a fault he could learn to live with. She had a stubborn streak, and that was something he would not tolerate.

All he had to do was close his eyes to see the image of her alighting from the stage, eyes wide and staring, unaware that the entire male population of Kingston was staring back.

She had stood there, looking lost, clutching a small wooden chest, when he had finally approached her. Nick was not proud of the fact that he waited until every passenger was off the stage before he had made a move. He had kept hoping that he was wrong, that she was not his bride.

She had taken one look at him, nodded and offered her hand. He could still hear the soft, musical lilt of her voice calling him "Mr. Dowling."

It was only right and proper that she address him as such. To his mother's dying day she had called his da Mr. Dowling. Why it irritated him now to think of it escaped him.

She wouldn't let him touch the chest. Not then, and not later when they reached the ranch. Her dowry she claimed, given to her by her sainted mother as a gift of remembrance. The hell with it. He'd be petty and mean to deny her a comfort of the old country in his home.

Their home, he amended. The jug of whiskey, good Irish whiskey that was a gift from Patrick, beckoned him over to the table. He didn't hold with a man get-

ting drunk on his wedding night, but then he'd never
had a bride before this. The rustlings had long since
ceased behind the curtain. Since his bride was slender,
he wasn't surprised that her weight hadn't made the
rope springs creak on the bed. He'd have to fatten her
up if he was going to get a fair day's work out of her.

What devil had prompted Patrick to send him someone so unsuitable for a wife?

He yanked the cork from the jug and poured out a
cup, then tilted the jug until the liquor brimmed the
top. He stared down into the liquid whose scent
brought memories of the home he'd left long ago. Nick
suddenly realized that Brianna's hair was nearly the
same reddish-amber shade as the whiskey. Surely it was
a wanton's hair color. He'd almost said as much when
she finally removed the serviceable bonnet and revealed the thickly braided hair, twisted and pinned
tight to the back of her head.

She was so damn young.

Nick tossed back a healthy belt of the whiskey, relishing the bite of the liquor.

Unpinned and loose, her hair would surely fall past
her waist. Was it silky soft? His fingers curled around
the cup.

She was waiting for him, likely wondering what was
keeping him from his marriage bed.

You! he wanted to shout. The whiskey slid down his
throat, the cup empty with a few swallows.

He was not fooled by the meek way she kept her
eyes from him. He wasn't even sure what color they
were. But he knew the shape and color of her lips.
Dusky rose, like the heart of a flower. Her mouth was
wide and her bottom lip full, just ripe for a . . .

Nick cut off his thought. He looked at the empty cup

then at the jug. *No more for you, boyo.* It was the whiskey that formed such fanciful thoughts. He pushed the
cork back into the narrow neck and set the jug high on
the open shelf above the table.

He'd delayed as long as he could. Nick moved to the
blanket.

Huddled beneath her wedding quilt on a lumpy mattress, Brianna felt smothered by the mobcap, and the
high, ruffled lace neckline of her nightgown. She bit
her lip as the edge of the blanket moved back. The
banked fire's glow revealed the tall, powerful shadow
of her husband.

Husband. The fine trembling in her limbs could not
be helped. She closed her eyes, envisioning again the
silver-tongued Patrick Dowling seated in their small
farmhouse parlor, reminding her and her mother of the
wonderful marriages he'd arranged for Sheila O'Leary,
Flory Connolly and Kathleen Kildare. All by proxy, all
shipped off to this strange land.

Patrick had performed a grave disservice to her. He
had married her off to a man who didn't believe in
. . . anything, not a wee dram of luck.

And she did not please him. Not a grave disservice at
all, Patrick had committed a grievous sin pairing her
with a man who couldn't hold his tongue. Tell her,
would he, that a fair wind would blow her away! Her
fingers worried over her carved rosary beads. The
prayers were for Nicholas. Perhaps the Lord would
have mercy and protect a man who incurred the anger
of the daoine sidhe.

It was *her* fault. *Her* careless remark as he drove his
fine wagon up the road to his home. The setting sun
had spread a wondrous glow over the tall pines shelter-
ing the cabin and the clearing around it. A place where

the fairy people would be welcomed. She foolishly said as much. And his husky voice—already sending strange shivers deep inside her to heighten her awareness of his powerful male presence—had replied that he'd not stand for that superstitious nonsense in his home.

His home. It had been a sharp warning and a painful one, but she was entranced by the majestic rise of the mountains, and half in love with a land near as beautiful as the one she'd left behind. A land that called to the wildness within her, reassuring her that Maggie Shay's cast of the runes had been right. She'd been promised riches and happiness. She couldn't wait to explore in the morning.

But first she had to get through the night. The mattress depressed on the other side, and she clung to her edge as he sat down. The soft thuds told her his boots were off. He was up again, and she strained to hear the whisper of cloth that warned her he would be joining her in bed soon. Very soon.

She squeezed her eyes tight and clutched the rosary to her chest. Dense she was not to have understood his first warning.

After a silent supper, which he'd been kindness itself to prepare, she had asked for a wee bit of milk to set upon the window sill as an offering to the gentry, as the daoine sidhe liked to be called. The fairy folk were easily pleased by small gifts to keep misfortune away.

She couldn't bring herself to explain to the man she had promised to cherish and love, that the offering was for his protection. It wasn't wise to anger the gentry. If she could call back the moment she had set aside the cloth she used to dry their few dishes and turned around to look at him, she would do so in an instant.

But she had looked. He had been seated on the

rough-hewn bench, facing her, one hand raking back the thick black collar-length hair, the other drumming on the table. His dark eyes, Black Irish eyes, she thought, fairly snapped with anger. A dull flush stole up lean, sculpted cheeks beneath tanned skin and the fine set of his lips pulled tight. She had felt herself bristle to see the flaring nostrils at the end of his slightly crooked nose.

His voice, that delicious husky voice, had not borne a hint of home in the little he had spoken. But it was thick, and rough with an Irish lilt then. " 'Tis a bad an' sorry state of affairs I got meself into marryin' a colleen. I'll no' be sayin' this again. I'll no' have that heathen gibberish in me home."

Stricken by his tone, hurt that he'd called her a girl when she was near an old maid at twenty-two, Brianna ended the night in silence. When he'd gone off to see to the evening chores, she smeared honey on the window sill, and left her sewing thimble filled with the precious whiskey Patrick had sent him as a gift. Now she had to finish her rosary and hope that she had appeased all to protect the foolish man from himself.

She slid her right hand out of the covers and made the sign of the cross, kissed her beads and tucked them beneath her pillow.

"I'd thought you asleep."

She nearly jumped from the bed. She had been so occupied by her thoughts that she never felt his presence beside her.

"This is all wrong," Nick murmured, feeling her fear stretch across the bed that suddenly appeared too small for both of them.

"Wrong?" she repeated. *What?* she wanted to demand. *Me? The marriage? The bed? What?*

He turned to his side and propped his head on one hand. He had deliberately left the blanket drawn aside to allow the faint light of the banked fire to penetrate the dark corner, as well as to allow the heat to warm them. The nights were cold in the mountains, despite the early arrival of spring.

In the faint light he could barely make out her eyes. They were the only feature not smothered beneath cloth. She had the covers pulled up to her nose, a silly cap draped over her head and it annoyed him that she was more covered now then when she had arrived here.

"You won't be needing this." He plucked off the offending cap and tossed it across the room, lightly batting away the hand she raised to stop him.

The small scuffle freed the glorious wealth of her hair. He was quick to take advantage of it, tunneling his fingers deep within the silken mass, releasing a scent of a dewed Irish morning. He could describe it no other way, and leaned closer even as he raised her hair to his nose. It was the scent of home, and of woman, and his blood heated to hear the catch in her breath.

"Did they bother to tell you of the marriage bed, wife?" The word rolled easily off his tongue. In the minutes it had taken him to join her, Nick had made up his mind that wife she was, wife she would be, until death did they part. It was no more her fault than his own. Patrick could bear the blame to his grave for pairing him with an ill-suited girl when he had wanted a woman.

Brianna stilled. She thought of her proxy wedding at home. *Married in August's heat and drowse, lover and friend in your chosen spouse.* Would Nicholas Dowling be her lover and her friend? Her arrival and proxy wedding with his cousins had taken place in March, and married when March winds shrill and roar meant a home on a distant shore. She had that. She had worn a green velvet gown, the color of the sod, an added piece of good luck for her marriage. And her mother had added a last stitch to her gown just before she left for the church. But in the midst of celebrations, of good wishes and packing, had any given her more than words of wisdom?

"Brianna." He cupped her cheek to turn her toward him, cursing the shadows that lay so deep he could barely see her. "Won't you answer me? I need to know if they've filled your head with silly nonsense, or frightened you with tales of pain."

"I intend to be a good, dutiful wife to you, Mr. Dowling."

"And if a man wanted more?"

She strained to see him, but it was impossible. "More? What more could you be wantin'?"

His breath warmed the chilled skin of her face. "Willingness to learn to please me."

It wasn't a question, but she answered him with honesty anyway. "Mary Alice said there is pleasure to be found in a marriage bed. And Meave, me sister, married three months afore me, claims no man's yet born that can please a woman." She worried the edge of the quilt with her fingers. "Sosanna, now, she winks an' smiles an' tells us all that betwixt a man an' a woman . . . there's pleasure, an' then there's pleasure." She spoke faster, as if getting as much as possible said would hold off the moment she both dreaded and, honesty demanded, anticipated.

Nick curved two fingers over her mouth. "I think that of all, Sosanna has the right of it. Betwixt a man and a woman there is a great deal of pleasure to be found."

Brianna suddenly remembered what she had forgotten to do. She squirmed, feeling the glide of his fingers from her mouth to beneath her chin where they came to rest on the ruffled lace that encircled her parched throat. She restlessly stirred again, unwilling to upset him, but the need was an urgent one. His breath was scented with whiskey, and somehow warmer, almost hot as his head came closer.

"Let me teach you, wife." Nick used the word deliberately to remind both her and himself of her place. Her squirming did not fool him into believing that passion had suddenly aroused her, more likely her wiggling about came from fear. He swore he would be gentle, he vowed to himself that he would take care and use tenderness to initiate his bride. Nick touched his lips to hers.

She slid out from beneath him and promptly fell on the floor.

Chapter Two

"What the hell?"

"I've a need to see to."

Her whispered words held a world of frightful shame. She tripped on the hem of her nightgown as she scrambled to stand, caught herself from falling and whipped the excess folds over one arm as she made her way to the corner. Her belongings were neatly stacked, and she had no trouble finding her small wooden chest. Without a glance at the bed, or the man in it, Brianna backed out of his sight.

How could she have forgotten to tend to her most precious dower gift? It was for fair and certain Mr. Dowling's fault!

With a groan born of too many frustrations to name, Nick yelled out, "For God's sake, take a lantern with you! I've no intent of searching for you if you get lost. And the outhouse is to your left, behind the stand of cedars."

Had the fool girl taken her shoes? He plumped up his pillow and slammed his head against it. Faith and begorra, hanging was too good for Patrick! A waste of good rope. She didn't have the sense to tend to herself before . . . He cut himself off, listening to what he knew was the screech of the pump being primed.

She'd run from him like a scalded cat to get a drink
of water!

Brianna threw a worried glance over her shoulder,
working the pump handle as fast as she could. It
wouldn't do to show Mr. Dowling her dowry gift. The
man hadn't the soul to appreciate it. She traced the
gilded shamrock that enhanced the small chest's cover,
then whispering the words her mother had taught her,
she lifted the lid. Into the specially copper lined base,
she slowly poured cup after cup of water.

A noise, a sense, she wasn't sure what made her slam
down the lid and fix the catch before spinning around.
But she had been right to do it. Her husband stood,
hands on narrow hips, not ten feet away, wearing nothing but shadows. Faith be!

"Drink your fill," he muttered, finding his way to the
shelf and taking down the jug. "I've a need for a drink
myself."

"The whiskey?"

"Aye, the whiskey."

She kept her back toward him, set the cup down in
the dry sink, and inched her way past him. Her husband was not inviting a comment from her, nor extending an invitation for her to stay. She could use a
brace of the water o' life herself. It was just as well that
she didn't partake, she'd likely give Mr. Dowling what
for. And she needed to find a safe place to store her
dower chest.

She hugged it tight, shivering a little from the cool
drafts that crept beneath her nightgown.

"I'll join you in a minute."

His announcement was warning that she'd best be in
bed, ready for his teaching. 'Twas a grand pity that her
ma had spent all her time embroidering tablecloths and

linens, going on about minding her housekeeping duties. Far better if she had explained how to willingly
please a man. She edged her way a little farther from
him.

Nick raised the jug to his mouth, but did no more
than touch it to his lips. The sight of his bride's timid
retreat arrested him.

"Don't skulk about like a mouse. You need have no
fear that I'll beat you."

"Beat me?"

"You heard me right. Are you a parrot or a wife?"

"A wife, Mr. Dowling. Yes, a wife." Beat her indeed!
As if she'd let him get his hands within an inch of her.
Saints be, what was she thinking? Of course he would
get within an inch of her. And a lot closer besides!
Despite his warning, she scurried back to the alcove
where the bed waited. The dark corner was the only
place for her chest. She set her hatbox before it, offering a quick, fervent prayer that he would respect her
privacy and not peek at it.

"Come to bed, Brianna."

She spun around at his demand, and Nick was struck
by the settling cloud of fiery hair that ended below the
waist of her voluminous nightgown. Poised to flee, like
an animal at bay, it was not the mood or image he
wished for his bride. He cursed her youth, and for good
measure his own arrogance, then his cousin once again.
His sigh was born of frustration melded with his suffering.

"Shall we begin again?"

Brianna admonished herself for behaving like a
ninny, and came to stand beside the bed. Night-ad-
justed, her eyes confirmed that Nicholas Dowling did
not wear a nightshirt like a proper man. The heathen.

Her wedding quilt, lovingly stitched with pride by every woman in the village, had been kicked to the foot of the bed. The linen sheet draped him from the waist down. It was an old, worn sheet, conforming to his body like a glove to the hand it was made for. Her eyes widened. It wasn't a hand that sheet gloved. Both of his hands were tucked behind his head as he lay there, watching her.

"Come to bed," he repeated, his husky voice soft. "I promise I won't pounce on you. But you must be chilled through standing barefoot on the floor."

As the fiery torrent of her hair fell back from her face with a toss of her head, Nick could almost feel her breathless, controlled fear in the faint firelit room like a short jab to his belly. God, she was so young. But the longer he waited, the longer fear would have to imbed itself.

"Come," he coaxed.

Brianna hesitated a moment more. "I'm no' fearin' that you're a cat to be pouncin', Mr. Dowling, but a man wantin' his due. I'll no' be denyin' you the husbandly rights you've paid dear for."

Nick didn't move. If she had taken a stick to him, she couldn't have more thoroughly squelched his desire. "Get into bed." This time it was a growled command. Remind him, would the chit, that he had paid her way from Ireland, paid dear for the loss of her services to her poor widowed mother, too? And he couldn't forget Patrick's hefty fee for making all the arrangements.

The temperature in the room dropped to a chilling degree. There was no more give in her than the walnut headboard that he had so lovingly crafted in honor of his bride. And simply for his statement that he would not pounce on her, Nick now refused to touch her at all.

Brianna bit her lower lip. She had said the wrong thing. Beside her lay a frost-shielded man. Her husband. Nicholas. She repeated his first name to herself, savoring the sound, the strength it conveyed. But as the tension lying between them became an almost tangible barrier in the middle of the bed, Brianna knew it was up to her to make amends.

"Mr. Dowling?" she ventured.

A snort was not the response she hoped for, but at least he was awake and listening.

"Likely, you're regrettin' the poor bargain Patrick made for you?"

"Am I?" Clipped and short as a shorn sheep, his voice was not inclined toward charity and forgiveness.

Brianna noted that. "Ah, but it's a sorry mess. I won't be claimin' to have the sight, but in your place I'd be havin' a wee bit of second thoughts. 'Tis a fact that in the eyes of the Lord and man we're married. 'Tis sorry I am not to be the woman you wanted."

"You're not even close to my needs in a wife."

Like the snapping of a whip, the emotionless delivery of his opinion pained her. Tears rose. She brushed them away. But they filled her eyes and slid down her cheeks.

Aware of her moves, as he was aware of every inch and breath she took, Nick winced to hear her sniffling noises. He'd never been a cruel man. How had he come to such a sorry pass that he would injure one so young?

"I'm sorry," he whispered, turning to his side. "It's the God's truth, but I never meant to hurt you over something that's not your fault. Patrick's the one to blame. He knew I wanted a woman to wife, not a colleen."

"Colleen?" She turned and found herself nearly nose to nose with him. Rearing back as she braced herself up on one elbow, Brianna blinked and sniffed. "Colleen? Are ye daft an' blind, Mr. Dowling? I'm no' a girl. Here I'm thinking you're angry that Patrick sent you an old maid."

Nick disliked her looming over him and rose to a half-sitting position. "Old maid? What tale are you spinnin'?"

"None. I've the right of it. That's what you call a woman who's long past her prime for marryin'."

The reaction was instantaneous. His body accepted her claim out of neediness long before his mind did. "Past your prime? Just how old are you?"

There was never a thought to lie to him. "Twenty-two. Didn't he say as much?"

"No." He flopped back to his pillow. "Here I am, beating myself for desiring a girl when I've a woman grown in my bed."

There wasn't an ounce of sense in her to be pleased by his remark, but Brianna was pleased, very pleased. "Patrick said you've got twenty-nine hard years behind you. Did he—"

"Lie? No. But I've had a birthday come and gone since he began." *She wasn't too young. Not sixteen but a woman grown.*

She half turned and relaxed against her pillow. Her heartbeat quickened. A warm, giddy feeling spread inside her. Laughter bubbled up. Its joyous sound invited him to join her.

In the darkness he enclosed her smaller hand with his. The guilt that had gnawed at him fled. The desire he felt had not been for a child. She was old enough to become his wife.

"You thought I was too young." Breathless, she slowly turned her head to look at him. So simple a thing. A little of her fear took flight. "Would you have bedded me despite thinking me too young?"

"You're my lawful wife."

"Not so, Mr. Dowling. I'm a woman grown and in your bed, but you've not yet made me your wife."

Her low voice soothed him like honey seeped with whiskey. The words, the bold meaning behind them, drove themselves into his senses like an exploding stick of dynamite. The dark came to life with desire, thick and hot and simmering. Nick had to swallow before he could speak.

"No. I've not yet made you my wife."

He lifted the hand he held, bringing it to his lips. He knew she thought the only objection he had to her was her age. He'd not handled their beginning very well, but he wasn't about to spoil the mood that settled warm as porridge on a winter's morn between them.

Her lips were sweet and trembling beneath his own. He was gentle. Infinitely so. He tutored. She proved an apt pupil. Nick found a depth of tenderness he didn't know he possessed. Patience. Understanding. He uncurled her fingers one by one with his own, with kisses, until she released her clutching grip on the ribboned ties of her nightgown.

There was a heated, womanly scent that enticed him to taste. She was shy, and rightly so. He coaxed. He seduced and smiled as he measured the pounding beat of her heart with his mouth. She held his head as his tongue bathed and teased skin made sensitive by the growing ache that excited even as it bewildered her.

Alert to her every sound and move, Nick lifted his head. His loins were blazed into a desire so intense he caught his breath, but he sensed the tension coiled tight within her, the very tension that had made her cry out.

"What is it, little one? Have I made you afraid?"

His voice was a warm wash of caring. Brianna shifted restlessly beneath him. "Do not think me too bold, but I've a question to ask."

"Anything. Ask me anything." The dark tendrils of her hair were spread beneath her, her skin as creamy white as her gown. Nick reined in the passion that seethed through his blood making its own demands.

" 'Tis wonderin' I am if you're mother naked beneath the sheet, Mr. Dowling?"

"If I wasn't," he murmured, amusement evident, relief flooding him that it was only virginal curiosity prompting the question, "we'd be having a grand problem making you into a wife."

"Are ye in a bloomin' rush to have it so?"

Nick leaned to one side, cradling her cheek, his thumb spread to rub the swollen fullness of her bottom lip. "It's a man's nature to be so. Does that frighten you, little one? I'll temper my desire for you till you're ready to accept me."

" 'Tis kind of you." *But no' what I'm wantin'!* It was too late. Once again the gentle kisses began. The tender touches that spread a coiled ache inside her. She felt petted and wooed. She couldn't seem to draw enough air, for the panting sounds were her own. She twisted toward him, not understanding why the solid weight of him eased and tormented her at the same time. A fine sheen of sweat covered her just as he did.

With devilish care he set a fire burning, deep and

low, and she tried to close her thighs against the nestling of his hips. The quilt was long gone, the sheet shoved to the foot board and still heat consumed her. She had only envisioned the suckling of a babe, never a man, never the strong pull that reached down inside her to make her moan.

"Kiss me," he whispered, sliding his body up over hers, his mouth hot and open, slanting to find hers yielding like a flower to the sun.

She tantalized him with her curious mix of innocence and ardent response to his lovemaking. He wanted to discover every feminine secret hidden from his eyes, his touch, his lips. His tongue stole what it could, until her mouth bloomed with a woman's hungry passion. She was fetching enough to tempt a saint, but Nick had never aspired to be one.

His murmurs grew huskier, darker, by turns cajoling and praising until he had divested her of the nightgown.

The fierce desire to couple with him made her shudder as the cool night air touched her skin. She was quickly warmed by his large caressing hands and the roughened sound of his voice. She sensed his growing impatience and measured it against her own. She was encouraged to touch him with a groan that rose from deep within his chest.

His breath was ragged in her ear. The slide of his male body intimate against hers. He stilled the restless moves of her thighs with a touch. She knew the pain was coming. Too soon, she wanted to call out.

He kissed her lips, her throat, her breasts, whispering words of pleasure until her legs parted in welcome for his first slow thrust.

The sudden, unexpected sharp pain of his teeth on

her lobe made her cry. Dazed, it took her long moments to understand he'd replaced one pain for another.

Nick brought his mouth down hotly on hers, stifling her breathless gasp of surprise. She struggled feebly, but each slow, deep stroke of his manhood intensified the burning, pulsing ache within her. Brianna lifted her arms to hold him. Now she was a woman. Now she could truly claim to be his wife.

Her tight gloving lured him. Her hard nipples rubbed against his chest and he wanted to lose his soul in her softness.

Fulfillment beckoned. The quickening rhythm of his desire enticed her with its promise. She arched to its driving force, aware of his long body, the smooth, powerful muscles that coiled and uncoiled in the flat, hard belly moving against hers. A wildness took hold of her, her nails digging into his back in an effort to find the intense pleasure promised. In a moment when darkness held sway, when there was no breath, no sense of self, the compelling rhythm ceased with a molten explosion and slowly, the pleasure seeped away, leaving her confused.

Nick gathered her close, hiding his disappointment. He was unsure if he should explain what had happened. His finger traced her features as if she were precious, his kiss cherishing before he tucked her head against his shoulder. His sigh was sheer contentment. Patrick deserved a bonus. He'd send him one after the spring calves were sold.

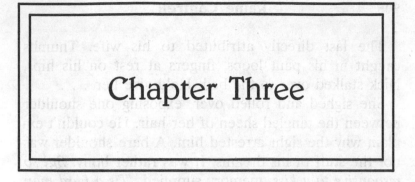

Chapter Three

When morning came, ants were everywhere. Drunken little columns of tiny brown bodies weaved to and fro as Nick blinked the sleep from his eyes. He shook off the water he'd just pumped over his head, sending it flying in a wild spray. The blissful, whistling mood that made him leave his bride to sleep in this first morning took a turn around a corner and disappeared. There was no denying what he was seeing crawling all over the dry sink. He leaned closer to the window sill and sniffed.

If he wasn't smelling wild, sweet honey, and the fumes of good, sainted Irish whiskey, then he'd been born a bloody Englishman.

He knew—even before he straightened and looked at where he'd left his bride asleep—that this had something to do with her heathen nonsense. Ants, for pity's sake!

His fingers dug into the wood of the sink's edge. Start as you mean to go, his da had always said. Advice Nick had taken to heart. He'd given his wife plain enough warnings. Gone were his thoughts of his relished morning coffee before he began chores. Gone, too, was the feeling of well-being that had him thinking he could ride eight green broncs without tiring.

The last directly attributed to his wife. Thumbs caught in his pant loops, fingers at rest on his hips, Nick stalked over to the bed. He'd give her . . .

She sighed and rolled over, exposing one shoulder between the tangled sheen of her hair. He couldn't explain why the sight arrested him. A bare shoulder was not the stuff of his dreams. It was rather bony. *But so responsive to a kiss,* memory supplied. *'Tis a hard man who'd take a woman to task after she pleased him.*

Maybe so, he answered his conscience, but I'll not live with superstitions governing my every breath and move. Why the devil didn't Patrick give him some warning? *'Tis foolish you are, for asking. You wanted an Irish bride, born an' bred on the sod. You knew what'd come along with her. Beliefs steeped in mother's milk, blood and bone. Have you no thought, man, that there's something verra wrong with you?*

No! The denial and conversation's end were quick and sharp.

"Brianna. Wake up, woman. I've a powerful urge to throttle you, but I'll be kindness itself this morn an' contain myself." He leaned over, braced one hand on the bed, and roughly shook her offending shoulder. "Wake up now. You are going to have another wifely lesson."

Untold riches . . . Startled from her pleasant dream, Brianna stirred hearing a man's gruff-voiced demand. No' a man, silly creature, she reminded herself. 'Tis your very own husband who's calling you to wake. With a sigh, and a smile, she flopped over to her back and opened sleepy eyes.

Sweet heaven! With his upper lip curled back from his teeth, 'twas Lucifer himself come to wake her! His eyes were glazed like a sot's. Seeing where they

strayed, she snapped the quilt up to her nose. If his
eyes could leap across the bed, she'd be flayed by the
crackling anger within them. Oh, Lord, what've I done?

"Mr. Dowling?"

"An' none other. Get up—"

"You're frightenin' me with your snarl an' scowl."

"Thank the goodness that you've the sense to see
that."

She angled her head to the side, peering up at him.
"You mean to frighten me? I've no understandin' of a
man's way of thinkin', Mr. Dowling. Why ever for?"

"There's a grand mess your meddling with heathen
notions has left in the kitchen. Up with you now. I'd
have you clean it up. Then we'll have us a talk."

She didn't like the sound of that. No more than she
liked having a muscular, hair-matted chest, un-
ashamedly bared and looming above her. 'Twas all for
naught. The gentry were deeply offended if there was a
mess to clean. If they were not, Mr. Dowling would
never have known what she'd been about. The man
obviously had sins untold upon his furrowed brow, else
her rosary wouldn't have failed her, too.

"Would you be mindin' to give me a bit of privacy
so's I can join you directly?"

Mollified by her penitent tone, Nick backed off the
bed. "See that you're quick about it." In passing, he
jerked the blanket across the rope.

Minutes later, having donned nightgown and shawl
and fidgeting like a fly about to land in a trout-laden
stream, she joined him near the sink. His pointed look
from her face to the window sill, then back again at
her, left the need for words unsaid.

"The ants—"

"I'm glad you're not blind, but we'll work on the daft part after you've gotten rid of them."

"Rid of . . . oh, no, Mr. Dowling. I cannot do that. 'Tis unlucky to destroy them, for their building a nest means you can expect riches to come."

Wagging one large, blunt finger under her nose, Nick gritted his teeth. Patience, man, have patience. "Just . . . do . . . it." He jerked his shirt from the bench where he'd tossed it, jammed his hat on his head with the brim canted low over his eyes, then stomped to the door. "*I'll* see to my stock, *you* see to cleaning this mess. *You* tend to having hot coffee an' food waiting my return. As for riches, woman, *I'll* tend to that with my own two hands."

"Aye, Mr. Dowling . . . sir!"

He shook his head. "An' a damn vinegar tongue besides." Muttering, he slammed the door behind him.

"Ah, he's gone an' done it now. Sainted mother, has he no' a wit of sense? I'll be havin' me hands full coverin' over for him, an' a scrubwoman's knees for prayin'. What to do?" Always so careful not to anger *them,* Brianna racked her mind.

He'd be plagued with all sorts of ill luck if *they* were of a thought to teach him a lesson. He could find their sharp thorns in his bed, for all knew how the wee folk loved their thorn-trees. Shivering to even think about it, she knew they could call up the *pooka.* An angry one could use fairy darts on beast and man alike.

"An' where would the bletherin' Mr. Dowling be then, without the use of his braw hands to gain his riches?" Her head tilted back, and her eyes closed. "I'm beginnin' to understand why you've sent me here. I'm to save the poor man from himself. 'Tis no' an easy task you've set me, so be merciful an' lend a hand."

Her gaze was drawn to the window. Beyond the edge of the tree tops, the rising sun sent a brilliant dart of sunlight to rest on the sill. The corner where she had put her silver thimble filled with whiskey was empty. A deep smile creased her lips.

"Saints be praised. Ah, but you're a sly lot, takin' the gift that pleased you most. I'll see to findin' a home for your creatures where they'll be safe from the man."

The eggs were runny. He liked them hard. The bacon was crisp. He liked it soft. The biscuits were fine tasting but fell apart into a crumbly mess. The coffee was hot, black as a miner's heart and thick as his skull. He liked that just fine.

Brianna didn't eat. But she had plenty to say.

"Did you know that bacon is believed to be a powerful curative for fever and constipation, Mr. Dowling? But it only works if it's stolen."

Nick grunted, and once again attempted to butter a biscuit.

" 'Tis sorry I am, that your biscuit's too light. I'll be needing to fix my measurements as quick as can be."

He slowly looked up at her. From where he sat, her *measurements* were fine. Just fine. He gave up the crumbs to his plate and ate with his fork.

"I suppose I should be mentionin' that bread falling apart means there's to be a fight."

"That so?"

"Aye, Mr. Dowling. We could have ours right quick if you're of a mind to."

"If I'm of a mind to?"

"Are you havin' trouble with your ears? 'Tis what I said."

Nick wrapped his hands around the coffee cup. It

was not as satisfying as holding her lily-white throat, but far better for his constitution. It wouldn't do to murder his bride of less than a day. Provoking little vinegar mouth that she was.

It was not the only provoking thing about her. Her lovely hair was braided and wrapped up tight. He finally understood why they called it a woman's crowning glory, it was the form of the braids. Like a dew-fresh milkmaid, she faced him across the planked table. He'd seen friendlier eyes over a rifle barrel. Challenging him. That's what the woman was doing.

He set his cup down, and she was up at the stove before he could ask for more coffee. Her plain, serviceable brown skirt brushed against his bare forearm, and Nick wished he had kept his sleeves rolled down. He didn't want to be made so . . . aware of her. That was it. She had him on a leading rein, a place he'd never been.

All because of last night. If she hadn't been so eager, so responsive, he wouldn't be tempering his anger a bit.

Ah, but she had been eager to be his wife. He came to and found that she was still beside him. Holding the battered pot, she stared into his cup.

Nick didn't want to ask. But he did. "What are you doing? Looking to see if any of those ants ended up in my coffee?"

"I'm watchin' the bubbles, Mr. Dowling. If you . . . well, never the mind."

Back to the stove she went. And he sat there, feeling her behind him. Smelling the sweet spring morning scent of hers, and waiting for the pronouncement of another one of her heathenish beliefs. None were forthcoming. He drummed his fingers against the table. Not a sound did she make. Not a move.

Once more he found himself struggling not to ask. He lost. Again. "So, you'll let me sit here wonderin' what it was about the bubbles in coffee that held your attention so long?"

"Are you wonderin', Mr. Dowling?" Brianna fought to keep the laughter from her voice. "I didn't mean to impose me heathen nonsense on you again."

Patience, man, have patience. But Nick knew he had warned himself before this. It hadn't done a lick of good then. It certainly wasn't working now.

Standing behind him, Brianna's view of his faded gray shirt back revealed muscles rippling with tension. His drumming fingers increased the tempo. Step lightly, she warned herself. But she had already taken the measure of her husband's temper.

"I've never angered someone so many times in so short a time," she announced.

"That so?"

Glaring at his back, she fought the urge to make the evil sign against him. "The admission cost me a great deal, Mr. Dowling. Respect that, if you will not respect that I'm your wife."

Nick's fingers stilled. Calling her vinegar tongue was far too mild: she was sharp as a spike. But as he repeated her words to himself, he realized that she wasn't spoiling for a fight. Or was she? This marriage business was new to him. To his surprise, he said as much.

"An' to me," she whispered, coming to stand at the opposite side of the table. " 'Tis an admission that only a *man* could be makin'. I thank you for it."

Man as opposed to woman. Man as opposed to boy. Nick chose the latter. Beneath the tiny flowered print cloth of her shirtwaist, her shoulders were mantled with pride. Staring at her, he wasn't sure if it was pride or the starched high collar that kept her lily-white neck and her head rigid. He met her steady regard and for the first time saw the color of her eyes. Like a field splintered with sunlight, they were green and brown, flecked with gold. Her lashes were pale, short spikes matching the shade of slightly arched brows.

And her mouth . . . ah, there was a place to settle his gaze. Like a flower bursting to bloom, the pouty swell of her lips were an invitation to sip honey. Honey?

Why? Why had his thoughts taken him directly where he wished to avoid? Start as you mean to go . . .

He cleared his throat. Sipped his coffee. Set the cup down and turned it around and around. He glanced out the distorted glass window and saw that time was wasting. There were cattle to check now that his barn chores were done.

The kettle whistled on the stove behind him. Almost in warning. Brianna didn't move.

"The water's boiling," he said.

"Ain't it now," she answered, forcing her feet to keep still, for there was a need to express her impatience with a bit of toe-tapping.

"I see you cleaned up the ants."

"Caught every last one of the wee creatures. They'll not be plaguing you again."

"I'm glad we understand each other." Nick shoved back the bench and rose. He stretched his arms high, then turned to snatch his hat from the peg near the door. "I'll be riding out for a time. Seeing to the cattle," he added, though he couldn't have explained why. He opened the door, then turned back. She still stood in the same spot, just staring right at him. "You know where the smoke house is? Remember, I showed you yesterday?"

"I remember."

"Yeah, well, ah . . . you have everything that you need?"

Brianna smiled at him. It was the first time. A wide, generous smile, the kind that lit up her eyes with sparkle. "Aye, I've got everything that I need, Mr. Dowling. What you need to be askin', is do you?"

She turned aside to scrape the plates, leaving him with a frown. Moments later the door closed behind him. Quietly this time.

Her smile, and the mischief-making sparkle in her eyes, wouldn't leave Nick's mind. He'd handled the whole business of the ants badly. If he hadn't been thinking about her mouth, about the soft satiny feel of her lips opening beneath his, he would have been firmer. *For sure, man, you'd have given the woman a tongue lashing she'd not soon be forgetting.*

Well, it was true. He would have. She was interfering with his work. He had roped a cow too far out in the muddy pond, her calf bawling to wake the dead, when the look on the dumb animal's face had him picturing his wife. She wore that long suffering, patient, he'll-come-to-his-senses look, too.

Minutes later he realized he'd been daydreaming. If it wasn't for his horse, who despite the rope Nick let go slack in his hand, had kept backing up until the bogged cow was nearly free, he would have lost the animal. He had not yet attained the riches he'd boasted about to Brianna that he could afford to lose one cow.

Nick finished up quickly, watching the ungrateful pair lope off with their tails in the air. "Ain't that just like a female." He laughed when the calf began butting its head in a quest for milk and the cow stopped instantly. "Watch out there, critter, that little one'll have you jumping through hoops."

He snapped his brim lower, took a hurried look around to make sure he was alone. He had the most uncomfortable feeling that he'd been talking about himself.

With a jerk of the neck-rein he turned his horse for home, sitting up a little straighter, urging the horse a little faster. He found himself anxious for supper and sass.

At least he hoped he'd have supper. There was no doubt about the sass.

Chapter Four

Nick was still brooding over his wife's lack of spirit. Five days. He'd had his suppers, his breakfasts, and even two surprise picnic lunches, all lovingly presented by his wife's hand, but no sass. Not even a whisper. Frustrated didn't come near what he was. She didn't leave any needs untended, none that is that a hired woman couldn't perform.

What had happened? he asked himself, forgoing the count of how many times he'd questioned himself.

That second night, he had not pushed her to come to bed, thinking he'd left her sore. Although what had her lingering in the kitchen for so long was a mystery. After an agonizing night of lying beside her, she had given him a sweet, morning smile that hinted of things to come. He'd set off with a jaunty step, almost doing a jig at the thought of the night, and the lessons he had planned to teach her.

He *knew* that she was a passionate woman. He'd been pleased with his part in making her so. And he had made a promise to himself to try and have more patience with her. After all, she was new to the role of a wife.

Taking courage in hand, he had faced her in the morning, and asked right out if he had hurt her. "Nothing lasting, Mr. Dowling," was her reply along with a steady level look that seemed to challenge him to ask more pointed questions.

He found he couldn't do it.

After all, he was new to the role of a husband. But he was trying.

Somehow, he'd ended up in bed, alone, gritting his teeth.

"Jus' be lettin' me finish this rosary now, Mr. Dowling," he mimicked, having heard the same for the past three nights.

His horse snorted as if he agreed with his mocking tone.

Nick reminded himself that he had waited. He had mentioned to her that he was waiting. Her answer: "Another few beads, an' I'll be done."

He wanted to know what she prayed for that required such devotion. He knew he had sounded like a quarrelsome little boy, but it couldn't be helped. He felt like one who had his new treat taken away. And how was he to argue with a woman who prayed to correct grievous sins to protect one dear to her?

He could not. That was the truth of the matter.

Those few more beads had stretched and stretched, until he had dozed off. A little frustrated, he recalled that he had worked it off, maybe too hard. He had listened to the same excuse after a supper that his saintly mother would have been proud to set on her table, and promptly fell asleep.

What the devil had Patrick sent him? A novice from the convent? Ah, patience, man.

Patience could be as dangerous as working with barbwire. If he didn't exert all his strength when stringing fence, the damn wire would snap and entangle him. A most painful experience.

Nick shifted his seat. Painful, indeed. He felt as if he had slipped into a large barrel of blackstrap molasses.

What had he married? She had to have put a spell on him. Hexed him, but good. Evil-eyed him.

Lord, look where she took his thoughts. Stuff and nonsense that he didn't believe. But what then could explain how she managed to tie him in knots and avoid her wifely duties?

"Horse, I tell you, if she keeps this up, I'll shrivel like those apple rings she's drying."

Keeping to an ambling walk toward home, Nick worried over this sorry mess. He was a man, wasn't he? Made of sterner stuff than a woman? He'd show her a game of wits. And while he was at it, he'd see that she stopped hovering fussily over that damn dower chest in the corner.

Treating it like it was gold. She didn't fool him. He'd never heard of anyone whispering gibberish to gold. Well, he amended, there had been a few miners who coaxed and teased, as if ore would answer and give itself up to them.

But for sure, he'd never seen anyone water it.

Have yourself a look, a little voice urged.

The thought was tempting. Nick resisted. A man should respect his wife. And he remembered Brianna telling him so. Well, it did no harm for a woman to have a few secrets of her own. She had come a long way, to a strange new country, to marry a stranger. He'd . . .

You're a glutton for punishment, boyo.

Maybe so, but he had a few tricks of his own.

* * *

Brianna waited anxiously for her husband's return. He had promised her that after supper, he would walk with her to find a spot for her garden. True, his mood of late had not been of the best, but she hoped to change that.

She noted the change in him the moment he stepped into the kitchen. Jeweled drops of water nestled in his neatly combed hair. He didn't bring the smell of the barn inside tonight, and a quick peek revealed a clean pair of boots. My, my, but he's spruced up fine. Shaved, scented with bay rum, a cocky grin and a hand hidden behind his back. She stirred the pot of stew with vigorous motions.

"Supper'll be ready in a few minutes."

"No rush," Nick answered, tossing the hat he carried onto the peg. "So tell me, how was your day?"

Did you ever hear the like? she asked herself. She could not ever remember hearing a man of her village ask such. " 'Tis the same as the day before, and the one before that. A woman's work only varies with the weather and the seasons, Mr. Dowling."

"I've been thinking about hiring someone to help you."

That brought her head up from sniffing the stew. She saw that he rocked back on his bootheels, still standing just inside the closed door.

"Are you believin' you made a poor bargain then, an' I can't be carin' for my own home meself?"

"Stop twisting what I said." He had to remind himself to temper his voice. Shouting at her was not going to achieve his ends. "I meant no such thing. I can afford to hire a girl to help you."

"Mr. Dowling—"

"Nick would be nice. There's no one but the two of us. You could use my first name."

" 'Tis respect I show you. Mr. Dowling you began, and Mr. Dowling you'll stay." *For now.*

Nick took a menacing step forward, then caught himself. "Listen, wife. I won't argue the matter." *For now.* "I've brought you something. A present."

Brianna nearly dropped the tray of biscuits. "A present? Why would you be doing that? 'Tis no' my—"

"A man," he said, fighting not to grit his teeth, "does not need a reason to bring his wife a present."

"I see." Her hands slid down and played with the edges of her apron. How could he have known? She'd been so careful, having no idea how to explain to him.

"No, you don't. I mean, you haven't yet. Sit down and I'll show you what I've bought you."

Brianna sat. Her head was tilted slightly to one side, her look expectant, her hands folded in her lap, and Nick was struck once more by the sweet innocence of her.

He came to stand before her, and drew his hand out from behind his back. "Here," he said, offering the paper he held.

Her hesitation sent a prowl of impatience across his face. With a it-might-burn-me-if-I-touch-it look, Brianna held the paper.

Nick whistled, he rocked, he smoothed his hair. He sniffed appreciatively at the aroma of the stew bubbling on the stove. He hummed. He waited. He stared at her bewildered expression.

"Doesn't it please you?"

She had to force herself to look up at him. It was almost beyond her to meet his penetrating dark eyes. She cleared her throat, straightened her shoulders and slowly rose.

" 'Tis a fine present I'm sure, Mr. Dowling."

Nick stared at her, then at the paper she thrust at
him. "That's it? That's all you have to say? I thought
you would be pleased, going on the way you have about
having a bit of cream or your own butter."

There was no help for it. She had to tell him. He
looked hurt by her lack of excitement over his present.
"Mr. Dowling," she began.

"Nick. Call me Nick, dammit."

"There's a fightin' mood upon you an' I've no wish
to fight." She placed one hand on his arm that was
raised and holding the paper. " 'Tis shamed I am to be
admittin' this, but I cannot read."

Still caught up in his anger over her reception of his
gift, Nick bellowed, "You can't—" he cut himself off,
saying the rest silently. *Read. She couldn't read.* He
caught her hand and held it in place on his forearm.
"No, stay right where you are. And there is nothing to
be ashamed of. I didn't learn till I was a man grown.
An' only then, 'cause I was cheated badly."

An understanding passed between them. Brianna
knew there was no other way to describe it. The
warmth in his eyes, the way his hand covered hers,
pressing it to him, and the smile that invited her to
share her own, diminished her shameful admission. He
didn't seem to care. It didn't lessen her in his eyes. He
was a kind man, a good one. And she stood on tiptoe
to kiss his cheek. Nick turned his face and caught her
lips with his. It was a sweetly chaste kiss as far as kisses
went when compared to those passionate ones they had
exchanged. But Brianna knew it marked a wondrous
change between them and couldn't resist teasing him.

"Were you really cheated?"

He didn't know how, or even why sharing the story
with her was necessary, but it was important. "I'll tell

you while we eat, if you promise not to laugh too much.
Then we'll find a spot for your garden."

"An' your present? Will you be tellin' me what it is?"

Nick tucked the paper into his pants pocket. "I think
I'll let you see it for yourself. Somehow reading about
it wouldn't make the same impression."

Looking as joyful as he could want, she hurried to
set the food on the table. "Will it be soon, do you
know?"

"Tomorrow. You'll have your present tomorrow." He
ate and spoke to his wife with relish. *His wife.* Unex-
plainedly the admission that she couldn't read, and his
own admission that he'd been a fool because he signed
a paper without knowing what it said, had made him
feel more like a husband. Listening to Brianna hum as
she washed the dishes while he waited by the door,
made her seem more like a wife.

And the painful frustration that had marked his days
slipped away, just as she slipped her arm through his to
take their walk.

It was a new moon, as weak as Brianna felt when
Nick raised his head and broke the tantalizing kisses
they'd shared. Standing in the middle of what would
become her garden, Brianna welcomed the tendrils of
warmth that curled inside her.

"Now tell me," he asked, sliding his arms around her
waist and rocking her to and fro against his body,
"where you want your fence posts set?"

"Fence posts?"

Pleased with her distracted air, he kissed the tip of
her nose. "You'll need to show me so I can mark them
off. No garden would be safe from the wild creatures
without a fence."

Wild. There was a word to latch onto and Brianna

held on tight. The way his thumbs rubbed and circled the small of her back had her ready to suggest they retire. It would be unseemly for her to do so. Not proper at all. But as she lifted her hand and touched his chest, she wondered why. Firm muscle and heat met the palm of her hand, and with them, the steady beat of his heart, as she told him she wasn't sure how big the garden should be.

"I've not had so much land to pick an' choose from."

"I should have remembered," he answered.

" 'Tis a dream you've given me. There's so much I want to grow. Could we have trees?"

"Trees?" Even with the shadows deep on the land, Nick knew she had to see the thick forest that nearly encircled the clearing they had chosen.

Brianna laughed at his questing tone, then explained. "It's not these trees that want plantin', but sweet fruit ones." She toyed with the button on his shirt. "I could can the lot an' you'd have your sweet tooth full all winter long."

"Just mine?"

"Oh, I've a sweet tooth, too."

"Then, by all means, we shall plant your fruit trees, but till then—"

"Till then?" she asked with a catch in her voice.

"I've got you." With his words the mood changed to one of sharp, sensual awareness. He knew she was aware of it, for her head came to rest against him. Nick rested his chin on the top of her braided hair.

"Brianna, I haven't wanted to pry, but I must know why you've kept yourself from me these past nights. Will you trust me? Will you tell me if I've frightened you or hurt you or . . ." He hugged her close, unable to find the right words.

She waited so long he thought she wasn't going to answer him.

" 'Tis not that I don't want to say, but I'm strugglin' for the way." *Tell him, he's your husband.* "Does it matter a great deal to you?"

"Does it matter—yes, damn, pardon me, but yes, it does matter. I need to know if I've made you afraid of me."

She appeared suddenly smaller, more fragile in his arms. He couldn't hear what she was murmuring, only faint sounds reached him. Nick curved one hand over the back of her head.

"You can tell me whatever it is," he encouraged.

" 'Tis a woman's thing."

He repeated her whispered words to himself, trying to making sense of them. He was distracted by the feel of her soft breasts pressing against him, and the scent of her that warmed with the slow heat spreading from where they joined at chest, hip and thigh. He bent to kiss her ear.

Brianna angled her head back to look up at him. Shrouded in shadows, she couldn't make out his features. Why didn't he say something? It dawned on her that he had not understood what she told him.

"Mr. Dowling, 'tis a monthly woman's thing."

Once more lowering his head to explore the little bare skin revealed by her high-necked shirtwaist, Nick took a few moments before lightning struck. His head jerked up.

"Oh."

Brianna caught him by both his ears and brought his head down. "Oh? Is that all you'd be sayin' after makin' me blush an' stammer like I was still in swaddlin'?"

Nose to nose with her Nick couldn't hide his wide grin. " 'Oh' is what I said. Oh, ain't it grand 'twas the only reason. Oh as in, O Lord, thank you I didn't scare her out of me bed." He kissed her nose, her cheek, her temple and whispered in her ear, "I've stood here an' planned and plotted your garden with you. Now, wife, while I'm not claimin' to be a farmer, there's a wee garden of me own that I'm wantin'—"

"Mr. Dowling!"

"Aye, you've got that right." He lifted her up by the waist, holding her above him. Her shrieks melded with his laughter. "Are you ticklish, Mrs. Dowling?"

"Put me down an' see."

But he brought her up against him, his lips pressed to the valley between her breasts, and heard the hitch in her breathing. Slowly then, he lowered her body, sliding it tightly to his own. Need came with a forcible hunger as his mouth claimed hers and beneath the new moon Nick learned his new role as husband while he taught Brianna more of hers as wife.

Chapter Five

Brianna's present announced its own arrival before cock's crow in the morning.

The brown-eyed cow, left tied to a corral fence as Nick had arranged, created a racket that couldn't be ignored. Brianna, running outside in her nightgown and shawl, promptly washed her, flipped over a bucket and sat to milk her. From the sweet crooning noises his wife made, he knew she was pleased with his gift. He was certain of it when she was done, for she hugged and scattered kisses where she could, her happiness infecting him.

"Ah, 'tis cream for your porridge an' butter for your bread, boyo. That's what your wondrous gift'll mean." She smacked her lips and licked them. Her husband, ever a man to take advantage where he could, swept her up into his arms and carried her back to bed.

When Nick drove the wagon into the yard, having spent the day repairing fences, he found that his wife had tied a piece of mountain ash to the barn door, and was fretting that she couldn't find primroses to scatter in the cow's stall. He found it difficult to ignore her superstitious mutterings. Unwilling to spoil the earlier, happier mood in which they parted, he kept silent.

Over supper, she shared the small happenings of her

day, and he relaxed, listening to her, and seeing his land through her eyes. Everything was new to her, and she made it so for him.

"I was thinking we should go into town and place the order for your seeds and trees. By the time they arrive, we should have the ground cleared and ready for planting."

"Just like that?"

"Just like that," he returned, chuckling at her wide-eyed look.

Brianna finished mending the tear on one of his shirts. She pricked herself with the needle on the last stitch, wishing she still had her thimble. But Nick was beside her in a moment, kissing the tiny drop of blood that welled up from her fingertip.

Hunkered down beside her chair, he held her hand, and looked up at her. "There, it's all better now, isn't it?"

She regarded him most seriously, for his level look and husky voice suggested a deeper meaning to his question.

She thought of her fears and doubts when making the long journey to marry a stranger. She knew he regretted Patrick's choice of her for his wife, not that she doubted his desire for her. Of that, there was no question standing in her mind. He'd been kind and thoughtful and willing to share bits and pieces of his past with her. Of late, he had held his wicked tongue about her beliefs.

But she found herself wanting more. She wanted Nicholas Dowling to love her.

"Brianna?"

She looked into his eyes. "Aye, 'tis much better now."

Drawing her up from the bench, Nick picked up his shirt that fell from her lap. He glanced at it, then placed it on the table.

"Your tending to wifely duties is a credit to you, but I've a need of your delicate hands elsewhere." The tiny tendrils of hair that escaped their bonds and lay curled against her cheek made him want to smooth them back, very slowly, very gently and plant kisses over her flushed face.

While he gave in to his want, she answered him. " 'Tis a fine thing when a man *asks* his wife, Mr. Dowling."

Sucking her lobe into the heat of his mouth, Nick scraped his teeth against the sensitive flesh, then gently bit her. He found it quickly aroused her. It was trial and error on his part to find what his wife liked and didn't, for Brianna was still far too shy to tell him. An undertaking that he never tired of, and one that brought him as much pleasure as he gave in return.

"Did you hear me?" she asked, angling her head to give his lips better access. She knew the fine trembling that beset her pleased him. It was in his voice, in his teasing growl before his mock attack was complete.

" 'Tis a feast you are with your sweet scent and soft skin. An' it sorely tests me to ask when the desire rises higher than the smoke from the chimney, and for sure, hotter."

She caught his cheeks with her hands, holding him off from kissing her again. "Why do you do it then? Ask me, I mean?"

" 'Cause I grew to hate the sound of me ma being forced when she had more bairns that couldn't be fed, an' him awantin' his rights. I swore I'd never take an unwilling woman. And I never will."

" 'Tis the way of things in the old country, husband.
I'd no more—"

"Hush. I'll no' be takin'—"

"An' I'll no' be refusin' you."

They woke later to the sound of rain, and its gentle
beating on the roof set a rhythm for their lovemaking.
Spoon fashion, Nick held his wife tight. Just before
sleep overcame him, he realized they had forged another link in the bond that held them.

Brash and new, Kingston's long, curving main street
grew down the canyon high above Middle Percha
Creek. The town was edged with boardwalks and solid
with brick and stone buildings. Nick, driving the wagon
toward the livery, reminded Brianna that it was still a
mining town. There were, he recalled, at last count
over twenty-two saloons, and fourteen merchants.
There was no church, but with more and more men
bringing in their families, a church and schooling
wouldn't be far behind.

When she asked why he'd paid for a full day of feed,
he replied, "Because we've had no wedding supper, but
I intend to make up for the lack of one." He proceeded
with her to the Percha Bank to arrange the transfer of
funds to Phil Wares' account for the purchase of the
cow, very aware of the men who cast admiring looks at
his wife. He didn't even try to deny his pride that she
ignored the lot of them.

"You're pretty as a picture, Mrs. Dowling," he
leaned down to whisper as they left the bank. Her eyes,
meeting his, sparkled with pleasure beneath the short
brim of her straw hat. He touched the velvet forget-
me-nots spray pinned to the hat's crown. "It pleases me
that you wore these."

With the light, teasing mood that had prevailed from the moment they had awakened, Brianna, holding out the flare of her plain blue-grey poplin day dress, dipped him a curtsy. "As if I'd be forgettin' a man so fine as yourself, Mr. Dowling."

"See that you don't, wife. An' now, do you want to visit the mercantile and get your order for seeds in, or stroll about the town?"

Both appealed to her. He saw the indecision and her careful consideration as her gaze swept the street. "It doesn't matter which we do first, Brianna. We do the other next."

"The mercantile then. Your cousin Mary showed me the wonder of looking in a little book an' pickin' out things to buy. I've a desire to see more."

Settling her arm within the crook of his, Nick waited for a group of horsemen to pass, then crossed the street. "The catalogue is not just for looking now. Anything that you want can be ordered."

"Anything?"

"Anything but a corset. I've no liking for you to begin wearing one of those."

She laughed because it was expected, because he was so generous with her, and for the love that was filling her heart. If only she could get him to believe as she did, life would be a dream come true. It was harder and harder to hide from him the scattered offerings she left to keep the gentry pleased and happy. There was no doubt of the days that he angered them. He'd return near evening for supper and tell her of the strange fraying in a new rope, or the slipping of the hammer to strike his thumb. She cooed and fussed, then redoubled her offerings.

As they neared Munson's Mercantile, proudly dis-

played by a fancy-lettered sign that Nick read to her,
Brianna winced at the whine of the saws from one of
the mills. Seven, Nick yelled, seven sawmills the town
had to keep up with the building demands.

She nodded, her gaze straying to the meat shop. She
did not need him to read the sign. Turkey carcasses
were tied to a rope near the doorway, and a young boy,
no more than eight, called out the meats available.

Tugging on Nick's arm, she asked, "Do they really
eat bear meat?"

"If you're hungry, you'll eat anything."

"A great shaggy beast can't be fit for the table. I
hope you'll not be thinking to hunt one an' bring it
home."

"You're nagging like a wife."

He sounded so pleased, that she was pleased, too.
" 'Tis a skill learned at me mam's knee an' don't be
forgettin' that."

Nick blinked to adjust to the dimly lit interior of the
store after the bright sunlight outside. The aisles were
crowded, for Munson's was the largest and the oldest
shop in town. Nick had to wait his turn to give the clerk
his list, then wait with his wife for a turn at the catalogues. Usually, he would leave and spend his time at
one of the saloons with a drink and conversation. But
he was reluctant to leave his wife on her own.

He had a feeling that she couldn't take it all in, that
she didn't quite believe that she could buy the items
she looked at and touched, then walked away from. He
tried to note what really caught her fancy, mentally
making a list of what he would add to his order. But
she never said, and he was forced finally to ask what
she wanted.

"There's a great deal to choose," Brianna answered,

her eyes scanning the rafters where farm implements hung alongside harnesses, coffee pots, dippers and pans. The shelves were enough to make her eyes hurt, for they were filled to overflowing with more items than she could name. Tables piled high with bolts of cloth, blankets, and assorted baskets made movement in the aisles a little dangerous. One bump and the piles threatened to topple.

"Well, has anything caught your eye?"

"I'll be needin' a bit more sewin' thread an', if you're of a mind, a thimble."

"Done. But that can't be all?" Waving one arm around, he indicated all there was to buy. "Surely there's something else you want to bring home?"

"Orderin' the seeds an' the fruits trees for our garden is all I want."

Nick nodded, and having used up his small store of patience waiting for a chance at the catalogues, whispered to the man next in line.

Brianna wondered at the man's strange look as he let them have the place in front of him. The devilish smile that her husband wore hinted she wouldn't like what he said. Unwilling to put it to the test, she sat in the chair before a small table that Munson provided for his customers. The arrival of new booklets and catalogues meant careful study for one and all. None wished to be rushed.

Hovering close by his wife's shoulder, Nick thought it was a stroke of brilliance to tell the farmer that his wife was expecting their first child and grew faint in the crowded store. Staring at her profile, watching the play of expressions across her features as she marveled over the woodcuts, so that he didn't need to read everything to her, he found himself wishing that it was true. He wanted to see her grow big with his child.

It did not cross his mind that his thought could have somehow become hers when she stopped on the page that showed rockers. It wasn't the one with the fancily carved oak, richly appointed with a silk tapestry seat and boasting of its comfort that her finger traced. He knew she couldn't read the tiny print beneath the woodcut. But she lingered over the Nurse rocking chair with its maple-stained imitation walnut finish and caned back. The fancy rocker cost five dollars and eighty cents, the one Brianna was drawn to, one dollar and forty cents. Nick rapidly figured the two percent discount allowed, then added in shipping costs. He waited for her to ask for the chair.

She closed the catalogue and drew the one for the seeds forward.

Ah, so that's the way of it. She won't believe I can provide for her wants. And a little voice countered, but you don't believe in her superstitions. *Gibberish and lore. One has nothing to do with the other. Nonsense to think that providing real comfort was one and the same.* But the most uncomfortable thought surfaced in his mind. Her beliefs were a *real* comfort to her.

Brianna drew his attention to the trees. He dismissed his thoughts and wrote their order for two each of apple, cherry and peach trees. As she left the seat, he flipped open the page and added the rocking chair to his list of seeds.

With a forced smile, he led her from the store, directing her attention to the Lady Franklin Cafe where he promised they would have their supper. Brianna had never eaten a purchased meal, and he was determined that this would be another of the firsts she'd share with him.

The cafe was nearly empty as Nick escorted his wife inside. He headed for a window table where the half curtains would give her a view of the street. A booming voice, belonging to Rita Franklin herself, announced his arrival.

"So, you've finally floated down from your mountain to let us get a look at the gal that hitched you to her wagon."

He endured Rita's bear hug, and his wife's quirked brow until he managed to free himself, but not before the only woman who was eye-level with him planted a smacking kiss on his lips.

"Rita, my wife, Brianna."

Shaking her hand as if it was a pump to be primed, Rita made a quick study of the Black Irish's wife. She never called Nick that to his face, but she had a fond spot for him, since he'd worked for meals when she needed help to finish the roof before he'd bought his ranch land. Nick was one of the few men who didn't make fun when the cafe's sign went up in front.

"She's a one to lead you a merry dance, Nick. Pretty, too. But you'd best get some meat on her bones if you want her to last a time."

There was a spark in Brianna's eyes, and Nick offered his profound thanks to whatever made her hold her tongue. She smiled like the gracious lady he thought her, and nodded at Rita.

Accepting the big woman's squeeze on his shoulder, Nick asked her what was on the menu today.

"Chicken gumbo soup, lamb stew or roast turkey, chili, but you know I've always got chili, and elderberry cobbler."

They both chose soup and turkey, and Rita, merely
standing in the archway leading to the kitchen, called
out their order in her loud voice. Nick didn't have the
heart to ask her to leave them alone when she
promptly rejoined them.

There was local gossip to share, but he watched his
wife. When he saw that she really was interested, he
began to enjoy hearing what Rita had to say.

"There's a bluecoat up by Fort Bayard that figured a
way to use flashing sunlight on mirrors from station to
station as a warning about the raidin' Apache. Some of
the miners got hold of the code an' are usin' it, too.
Wouldn't be a bad thought if you was to learn yourself
an' the little missus how to use one, Nick. Your ranch is
a far piece from any neighbor."

The talk went on, about Toppy Johnson's slaughter-
house, and the persistent rumor that he rustled the
steers he sold. Rita told them that lots were selling for
five hundred dollars each in town, and they were getting a new monthly paper in addition to the two weekly
ones.

Brianna asked questions, Rita answered and the
meal passed in pleasant company. They parted in late
afternoon, having lingered over more cobbler and coffee, had the wagon loaded and turned for home.

"Was she ever your woman?" Brianna asked him
once town was behind them.

Nick didn't make the mistake of misunderstanding
her question. "No. Rita and I are just good friends."

She slipped her arm through the crook of his and
rested her head on his shoulder. "That's good. I truly
liked the woman and want to be friends with her, too."

He couldn't have explained why the unspoken jeal-
ousy pleased him no end. But it did. Glancing beneath

his hat brim at the contented look on his wife's face, Nick decided that his marriage may have started off with regrets on both sides, but it was on firm ground now. But he didn't think himself lucky. He *knew* it was his own hard work that formed the strengthening bond between them.

Who said a man couldn't make his own luck, if any name had to be attached to it?

With Brianna shifting a little and sighing beside him, he never felt her patting the dried four-leaf clover she had sewn into the lining of his vest pocket.

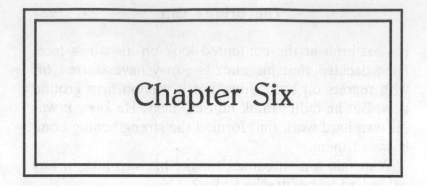

Chapter Six

At first indulgent, Nick caught Brianna's excitement over her garden. He helped when he could, hauling the buckets of rocks she gathered to the edge of the clearing where he built a rockwall overlooking the bluff above the stream. Even as he cautioned her they were late getting started, he labored to dig the plot, bringing straw and rotted manure to mix into the earth to make it fertile.

He discovered that a fair wind wouldn't blow his slender wife away. Patrick had written that she worked as a housemaid but Nick heard from her lips that she had been let out at six to scrub the gentry's fireplaces. It was the way of life in a land he'd escaped as soon as he could.

She toiled as hard as he did, not only working on the garden, but making his cabin into a home. Curtains appeared on the windows, wildflowers always filled a crock on the table and in the evening, she began turning his old quilt into a rag rug.

And they talked. That became the second best sharing time of all. He could freely share the encounters of his day with her, from sparing a few minutes to watch twin fawns gamboling in a field, to the helpless anger of burying a foal bloated with rattlesnake venom.

She named the cow Malvina, for she was a sweet friend, following Brianna around like a puppy, and her rich milk was, according to his wife, as sweet as any wine. She asked him incessant questions: What bird was that? What tree? What wild plants were edible?

He never knew he had been lonely, until he caught himself one day rushing because he'd been too long away from her, anxious to get home.

Every two weeks, they made a trip into Kingston, with a stop at Lady Franklin's cafe for dinner. Spring days slid into summer.

His temper mellowed. Brianna revealed she had one that more than matched his.

It happened the night he discovered her gone from their bed. He never knew what woke him, the seeds and fruit trees had been planted at last, they'd both fallen asleep from exhaustion. He couldn't dispell the feeling that she had gone out to the garden, and went looking for her.

He didn't need to light a lantern. The moon was as round and glistening as a perfect pearl suspended in a dark velvet sky. He cursed himself for not putting on his boots, but something powerful drew him to keep walking until he stood at the edge of the trees and saw his wife.

She was gowned in moonlight and shadows and nothing else. He stared, transfixed by the incredible beauty of her body, unaware that he gripped her discarded nightgown with both hands. He listened to the soft, crooning lilt of her voice, but could not make out the words. Her arms were spread wide. Free of the braids, her hair fell below her hips, a shawl of fire that covered her. There was a scent of something . . .

herbs, he thought, inhaling deeply to discover they had a burnt smell.

Anger rose within him. Every promise he'd made to ignore her heathen beliefs was forgotten in an instant.

"Brianna!" he called once, twice, a third time. She didn't answer, didn't acknowledge his presence at all. He started to climb the wooden pole fence when she turned around.

Proud and defiant, Brianna stared at her husband. " 'Tis no' a place for the likes of you now. If you dare to belittle what I do, what I believe, I'll never forgive you."

The chilling hardness in her voice, the fury he could feel from her glare made him drop back to the ground. He spied the open dower chest, the hated, secret thing that she guarded like hoarded gold, and his anger churned into fury that she would cast aside what they were building together for its heathen content.

"What devil's toys are hidden in that chest?" he shouted, needing to vent the strong emotions that gripped him. "You haven't the sense of a week-old babe to think this heathen nonsense will bring you riches, or anything but grief and anger."

"Look at me. Do you see the mark of the devil on me? 'Tis no devil's work I do."

He looked and fought the hot tide of desire that flooded his loins with heat. He wanted her. Now. As she was, grand and glorious with temper crackling around her.

"I can see the wantin' in your eyes. But 'tis grief, my grief, that you cannot believe as I do. You force me to hide. You make me keep secrets. An' 'tis anger of your own making that will see you end a bitter man, Nicholas Dowling. Go now, for you risk all we share, all the

love I hold within me heart for you. Go an' leave me be
this night."

"Love?" It was all he heard.

"Aye. 'Tis a woman's word, soft an' sweet. A
woman's deep abiding need to have and to give. Go
now, my husband, an' leave me to my woman's things."

He left her. The only reason was that he didn't trust
himself not to do or say something that would hurt
them both, there'd be no recovery from it. Love? She
had spoken of love. The word slipped easily from his
thoughts to his lips. And he knew that anger had no
place within the thought of love, not when it took root
as easily as the seedlings they had planted.

She returned near dawn. He was still awake, and listened to the prime of the pump, the sounds of her
washing, his own heartbeat. Without shyness, without
pretense, Brianna came to him in their bed, bringing
with her a wild passion that was made from a man's
dreams. But she flesh, heated and wanton, and the sun
was high when he left her.

He remembered thinking that she should have her
woman's secrets, and in the aftermath of a desire not
quite sated, he vowed he would hold his tongue. Some
matters, he had discovered, were best left unspoken.
He put the incident from his mind. So easy to do when
the first bud of love for Brianna began unfurling.

There was a letter from Patrick to Nick the next time
they went into town. By mutual decision they decided
to wait until they were home before reading it.
Couched in vague terms, and colorful Irish phrases,
Patrick wrote asking how they were getting on. Com-
posing an answering letter sent them into gales of
laughter as they sat on the completed rag rug before
the clean-swept fireplace. The nights were too warm to

build a fire, but then, they had learned to build one of their own.

Rita told them of the increasing raids by the Apache throughout the territory. She had taken them up on their invitation to dinner. Brianna fussed and fretted, until Nick begged her not to be so hard on herself. Nick ordered two mirrors and, with Rita's help, found a miner to teach them the codes.

A stifling summer's heat blanketed the land and with it came drought. Nick set four stout barrels in the corners of her garden, filling them with buckets drawn from the stream. He refused to step inside the fence, and she never asked him to.

He had to leave her for a few days. There was no choice. His cattle had to be moved to water. She helped him pack his saddlebags, listening and nodding to his warnings and his many instructions of what she was to do if there was trouble.

Kissing him, whispering that he was to be careful, she sent him on his way.

Two days past, then three. By the fourth morning, Brianna knew she would have to replenish the water in the barrels. Her plants flourished, despite the drought, but they were thirsty beggars that required constant care. She couldn't bear the thought of losing her fruit trees, or the herbs. Vegetables they could buy, even if her thrifty ways rejected the idea of spending money on what she could save with hard work. She had to protect the special place in the center of the garden. She didn't dare let lack of water kill her piece of Ireland.

She made her way to the path her husband had cut into the bluff, carrying two buckets and his loaded shotgun. Nick had said she didn't need to aim with great accuracy, just point and shoot.

Dismay filled her. The stream bed was dried up in places.

Flies were thick around the dead fish and she was forced to walk until she saw a pool deep enough with water to fill her buckets.

Her skirt hem dragged in the dust and twilight had fallen before she was done with her watering and made her way back to the cabin. There were two wells, one for the house, and one for the stock near the barn. The animal's care had to come first, before her plants, so she couldn't use their water.

" 'Tis a quandary for sure," she pondered, pumping water into the trough for the horses and Malvina. Scratching the small white spot between the cow's ears, she stared into her large brown eyes. "If I could divine your thoughts . . . divine . . . oh, 'tis a grand, beautiful lass you are!"

A divining rod! That's what she needed. She would dowse for water near the garden. Wouldn't that please Nicholas to no end that he wouldn't be hauling water for her again?

"A tree," she muttered, searching the deepening shadows. It was too late tonight to begin, but come morning she'd set off on her search for the perfect forked branch.

Her prayers were fervent, her offerings left openly on the table; a bit of sugar, a bit of honey, a little water of life and a sweet taste of cream, all for the gentry's favor.

In the morning, Brianna had worked up a sweat dressing in the thick, sultry air. She set off without eating, in a fine, tearing hurry to find what she needed. Nicholas's axe was heavy, and she found it awkward to carry, but determination lent her strength. There were saplings aplenty to choose from, but Brianna went from tree to tree, waiting for a whisper to tell her she'd found the right one. Tales came as the hours passed, of men alone being the only ones who could dowse for water. Her need made her dismiss them. She did pay heed when she recalled that in a nearby village, the dowser used a knife with his forked stick, claiming it made it easier for the water to be found.

She was all for that. The very air seemed to suck the moisture from her body, breathing became difficult, and the day remained overcast with clouds that promised everything, and delivered nothing but heat.

Temptation loomed to give it up, but she was driven now to complete her task. Resting beneath the spread of a walnut tree, she closed her eyes, tilted her head back and prayed.

There above you.

Almost fearing that she wanted it so badly her mind was playing tricks, Brianna opened her eyes. A forked branch, the width of Nick's fingers, the length of his arms, hung above her.

Nick found water for his thirsty cattle in a hidden canyon high in the San Mateos. The grass was lush, nearly knee-high, and not one tip showed signs of burning. Two cottonwood trees, as ancient as the canyon walls that protected this place, spread their limbs in thick-leaved abundance to give the animals needed shade.

He worried over the four days that he had been gone, but he couldn't ride away without first building a secure brush and rope fence to keep his cattle safe. There was no choice about his need to hire another man to help him. Resentment surfaced constantly for each hour away from his wife.

He missed her. No longer did he hold the belief that she had bewitched or hexed him. He had turned the idea of love around and around in his thoughts.

What did he know about love? A woman's word, she had called it. A woman's need to give and to receive. But what, he wanted to know, was love?

Was it the sound of her voice when she praised him? Or the shimmering glow in her eyes when they woke to a new day with soft murmurs and gentle touches? Was love what brought him the impatient anticipation of seeing her surprise when the rocking chair arrived? And the measuring eye he cast around both cabin and land to please her more?

Was love what he felt, that he wished he could soar with the span of an eagle's wings to rush back to her side? Was it the intense need he had to hold her within his arms, dwelling in a cocoon of their own making where spirit and soul were one?

He worked by firelight, and continued his questions, nearly killing himself and his horse to get back to her.

Chapter Seven

Silence answered the wild, whooping shouts he made of her name. Nick came off his horse at a run, bursting into the cabin when she didn't open the door. The air was stale, as if no one had been inside for days.

"Brianna?" he called, forcing himself to walk inside. The stove was stone cold. The bed neatly made. And his shotgun was missing. "Brianna!" His shouts, repeated as he ran to the barn, brought him no answering call.

Fear, the like of which he'd never known, coiled tight in his belly. He fought to keep it from his mind, from the places where terror would take hold and envision—no! He would not panic.

Step by step, he examined the yard, the barn, the cabin. There were no signs of a struggle, other horses, or, Lord forbid, blood.

The half-full water trough told him she had watered the horses not too many hours past. The wagon was as he left it, on the side of the barn. There was no point in checking the chicken coop they had built together, for they were to pick up chicks next week to start their own flock, but he dipped his head low and looked inside anyway. Habit made him carefully latch the gate behind him as he retraced his steps into the cabin.

It was then that Nick realized the wedding quilt she had brought with her was missing. His gaze made a quick scan of the wall pegs, but her clothing was there, hung neatly beside his own.

Breath he had not realized he had held, whooshed out with relief that she had not left him. But where was she?

The garden? Had she somehow hurt herself and been unable to get back to the cabin? Fear lodged itself in his gut, dried his throat, and sent a fine trembling through him.

He ran then, her name a silent scream on his lips, the vision of her lying hurt, broken and bleeding fixed in his mind.

So firmly entrenched was the thought that she was hurt, that Nick wouldn't believe his own eyes when he saw her in the middle of the garden. He mouthed her name, scrubbing his knuckles across his eyes, one hand pressing against his chest as if to contain the furious beating of his heart.

He couldn't seem to draw one breath that wasn't tainted with the fear still streaming through his body. She appeared lost in a world of her own as the clouds darkened and heat lightning ripped the sky.

Slowly then, Nick took in her bedraggled state. There was a tear in the sleeve of her gown. Another jagged one in the skirt. Mud stained the cloth. He fought to leash his need to shout in fury at her. His eyes moved from her still figure to beyond the garden fence. There lay their wedding quilt, beside a stone ring where coals still glowed beneath a coffee pot. His shotgun rested upright against the fence post. His scanning gaze touched upon the straight stalks of corn, their leaves the bright green of well-tended plants. Everywhere he looked, her garden had flourished.

There was no danger that he could see. No reason for the lingering fear, the growing fury. None at all, he warned himself as he braced a hand and leaped over the fence.

"Brianna!"

She spun around, dropping the bucket she held, her mudstained face lit with joy. "Nicholas! Oh, Nicholas, you're home at last!" Her few running steps faltered, and she stopped, arrested by the look of him bearing down on her.

"What's happened? Are you hurt?" she cried out, seeing with bewilderment that he too stopped short.

"What's happened? Are you hurt?" he mimicked in her thick brogue. "I've nearly killed myself and my poor horse trying to get home to you. Are you there waiting where you should be? No! You're here in this damn—"

"Let me tell you—"

"I don't want to hear it! I thought my heart would stop with fear that something had happened to you."

Brianna raised her arm in a pleading gesture, only to let it fall to her side. "What is it you're wantin', Mr. Dowling?"

It wasn't until now that she addressed him so, that Nick recalled the joyous moment she had turned and used his first name. But there was no joy in her gaze. Like a fire that had been smothered, the light went out from her eyes.

He had killed it with his shouting, with his fury bubbling hot in his blood. And he couldn't help it. Couldn't stop it from coming from his lips.

"I thought you dead. I thought you taken by the savages. I pictured you hurt, alone and bleeding, with none to help you, none to call. And here I find you, looking like a lass playing with mud pies."

"I've no been playin' while you were gone. The stream dried. I had to find water. I've been digging a well. An' just this morn had the first of it come bubbling up."

"An' I suppose it was your heathen gibberish that led you to a spot to dig?" Fists planted on his hips, Nick bit back the curses that formed. She had dug a well? His slender slip of a wife? Guilt flooded him, and he looked away from her.

"I used no gibberish, Mr. Dowling," she explained in a deadened voice. There were aches in every part of her body from the laborious job she had set for herself and managed to complete. But none hurt as much as his turning away.

"I found a dowsing fork—"

"A dowsing fork?"

"Don't be tellin' me you've not heard of such? 'Tis a gift that many have across the lands. I cannot say that my being a woman didn't take me longer to find water, but I had to do it."

Unable to keep still, afraid that he would hurt her if he touched her, Nick paced, unaware of her stricken look when he crushed the tender shoots beneath his boots. "The fact is you're a woman. This is not something for you to do. Laborin' like a gold miner, digging a well! You should have waited for me."

"Waited? Aye, you'd have liked that. You worryin' 'bout losing your cattle wouldn't have cared that my precious treasure died for lack of water."

"So it's mine and yours now?" He stopped and faced

her. At his forward step, she moved to the side, as if blocking his way. It infuriated him all over again.

"I'll gather my things an' come up to the cabin an' fix you supper."

"Oh, will you now? An' would you be thinkin' to bed me like a wanton from a man's dreams to keep me from seein' what you're hidin' behind your skirts?"

She backed up two steps to the ones he took to close the distance between them. But she refused to cower. "If my ways are no' pleasin' to you, Mr. Dowling, I'll no longer bed you at all."

"Threaten me? You'd dare?" He towered over her, using his size, his height, his maleness to intimidate her. "Step aside, *wife.*"

The word was a curse, a reminder of her place. Brianna thought of her vow to obey him, to love and to cherish this man who cast away the past months as if they had never been.

"What's here is mine. I'll no' let you touch it."

"I'll tell you again. Step aside for me. I would see what made you run from our home, and lose sleep to find water. Save your breath to deny it. I can see the shadows beneath your eyes and the pale look of you. I've no wish to hurt you, but you will do as I say."

"If you've no wish to hurt me, then leave."

"No. Once before I let you order me from this place. I'll destroy whatever it is that makes you defy me."

"Destroy? No!" She flung herself at him, trying to force strength into a body that had been depleted of it, needing to stop him. "Why should it matter that I found more water? Or how? Surely your other wells were found by the same?"

She couldn't budge him. He made no move to touch her, bearing with her fingers digging hard into his muscled arms in her weakening effort to dislodge him. Some instinct made her look up at his face. The words weren't needed, she knew he'd never admit to it, but she just sensed that she was right. He had used a dowser to find water.

"Why is it only a heathen thing for me?" she screamed.

The leash on his temper snapped and he swept her aside, where she stumbled and fell. Nick would have reached out for her, ignoring the fear on her face, but his gaze fell upon the center spot of the garden.

Lightning forked above them. But he didn't look up at the black roil of clouds as thunder quickly followed, rolling across the land to herald the coming storm. Nick couldn't take his eyes from the grass that grew in lush, emerald splendor.

" 'Tis a dower gift from me mother! Don't be touchin' it!"

"Sod? You've near killed yourself over a piece of sod?" He turned on her, feeling the eruption of rage that he couldn't contain. "This is what you've whispered to? What you hid in that damn chest, protectin' it like it was gold? Damn Irish sod!"

Brianna flung back her head. There were no prayers on her lips. No pleading left in her eyes. She faced a man who was suddenly a stranger. His hands that covered her with tender, loving touches were curled into fists. His eyes were as black as the sky, filled with the same fury as the storm about to unleash its wrath on them.

" 'Tis precious as gold to me, Nicholas. Don't destroy what me mother gave me with a promise of riches."

The first fat raindrops fell. He watched her struggle

to her feet. He couldn't begin to measure what possessed him. He only knew he had come home to her, his lovely Irish bride, ready to give her a rich gift. His heart. For he had finally discovered what love was. All the feelings he shared with Brianna. And there she stood, ready to tear him apart over a few worthless inches of sod!

He moved without thought, without warning to rip the sod from its place.

The storm caught her cry and whipped it into a mourning wail. But he heard it. Heard it and ignored it as he used his strength to hurl the small emerald carpet of grass out over the bluff.

Chapter Eight

"No! By all the saints, no!" She hurled past him, sliding between the poles of the fence.

Nick was blinded by the downpour and lost sight of her for a few minutes.

"Brianna! Don't move." Slender as a sapling, her body was revealed to him, poised on the edge of the bluff. In the blink of his eye she disappeared.

He tore after her, shoving aside rocks to make a space for himself, ignoring the ripped, bleeding flesh of his hands. Fear had gripped him before, but that was imagined. This was real. And ten times more powerful. His chest felt as if iron bands prevented him from breathing. He was shaking from the inside out. His legs threatened to give way.

He couldn't see her! The earth beneath his boots suddenly gave way to the fury of the storm. A stream of mud carried him and half the rockwall down to the once-dried stream bed.

Slipping and sliding, he struggled to regain his footing. The rain came down with a pounding force that was too much for the parched earth to absorb. Holes filled and overran into puddles, building a current that was treacherous.

He shouted her name and the wind tore the sound from his lips, shredding it into its own howl.

His head snapped from side to side, trying to find her. He couldn't believe the rain had swallowed her up in its black blanket and kept her hidden from him.

Nick prayed. He wanted his wife. Wanted her within his arms, safe and warm. And loved.

"Aye," he bellowed, "I love her! Do you hear me, Brianna? I love you." It was a challenge flung to the very heavens, just daring them to stop him from having her safe.

He slogged through water nearly at the top of his boots. His clothes were sodden weights, plastered against his skin by the continuing beat of the rain. Nick tried to get his bearings, to remember where it was she went over the edge. How far could she have tumbled? Had the water carried her off without him seeing? *She had to have been unconscious for that to happen.*

He fought the guilt that swamped him with the thought that she could have hit her head when she fell.

"Just let me find her," he begged. But his search upstream proved empty. He turned and began again.

He lost sense of time, of place, even of himself. He was alone, the only inhabitant of a dark, gray world.

You know what you need to say.

No!

She's your wife. You claim to love her.

"I do! By the Lord in heaven, by all the saints, I do love her!"

Then say the words. Make the promise.

He'd kill for the precious sight of her. But emptiness surrounded him.

'Tis no one's death that's needed, boyo. A promise. Just a promise.

"Brianna!" He felt the rawness of his throat, but the pain was small to the one tearing him apart. Where was she?

Would you be running into the arms of the one who trampled a precious treasure?

"Answer me. I swear on my life that I'll find your precious sod. I'll get Patrick to send a gilded chest full of emerald green to please you. Only answer me, love! Just answer me."

Water streamed down his face, but Nick felt the hot sting in his eyes. There was a sound above the rushing water. A faint thread that rose over the wind. He felt as if his strength was beaten into the mud, but he heard it once more. Heard a sound of a cry. Hope filled him.

He fought his way downstream. The wind filled his shirt so that it billowed like a full sail around him.

There! Against the gray void, he saw Brianna huddled against a blacker hole, struggling with her bundled skirt.

"Love! Stay there. Wait for me."

He could barely make out the tilt of her head, and hoped that she heard him.

When he first touched her, then grabbed her tight, his head buried against the curve of her shoulder, prayers and promises fell from his lips.

"Nicholas! Nicholas, look what I've found." Brianna had to scream the words over and over before he lifted his head. She had to close her eyes, for the rain had not ceased.

"Safe. You're in my arms. Safe." He mouthed the words against her lips, tasting rain, tasting love as her mouth so warmly welcomed the touch of his.

And he had a taste of forgiveness that seeped into his soul. He had not lost her, not to the storm, and not to his own thick-headed stupidity. What did her beliefs matter? He knew what he held: love.

But he needed the words, needed to hear them, needed to confirm what he sensed, what her kiss told him. He didn't trust his instinct, or the world around them, not when it could rip her from his life.

As suddenly as the storm had begun, the rain suddenly lessened. He smoothed back her hair from her face, cradling her cheeks. "I love you. Love you, loveyouloveyou—" The words ran together with those begging her forgiveness.

"Ah, Nicholas, heart of my heart, how can I not forgive? I love you."

He angled his head for a kiss, sliding his hands over the curve of her shoulders, rubbing her back, and trying to bring her fully against him. Her bundled skirt that she yet held stood between them.

"Let it go, love. I've a need to celebrate the gift of your love, of life itself."

"You're Black Irish for sure, Nicholas. 'Tis no less than in my own mind to do the same, but first see what your temper had brought us."

He let her lean back against his arms, but he was afraid to look.

" 'Tis no' a thing to be fearin', man. Go on with you. Look what fills me skirt." She held his steady gaze, willing the joy of her heart to tell him the anger was done. "Look, Nicholas. See the wondrous gift your temper has given us."

There in her skirt was the remains of the sod. Broken bits of grass clumped in mud. But she coaxed him to look again, closer this time. And he saw the glimmer of flakes. With an unsteady hand he reached into the pocket of mud and lifted up a stone.

"Rub it, Nicholas. See the riches I was promised by me mother if I planted the sod."

He knew what it was before he rubbed it clean on his shirt. The nugget was nearly the size of an egg. For a moment it tempted him, but his gaze locked with that of his wife and he knew all the gold in the world couldn't equal the sparkle of love in her eyes.

"Come home with me," he whispered, sweeping her up, bundle and all, into his arms. "I would measure the riches found this day. Mine to yours. And mine, love, will tip the scales with their measure as richer by far."

In the years that passed there were whispers about the Shamrock ranch and the Irish bride who made it a home.

Tales spread and grew of golden riches hidden within its boundaries.

Rumors and murmurs that none of the Shamrock's brood confirmed or denied. But they often smiled. Only Brianna and her Nicholas would laugh to hear the most persistent story.

For 'twas said of a midsummer night when the moon waxed full the shadows of two lovers could be seen in their private garden. If you were peeking, they'd be gone in the blink of an eye. An' if you waited till the bright morning sun showed the place where they stood, a silver thimble filled with the Irish water of life would remain. The bride's gift.

THE LADY IN GREEN

Bonnie Pega

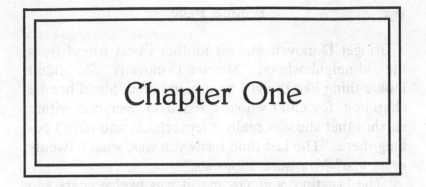

Chapter One

Richmond, Virginia, 1995

The lady wore green—a veritable smorgasbord of green. Lime green, grass green, emerald green, forest green. She looked like a girl scout run amok.

Michael Connor shoved a hand through his sleep-disheveled hair and cast a quick glance over his shoulder to the electronic numbers on the VCR clock. Six a.m. "May I help you?" He thought he sounded remarkably civil for someone awakened from a dead sleep by a normal-sized relative of the Jolly Green Giant.

"Michael? Dear ol' Michael! Don't you remember me?"

He didn't. He peered at her closely. Of course, her hair was covered by a green knit stocking cap, her face was partly covered by the lime-green scarf swaddling her neck, and whatever figure she had was covered by a large, bulky dark-green sweater. Even her legs were covered by green tights. But what he could see, he didn't recognize. "I don't . . ."

"It's me. Your cousin. Shannon."

"Shannon?" Did he have a cousin Shannon?

"We're not actually cousins. More adopted cousins, really. I'm Bridget and John Donovan's daughter."

Bridget Donovan was his mother's best friend from
the old neighborhood. "Skeeter Donovan?" She didn't
look a thing like the girl he remembered. She'd been a
charming, fey child who'd insisted to everyone within
earshot that she was really a leprechaun and didn't be-
long there. "The last time I saw you was, what? Twenty
years ago? You were about six."

"The last time you saw me, it was twelve years ago
and I was fourteen, but who's counting? Are you going
to invite me in? It's blasted cold out here and snow's
sifting down the back of my neck."

"Oh, yeah. Sorry." He stepped aside and she entered
the living room, tugging several pieces of luggage—as
well as a cat carrier—with her.

"Is that a cat?"

"Yes. He won't be a bit of trouble. What a lovely
warm room this is. Which bedroom is mine? I'll just
put these things away."

"Wait a minute. What do you mean, which bedroom
is yours?"

"If you don't have an extra, I can sleep on the sofa. I
can sleep most anywhere. I'm not picky."

"You think you're staying here?"

The frenetic green blur who'd been moving about
the living room, examining first one object, then another, stopped. "Didn't your mother call you?"

Michael had a sinking feeling in his stomach. "I
haven't spoken to my mother since she and Dad left on
a Caribbean cruise four weeks ago."

"Oh, dear. That does present a problem. I'm supposed to stay here for a few weeks and help out until
you have a chance to find another housekeeper. Your
mother thought it was a wonderful idea."

She would. Well, he didn't. He needed peace. He

needed quiet. He needed . . . he watched as Shannon pulled off her knit cap and a waterfall of strawberry blonde fell to her waist . . . he needed to think about this some more.

Shannon tossed the hat, scarf, and the oversized sweater over the back of a chair and Michael couldn't help but notice that the fey child had grown into an astoundingly attractive woman. She still had dainty, almost elfin, features, but her eyes were the most incredible shade of green. She was still daintily built, topping out at a hair over five feet, but came packaged with soft round curves in all the right places.

All the right places, he thought again, as he followed the sweeping curve of her green-clad calf up to a shapely knee, then to an even more shapely thigh. Lots of thigh. It looked for all the world like she'd put on only half a skirt.

"I hope it's not going to be a problem."

"What?" Those legs could present a problem to any red-blooded male—with his concentration, anyway.

"Staying here."

Staying here? That would be a problem, all right. A big problem. He and his daughter Jenny had just begun to get their lives back on track. They needed the reassuring boundaries of routine and order after the turmoil of the past year. It was something to cling to.

Especially for Jenny. Jenny was still so fragile. Losing her mother had shattered her safe little world. And, Michael knew, moving to a new city had only compounded her insecurity. He felt guilty about that, but he'd needed to start over, too. The old house, the old neighborhood, had been full of too many bittersweet memories.

He did need a new housekeeper, but really wanted a

nice motherly older woman. He didn't need some bouncy and thoroughly distracting young woman disrupting his house. "Shannon, I think that—"

"I had planned on being able to stay here, you know. I don't start my new job for a month yet and money's liable to be a bit scarce. But if it's going to be a problem, then don't worry about me. I'll manage."

She'd delivered that speech with just the right amount of pathos. Michael doubted whether Katharine Hepburn could have done any better. He sighed. "You're welcome to stay here." He could hardly turn her out into the street. And, after all, it would only be for a few weeks.

He showed Shannon to the guest room and went into the kitchen to put on the coffee. He stared at the coffee-maker, trying to will the coffee to drip through faster than usual. Not a morning person on the best of days, he had a feeling he was going to need twice his normal boost of caffeine today.

His half-awake mind tried to scrape together all the bits and pieces of information he'd heard about Skeeter Donovan over the years. He remembered hearing that she'd hung onto that leprechaun story until she was nine or ten. She'd insisted that was why she didn't look a thing like her brown-haired, brown-eyed parents.

She'd been athletic in high school. His mother had always mentioned awards won for various things: swim team, girls' softball, tennis. He wondered briefly if she were still interested in sports. Her legs had the same trim muscular curves of an athlete.

Her senior year, she'd been an exchange student to Ireland and had gone on to stay there long enough to graduate from the University of Dublin. She was supposed to be working with some Irish clothing design house that had decided to open up an American branch. He didn't have any idea what kind of clothes Shannon designed, though. Probably green ones.

Michael had heard all sorts of things about Shannon. She was one of his mother's favorite subjects—especially this last year after Anne's death.

He'd heard how bright she was, how attractive she was, how sweet she was, how much she loved children. He had no doubt that his mother had set this whole thing up. He also had no doubt that her "forgetting" to tell him about Shannon's visit was no accident. But his mother was going to be sorely disappointed. His heart was still too full of pain, bitterness and guilt. He didn't think he'd ever have room for anything—or anyone—else. Except Jenny.

He did remember seeing Shannon at fourteen. He'd been home from college for the weekend and Shannon had been staying with his parents for a few days while her parents were out of town. She'd been awkward and ungainly—all legs and eyes. Her figure hadn't yet begun to bud out, but she'd been bright and well-read and they'd had several long conversations before he'd gone back to college Sunday night. He could remember thinking, condescendingly, that she'd been relatively intelligent—for a child.

"Coffee ready?" His new house-guest poked her head into the room.

"Um, not quite yet. It'll be a couple of minutes. Is your room all right?"

"Oh, it's beautiful. I love the wallpaper. I've always liked green."

Michael couldn't prevent a little smile from tugging

at his lips. "Is that a holdover from your leprechaun days?"

"Actually, leprechauns prefer red, red jackets, red trousers." Shannon gave him a sidelong glance.

"Red? How come pictures always show them in green?"

"I guess people think it suits them better than red. After all, they've tied them in with St. Patrick's Day and green's appropriate for that. But leprechauns really wear red. I just love red."

"I thought you liked green."

"Oh, I do. But red's my favorite color."

"So why are you all decked out in green this morning?" He nodded at her attire.

"This is in honor of St. Patrick's Day." Her lips curved merrily. "Any leprechaun worth his shamrock dresses out in honor of the good Saint's day."

"Good morning, Daddy," a small voice piped up from behind Shannon.

"Good morning, pumpkin," Michael greeted his six-year-old daughter.

"Daddy, you're supposed to introduce me."

"You're right. I'm sorry. Jenny, this is Shannon Donovan. She's a friend of Grandma's. Shannon, my daughter, Jennifer."

As if she'd had to be told this was Michael's daughter. Jenny had his shiny dark curls and a daintier version of his determined jaw. The only thing that didn't match were their eyes. His were heart-stopping blue. Hers were chocolate-bar brown. Like her mother's?

"Pleasedtameetcha." Jenny solemnly stuck out her hand.

Equally as solemn, Shannon grasped Jenny's hand

and shook it. "I'm very pleased to meet you, Jenny. Your grandma has told me all about you."

"About my being smart, I suppose. Why are you and Daddy talking about leprechauns?"

Michael said, "Well, Jenny, a leprechaun is kind of like an elf and . . ."

The little girl sighed patiently. "I know what a leprechaun is, Daddy. I just wanted to know why you were talking about them. Is it because it's St. Patrick's Day?"

"Shannon and I were just remembering when she was a little girl about your age. She thought she was a leprechaun."

"That's silly," Jenny said with a superior air. "There's no such thing as leprechauns and fairies and elves. Everyone knows that."

"And do you know that for a fact?" Shannon asked, her eyes wide.

"Sure I do. Just like there's no Santa Claus or Easter Bunny."

Shannon shot Michael a reproachful glance. Every child ought to believe in the whimsical and remarkable. But then, maybe Jenny's daddy no longer believed himself. Maybe losing his wife had taken all of the whimsy out of him. It was a real shame. Shannon believed that the whimsy in one's soul was what made life worth living.

"You don't believe in any of that stuff, do you?" Jenny asked.

"Every bit of it," Shannon said with another smile at the earnest little girl. "But especially in leprechauns. Every Irish Donovan has believed in the little people."

"Shannon." Michael's low voice held a warning. "Stop teasing Jenny."

"Who's teasing?" Shannon reached out toward Mi-

chael's ear and pulled her hand back, with a coin between her fingers. She handed the coin to Jenny. "It's
an Irish pence. You may keep it."

Jenny's eyes widened. "How'd you do that?"

"Leprechaun's magic."

"That's silly," Jenny said again, but Shannon could
see the slightest bit of doubt in her eyes.

"Jenny, what do you want for breakfast?" Michael
asked.

It was clear to Shannon that he had interrupted because he didn't like the direction of this conversation.

"Can I have pancakes?"

"We don't have time to fix those, sweetheart. You
have to get ready for school."

"But there's no school today. It's all snowy."

Michael fell silent, as if just now remembering that it
had been snowing when he opened the door to find a
green-clad Shannon on his doorstep. He reached over
and turned on the radio, glancing out the kitchen window as he did so. "There does seem to be a few
inches." He turned a questioning gaze to Shannon.
"How did you get here?"

"A taxi, but he had some trouble. He barely made it
up that hill around the corner."

Michael turned his attention to the radio, listening
for school cancellations, and Shannon allowed her gaze
to wander freely over him, noting the changes that time
and life had made in him. He was, perhaps, average
height—maybe five-eleven, six feet—but that was still
tall compared to her diminutive stature. With his tousled dark hair, blue eyes, and olive-toned skin, he had
to be Black Irish, she thought, though he'd probably
deny it. However, she knew. The Irish in him called to
her.

But he had such sad eyes. And though he wasn't more than thirty-two or thirty-three, he had lines heavily etched into his forehead. Lines of sorrow. Lines of pain. He was so different from the way he'd been that fateful weekend—the weekend she'd fallen in love with him. Not that he'd ever noticed. She'd been a gawky and awkward child-woman who was just starting to blossom. He had been twenty—full of energy, excitement, intensity, tackling life with ferocious enthusiasm.

Just being around him had awakened her to the passion for life that bubbled inside her, too. The promise and the possibilities. Now, with any luck, she could give some of that positive energy back. She owed him that. But the crush was gone. She'd outgrown it years ago.

Her gaze lingered on his face a moment longer, then fanned down over his shoulders. His shoulders were broad, but covered by a shabby terry robe over pajamas. For a moment her gaze lingered wistfully on those pajamas. Maybe he wore them in deference to his daughter.

"School's closed," he said suddenly and turned to Jenny. "Looks like I don't have to teach today and you don't have to take that spelling test."

He glanced over at Shannon and, from the way he suddenly murmured something about getting dressed, she knew he'd been aware of her watching him. She sighed. This wasn't going to be easy.

By the time Michael had showered and dressed in jeans and a sweater, Shannon had already heated a frying pan and was stirring batter for pancakes.

She looked up when he entered the room. "These'll be ready in just a couple of minutes. Why don't you sit down?"

Michael sat at the kitchen table and watched as she oiled the pan and added spoonfuls of batter. She moved with a graceful economy of movement, her body a curious blend of lithe, supple muscles and voluptuous curves.

He didn't care what she said about leprechauns preferring red, she still looked like one—a very sexy one—in her green sweater, delightfully short green skirt and green hose. He paused to study those green legs again. She had long legs for such a petite woman. Great legs, even. His gaze swept the curve of her calf down to her ankle and stopped at her shoes. Her shoes looked like—

"Do you like them?"

"Huh? What?"

"My shoes. I noticed you looking at them." Shannon held out her left foot. Her ankle-high soft suede boot was topped with a shiny gold buckle. The real kicker was the pointed toe that curled up just slightly on the end. "I call them Elfin Fantasy."

"You call them . . ." his voice trailed off. She named her shoes? He had to admit the name was appropriate. They looked for all the world like a leprechaun's boots.

"I designed these. That's what I do. I design shoes."

"I see." He digested this bit of information.

"Appropriate occupation, don't you think?"

"Appropriate for what?"

She looked at him with wide-eyed innocence. "Did you know that the word 'leprechaun' comes from the Irish *leith bhrogan?* That means one-shoemaker. That's how a leprechaun gets his pot of gold, you know. He earns it by making shoes."

"And you make shoes," Michael said slowly.

"And I make shoes. Whoops! Pancake's ready. Do you want Jenny to have the first one?"

"Sure." Michael called Jenny, who slipped into her chair almost immediately.

Shannon set a plate in front of Jenny with a flourish.

"What's this? It looks like a green clover."

"It's a shamrock. In honor of St. Patrick's Day. And here's some green maple syrup to go with it."

A green pancake. Michael watched his daughter take a cautious mouthful. "How is it?"

"It's terrific. It doesn't taste like an ordinary pancake."

"It's the special leprechaun spices." Shannon winked at Jenny and the little girl took a bigger bite. "How many would you like, Michael?"

"Ah, none for me, thanks. I'm not a big breakfast eater."

Jenny looked at her father. "But you usually eat five or six pancakes, Daddy."

"I, ah, I'm not very hungry this morning."

"Oh, come on. Have a bite. It'll do you good." Shannon set a plate in front of him.

Michael smiled weakly and took a tiny bite. His eyes widened. It was good. It was very good. But Jenny was right. It wasn't an ordinary pancake—besides the fact that it was green and shaped like a shamrock. "It's very good."

"Don't sound so surprised, Michael. I've learned a thing or two about cooking since I made you that sandwich."

Michael held his fork suspended in mid-air. "I'd forgotten that."

"I don't see how you could possibly forget. I thought we'd never get you away from the water fountain."

"What happened, Daddy?"

Michael and Shannon exchanged glances and Michael suddenly grinned. "She was about your age, pumpkin, and I was, oh, six or seven years older, but she kept following me around like a puppy. I kept shooing her away but she kept coming back."

"Why'd you shoo her away?"

"Well, you know how you like to play with Kimmie but you don't like it when her baby brother gets in your things? That was the way I felt."

"She followed you 'cause she liked you, huh?"

Michael looked back at Shannon who was watching him with undisguised interest. "I guess she did. Anyway, I think she thought I'd pay more attention to her if she brought me a present. So she fixed me a sandwich—peanut butter, grapes, and bologna on rye bread."

Jenny made a face, then said, "It doesn't sound too good, but it did have a bread, a fruit, and protein. That's three of the four food groups."

Shannon quirked a strawberry-blonde eyebrow. "See, I didn't do as bad as you thought."

"It might have been better had you left off the cayenne pepper."

"But you can't deny I got your attention."

"You got my attention, all right."

"I had a horrible crush on you, you know, and you were positively rotten to me." She shoved a strand of hair back behind her ear.

Michael followed the movement of her hand and found his gaze lingering on her hair. He seemed to remember it being a rather unattractive carroty tangle, not this silky tousle the color of a new penny. "I acted the way any normal thirteen-year-old boy would have under the circumstances."

"I never said you weren't normal, just rotten."

"It was because you kept saying you were a leprechaun. I thought that was just too weird. By the way, how did you think a Maryland girl got to be an Irish leprechaun, anyway?"

Shannon sat down at the table with her own plate of pancakes. "I was born in Kilkenny."

"Ireland?"

"Sure. You didn't know?" When he shook his head, she continued, "Mom and Dad were visiting his parents and I came along six weeks early. I was delivered by emergency C-section." She paused, then, with a sly smile, said, "There was quite a mix-up in the hospital right after I was born."

"What kind of mix-up?"

"They lost me for a couple of hours. And when I finally turned back up in the nursery, I was missing my ID bracelet."

"How'd that happen?"

"Nobody knows." Shannon continued to look at him, waiting for him to make the connection. She could see the awareness dawn in his eyes.

"So that's why you believed you were a leprechaun. Your parents told you that story and you thought you'd been swapped."

"Who's to say I wasn't?" Shannon took a bite of her pancakes and winked again at Jenny, who'd been watching this exchange with fascination. "There are quite a few tales in Ireland about changelings."

"What's a changeling?" Jenny asked, as she licked maple syrup from her fork.

"A changeling is a fairy child that's been swapped

for a human baby. Of course, the parents don't know it until the baby grows up and begins using magic."

"Jenny, why don't you go change out of your nightgown now?"

Michael waited until his daughter had left the room, then turned to Shannon. "Look, I wish you wouldn't go into that leprechaun stuff with Jenny. I know you're just teasing, but she might not."

"Maybe I'm not teasing." She laid down her fork and watched him through lowered lashes.

His jaw tightened. "If I thought for one minute you still believed that nonsense, I'd ship you out to the nearest hotel."

"Now, now, don't go getting yourself into a state. It's just that it wouldn't hurt for the child to believe in something. She doesn't believe in any of the things young children usually believe in."

"She's been through too much reality in her young life."

"All the more reason for her to believe in fantasy. When you've lost everything else, you need something to hold on to. A child needs magic. It helps cushion them from the rest of the world."

"It's better that kids learn about real life early on."

"You're wrong."

"And I think it would be best if you don't question my methods of raising my daughter. You don't know what she and I have been through."

"I think I do."

"Oh?" He smiled sardonically. "And who have you lost recently?"

She looked at him with compassion. "Michael, you don't have to lose someone to know how it feels. All you have to do is love someone. And imagine the possibility."

Michael stood abruptly, the legs of his chair scraping against the tile floor. "I'll do the dishes."

"Nonsense. I'm going to be keeping house for you for the next few weeks. That's part of my job." She got to her feet in one fluid motion and began carrying the dishes to the sink.

Michael went into the living room and flopped heavily into his favorite chair. He watched his daughter work a jigsaw puzzle. Jenny had been much quieter since her mother died. That was normal, he told himself, just as the solemn way she now faced life was normal. He couldn't deny, though, that he missed her gleeful giggles and her cheerful off-key songs.

Could Shannon have been right about . . . ? No. It was far better that Jenny learn the world wasn't necessarily a kind or safe place. If you forgot that for even one minute, you wound up kicked in the teeth. It wouldn't be doing Jenny any favor to let her grow up with unrealistic expectations. Children who were sheltered didn't grow up prepared for the harsh reality. He hadn't been.

He hadn't been at all prepared for the catastrophic illness that would take his wife and all his savings and leave him with a young bewildered child to raise alone.

And Shannon expected them to bite into her fantasy about leprechauns? Not a chance.

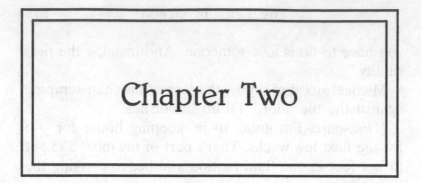

Chapter Two

Michael plopped his briefcase on his lap and pulled out a stack of papers to be graded. He tried to concentrate on his students' evaluation of their latest chemistry experiment, but found his thoughts wandering. Wandering right back to the kitchen where the aggravating Miss Donovan cheerfully whistled some vaguely Irish sounding tune.

With a sigh, he tucked the papers back into the briefcase and closed the lid. He knew this wasn't going to work. She'd been here all of two hours and she'd already disrupted his concentration. Something about her got under his skin and made him conscious of every move she made, the way she smelled, the lilting inflection of her voice. He lay his head back against the chair and shut his eyes for a moment, trying to herd his thoughts back into the corral.

Something tickled his ear and his eyes flew open again. He turned his head and met the disdainful green eyes of a cat. Her cat. How could he have forgotten her cat?

It was a large black cat. It was, quite possibly, the largest cat he'd ever seen. He didn't know how Shannon had carried it in with such ease, the critter must weigh a ton. And how had she managed to find a cat that had eyes the same spooky green as hers?

The cat gave a superior sniff and walked down Michael's chest to his lap. He leapt from lap to sofa with ease and sprawled out in regal splendor. Jenny was entranced and made a beeline for the animal.

"Be careful," Michael warned his daughter. "He might scratch."

"He will not," Shannon said from the kitchen door. She sounded affronted. "Puca is very well-mannered. He knows he's a guest here and wouldn't do anything to abuse the privilege."

She spoke like the cat was another person, he thought. "Just the same, Jenny, be careful."

The cat raised his enormous head and watched the child without blinking. When Jenny put her hand out, he butted against it and gave a kittenish mew, obviously begging for attention.

"I told you he'd behave." Shannon, a satisfied smile on her face, sat in a rocking chair across from Michael.

For a moment, Michael lost himself in that smile. It was a smile that belonged on a man's pillow the morning after a strenuous night making love. The biggest problem would be that any man waking up to a smile like that might never get out of bed. He pulled his gaze away from her smile and it fell on her green-outlined legs. Her skirt had ridden up when she sat, exposing a lot of thigh. A lot of very well-shaped thigh. Any man waking up to thighs like that might never get out of bed, either.

Shannon looked curiously at him and he felt that she'd read his every thought. It would be best to turn his attention to something besides her. He looked at the cat. " 'Puca' is an odd name. Does it mean anything in particular?"

"A puca is an Irish spirit. An animal spirit. It's usually a horse, but can also be a goat or an eagle or some other animal. I named him Puca because I found him in November and November is special to Pucas. That's when they appear to humans and tell their fortunes for the next year."

"That's when *legend* says they appear to humans," Michael said, for Jenny's benefit. Amusement flitted across Shannon's face, letting Michael know his reasoning hadn't escaped her. He made a mental note to discuss this make-believe nonsense with Shannon later. She was going to have to stop it before Jenny wound up thoroughly confused. God knew, it confused him.

Michael determinedly opened his briefcase again and turned his attention back to the test papers while Jenny crooned to the cat, who lay on his back thoroughly enjoying the attention.

"I like cats," Jenny confided.

"So do I." Shannon gave the child a conspiratorial smile. "And Puca is pretty special."

"You're lucky to own such a nice cat."

"Oh, I don't own him. Cats are very smart and very independent. You can't ever own them, but you can be friends with them."

"Do you think he'd be friends with me, too?"

Shannon looked at Jenny's wistful brown eyes and vowed that Puca would be her friend, even if she had to hog-tie and muzzle him. From the way he was revelling in the young girl's attentions, however, Shannon didn't think that would be necessary. "I think he's already your friend," she said gently and was rewarded by a shy smile. She just now realized this was the first time she'd seen Jenny smile.

She glanced over at Michael, but he seemed to be engrossed in his stack of papers. She hadn't seen Michael smile all that much, either. She wondered if he smiled often. She didn't think so. And she'd bet her life savings—as meager as they were—that he never laughed. He used to, though. A lot. That was what she'd fallen in love with at fourteen. His laugh.

She watched Jenny for a few moments more then picked up a magazine from the coffee table and pretended to read it, though she couldn't say she was all that interested in *Modern Chemistry Today*.

She finally put down the magazine and let her gaze wander around the room, wondering what it would reveal about the man who lived here, the man she knew and the one she didn't know at all. She'd heard all the usual stuff from his mother: how devoted he was to his daughter, what a terrific teacher he was, how he'd changed since the illness and death of his wife last year. But she wanted to know more. She wanted to know all the things his mother hadn't told her—or didn't know.

There were a lot of technical books on his bookshelf. She assumed they were either old college textbooks or reference materials he used to prepare for his students. That simply reaffirmed the "terrific teacher" part. But there was also a shelf of the latest spy and science-fiction novels. So he did have an active imagination, even if he kept it firmly in check. That was more like the old Michael. The one she remembered.

She eyed a stack of CD's next. His taste in music was nothing if not eclectic—progressive jazz, rock and roll, classical, Broadway show tunes. She wondered how he listened to it. Did he lay on the comfortable over-stuffed sofa and close his eyes? Did he play it in the background while he read or graded papers? Did he sing along or tap his foot in time to the beat, as she did? He used to sing along, sometimes off-key, but always enthusiastically. She certainly had a healthy curiosity about him, she admitted to herself. Maybe more than healthy.

A change in scenery was definitely in order here. She stood abruptly. "Jenny, why don't you go get bundled up and we'll go outside to make snow angels."

"I've never made a snow angel," Jenny admitted before running to her room.

"It's cold outside," Michael said, looking up from his papers. "I'd rather she didn't get chilled."

"Then maybe you'd better come outside with us so you can hurry her in when you think she's too cold," Shannon said, with challenge in her eyes. When Michael began to methodically put his papers away, she sashayed to her room, hiding her look of triumph.

Shannon came out of her room while Michael was helping his daughter into a pair of boots. Only this time Shannon wasn't wearing all green. She still wore her green tights, skirt, and sweater and had even tugged on her green knit hat. But now she'd added bright red leather boots that came up to her knees and a fuzzy red scarf around her neck. She didn't look quite so much the leprechaun this time as she did a Christmas elf.

This image stuck in his head when they went out into the backyard and snowflakes dusted her hat, clung to her eyelashes, frosted her cheeks. He had a sudden desire to taste the snowflakes that melted on her skin.

Would they taste like Irish cream or Christmas eggnog? And her skin, would it taste sweet or would it have her own unique woman's flavor?

It was with an effort that he pulled his attention away from Shannon. He forced his gaze to wander about the backyard, mentally measuring the amount of snowfall they'd had. Six inches, maybe seven. Enough to make a credible snow angel. He watched as Shannon explained to Jenny how to lie down in the snow and wave her arms to make the wings. And it nearly broke his heart to see Jenny try it with such an earnest expression on her face.

She should be laughing, her eyes bright, her cheeks rosy, but she still looked so solemn, even at play. Again he wondered if maybe Shannon was right, after all. Was the fantasy a necessary part of being a child?

And yet, how could he let Jenny believe in fantasy when real life was always waiting just around the next corner, ready to pull out the rug from beneath her? There always seemed to be more clouds ahead and clouds didn't always have silver linings. Sometimes clouds simply hid other clouds. No, it was better to be armed and ready. And Jenny was armed with the truth.

Still he couldn't help but contrast Shannon's face with the thoughtful, serious one belonging to his daughter. Shannon's eyes sparkled, her lips curved with sheer joy, her face was so animated, so alive.

As his gaze lingered on her face, he was hit with a surge of desire so strong it felt like a kick in the gut. He wanted to taste that *joie de vivre,* to hold it in his arms until it became part of him, to hold *her* in his arms until she became part of him.

He wondered what she wore beneath all that green.

More green? Green lace? Green silk? Green satin? And beneath the green lace . . .

Michael took a deep breath. This wouldn't do. This wouldn't do at all, he told himself and tried to cool down his overactive imagination. He tried visualizing cold things—ice cubes, a frigid shower, a snowball. For a split second, he thought he'd visualized a snowball out of thin air, but the icy slush slipping inside the collar of his coat was real, as was Shannon's laughter.

When he looked at her, she tossed another snowball up into the air, catching it again. "Girl's fast-pitch softball. Regional All-Stars," she said with a smug smile.

Michael's look of surprise gave way to a sudden wicked grin. "Varsity baseball," he remarked casually as he scooped up a gloveful of snow, forming it into a ball. "Tournament champions. Pitcher," he added just before he let loose a snowball that caught her neatly on the shoulder. "Bingo!"

The snowballs had flown with deadly accuracy and with shouts of glee. Even Jenny had gotten into the act, after watching the strange antics of the two adults. When she had joined in with girlish giggles, Michael had felt unaccustomed tears sting his eyes. So long. It had been so long since he'd heard that sound. He wanted to stop and just listen, to store up the sounds so he could take them back out when times got tough again.

When the sounds of his own laughter rang out, it had startled him. It had been a long time for him, too. He wondered if his laugh were a little rusty from disuse. There hadn't been much reason to laugh. Until Shannon.

Now he sat in front of the fireplace, thawing out. He wondered when Shannon had found time to make the fire that crackled so merrily. Jenny, who Shannon had helped change into warm dry clothes, was crooning to the cat perched on the hearth. Michael sipped the cup of hot cocoa that Shannon had placed in his hand and listened to the homey sounds of her moving around in the kitchen.

He could hear the clatter of dishes on the counter, the tinkle of the silverware, but over and above all of that, he could hear Shannon's footsteps, he could hear the whisper of her sleeve as it brushed against her side, he could hear the melody she hummed as she worked. He could almost hear each breath she took.

It was almost as if she were some other-worldly creature who had enchanted him. He didn't believe in leprechauns, but he could almost believe she was a witch. A witch who had cast a spell on him to make him hypersensitive to her every nuance.

A drop of hot liquid that sloshed on his pants' leg reminded him that it would be safer to keep his mind off witches and elves—and Shannon. He reached over to place his cup on the coffee table before he did any more damage and nearly knocked over the strange plant with three-lobed leaves and small white flowers that had been set in the middle of the table. "Jenny, where did this flower come from?"

"Shannon put it there. She said every Irish house had to have a shamrock for St. Patrick's Day. It's supposed to be good luck."

"Where did she get it from?" He hadn't been aware of any deliveries.

"She brought it from her room."

Her room? Did she routinely carry blooming plants around in her luggage? He wondered what else she had in there. Maybe a negligee? He took a deep breath and brought his thoughts to heel, promising himself he was not going to do any more speculating about Shannon. He knew all he needed to know about her. He knew more than he wanted to know. He knew she was a few ounces short of a pound. She was exasperating, distracting. Disarming. Beautiful.

It was a miserable afternoon. Lunch was a perfectly cooked broccoli quiche that even Jenny liked. In no time at all, Shannon had done the dishes and put them away. She got Jenny to clean her room and make her bed with absolutely no argument. She even managed to get a mustard stain out of his favorite T-shirt. Yes, it was a miserable afternoon. The worst.

Michael sat in his chair and fumed as she did one right thing after another. He didn't want her here, didn't want her to fit in so easily. But she was and she did. And you couldn't exactly get rid of somebody because they cooked too well, or cleaned too perfectly, could you? So it looked like he was stuck with her. At least for the next few weeks. Damn!

His concentration was shot to pieces and his brain in a muddle because of her. Too much more of this and he'd be fair game for the men in the little white coats. Hell, he'd be the one to call them. She made him crazy. She made him smile. But mostly she just made him crazy.

Chapter Three

This was going to be harder than she'd thought, Shannon realized. She'd gotten both Jenny and Michael to let down their guard for a few precious minutes this afternoon. But now the walls were back up. At least Michael's walls were back up. Shannon's attention lingered on the man who was gazing moodily at the crackling fire. His walls were up stronger and higher than before.

He'd barely spoken since they'd come back inside. He'd eaten his lunch in silence, then spent the rest of the afternoon staring down at the stack of school papers in his lap. She hadn't seen him mark a single one.

Why was he so reluctant to relax and have fun? She knew it wasn't because he'd forgotten how. She'd seen this afternoon just how much he remembered. For one split second she'd seen the young college student, trying to cram twenty-six hours' worth of living into twenty-four. That was the Michael she'd fallen for.

She didn't think Jenny was going to be as tough a nut to crack. Jenny so desperately wanted to laugh again, to feel like a normal little girl again, that she'd begun to open up, even in this one short day. True, it was like a tight rosebud just unfurling one small petal but, the good Saint willing, it was a start.

After supper, the rest of the quiche from lunch,
Shannon sat on the floor playing a game of checkers
with Jenny. Every time she glanced up at Michael, his
eyes were trained on the television, but when she
turned away, she could feel his gaze on her as surely as
if he'd been touching her with his hands. She wanted to
shake off his gaze like a dog shakes off water droplets.

This was ridiculous, she kept thinking. One would
think she still had a crush on him. But she'd gotten
over it years ago. She really had.

She was relieved when Michael took Jenny into her
bedroom to get her ready for bed. At least she didn't
feel like her every move was being watched. Shannon
poked her head into the bedroom door a few minutes
later to ask if she could help and saw Michael sitting on
the edge of the bed brushing Jenny's hair. His face was
suffused with such tenderness that her breath caught in
her throat. She watched for a moment as his large gentle hands smoothed over his daughter's hair.

Some men might have looked clumsy and awkward
performing such a task, but he looked so natural. It
reminded Shannon that he'd had to be both mother
and father to his daughter. Obviously he was doing a
good job at it. Except for that reality business. She'd
have to work on that some more. Silently she stepped
back, loath to disturb this quiet moment between them.

She went back into the living room and sat on the
footstool next to the hearth. All of a sudden, she felt
cold. She wrapped her arms around herself and sup-
pressed a shiver. The cat came and sat beside her while
she absently watched the flames flicker and dance. The
cat meowed once and she looked down at him. "You
may be right. I am afraid. I came here to help him

rediscover the laughter he's forgotten, but I may discover something I wish I hadn't."

"Who were you talking to?"

Shannon looked around at Michael, keeping her face carefully blank. "Um, Puca."

"The cat?"

"He's quite a conversationalist," she said with a feeble attempt at a smile.

"I'll bet. Uh, speaking of talking to cats and such, I think we need to have a talk. I—"

Shannon stood abruptly. "Could we do it in the morning? I'm really tired and I thought I'd get ready for bed. Do you mind if I use a couple of towels?"

"Uh, no, but—"

"Thanks." Shannon all but ran out of the room. Without Jenny in there with them, she had suddenly realized how alone they were. And some deep-rooted self-preservation instinct made her decide that being alone with him right now was the last thing she needed.

It had been twelve years since she'd fallen for him and she'd been such a child at the time that she was sure she'd outgrown those feelings, but it was as if they had simply been dormant and were now reawakening. No, it was that it had been a long day and she was tired. A hot shower and going to bed early would do wonders for her equilibrium. She hoped.

Michael sat on the stool Shannon had been sitting on and listened to the water running in the bathroom. Against his will, he began imagining Shannon undressing for the shower. Her clothes would be tossed into a little green pile on the floor, her hair would cascade down over the creamy skin of her bare shoulders.

She'd step beneath the steaming spray of the shower,

water sluicing over her up-tilted breasts, channeling in the valley between, dripping from the rosy tips. She'd close her eyes and turn her face into the water, enjoying its warm caress as it ran down over her. No, it shouldn't be the water's caress, but the touch of a man's hand. His hand.

He jumped to his feet, startling the cat who'd gone back to dozing on the hearth. He headed for the kitchen to make himself a cup of coffee, though he'd probably regret it. He didn't need an extra dose of caffeine keeping him awake tonight. Thoughts of Shannon would do that well enough. On second thought, he pulled out a jar of instant decaf. No sense taking any chances.

Three a.m. Michael scowled at the clock and punched his pillow down for what must have been the hundredth time. He may as well have had a cup or two of fresh-brewed. He couldn't be any more wide-awake than he was right now.

She'd only been here one day. One day. How had she managed to turn his life upside down in one day? She'd made him forget, for a moment, this afternoon. But that couldn't happen anymore. That left him vulnerable and he'd vowed to never leave himself wide open again. He'd have to steel himself against her charming eccentricities because they made him lower his guard. And that wasn't safe.

The last time he'd been open and trusting, he'd had his heart handed back to him in pieces. His marriage hadn't been perfect, but finding out Anne had an incurable disease had nearly killed him. And when she died, that had frozen him inside. He didn't believe he had any feelings left. Except for Jenny. But never again for anyone else. Never.

Michael wearily sat up in bed and lookcd at the clock again. Three-fifteen. Damn. Thank God it was Saturday. At least he wouldn't have to get up at seven —providing he got to sleep by seven.

Maybe a glass of milk and some dull reading would help. He got out of bed, tugging at the cuffs of his soft cotton pajama shirt. He preferred sleeping in the buff but wore these because of Jenny. Still there was nothing like bare skin between crisp clean sheets. He wondered what Shannon wore to bed. A green T-shirt? No, she'd said leprechauns preferred red. Maybe red silk. And maybe he should quit speculating about things like this and get his glass of milk.

When Michael opened his bedroom door and stepped into the hall he noticed the faint flickering of light. He'd banked the fire before going to bed, had it flared up? He went into the living room and stopped dead. He'd been wrong. Shannon wore neither green T-shirts nor red silk. She wore white, the demurest of white-cotton nightgowns with a high beribboned neck and long sleeves ending in lace-edged ruffles.

She sat on the floor in front of the sofa, her gown swirled around her. With her hair fanned over her shoulders in gold-shot waves, she didn't look a thing like a leprechaun. She looked like an angel. She looked sweet, innocent—that is, until she looked around and he saw the flames reflected in her green eyes. Those were the eyes of a sorceress, a seductress. They promised, they beguiled, they tempted a man beyond endurance.

"Couldn't sleep?" Her voice was soft, husky. "Me either. I came in here to watch the fire. Grandda, my father's father, the one in Kilkenny, used to say that you could see your dreams in the flames."

Michael sat down on the sofa. "And do you see your dreams?"

She smiled a little, a slow smile that beckoned him closer. "Yes. Do you?"

"I don't dream anymore."

"You should. The world is full of possibilities. You used to believe that. Remember?"

"When?"

"Twelve years ago. You were home from college and so full of ideas you could hardly contain them all. You bubbled over with excitement."

"Men don't bubble."

"Boiled over, then."

"So I grew up. You can't live like that forever."

Shannon rose from the floor, in a drift of white ruffles. Again he thought of an angel—with devil eyes. She sat next to him on the sofa. "Can you live without laughter forever?" she asked gently.

"If I have to."

"You shouldn't have to."

Michael watched the warm light from the fire play over her face. Her skin looked creamy, silky, her lips a rich soft pink. He could live without laughter if he had to but he didn't know if he could live without knowing how those lips tasted. He bent his head closer, almost hoping she would realize his intent and back away. She didn't.

Oh, she knew what he intended, all right. He could tell that by the catch in her breathing. But she didn't pull away. Instead, her lips parted slightly and she tilted her head back. It was as if she were inviting him to kiss her.

He'd never been one to turn down an invitation.

His lips brushed against hers once, twice, then settled down in earnest. The kiss was slow, almost leisurely, as he learned the shape and feel and taste of her lips. He sipped, he savored, he drank.

Ah, he should have known. The taste was sweet, exotic, intoxicating. It went to his head like wine. No, he thought hazily, like Irish whiskey. Suddenly he didn't care about keeping his distance, playing it safe. He didn't want to be safe. He wanted to walk on the edge, hell, he wanted to dance on the edge.

Shannon moved into his arms as if there were no other place on earth to be but there. When she threaded her fingers through his hair, he answered in kind, gathering his hands full of silky waves. Their tongues touched, tasted, then touched again. He heard a breathless moan of pleasure, but didn't know who it came from, her or him. He didn't care.

But he did care. Somewhere deep inside him little voices were clamoring to be heard. Little voices of guilt, wariness, pain. This had to stop. His lips stilled on hers, his hands slowly flexed, releasing her hair from his grasp. He pulled away, wanting to grimace at the ache of separating from her.

"This shouldn't have happened," he murmured. "I never meant for this to happen. You're a guest in this house and I—"

"If you apologize, I'll hit you," Shannon interrupted.

"I won't say I'm sorry," he said softly, "but it won't happen again. It can't." With that he got up and left the room, without a backwards glance.

Shannon awoke to a crystal world. Sometime during the night, the snow had changed to sleet and freezing rain, encasing everything in a glittering layer of ice.

The sun sparkled brilliantly as she looked out the window. It hurt her eyes.

She hadn't slept well. She didn't need a lot of sleep, only four or five hours a night, but without that she became distinctly out of sorts. After Michael had left her, she had stared at the fire for a long time, going over things in her mind. He'd said he hadn't meant for this to happen. Well, neither had she. She had been walking such a thin line where her feelings for Michael were concerned. What she didn't know was whether this had pushed her over the edge. That was the question that had kept her awake until nearly dawn.

She'd been trying to convince herself that she'd gotten over her long-ago crush, but now she wasn't so sure. She wasn't sure about anything anymore.

Faint sounds came from the living room and Shannon glanced at her clock. Nine o'clock? Some housekeeper she was, she thought as she hurriedly changed clothes. It was her job to get up before everyone else and have breakfast ready.

She had an "I'm sorry" poised on her lips as she entered the living room, but the only person there was Jenny. She sat on the floor in front of the television with a bowl of cereal in her lap and Puca sitting attentively at her knee. "Morning, Jenny," she said when the child looked up with a smile.

"Puca likes cereal," she said, holding a frosted puff out to the cat. He daintily removed it from the child's fingers and ate it.

"I think he likes the milk on it," Shannon said and peeked around into the kitchen. "Where's your Daddy?"

"Oh, he's not up yet. Saturday rules: don't keep the

TV too loud and don't wake up Daddy until ten unless there's an emergency."

"And have you ever had an emergency?"

"No. Not unless you count the time Meggie Watkins next door shinnied up the drain pipe and got stuck on the roof and Mrs. Watkins ran over here to borrow Daddy's ladder."

"Meggie Watkins is a friend of yours?"

"Nah. She's too bossy. Besides she's too little to play with. She's only four or five."

"But you're only six, aren't you?"

Jenny sighed. "Yeah, but sometimes I feel older."

"I know what you mean," Shannon muttered as she went into the kitchen to make a cup of tea. This morning she felt positively ancient. A nice cup of tea would help put things into perspective. That's what her Irish grandparents always said.

She'd spent weekends from college with them in Kilkenny. It had helped ease some of the homesickness. And yet, when she'd come back to the States for the summers, she'd been homesick then, too. She was truly a woman of two countries.

When she began to realize that home was where the heart was, she became a woman without a home because her heart belonged to no one. Not once had she fallen in love. Not once had any man touched her heart. Except Michael. She sighed, stirred a touch of cream into her tea and took a sip.

She used to believe that she'd kept in touch with Michael's mother, Catherine, over the years because it was one more tie to "home." Now she began to see that it was one more tie to Michael. Michael was Catherine's only son, therefore her letters had been full of him.

Shannon absently started a pot of coffee for Michael, remembering when she got the letter that said Michael had married. Mrs. Connor hadn't seemed especially thrilled about it; Shannon had been decidedly un-thrilled. She'd been a sophomore in college and had skipped nearly a week's worth of classes to go to her grandparents and sulk.

Somehow she had cherished the faint hope that one day she'd go back home and Michael would notice how grown-up she was. He'd take her out for dinner and then, reluctant to let her out of his sight, would suggest dancing. He'd whisper that he had always wanted to hold her in his arms. Mrs. Connor's letter had put an end to all that. So Shannon had hung up her girlish dreams.

Until she'd come back to the States and found out his wife had died and Mrs. Connor was worried about her son. Worried that he'd lost his laughter, his dreams. And Shannon had convinced herself that she'd owed him something because of all those years he'd unknow-ingly fueled her childhood fantasies. Now she knew she'd only been fooling herself. That wasn't why she'd come. She'd really come hoping he'd look at her, no-tice how grown-up she was, take her out to dinner . . .

A footstep on the kitchen tile made her look up from the tea leaves she'd been contemplating in the bottom of her cup. "Um, good morning, Michael," she said with a bright smile. "Coffee's ready. Shall I fix breakfast? What would you like? Cereal? Toast? Eggs?"

"I'll just fix a bowl of cereal, thanks. I don't eat a big breakfast on Saturdays."

"I don't mind scrambling a couple of eggs. Really."

"Well, if you want to—"

"It's my job," Shannon said as she prepared the frying pan and added the eggs.

Silence fell until Shannon finally said, "Ah, it looks like just snow flurries this morning."

"Yeah. Maybe the snow will let up now."

"How much do you think we got?"

"I don't know. Eight or nine inches, I guess."

Shannon set a plate in front of Michael. "Are we really discussing the weather?" she asked.

He grimaced. "Looks that way. What's this green stuff on the eggs?"

"Just chives. A little green in honor of Saint Patrick's Day," she said with a weak smile.

"That was yesterday."

"The Irish never just celebrate one day, you know."

"Right."

Shannon noticed how neatly he avoided looking at her while he finished his eggs. She looked back down at her teacup and took a deep breath. "Michael—"

He turned to face her, still without meeting her eyes. "Yeah."

"I think we need to talk about, well, about what happened last night. We need to. I mean, we're actually reduced to discussing the weather."

Michael shrugged. "What's to say? We both had errors in judgment last night. All we need to do is agree not to let it happen again."

"Can you do that?"

"Sure."

"Well, I don't know if I can. You can't deny there's something between us, Michael. Some kind of weird electrical energy—"

"It's just proximity." He set his coffee cup down a

little harder than necessary, as if to add emphasis to his words.

"You think so?" Shannon asked, almost hopefully.

"I'm positive."

"I hope you're right."

Chapter Four

By Monday the roads were clear and the schools were open. Shannon got up to fix breakfast for Michael and Jenny and found herself charmed by the morning routine. Jenny got herself ready for school, all but her hair and her shoes. "Daddy likes to feel useful," she confided to Shannon over buttered toast and hot oatmeal. "So I leave him something to do, even though I could do it myself."

Shannon's heart turned over. She hadn't been around other children much in her life, but thought Jenny must be an especially remarkable specimen. She was bright and thoughtful and eager to please. She just needed to laugh more. And Shannon desperately wanted to be the one who gave joy back to her.

Michael, looking rumpled and only half-awake, dragged himself into the kitchen about fifteen minutes later. It was obvious morning wasn't his favorite time of day, Shannon thought with tender amusement. He didn't say a word, just made a beeline for the coffee maker, stopping only long enough to drop a kiss on his daughter's head. He downed a cup of black coffee before heading to the bathroom for his shower.

When he finally made it back to the kitchen, he'd dressed and shaved and looked slightly more awake.

Shannon found her gaze lingering on the still-damp hair that curled over his collar. She wanted to reach out and touch that hair with a desire so fierce it was almost physical. But it was more than that. She wanted to have the *right* to do it, to know that he was hers to touch and to hold. With an effort, she shook those thoughts away and set a bowl of steaming oatmeal in front of him.

"Thanks." He picked up his spoon. "What, no green?" he murmured, almost to himself.

Shannon grinned suddenly and, with a flourish, set a cup on the table.

"What's this?"

"Cinnamon and sugar. To sprinkle on top, you know."

Michael sprinkled some on top of his oatmeal, then paused. "It's green," he said with a sigh.

"I didn't want you to be disappointed. I just used colored sugar, that's all."

"Don't you like green, Daddy?" Jenny asked.

"I used to," he murmured with a telling glance at Shannon.

She couldn't tell if he were joking or not, but she gave a bland smile anyway and offered him a piece of toast.

"Thanks." He propped it on the edge of his cereal bowl. "If you need to go anywhere today, you can use the Mazda. I'll leave the key."

"You don't need it?"

"I'll take the station wagon. We got that when Jenny was about two. Figured we'd need more room." He fell silent, lost in thoughts. Not happy ones, Shannon judged by the shadows that fell across his face. She wondered if he'd ever get over losing his wife.

After breakfast, she watched as Michael brushed and carefully braided his daughter's hair, finishing up with a bright yarn bow on the end of each plait. He tickled Jenny's chin with the end of one braid until she smiled, then kissed her nose. The obvious love between father and daughter left Shannon feeling more lonely by comparison.

She washed the few dishes, wiped off the table and set a bowl of shiny red apples in the middle. Jenny grabbed one and stuffed it in her coat pocket. "I love apples. I'll eat it at recess. We're allowed to have snacks, you know."

"Nice looking apples. Where'd these come from?" Michael picked up one, admiring the unblemished surface.

"Oh, I had a few in my things. I just decided to bring them in here."

Michael set the apple back in the bowl. "First shamrocks, now apples. What else do you carry in your luggage?"

"Maybe that's where I keep my pot of gold." She gave a sly smile and winked at Jenny, then handed the little girl her lunch bag and wrapped her own red knit scarf around Jenny's neck. It added a bright note to Jenny's rather somber navy blue coat.

"Michael, can I fix you a lunch?"

"No, thanks. I'll pick something up in the cafeteria. Jenny, it's about time for your bus, sweetheart."

Jenny gave her father a hug, grabbed her bookbag by one strap and skipped down to the end of the meticulously shoveled sidewalk. Michael followed along behind her, got in his car and waited in the driveway. When the bus came, Jenny stepped up on the first step of the bus, then turned and waved at her Daddy. Shannon was touched when Jenny waved at her, too. As the bus pulled away, Michael backed out of the driveway and headed in the opposite direction.

Apparently this was a normal part of their morning routine, Shannon thought as she watched out the picture window in the living room, then sat morosely on the sofa, the cat jumping into her lap. An endless day stretched in front of her, the house seeming so empty that she half expected echoes to ring when she spoke to the cat. Was it Jenny's timid smiles and shy chatter that she missed? Or was it that Michael filled each room up so much that when he was gone his absence seemed almost palpable?

With a sigh, she gently plopped the cat on the floor and grabbed the portable phone, taking it into the kitchen with her. She could take care of some business for ErinWear and it just might help fill up a little of the day. She made some phone calls, making a mental note to warn Michael before he saw the trans-Atlantic charges on his phone bill. She'd pay for them, of course. She just hoped he had a good long distance company. Her funds *were* limited until the new branch officially opened here in a few weeks. Then she hoped funds would be plentiful.

With the hottest young Irish clothing designers on the roster, the initial response to ErinWear had been positive. And with so many of the clothes making use of genuine Irish linen and lace and in her case, leather, she felt the demand for their products would be high. At least she hoped it would.

Now that business had taken up all of an hour, she only had another five or six to go. She decided to do laundry first. She stripped the sheets and pillowcases from her bed and Jenny's then went into Michael's bedroom. She stopped dead just inside the door. The room was sparsely furnished with a dresser, nightstand and bed, but what a bed. A king-sized bed. Her gaze locked on that bed for long breathless moments as her imagination went into overdrive. She could imagine all kinds of things to do on a bed like that, but most of the activities involved just Michael and her.

Scene one: Michael, fresh from a shower, wearing nothing but a towel, with water droplets in strategic places. She'd find and catch each and every droplet with her tongue, before she and Michael fell together on the tiger-striped sheets.

Scene two: Candlelight everywhere. Her, in black silk, Michael wearing nothing but the wickedest of grins. She'd lay back on the red silk sheets, Michael stretching out beside her.

Scene three: Shannon wearing virginal white, perching nervously on the edge of the Victorian lace comforter, Michael striding purposefully toward her.

But the fantasy she liked the most was the one with her and Michael waking up in each other's arms, after a wonderfully exhausting night, as their kids brought in a breakfast tray.

An older Jenny, a confident and happy Jenny, would say, "Happy Saint Patrick's Day." All the kids, twelve-year-old Jenny, six-year-old Sean (who had his mother's green eyes), and four-year-old Siobhan (who had her father's nose) would all climb up in that king-sized bed and chatter happily while their parents ate their breakfast.

Still caught up in her daydreams, Shannon stripped the sheets—plain white ones—from the bed. As she filled her arms with the linens, she held them close, as if she were somehow holding Michael nearer as she did so. She lifted her head and looked at the cat, who'd brushed up next to her ankle. "Well, now, that's enough of this nonsense! By the Good Saint, it'll not happen again." The cat meowed and Shannon stopped and looked down at him. "Okay, so I'll try not to let it happen again. Satisfied?"

When Michael got home late that afternoon, everything seemed the same, at least on the surface. But there were things, small seemingly insignificant things, that gave the house a whole different feeling. A homier, even more welcoming, feeling.

New smells greeted him: basil and tomato, with a hint of vanilla. Something Italian, he guessed, with fresh-baked cookies? Cake? Brownies? The living room held the fresh tang of lemon from the furniture polish that left the dark wood gleaming. But over it all, he could still detect the soft floral scent that was uniquely hers.

There were other homey touches, too. The crackling fire in the fireplace, with the cat sleeping on the hearth in front. The throw pillows on the sofa had been plumped up invitingly, the newspaper lay ready on the coffee table, a green vine trailed from the window sill of the picture window. He didn't even bother to ask where it came from, probably from that bottomless bag of tricks she called a suitcase.

Now this was what a housekeeper was supposed to do. If Shannon could keep this up for the next few weeks, it wouldn't be so bad. As long as she left off the leprechaun stuff. Housekeepers weren't supposed to pretend to be leprechauns and have cats named after Irish spirits. And they certainly weren't supposed to look like an angel in white ruffles and kiss like the devil's mistress.

He couldn't help but breathe a sigh of relief when he sat down to dinner and found marinara sauce over pasta, regular ol' white pasta, and garlic bread, white bread spread with ordinary butter. Nothing green in the bunch. All weekend long, something green had turned up at every meal. In honor of Saint Patrick's Day, she'd said.

Friday night had been that quiche with broccoli, Saturday had been scrambled eggs with chives for breakfast, split-pea soup for lunch and chicken stuffed with spinach for supper. Sunday had been more of the same. He wouldn't deny that it had been tasty, but enough was enough.

By the time for dessert, he was feeling relaxed. The meal had gone well. Jenny had been full of excited chatter about a sleepover she'd been invited to that weekend, and he and Shannon had been able to carry on a light and pleasant conversation. No meaningful looks, no uncomfortable silences, no electric touches. Just a nice ordinary meal.

With green sherbet for dessert.

"I thought I smelled cookies baking," Michael found himself saying in disappointment.

Shannon whipped out a plate. "Sugar cookies. I knew you were a cookie man the first time I ever met you. I think you had the equivalent of half a bag of chocolate chip cookies stuffed in your back pocket. I kept hoping you'd give me one. That was the real reason I followed you around, you know."

Ignoring the green sugar sprinkled on top, Michael bit into a crisp cookie and chewed appreciatively, then indicated the dishes of sherbet. "Did you go to the store today?"

Shannon gave him a quizzical look. "No. Everything I needed was right here."

Somehow, Michael doubted he had lime sherbet in his freezer. Because if he did, he had no idea how it had gotten there. Maybe it came out of her suitcase. It bothered him how easy it had become to accept the strange and unusual when he was around her. But then she was pretty strange and unusual herself.

After supper, Jenny went into the living room to watch television and Michael rinsed the plates while Shannon loaded the dishwasher. The cat wandered into the kitchen and investigated the floor beneath the table, looking for crumbs. When he didn't find any, he sat and began grooming himself as if it didn't matter to him one way or the other.

"Did you come here straight from Ireland?" Michael asked suddenly.

Shannon stopped and turned at Michael's abrupt question. "No, I spent a couple of weeks visiting my parents. Why do you ask?"

"I was just wondering if that's where you found your cat."

"Not exactly." Shannon paused, wondering if he'd believe the real story when she wasn't sure *she* did. Well, why not? He'd already decided she was a few eggs short of a dozen. "I found him, or rather he found me, on November first of this past year. Do you remember I told you that November is a special month for Pucas? Well, I'd been out riding my bike and stopped into a little shop to have some tea. When I came back out to my bike, there was this huge black cat sitting next to it. When I got on my bike, he jumped up in the basket."

To Michael's credit, he raised an eyebrow, but didn't verbally express his disbelief.

"I know it sounds farfetched, but it really happened. I went back in the shop and asked if anyone knew anything about the cat and no one did, so I took him back to school with me until the end of the term. When I decided to come back to the States to help ErinWear set up their American branch, I made arrangements to leave him with my grandparents."

"So why didn't you?"

She gave a sheepish smile. "I thought I had."

"What do you mean?"

"I mean, that I left him at my grandparents' house just before I flew home. But when I arrived in New York and went to pick up my suitcases, Puca was sitting on my luggage."

"In New York? How'd he get to New York? Don't animals have to go through customs or something?"

Shannon shrugged. "No one at the airlines seemed to know how he got there."

Michael stared at her for a long moment, then turned to look at the cat. Finally, comprehension dawned in his eyes. "I see. This is one more of your cute little stories, isn't it?"

Shannon sighed a little. "No, it isn't. That's really what happened. Believe it or not, as you choose." She turned back to the dishwasher. "I'll finish these dishes. Why don't you go relax?" She couldn't keep the tiniest bit of pique out of her voice. She was getting tired of having him second-guess everything she said.

As if he picked up on her frustration, he turned back to her. "It really happened that way?"

"I swear by the Blessed Saint Patrick."

Michael nodded and looked thoughtfully at the cat who gave a bored sniff and strolled casually back into the living room.

"Do you believe me?" Shannon had to know.

"I'll admit you certainly have an unusual cat," was all Michael would say.

Somehow that was enough for Shannon.

The next two weeks went pretty much the same way Monday had gone and Michael grew more and more comfortable as they got into a routine. He felt the most comfortable when he knew exactly what to expect from his day. It was just that around Shannon, he'd gotten used to expecting the unexpected.

He'd gotten used to eating green food, even when it was food that ordinarily didn't come in green. He'd gotten used to having more things show up from out of her magic luggage: a pink flowering shamrock to sit beside the white flowered one, a basket of kiwi fruit (more green, he thought), a beautiful Irish lace table-cloth which dressed up the kitchen table, even a large green teddy bear for Jenny.

He'd gotten used to laying in bed at night and listening to her moving quietly about her room next door. He could almost hear her hairbrush as it pulled through her hair, hear the rustle of her nightgown as she pulled it over her head, hear the soft squeak of the bedsprings as she got into bed. He'd gotten used to lying in his bed, aching with need.

He'd gotten used to sorting through her sweet-smelling toiletries on the bathroom counter to find his razor. He'd gotten used to seeing her face across the breakfast table in the morning. He'd even gotten used to the lilting Irish melodies she hummed, even when she wasn't aware of doing it.

The truth of the matter was, that even though he'd convinced himself that he'd liked his safe and secure existence the past year, she had spent less than a month in his life and made him aware of how staid and sterile that year had been.

Damn!

Chapter Five

On Friday, Shannon helped Jenny pack an overnight bag for the sleep-over she was going to at Kimmie's.

"You don't suppose I could pack Puca, do you?" Jenny said with a giggle. "I'll bet everybody would just love him." She glanced at the cat who was stretched out on her bed, lazily watching the activity.

Shannon smiled and ran her hand over the child's glossy curls. "I don't think he'll fit in your suitcase."

"Maybe I should take yours. The magic one."

Shannon's smile widened. "It's still too full of all kinds of magic stuff."

From the living room, Michael called out, "Jenny, sweetheart. Mrs. Parks is here to pick you up. Don't forget Kimmie's birthday present."

Jenny pulled on her coat while Shannon grabbed the overnight bag. "Don't torture Kimmie's little brother too much, okay?" She dropped a kiss on the child's cheek and followed her into the living room. Jenny gave her father an enthusiastic hug and ran down the sidewalk, Michael following behind with the overnight bag. When Michael came back in the house, he and Shannon turned toward each other with awkward smiles. It was as if it had suddenly dawned on both of them that they were alone together.

Shannon stepped back. "I-I think I'll start supper now."

"Great," Michael said. "I think I'll, uh, grade some papers."

He pulled out his briefcase with the same expression that a knight might wear as he donned his suit of armor, Shannon thought. Certainly he used his briefcase as a form of protection. Every student's paper he pulled out was like another brick in his wall.

But what was he protecting himself from? Did he really find her so threatening? Or was it what she represented? Was it the fun, the laughter, the joy in living? No, she believed it was the feelings. Deny it as he might, or ascribe it to proximity, feelings were there between them—powerful, overwhelming, electric.

Her brows knitted in thought as she opened the refrigerator door and stared without seeing at the contents inside. Instead, what she saw was the way Michael would look if he ever let down his guard enough to laugh. Not a little laugh, a rusty laugh, but a full-blown hearty belly laugh. It was the kind of laugh that was therapeutic, medicine for the soul. And he needed that medicine. So, she'd have to see that he got it.

It was unfortunate that in helping him find his laughter, she might lose her heart in the process. She sighed philosophically and reached for a package of steaks. No point in worrying about that now. She had a feeling it might be too late, anyway.

As she glanced out the kitchen window at the rapidly darkening skies, she saw a whirl of snowflakes. The thought of being snowed in with Michael without Jenny there as a buffer made her feel unguarded, vulnerable. Those feelings intensified when she heard the ping of sleet against the windowpane. It was going to be a long, long night.

To her surprise, it wasn't nearly as uncomfortable as she feared. She and Michael wound up on the sofa, in front of the fire, reminiscing. They hadn't seen each other more than a handful of times as children, but still seemed to have hundreds of memories in common.

Shannon hadn't been there when Michael had had his front teeth loosened by a baseball in a Junior Varsity game, but she'd heard the story enough times to know all the details. Michael hadn't been there when she'd gotten her long hair tangled in the jungle gym and had had to have it cut off, but her mother had told that story dozens of times, so she knew he'd heard it. Probably more than once.

Shannon told Michael about the experiences of an American girl in an Irish university. She even found herself telling him about her first college boyfriend. It was less comfortable for her when Michael began talking about meeting Anne, but she never betrayed it by so much as a blink.

Then Michael pulled out a photograph album. Some pictures she laughed at—one of herself at six, with bedraggled pigtails and a big grin, highlighting her two missing front teeth, one of her and Michael posing awkwardly in front of his parents' sofa. He was looking down at her as if he didn't know how anyone could manage to look so gawky and she was looking up at him with her heart in her eyes. Shannon wondered why Michael couldn't see it.

There were other pictures, too. Pictures that tugged at her heart. Jenny's first smile, first tooth, first step, first everything. Some pictures were unbearably sad and she could hardly bear to look at them. Anne holding her baby or posing with Michael. They were poignant reminders of just how fragile life could be. All the more reason to squeeze every last drop of happiness out of it.

Michael grew quiet and stared at a picture of him and Anne holding a much younger Jenny by the hands. The silence stretched into long moments.

Shannon broke the silence. "Jenny was about three in that picture, wasn't she?"

Michael nodded. "It was just before we found out Anne was sick."

"She was sick a long time," Shannon said softly. "That must have been so hard on all of you."

"I think it was hardest on Jenny. The first year she was too young to understand why her mother couldn't pick her up anymore or take her for walks in the park. The second year, Anne was in and out of the hospital so often . . ." his voice trailed off.

"I know that was a devastating thing to have happened, Michael. I'm so sorry."

He looked up from the picture with a bitter twist to his mouth. "But that's life, isn't it? It's just all part of life. So we might as well get used to it. Even expect it."

Shannon nodded. "I guess it is part of life," she said thoughtfully. "And so is guilt and anger and grief. But there's also joy, laughter, love. It all comes tangled up together. We're not supposed to separate them because when we do, we lose the balance."

"Where was the balance in Jenny having to watch her mother suffer and die, Shannon? There was no joy in that, only pain."

"There was no joy in that," Shannon agreed. "But there *is* joy in other things, Michael, so many other things. Pain is, well it hits you on the head. You can't miss it. Joy can be much more subtle. Sometimes you have to look for it, but it's always there. You used to be able to find it. You taught me how."

"What do you mean, I taught you how?"

"That weekend you came home from college and I was staying with your parents. I was pretty depressed that weekend and mad at the world. My parents had gone to Ireland without me, I'd had a fight with my best friend, and I was the only girl left in my group of friends who didn't have a bra," she smiled a little, "and didn't need one. I found all this pretty overwhelming. I was sitting on the front porch pouting and you came outside and sprawled on the porch swing. Remember?"

Michael saw himself as he'd been then, tall, lanky, dressed in the ratty jeans and T-shirt he always wore, full of the self-confidence and conceit that only a twenty-year-old has. He remembered Shannon as she'd been. Her hair had been a little redder and pulled back in a swinging ponytail. It served to make her look even younger.

She'd been wearing pink, not a flattering color with her bright hair and pale skin. And though the clothes had been feminine in nature, the body they covered could have been that of a young boy. Her eyes, too big for her thin face, had been red-rimmed from crying. "I do remember," he finally said. "It was ninety-something in the shade and we hadn't had rain in weeks."

"That's right. It was late afternoon and you said it was going to storm. I didn't believe you and you pointed out all of the signs: the birds flying in low, the way the clouds were racing into each other, how still the air was. And when the winds picked up and the lightning flashed, you jumped to your feet and nearly hung over the porch railing in excitement.

"I remember an especially loud crash of thunder and, just before your mother came out to hurry us inside, you turned to me and said 'Isn't this glorious?' And you know what? I could begin to feel it, too. Out of what had been a hot boring July day, came this sudden excitement, a cool breeze, and the rain we needed. Everything just fell into place and I began to realize that sometimes joy just happens."

Michael stared across the room, the hard lines of his face softening a little with the memories. "I remember you turning toward me and your eyes were shining and you were wearing the first smile I'd seen on you all weekend." He could also remember seeing, for one instant, the promise of the woman she'd someday become and his hand had lifted to touch her cheek. "Cripes, man, she's just a kid," he'd thought in horror and had ended up flicking her lightly on the end of her nose.

And now he found himself looking at her again, noting all the differences. She was dressed much the same as she'd been then, though in green not pink—a green blouse tucked into a skirt. She even wore knee socks. But, Heaven help him, she wasn't the scrawny little thing she'd been then.

The green blouse caressed luscious breasts, her skirt flared over softly rounded hips, the knee socks hugged firm calves. Her cheeks were fuller, her chin still pointed, her eyes still big, but no longer too big. She'd grown into the promise. Hell, she'd grown past it.

Her hair caught the flickering light from the fireplace and seemed to dance with a thousand tiny flames. Her green eyes, too, reflected the fire, giving their depths a golden glow. Or maybe it was the way she looked at him that made her eyes glow. She was look-

ing at him as if she wanted nothing more in this world
than for him to kiss her.

To tell the truth, he wanted nothing more himself.
He knew it was crazy. He knew this would only compli-
cate matters. He knew he should listen to the little
voice that told him to stop while he still could, to play
it safe. But he wasn't in the mood to listen. And he
wasn't in the mood to play it safe. He was in the mood
to kiss her.

Just one kiss, he told himself. What harm could one
innocent kiss do? Only it wasn't innocent. From the
moment his lips touched hers, innocence disappeared.
That kiss was charged with sensual promise, sexual
need. And hunger.

God, he was so hungry. Hungry for the feel of her,
the taste. His mouth crushed hers, drinking greedily.
Her lips were sweet, so sweet, he didn't think he'd ever
get enough. It might have been minutes that he kissed
her, it might have been hours, but it didn't matter. He
needed to breathe, but he needed this more. It was an
elemental need, as necessary as air and water.

His hands swept restlessly up her back, pressing her
into him, but that wasn't close enough. Without ever
lifting his mouth from hers, he tugged his shirt free of
his jeans and pushed it up. he did the same to her,
growling in frustration as he encountered the delicate
lace of her bra. That, too, was pushed up and he gave a
satisfied groan as bare skin met bare skin.

Her soft full breasts nestled against the harder plane
of his chest as if they had been designed with just this
in mind. Their weight filled his hands perfectly, their
pebbled nipples teased his thumbs perfectly. The very
rightness of it drew him back to reality and he began to

pull away, feeling as if he were standing on the edge of a cliff.

Shannon made an inarticulate sound of dismay and pushed her breast more fully into his palm. That innocently sensual gesture chased sanity away again and Michael welcomed the absence of rational thought. He didn't want to think at all, he just wanted—needed—to feel.

He could hardly bear to relinquish her lips, but longed to taste more of her. With an effort, he pulled his lips from hers, then immediately fastened them on her skin, leaving a damp trail down to the rosy tip of one breast. Shannon moaned and clutched his head to her. So this, at least, was one way he could make her as crazy as she made him, he thought in savage satisfaction. No matter that in making her crazy with need, he was driving himself to the point of insanity as well.

He teased and tormented her breasts until she was quivering beneath his touch. Only then did he slide one hand under the hem of her skirt. Her thighs were so soft, silky velvet over the firm muscles beneath. Michael drew in a breath and forgot to let it out again as he teetered one step closer to the edge. When his fingers slipped inside the edge of her panties, he let out the breath he'd been holding. She was warm and wet and slick.

And demanding. With a movement that took him by surprise, she jerked his shirt up and over his head, tossing it carelessly aside. Her hands shaking with anticipation, she unsnapped his jeans, then fanned her hand over his pulsing need. Michael sucked in another breath and held it as she slid down his zipper. When Shannon opened her mouth to speak, he laid a finger against her lips. He didn't want anything to remind him of reality.

She gently pushed his finger aside and tried to speak again and this time Michael stopped her in the best way he knew. He kissed her, his tongue thrusting in and out as his finger mimicked the motion inside her body.

The rest of their clothes were tossed aside in short order and Michael pressed her down into the over-stuffed sofa. He wanted her so much he was shaking with the force of it. He'd never wanted anyone so desperately. Not even Anne.

The name was a dousing of cold water and he froze, then reluctantly levered himself to a sitting position. He couldn't do this and he opened his mouth to say so, but his gaze fell on her. God, she was beautiful, so beautiful it hurt.

Her creamy breasts were crowned with rosy nipples still moist from his mouth, her rose-gold hair tousled around her, the green eyes looking up at him were hazy with desire. His gaze moved to her beautiful kiss-swollen lips and he wondered if joy, real joy, could be found in her loving.

No, it was crazy. It was wrong. He'd made his rules and had to live by them. And, after Anne, rule number one was to never let his guard down again. With another woman he might have been able to share physical passion and never once lower his mental guard. But he couldn't do that with Shannon. Without ever asking for it, she somehow demanded total capitulation—not just a man's body, but his heart and soul. Only he couldn't give his heart. He'd locked it up a year ago.

Shannon's eyes fluttered open and she stared at his

face for a long searching moment, then sat up, not even trying to cover herself. "Wanna talk about it?"

Whatever he'd been expecting, this wasn't it. He'd expected piercing questions, frustration, maybe even anger, but not this almost cool sounding query and what looked to be nothing more than genuine curiosity in her eyes. Taken momentarily off-guard, he gave himself a few seconds of time by standing and tugging on his jeans. He sat down again, this time at the far end of the sofa.

He tried hard not to look at her, though it was difficult. She really did look like some other-worldly sprite with her mysterious eyes, her impossible tangle of hair, her perfect body. She should be perched on a rock somewhere out in the Rhine combing her hair with a seashell. A Lorelei luring unsuspecting men to sweet oblivion. Or, he found himself thinking as her cat gingerly stepped into her lap, a young beautiful witch with her familiar, bewitching mortal men and allowing them to purchase their freedom with the price of their soul. Or maybe she really was a leprechaun with their sense of magic and mischief.

Only magic and mischief had no place in his life and, while she was wonderful at fantasy and fancy, he doubted she'd hold up in harsh reality.

"This isn't going to work. It's wrong," he finally said.

She gave a little shrug, "It felt all right to me, but you be the judge." She stood, slender and proud in her nudity and scooped up her clothes. "If you'll excuse me, I'll just take a shower and go to bed. Alone." She gave him a distant smile. "Enjoy your solitude." She walked away, as regally as if she'd been wearing a velvet gown and golden tiara instead of bare skin and tangled hair.

Enjoy your solitude. That phrase played over and over in his head as he paced the room like a caged tiger. Enjoy your solitude. He stopped pacing and looked at the cat who sat like a statue on the hearth, tail curled around it like a fur boa. "Who the hell does she think she is?" he muttered to the listening cat. "Does she think I enjoy being alone, sleeping alone, raising Jenny alone? I do it because I have no other choice.

"What gives her the right to come waltzing in here with her magic suitcase and her laughter and her green everything and make me dissatisfied with my life? What right does she have to—" He stopped his murmured tirade and stared across the room, almost afraid to admit the last part. "What right has she to make me hate being alone?"

He forced himself to admit the rest. ". . . To make me hate being without her."

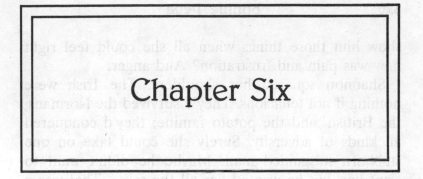

Chapter Six

Shannon stood under the beating water of the shower until it ran tepid, then cool. Try as she might, she couldn't get the feel of him off her skin. And she wanted to. There was nothing worse than almost-paradise. If she couldn't shake the memory of being in his arms, she'd spend the rest of her life wandering around the maze of might-have-beens. She felt as if something inside her had shattered and she was only holding the pieces together with the force of her will.

She loved him. She didn't know why that surprised her; she'd told herself this might—would—happen. She loved the young man he'd been, she always had. But she loved the adult he'd become even more. And she loved his daughter, too. She loved everything about him, except maybe his pigheadedness.

He wanted her, she couldn't deny that. Passion had burned in his eyes tonight, flowed from his fingertips, but he didn't *want* to want her. She'd set herself up. With eyes wide open and knowing full well what she was doing, she'd set herself up for the heartache of a lifetime. So where did she go from here? She'd come here on some sort of crazy quixotic mission to bring love and laughter back into his life, only how could she

show him those things when all she could feel right
now was pain and frustration? And anger.

Shannon squared her shoulders. The Irish were
nothing if not tenacious. They'd survived the Normans,
the British, and the potato famine; they'd conquered
all kinds of adversity. Surely she could take on one
stubborn misguided man. Maybe he didn't want to
want her, but he wanted her all the same. That was a
start. Light began to glitter in her tear-drenched eyes
and a slight smile curved her lips. Oh yes, that was
definitely a start.

She towel-dried herself until her skin glowed pink,
all the while her brain clicking away. It was going to be
a battle, but she had plenty of courage and never
backed down from a fight. It would take perseverance,
but that she had in plenty. It would take creativity and
she'd be able to come up with that, too. She tugged on
her robe and belted it tightly. Of course a little leprechaun's magic wouldn't hurt either.

When Michael awoke from a restless night's sleep, he
wasn't sure what to expect. Shannon had indeed taken
a shower and disappeared into her room last night and
had said nothing besides her parting "Enjoy your solitude." He could swear those words had echoed in his
dreams most of the night, vivid erotic dreams starring
her. What she'd be like this morning was anybody's
guess. He heard the clink of silverware in the kitchen
so he headed in that direction, deciding to get it over
with. Whatever "it" was.

He felt headachy and bleary-eyed, hardly a worthy
opponent for the cheerfully humming woman moving
about his kitchen. She was back in green garb this
morning. A short sexy dark green corduroy jumper

topped a silky light green blouse. She wore green tights and those impossibly silly shoes. She'd reverted to leprechaun status again. He wondered vaguely if there was some significance to it.

She looked up and gave him a bright smile. "Good morning, Michael. How many pancakes would you like?"

"Uh, two or three, I guess." He was determined not to let on that he was in anything other than top form, though he wasn't sure he'd be able to swallow a single bite. He felt like his mouth was full of sand.

"Great." She set a plate in front of him with three green shamrock pancakes on it.

He looked at them for a long moment, then said, "I see we're having green food again. What's the occasion this time? Is there some other Irish saint I don't know about?"

"No special occasion. I just thought pancakes would be nice. We haven't had any for a couple of weeks."

"So why didn't you leave out the green food coloring?"

Shannon looked at him, eyes wide, and a slight smile curving her lips. "There's no food coloring in it."

Michael's fork stopped midway to his mouth. "What *is* in it, then?"

Shannon's smile widened. "Secret family recipe. I promised I'd never give out the ingredients." She sat down with her own plate and dug in with seeming gusto.

How could she do that? She ate as if the most important thing she had on her mind was cleaning her plate. All he could think about, on the other hand, was the way she had looked lying naked on his sofa.

If he'd had any sense at all, he'd have taken her to

bed last night and loved her out of his system. Why on earth had he suddenly come up with an over-developed set of scruples? Was it because she was an old family friend? No, if she'd been a different type of woman that wouldn't have mattered at all. He'd called a halt because Shannon was Shannon. For all of her eagerness and undisguised passion, he had the feeling that she hadn't much experience, perhaps was even a virgin.

He wondered what it would be like to be her first lover, to teach her all the ways men and women pleasured each other. To tell the truth, his sex life had always been rather conventional, but he could think of all kinds of things he'd like to teach Shannon, or learn with her. Even traditional lovemaking was likely to be unconventional with her. He somehow knew that she'd approach it with the same curiosity and sense of adventure with which she approached everything else.

He found himself watching her speculatively and pulled his attention back to his plate, surprised to find most of his pancakes gone. Shannon had already finished hers and was rinsing her dishes in the sink. He wondered how long he'd been staring at her. Had she noticed? He wasn't the type to go around daydreaming about women and was more than a little piqued that this particular woman wouldn't stay out of his head.

It was too early for this, he told himself, as he felt the hot stirrings of desire. His hormones were as out of control as a sixteen-year-old's and it scared him. Sliding his chair abruptly back from the table, he exited the room before his wayward thoughts and unruly body could get him into trouble.

He flopped down into his favorite chair in the living room and picked up the morning paper, which lay conveniently on the coffee table. When he found himself staring at the front page several minutes later without having a clue as to what he'd read, he tossed the paper aside in disgust. He got to his feet, desperate to find something to occupy him. He poked at the embers in the fireplace, selecting a book from the shelf then tossed it aside, rearranged the pillows on the sofa.

This wasn't working. He needed to get out of the house for a while. Away from her. Maybe a little exercise and fresh air would exorcise her out of his mind and give him a fresh perspective on things. He tugged on his coat and gloves, intending to go out and shovel the additional sleet and snow that had fallen during the night, but when he opened the front door, it had already been done.

It was a nice thing for her to have done, he told himself. It was a lousy, stinking nice thing for her to have done. He slammed the door behind him and stomped down the sidewalk. What right did she have to be meddling with his sidewalk anyway? It wasn't any of her business if he slipped on his front porch and broke his neck. Sizzling with restless energy and finding no outlet, he stuffed his hands in his pockets and headed down the street.

He knew it was ridiculous to be angry with her for doing something so thoughtful, but every nice thing she did shook his tightrope and he was already having a hell of a time maintaining his balance. He heard footsteps crunching on the icy slush and, without turning around, knew it was her. His nemesis.

"Hi. I thought I'd walk with you a ways. Beautiful morning, don't you think?"

Michael grunted noncommittally and continued to walk, staring straight ahead. "Uh, thanks for shoveling the sidewalk. It was nice of you."

"Think nothing of it."

"It was nice of you," he repeated, "but I wish you wouldn't do it again. Have you even stopped to think how much a shovelful of snow and ice weighs? You're not very large, you know, and you could hurt yourself. If you've ever hurt your back or pulled a muscle then you'd know what I'm talking about."

"I'm stronger than I look."

"That may be, but as long as you're in my house, you'll leave the heavy stuff to me. That includes shoveling snow, moving furniture, hauling in firewood, etc. Got that?" He turned to look at her.

"Aye-aye, boss." Shannon saluted smartly, then gave a sassy smile.

He stared at the smile for a long moment and could feel its warmth and good humor tickling at the corners of his mouth. He didn't want to respond; he tried not to, but he couldn't stop himself from smiling back. Her good humor was as contagious as chicken pox.

He just wished he knew where it came from. If a woman had done to him what he'd done to her last night, he'd be frustrated and furious. He was frustrated enough right now and he'd been the doer.

He noticed she was wearing that bulky green sweater again and fuzzy green earmuffs nearly as big as dinnerplates. The idiot didn't even know how to dress correctly. "Don't you have a decent coat?" he asked mildly.

"Hm? Oh, sure, but this is plenty warm. It's made from handspun Irish wool. My best friend Kirsty O'Shea designed it. She's going to be working with me at ErinWear."

ErinWear. He seized on the subject eagerly. It was a nice safe one and one that would surely get his thoughts off how even that thick bulky sweater swelled nicely over her breasts. "We really haven't talked much about your company. Tell me more about it."

"We've got the brightest and the best of the Irish designers—clothing, you know—and, whenever possible, we're going to be using all-Irish goods."

"How did it all get started?"

"It all started with Finn and Megan McQuade, who had been selling Irish-made goods on consignment through a number of U.S. shops. The demand was so high that they decided to go at it full force and ErinWear was born."

"How did you get into it?"

"My friend Kirsty is Megan's younger sister and she showed her and Finn some of my designs. They tried a few on a trial basis and they did really well so I was invited aboard."

"And now you're handling the business end over here."

"When you work for a small company, you sometimes have to wear more than one hat."

"I know," Michael sighed.

"How? Did you used to be in corporate America? You don't seem the type."

"No, but I teach at a small parochial high school. I'm not just the eleventh-grade science teacher, I also coach ninth- and tenth-grade boys' tennis and head up the teacher advisory panel for the student council."

"Tell me about your students." Casually, Shannon looped her arm through his. It was such an innocent comradely gesture, that Michael could find no fault with it, except that her body sometimes brushed against his as they walked.

He was wearing a coat, she was wearing a thick

sweater, but that didn't matter. She might as well have been marching beside him stark naked. He didn't think he could be any more aware of her than he already was. Nevertheless he managed to hold an intelligent conversation. At least he thought it was intelligent. She didn't look at him with confusion in her eyes or go running to call for help.

They walked for miles, their footsteps leaving side-by-side tracks in the snow. They talked for hours, their breath mingling together in frosty white clouds. Michael wasn't sure how it happened, but gradually he found his guard eroded away. He chatted with Shannon as easily as if she were his best friend. Then the thought hit him. She was.

After Anne had gotten sick, Michael had shut himself away from everyone else. Everyone always asked after her and it hurt too much to talk about it. When she died, his wounds were too raw and seeing all the old familiar places and faces hurt too much, so he moved away. Now, except for amiable shop talk with the other teachers and the weekly call from his parents, he didn't really have any friendly contact with other adults.

Maybe that's why he felt the way he did. It wasn't Shannon in particular, it was that, without realizing it, he'd missed the contact with another adult. Then he looked at Shannon and that idea went straight down the tube. Her eyes sparkled, her cheeks and nose were rosy with cold. Her hair fanned over her shoulders in disarray, the way it had tousled over the sofa pillows last night.

She made him angry, she made him crazy, she made him want her with a need that ate at him. Most dangerous of all, though, she made him smile. An awful suspicion hit him, momentarily taking his breath away. Maybe he was falling in love with her.

God only knew she was all wrong for him. All wrong. She believed in magic and moonbeams, whimsy and wishes. He knew better. When he'd lost Anne, his heart had been cut to pieces. It had taken a year of careful routine and calculated moves, but he'd finally gotten the last piece glued back into place. He wouldn't survive a second loss. And lose Shannon he would. Maybe she wouldn't die, like Anne had, but she'd get bored with his order and routine. And with her head in the clouds so often, she'd learn to hate his secure grasp on reality. He couldn't bear the thought of her hating him.

He could feel a surge of desperation rising in him. For his own sake, he had to do something about it before he lost his not-so-secure footing on that tightrope. Now was as good a time as any, before he changed his mind or lost his nerve. "Shannon, I've been thinking and, uh, I don't think having you live here is such a good idea. I mean, proximity is-uh-is going to get us into trouble. Do you understand what I mean?"

"Like last night?"

"Yeah, like last night." He glanced at her out of the corner of his eye. She was looking straight ahead, chewing on her bottom lip.

"I see," she finally said, her voice expressionless. "So you think it would be best if I left."

"If you need money, I'd be glad to make you a loan or help in some way. After all, we are old family friends and what else are friends for?"

"What else?" Shannon echoed, gingerly removing her hand from his arm and stuffing her hands in her pockets. "I'll think on it and let you know. Now, if

you'll excuse me, I need to get back to the house. I
have a few calls to make." She turned on her heel and
walked back the way they'd come, leaving him trailing
behind.

He watched her walk away and was surprised by how
much it hurt. Dear God, but it hurt!

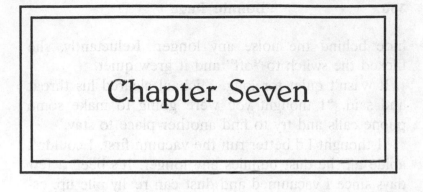

Chapter Seven

Shannon was so occupied with her thoughts, that she almost walked right by the house. She couldn't say she was happy with Michael's decision, but it was not unexpected. He was running hard and fast now; that had to mean she was getting under his skin. Of course, it wouldn't hurt to have a little talk with the good Saint to ensure that Michael ran in her direction.

The talk was more like a plea, but she felt a little better afterwards. The good Saint really did want all of Erin's children to be happy and Michael and Jenny would be happy with her, she knew that in her soul. Sometimes, though, heaven had other things in mind. Mentally she sent another plea winging its way as she unwound the vacuum cleaner cord and plugged it in.

When Michael walked in the front door a few minutes later, the air hummed with the roar of the motor. Shannon waved at him and turned her attention back to the task at hand. At least he couldn't say anything else to her while the noise reverberated around them.

That didn't stop him from sitting in his chair and glowering at her as she ran the machine over the carpet. He did oblige her enough to lift his feet so she could vacuum beneath them. She vacuumed every inch of the house, twice, before she realized she couldn't hide behind the noise any longer. Reluctantly, she flicked the switch to "off" and it grew quiet.

It wasn't quiet for long. Michael cleared his throat and said, "I thought you were going to make some phone calls and try to find another place to stay."

"I thought I'd better run the vacuum first. I couldn't abide all the dust bunnies any longer. It's been a few days since I vacuumed and dust can really pile up, especially when you have a fire going. It's the ashes, I guess. Anyway, I really need to strip the beds next." She knew she was beginning to babble, but didn't want to hear him say again that he wanted her to leave. She didn't think she could bear to hear him say it. "It's almost twelve. What time are you supposed to pick up Jenny? I don't mind going to get her if you've got something you need to do."

"I'll do it. Shannon, the phone book is in the—"

"I know where it is," Shannon said shortly.

"Like I said, I'll help you out any way I can."

You're already helping me right out the front door, she thought sourly. "I'm sure I can manage, thank you. Why don't you go pick up Jenny? I'll make those phone calls now." She made a big deal out of carefully winding up the vacuum cleaner cord, hoping he wouldn't see the tears welling in her eyes.

She stayed busy until she heard the front door shut, then sank down on the edge of the sofa. She wanted to cry, needed to cry, but couldn't seem to get out the gut-satisfying sobs she needed. So she just sat and let the tears run silently down her face. She tried to send another prayer up, but couldn't seem to choke out more than, "Please . . . please . . . ."

*   *   *

When Michael returned with Jenny, Shannon's suitcases were in the living room, the cat was in his carrier, and lunch was on the table. Shannon's green sweater lay waiting over the back of a chair.

Jenny bounded in the living room. "Shannon, they rented two movies and we played video—" Jenny stopped, then turned to Shannon, her eyes wide. "Where are you going?"

Shannon cast a quick glance at Michael. "I have to leave, sweetheart."

"But why?" Jenny wailed. "I like it with you here. You're my best friend now and I don't want you to go."

Shannon squatted down in front of the little girl. "I'll always and forever be your best friend, but best friends don't have to live together to be best friends. You can call me any time you need to talk and I'll come visit sometimes. I promise."

"But I like the house when you're here. It's like it used to be a long time ago, when I was really little. When Mom was okay. It's like the whole house is happy."

Michael looked sharply at his daughter, who had thrown herself into Shannon's embrace. It hurt to see the yearning on Jenny's face. He'd make it up to her, he told himself. He would. But this was best for everyone.

A car horn sounded and Shannon pressed a quick kiss to the child's nose. "I'll call you and give you my new phone number as soon as I get settled in. Okay?"

Jenny nodded, somewhat mollified. "But I'll still miss Puca. He can't talk on the phone. And he's been sleeping on my bed at night."

Shannon's eyes locked with Michael's and she said, "Then, if it's all right with your Daddy, maybe Puca can stay here. I think he'd miss you, too. Besides, I might not be able to keep him where I'm staying."

The car horn sounded again. "I'll help you with your luggage," Michael said and lifted a suitcase.

Shannon reached over and took it out of his hand. "I can manage, thank you." She stopped and opened her overnight bag, pulling out three cans of cat food. "These should get you through tomorrow morning. He likes the seafood flavors." She hoisted the strap of one case over her shoulder, and lifted the other two pieces.

Michael opened the door for her and she turned and fixed him with a cool smile. "Thank you for your hospitality, Michael. I'll be sure to tell your mother how kind you were."

"Do you need some money?" He felt as if he needed to do something to help her. He reached for his wallet.

"No, thank you," she said politely and turned to leave. She turned back long enough to say, "Enjoy your solitude." Head high, she walked down the sidewalk to the waiting taxi.

He bit back the urge to call her back and watched the taxi pull away. She'd used that damned phrase again. "Enjoy your solitude." He'd enjoy it all right, starting with a nice leisurely lunch. He called Jenny into the kitchen but she refused to come, so he sat at the table alone. He folded the newspaper and read while he ate the sandwiches Shannon had fixed, followed by dessert, an all-green fruit salad of honeydew melon and kiwi. Tonight, he'd fix a normal meal, maybe macaroni and cheese with hotdogs or something. Certainly nothing green, though, not even a green bean.

The afternoon seemed interminably long and boring, but Michael told himself it was because he had forgotten what peace and quiet was. He tried to get Jenny to tell him more about the sleep-over, but she answered in monosyllables and eventually left for her room, followed by the cat who turned a disdainful glance in Michael's direction as he walked by.

In desperation he turned on the television only to find *Finian's Rainbow* just coming on the Saturday afternoon movie and the only sports he could find was highlights of last season's college football. The focus this week was on the Fighting Irish of Notre Dame. With a sigh, Michael turned off the television. He turned on the radio next, only to find an afternoon of Irish folk music. He wondered, for a split second, if Shannon had put some sort of leprechaun whammy on the electronic equipment in his house. Hurriedly he spun the dial to another channel, relaxing as the throbbing beat of vintage rock and roll filled the air.

Jenny only picked at her supper, not that Michael did more than pick at his, either. She went straight back to her room afterward, leaving Michael alone again. He carried the dishes to the sink to rinse them and found himself expecting Shannon to come up behind him.

She'd been here only a couple of weeks, but they had rapidly gotten into a supper-time routine. One would rinse the dishes, the other stack them in the dishwasher, all the while chatting about heaven-only-knew what. Michael slammed the door shut on the dishwasher and stepped outside the kitchen door to take deep dragging breaths of the crisp cold air.

He went to bed early, hoping to lose himself in sleep, but sleep wouldn't come. Instead, he lay in bed and listened in vain for the soft rustling sounds Shannon had made as she'd moved around her room. Finally, in frustration, he sat up in bed and rested his forehead in his hands. How had she managed to become such a part of his life in such a short time? He'd been married to Anne for six years and she hadn't left this kind of mark.

His jaw set in determination, he lay back down. This was all just a temporary aberration. In a day or two things would be blissfully back to normal.

Only they weren't.

There didn't seem to be any reason to rush home after school, anymore. The house seemed so empty, but worse yet, Jenny had once again become the solemn-eyed quiet little girl she was before. Michael missed her giggles, her joy. He missed Shannon.

Thursday night, he cooked green peas for supper and Jenny burst into tears and ran into her room, slamming the door behind her. Michael removed the bowl from the table and tossed them into the trashcan. He didn't think he could ever eat another green vegetable again without thinking of Shannon. And to top everything, her stupid shamrock plants were dying.

He was getting angry. Shannon had promised to call and she hadn't. Then the thought hit him. Maybe she couldn't call. She'd turned down his offer of money, but maybe that was out of pride. Maybe she was living in one of those really horrible rooming complexes on the east side of town, sharing her mattress with roaches and rats. Maybe she'd been mugged. Maybe she'd found somebody else.

He called his mother who'd just arrived home from her cruise a few days ago. He didn't allow her to get a word in edgewise as he bellowed orders that she was to call him immediately if she heard from Shannon. After he hung up, he tried to get in touch with somebody at her company. The young woman who answered the phone curtly informed him it was one o'clock in the morning in Ireland and she hadn't heard from Shannon, but at this hour would be highly unlikely to tell him if she had. As he hung up the phone, he turned and found Jenny standing behind him. "What are you doing up, sweetheart?"

"Who were you talking to?"

"I, uh, was trying to find out where Shannon is. She hasn't called yet and I was a little worried."

"She's at Grandma's."

Michael sat, stunned. "Grandma's?" he repeated.

"Yeah. She called me Tuesday and yesterday."

"I just got off the phone with your grandma and she didn't mention Shannon."

Jenny just shrugged, then bit her lip. "Why did Shannon leave, Daddy? She was happy here. She said so. And she made us happy, too." She didn't seem to expect an answer. "I'm going back to bed."

"She made us happy, too. That's it in a nutshell, isn't it?" Michael said to the cat who sat in the middle of the floor eyeing him curiously. "She made me happy. She made me happy and I sent her away." He sank down on a chair and leaned his elbows on the table. "Only now I'm not sure why I did when it's so obvious I need her." He said the words slowly, feeling their weight on his tongue. "I need her." The cat stepped closer. "I need her." He said the words again, louder this time, then jumped as the cat leapt up in his lap, purring loudly.

He looked down at the cat. "I love her." The cat meowed as if in agreement. "Yeah, it took me long enough, I know." He stopped and looked at the cat, just now realizing he was talking to it, and it had seemed to answer him. He shrugged, not caring, as a grin crept over his face. So, she made him crazy. Big deal. Things here on the other side of sanity weren't bad. They weren't bad at all.

He jumped to his feet, dislodging the cat, who gave a disgruntled growl and left the room. He reached for the phone, then set it back down. He couldn't do this on the phone. He had to see her. He had his car keys in his hand and was on his way into Jenny's bedroom, then stopped. Tomorrow was a school day and she needed her sleep. He'd just have to go see Shannon tomorrow.

Damn! He stuffed his keys back in his pocket and flopped on the sofa, casting a curious glance at the two shamrock plants. They seemed to look marginally better. Of course, he realized it might be the rose-colored glasses he was wearing, at the moment. He got back up, too full of energy to sit for long. This night was going to be interminably long; he didn't know how he'd be able to stand it. He wondered just how upset his parents would be if he woke them up at five-thirty.

The cat suddenly jumped to his feet and walked over to the front door, turning to look at Michael. "You don't go out. At least, I never saw Shannon let you—" He broke off as a tap sounded at the door.

He swallowed, ran a hand through his hair, swiping it back from his face, and swallowed again. At eleven o'clock at night, it might have been a policeman coming to tell him his car had been broken into. It might have been a neighbor to tell him his roof was on fire. But it wasn't. It was Shannon. He knew because every nerve ending in his body was focused on that door.

His suddenly sweaty palm slipped on the doorknob,

but he managed to get it open. He smiled. The lady wore green. Again. He opened his mouth to speak.

"Michael," she said firmly, putting out an imperious hand. "You are the most stubborn, hardheaded, exasperating man I've ever met."

"I love you, too."

"You don't listen to—" She stopped. "What?"

"I love you."

Her mouth opened, then shut. She finally said in a voice barely above a whisper, "Don't make fun of me."

Michael reached out and took her hand, drawing her inside and shutting the door. "I've never been more serious in my life."

Shannon clutched at his hand as if she needed to hold onto something, but doubt still shimmered in her eyes. He gently tugged her over to the sofa, to sit next to him. "I need you, Shannon."

Her eyes still shimmered, but this time it was tears. "Are you sure?"

"More sure than I've been in a long time. You are my joy." He took both her hands in his and smiled again, shakily. "I'm not so dumb. I only need to be hit over the head three or four times before something sinks in."

Tears ran unchecked down her face, but she smiled through them. "I'll keep that in mind for future reference."

"Maybe I should get you a baseball bat."

"Tempting thought. I love you, too."

"I know. I need you in my life, Shannon. I can't sleep, I can't think, I can't eat a green vegetable anymore. Jenny's miserable and those damned shamrock plants are dying. We all need you." He reached out and caught a tear on his fingertips, then replaced his fingers with his lips. "Please come home," he murmured against her skin, just before claiming her lips.

"Yes," was all she had time to say before Michael swept her up into his arms and carried her into his bedroom, shutting the door behind him. He sat her on the edge of his bed and began to undress her, kissing each inch of skin he exposed. He shucked his own clothes in record time and, with slow deliberation, lowered his body onto hers.

His mouth moved over hers in exquisite, drugging kisses. His hands moved to familiarize themselves with her, to learn her body so thoroughly that it would ingrain itself in his very pores—and in hers. But he got sidetracked by her hands, her searching, seeking, wicked little hands. The wonderful things her hands were doing were going to push him too far and he tried to capture her hands in his.

"Let me," she murmured pleadingly. "I need to touch you, Michael. I really need to."

Oh, he wanted her to touch him more than he wanted anything, but a man could lose his soul in the pleasure of her touch. Taking a deep breath, he steeled his willpower, preparing himself to withstand her sweet, sweet torture. And he managed to take it when she caressed his chest, tugging gently at the coarse curls, teasing his nipples into tiny hard buds. He even managed to take it when her hands smoothed over his taut abdomen. But he couldn't take it when her light delicate touch feathered over him, wrapped around him.

With a soul-deep groan, he said hoarsely, "That's enough. Uncle. I cry uncle."

"If you think I look like your uncle, you're in real

trouble, young fella," Shannon said in a breathy whisper and lightly nipped his earlobe.

Michael threw back his head and laughed and, while laughing, joined his body with hers. The laughter faded quickly, burned away by the flames that engulfed him. His quick, deep thrusts didn't cool the flames either, instead they fanned them even higher, until he thought his whole body would burn with the intensity.

Dimly he could hear Shannon's breathless voice as she chanted his name over and over, her words falling like glowing sparks around him. He held onto the precious little that remained of his sanity until he felt Shannon tremble beneath him and cry out. Only then did he dive headlong into the fire and join her in pure light. Pure joy.

Sometime later he raised his head. "Did I hurt you?"

Shannon smiled a purely satisfied smile. "Those cries weren't exactly cries of pain."

"I love you." He laid his head next to hers on the pillow.

"How do you feel about children?"

He raised his head again. "I like them. Why do you ask?"

"How do you feel about having more?"

"Great. Sooner or later, I'd like more kids. A couple, anyway."

"That's good. How does sooner strike you? We didn't use any birth control."

Michael grinned and kissed her on the nose. "I guess we'll just have to bypass that big June wedding for an April quickie."

"No white dress, no bouquet of flowers."

"Are you going to miss those?"

"Not really. I'll find a suitable substitute."

Michael rolled over, pinning her beneath him and smiled down at her. "A green dress and a handful of shamrocks?"

"You're learning."

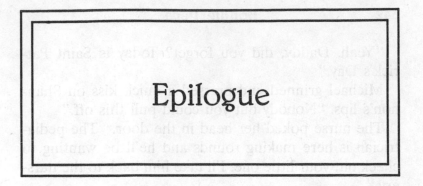

Epilogue

"Are you sure there's nothing to worry about? I mean, the baby's not due for six weeks." Michael clutched his wife's hands as she panted through another contraction.

She drew in a deep cleansing breath. "Everything's fine, sweetheart. I was six weeks early and I turned out okay."

"You turned out to be a leprechaun," he said mildly, keeping one eye on the monitor. "This hospital is prepared to handle a premature birth, right?"

"Relax. This is a great hospital. I was born here." She clutched his hands and panted for the next two minutes. "Michael, do check out in the hall to see if the doctor is on his way. I'm going to have this baby now, with or without him."

A couple of hours later, Michael watched his daughter hold her tiny red-haired brother. He sat on the edge of his wife's bed and held her hand in his. "Your grandparents will be in soon. Tell me, my love, did you plan to go into labor six weeks early just so you could have this baby in Ireland?"

Shannon smiled. "I think the good Saint had more to do with it than I did."

"Yeah, Daddy, did you forget? Today is Saint Patrick's Day."

Michael grinned and pressed a quick kiss on Shannon's lips. "Nobody but you could pull this off."

The nurse poked her head in the door. "The pediatrician is here making rounds and he'll be wanting to check out your little one. I'll take him back to the nursery."

Michael gave his wife another kiss and said, "I'll be back later, darling."

"You don't have to go."

"This is the same hospital that lost you, isn't it? I'm not letting my son out of my sight. One leprechaun in the family is enough."

DA. JUL 1 9 1995

DA JUL 1 9 1995